KT-134-472

midnight

Also by Stephen Leather

Pay Off
The Fireman
Hungry Ghost
The Chinaman
The Vets
The Long Shot
The Birthday Girl
The Double Tap
The Solitary Man
The Tunnel Rats
The Bombmaker
The Stretch
Tango One
The Eyewitness

Spider Shepherd thrillers
Hard Landing
Soft Target
Cold Kill
Hot Blood
Dead Men
Live Fire
Rough Justice
Fair Game (July 2011)

Jack Nightingale supernatural thrillers
Nightfall

STEPHEN LEATHER

midnight

HODDER &
STOUGHTON

First published in Great Britain in 2011 by Hodder & Stoughton
An Hachette UK company

1

Copyright © Stephen Leather 2011

The right of Stephen Leather to be identified as the Author
of the Work has been asserted by him in accordance with the
Copyright, Designs and Patents Act 1988.

All rights reserved. No part of this publication may be reproduced,
stored in a retrieval system, or transmitted, in any form or by any
means without the prior written permission of the publisher,
nor be otherwise circulated in any form of binding or cover
other than that in which it is published and without a similar
condition being imposed on the subsequent purchaser.

All characters in this publication are fictitious and any resemblance
to real persons, living or dead is purely coincidental.

A CIP catalogue record for this title is available from the British Library

Hardback ISBN 978 1 444 70066 4
Trade Paperback ISBN 978 1 444 70067 1

Typeset in Plantin Light by Palimpsest Book Production Limited,
Falkirk, Stirlingshire

Printed and bound in the UK by Clays Ltd, St Ives plc, Bungay, Suffolk

Hodder & Stoughton policy is to use papers that are natural, renewable
and recyclable products and made from wood grown in sustainable forests.
The logging and manufacturing processes are expected to conform
to the environmental regulations of the country of origin.

Hodder & Stoughton Ltd
338 Euston Road
London NW1 3BH

www.hodder.co.uk

midnight

I

It wasn't the first dead body that he'd ever seen, and Jack Nightingale was fairly sure it wouldn't be the last. The woman looked as if she was in her late thirties but Nightingale knew she was only thirty-one. She had curly brown hair, neatly plucked eyebrows and pale pink lipstick, and her neck was at a funny angle, which suggested that the washing line around her neck had done more than just strangle her when she'd dropped down the stairwell. She was wearing a purple dress with a black leather belt. One of her shoes had fallen off and was lying at the bottom of the stairs, the other dangled precariously from her left foot. A stream of urine had trickled down her legs and pooled on the stair carpet, turning the rust-coloured pile a dark brown. Death was always accompanied by the evacuation of bowels, Nightingale knew. It was one of the unwritten rules. You died and your bowels opened as surely as night followed day.

He stood looking up at the woman. Her name was Constance Miller and it was the first time he had ever laid eyes on her. From the look of it she'd stood at the top of the stairs, looped a piece of washing line around her neck and tied the other end around the banister, then dropped over, probably head first. The momentum had almost certainly broken her neck and she probably hadn't felt much pain, but even so it couldn't have been a pleasant way to go.

Nightingale took out his pack of Marlboro and a blue disposable lighter. 'Don't mind if I smoke, do you?' He tapped out a cigarette and slipped it between his lips. 'You look like a smoker, Constance. And I saw the ashtray on the kitchen table so I'm guessing this isn't a non-smoking house.'

He flicked the lighter, lit the cigarette and inhaled. As he blew a loose smoke ring down at the stained carpet, the woman's arms twitched and her eyes opened. Nightingale froze, the cigarette halfway to his mouth.

The woman's arms flailed, her legs trembled and she began to make a wheezing sound through clenched teeth. Suddenly her eyes opened wide. 'Your sister is going to Hell, Jack Nightingale,' she said, her voice a strangled rasp. Then her eyes closed and her body went still.

Nightingale cursed and ran to the kitchen. The back door was open the way he'd left it. Next to the sink was a pinewood block with half a dozen plastic-handled knives embedded in it. He stubbed out his cigarette, took one of the biggest knives and ran back to the hall. He took the stairs two at a time until he was level with her then he reached over and grabbed her around the waist. He grunted as he hefted her against his shoulder and climbed up the stairs to take the weight off the washing line. He held her tight with his left arm as he sawed at the line with the knife. It took half a dozen goes before it parted and her head slumped over his shoulder.

She was the wrong side of the banister and he couldn't pull her over so he let her weight carry him down the stairs until her feet were touching the floor, then he lowered her as best he could before letting go. She fell against the wall and slid down it, her hair fanning out as the back of her head scraped across the wallpaper. Nightingale hurried around the bottom of the stairs just as the woman fell face down on the carpet. He rolled her over and felt for a pulse in her neck with his left hand, but there was nothing. He sat back on his heels, gasping for breath. Her skirt had ridden up her thighs, revealing her soiled underwear, and Nightingale pulled it down.

'Get away from her!' bellowed a voice behind him.

As he turned he saw a burly uniformed police sergeant wearing a stab vest and pointing a finger at him. Just behind him was a younger PC, tall and thin and holding an extended tactical baton in his gloved hand.

'Drop the knife!' shouted the sergeant, fumbling for his baton in its nylon holster on his belt.

Nightingale stared at the knife in his right hand. He turned back to look at the cops but before he could open his mouth to speak the young PC's baton crashed against his head and Nightingale slumped to the floor, unconscious before he hit the carpet.

2

The superintendent was in his early fifties, his brown hair flecked with grey, and he studied Nightingale through thick-lensed spectacles. He was in uniform, but he'd undone his jacket buttons when he sat down at the table. Next to him was a younger man in a grey suit, a detective who had yet to introduce himself. Nightingale sat opposite them and watched the detective trying to take the plastic wrapping off a cassette tape.

'You've not gone digital, then?' asked Nightingale.

The superintendent nodded at the tape recorder on the shelf by Nightingale's head. 'Please don't say anything until the tape's running,' he said. He took off his spectacles and methodically wiped the lenses with a pale blue handkerchief.

'That could be a while, the way he's going,' said Nightingale.

The detective put the tape to his mouth, ripped away a piece of the plastic with his teeth and then used his nails to finish the job. He slid the cassette into one of the twin slots, then started work on a second tape. Nightingale figured the man was in his mid-twenties and still on probation with the CID. He kept looking nervously at the superintendent, like a puppy that expected to be scolded at any moment.

The custody sergeant who had taken Nightingale from the holding cell had given him a bottle of water and a packet of crisps and they were both on the table in front of him. He opened the bottle and drank from it, wiped his mouth on the paper sleeve of the forensic suit they'd given him to wear when they took away his clothes and shoes. On his feet were paper overshoes with elastic at the top.

The detective finally got the wrapping off the second tape and slotted it into the recorder before nodding at the superintendent.

'Switch it on, lad,' said the superintendent. The detective flushed and did as he was told. The recording light glowed red. 'Right.' He checked his wristwatch. 'It is a quarter past three on the afternoon of November the thirtieth. I am Superintendent William Thomas and with me is . . .' He nodded at the detective.

'Detective Constable Simon Jones,' said the younger man. He began to spell out his surname but the superintendent cut him short with a wave of his hand.

'We can all spell, lad,' said the superintendent. He looked over at the recorder to check that the tapes were running. 'We are interviewing Mr Jack Nightingale. Please give us your date of birth, Mr Nightingale.'

Nightingale did as he was asked.

'So your birthday was three days ago?' said the superintendent.

'And you didn't get me a present,' said Nightingale, stretching out his legs and folding his arms. 'I'm not being charged with anything, am I?'

'At the moment you're helping us with our enquiries into a suspicious death.'

'She killed herself,' said Nightingale.

'We're still waiting for the results of the autopsy.'

'She was hanging from the upstairs banister when I found her.'

'You were bent over her with a knife in your hand when two of my officers apprehended you,' said the superintendent.

'Your men beat the crap out of me,' said Nightingale, gingerly touching the plaster on the side of his head. 'I used the knife to cut her down.'

'One blow, necessary force,' said the superintendent.

'I was an innocent bystander,' said Nightingale. 'Wrong place, wrong time. They didn't give me a chance to explain.'

'Apparently they asked you to drop your weapon and when you didn't comply they used necessary force to subdue you.'

'First of all, it wasn't a weapon; it was a knife I'd taken from the kitchen to cut her down. And second of all, they hit me before I could open my mouth.' He pointed at the paper suit he was wearing. 'And when am I getting my clothes back?'

'When they've been forensically examined,' said the superintendent.

'She killed herself,' said Nightingale. 'Surely you must have seen that. She tied a washing line around her neck and jumped.'

'That's not what women normally do,' said the superintendent. 'Female suicides, I mean. They tend to swallow sleeping pills or cut their wrists in a warm bath. Hanging is a very male thing. Like death by car.'

'I bow to your superior knowledge, but I think I'd rather go now.'

'You're not going anywhere until you've answered some questions.'

'Does that mean I'm under arrest?'

'At the moment you're helping us with our enquiries,' said the superintendent.

'So I'm free to go whenever I want?'

'I would prefer that you answer my questions first. If you've done nothing wrong then you shouldn't have any problems talking to us.' Thomas leaned forward and looked at Nightingale over the top of his spectacles. 'You're not one of those Englishmen who think the Welsh are stupid, are you?'

'What?'

'You know what I'm talking about,' said the superintendent. 'Us and the Irish, you English do like to take the piss, don't you? Calling us sheep-shaggers and the like.'

'What the hell are you talking about?'

'I'm talking about you coming into our small town and causing mayhem,' said the superintendent. 'And acting as if it's no big thing.' He linked his fingers and took a deep breath. 'Because it is a big thing, Nightingale. It's a very big thing.'

'She was dead when I got there.'

'So you say.'

'What does the coroner say?'

'We're still waiting on the exact time of death, but it looks as if it's going to be too close to call.'

'She was swinging from the banister when I got there.'

'And her DNA is all over your clothes.'

'Because I cut her down. Trying to save her.'

'You said she was dead. Why were you trying to save a dead woman?'

'I didn't know she was dead. I just saw her hanging there. Then she moved.'

'Moved?'

'She was shaking and she was making sounds.'

'So she wasn't dead?'

'No, she was dead. Some sort of autonomic reaction. I got a knife from the kitchen and cut her down. I checked for life signs and there were none. That's when your guys arrived.'

'Which raises two questions, doesn't it?' said the superintendent. 'Why didn't you call the police? And what were you doing in the house?'

'I didn't have time to phone anyone,' said Nightingale. 'I'd just finished checking for a pulse when your men stormed in and beat me unconscious.'

'I'm told that you were resisting arrest,' said the superintendent. 'A neighbour called nine-nine-nine to say that a stranger had just entered Miss Miller's house. When they arrived they found you crouched over her, holding a knife.'

'They didn't say anything, just clubbed me to the ground.'

'You shouldn't have been in the house,' said the superintendent. 'It's not as if she invited you, is it?'

'The back door was open,' said Nightingale.

'Even so,' said the superintendent. 'You committed trespass at best, and at worst . . .'

'What?'

'A woman is dead, Nightingale. And you still haven't explained why you were in the house.'

'I wanted to talk to her.'

'About?'

'It's complicated,' said Nightingale.

'There you are again, suggesting that the Welsh are stupid.' He banged the flat of his hand down hard on the table and Nightingale flinched. 'Start talking, Nightingale. I'm getting fed up with your games.'

Nightingale sighed. 'I think she's my sister.'

'You think?'

'Like I said, it's complicated.'

'Complicated as the fact that her name is Miller and yours is Nightingale?'

'She never married?'

'Miller is the name she was born with. So how can you be her brother?'

'Stepbrother. Or half-brother. We've got the same father.'

'And would the father's name be Nightingale or Miller?'

'Neither. Gosling. Ainsley Gosling.'

'So you're telling me that Gosling was your father and hers and yet all three of you have different names?'

'I was adopted. So was my sister. We were both adopted at birth.'

'And so what were you doing at her house today? Surprise visit, was it?'

'I wanted to talk to her.'

'About what?'

Nightingale bit down on his lower lip. There was no way on earth the superintendent would believe Nightingale if he answered that question honestly. In the cold light of day he wasn't even sure if he believed it himself. 'I'd just found out that she was my sister. I wanted to meet her.'

'Did you call her first?'

Nightingale shook his head.

'For the tape please, Mr Nightingale.'

'No, I didn't call her.'

'You just thought you'd pop round? From London?'

'I wanted to see her.'

'So you drove all the way from London for a surprise visit?'

'I wouldn't exactly put it that way,' said Nightingale. 'It wasn't about surprising her. I just wanted to . . .' He shrugged. 'It's difficult to explain.'

'You see, any normal person would have phoned first. Made contact that way and then arranged a convenient time to meet. Not turned up unannounced.'

'I'm a very spontaneous person,' said Nightingale. He wanted a cigarette, badly.

'And what made you think that Connie Miller is your sister? Or half-sister?'

'I got a tip.'

'What sort of tip?'

'I was given her first name. And the name of the town.'

'And that was enough to find her?'

'I knew how old she is. Was. She was the only thirty-one-year-old woman called Constance in Abersoch.'

'Is that right?'

'You can check the electoral roll yourself. It's all computerised these days.'

'Well, I can tell you for a fact that Connie Miller isn't related to you. I know her parents. I've known them for years. And they've just been to identify her body.'

Nightingale rubbed his face with his hands. 'Okay,' he said. 'I was misinformed.'

'Yes,' said the superintendent. 'You most definitely were.

Connie was born in Bryn Beryl Hospital in Pwllheli, and I can assure you that there was no adoption involved.'

'If that's true then I was given a bum tip. It happens.'

'If it wasn't true then I wouldn't be saying it,' said the superintendent. 'I'm not in the habit of lying. So you're based in London?'

Nightingale nodded. The superintendent pointed at the tape recorder and opened his mouth to speak but Nightingale beat him to it. 'Yes,' he said. 'That's right.'

'And before that you were a policeman?'

'For my sins, yes.'

'You were with SO19, right?'

'CO19. It used to be SO19 but they changed it to CO19 a few years back. The firearms unit. Yeah.'

'You were an inspector?'

It was clear that the superintendent had already seen his file. 'Yes,' he said. 'I was an inspector.'

'Until that incident at Canary Wharf?'

Nightingale smiled sarcastically and nodded again.

'People have a habit of dying around you, don't they, Nightingale?'

'She had already hanged herself by the time I got there. I had never met the woman, never set eyes on her before today.'

'Let's leave Connie where she is for the time being,' said the superintendent. 'For now let's talk about Simon Underwood.'

'With respect, that's out of your jurisdiction,' said Nightingale. 'Way out.'

'Paedophile, wasn't he? Interfering with his daughter, according to the Press. She killed herself while you were talking to her?'

'Where are you going with this, Superintendent? I'd hate to think that you were opening old wounds just for the hell of it.'

'I'm simply pointing out that you have a track record as far as dead bodies are concerned. Simon Underwood went through the window of his office while he was talking to you. Sophie Underwood jumped off a balcony. Your uncle took an axe to his wife and then killed himself not long before you went around to their house. Bodies do have a tendency to pile up around you.'

'Can I smoke?' asked Nightingale.

'Of course you can't bloody well smoke,' snapped the superintendent. 'Last time I looked Wales was still part of the United Kingdom and in the UK we don't allow smoking in public buildings or places of work.'

'Can we take a break, then? I need a cigarette.'

The superintendent leaned back in his chair. 'You know smoking kills,' he said.

'Allegedly,' said Nightingale. 'Ten minutes? It's either that or you'll have to charge me because I'm not going to continue helping you with your enquiries unless I have a cigarette first.'

3

A cold wind blew through Nightingale's paper suit and he shivered. 'If I get a cold I'll bloody well sue you,' he muttered. He and the superintendent were standing in the car park at the rear of the police station. A patrol car had just driven in and large blue metal gates were rattling shut behind it. There were two white police vans and half a dozen four-door saloons parked against the high wall that surrounded the car park.

'You're the one that wanted a cigarette,' said the super-intendent. He took a pack of Silk Cut from his jacket pocket, flipped back the top and offered it to Nightingale.

'I'm a Marlboro man, myself,' said Nightingale.

'Your fags are in an evidence bag so if you want a smoke you'll have to make do with one of mine,' said the superintendent. He took the pack away but Nightingale reached out his hand. The superintendent smiled and held out the pack again.

'I wouldn't have had you down as a smoker,' said Nightingale. The superintendent struck a match and Nightingale cupped his hands around the flame as he lit his cigarette.

The superintendent lit his own cigarette with the same match, then flicked it away. 'I used to be a forty-a-day man when they allowed us to smoke in the office,' he said. 'These days I'm lucky if I get through six.' He smiled ruefully. 'The wife won't let me smoke in the house either. Tells me that secondary smoke kills. I keep telling her that the fry-up she makes me eat every morning is more likely to kill me than tobacco, but what can you do? Wives know best, that's the order of things.' The superintendent took a long drag on his cigarette and blew smoke at the sky. 'What I can't understand,' he said, 'is if the only two people in a room want to smoke, why the hell they just can't get on with it. Do you have any idea how many man hours we lose a year in cigarette breaks?'

Nightingale shrugged. 'A lot?'

'A hell of a lot. Assuming the average detective smokes ten during his shift, and each cigarette takes five minutes, that's almost an hour a day. Half a shift a week wasted. And do you know how many of my guys smoke?'

'Most?'

'Yeah, most,' said the superintendent. He took another long drag. 'My first boss, back in the day, kept a bottle of Glenlivet in the bottom drawer of his desk and every time we had a result the bottle came out. Do that these days and you'd be out on your ear. Can't drink on the job, can't smoke, can't even eat a sandwich at your desk. What do they think, that we can't drink and smoke and do police work?'

'It's the way of the world,' agreed Nightingale. 'The Nanny State.'

'Another five years and I'm out of it,' said the superintendent. 'I'll have done my thirty. Full pension.'

'It's not the job it was,' said Nightingale.

The superintendent sighed and nodded. 'You never

said a truer word,' he said. 'Tell me something. Did you throw that kiddy-fiddler through the window? Tapes off, man to man, detective to former firearms officer – you threw him out, right?'

Nightingale flicked ash onto the tarmac. 'Allegedly,' he said.

'Don't give me that allegedly bullshit,' said the superintendent. 'If you did do it, I'd sympathise. I've got three kids, and even though they're fully grown God help anyone who even thought about causing them grief. What about you, Nightingale? Kids?'

'Never been married,' said Nightingale. 'Never met a woman who could stand me long enough to get pregnant.'

'Yeah, I could see you'd be an acquired taste.' He chuckled and inhaled smoke.

'When can I get my clothes back?' asked Nightingale. 'I feel a right twat in this paper suit.'

'If your clothing is evidence, you'll never get it back,' said the superintendent. He grinned. 'I don't see what the problem is – white suits you.' He jabbed his cigarette at Nightingale's chest. 'Wonder if those things are flameproof?'

Nightingale jumped back. 'That's not funny,' he said, brushing off the ash.

The superintendent dropped what was left of his cigarette onto the ground and squashed it with his foot. 'This tip about Connie being your sister. Where did that come from?'

'A friend,' said Nightingale.

'How could he have got it so wrong?'

Nightingale shook his head. 'I've been asking myself the same question.'

'Who is this friend? Is he in the Job?'

'Robbie Hoyle. An inspector with the TSG.'

'One of the heavy mob, yeah?'

'Yeah. You could say that. But he was a negotiator too. Same as me.'

'I'll need Inspector Hoyle's number.'

Nightingale's eyes narrowed. 'Why?'

'To check out your story,' said the superintendent. 'If he confirms that he sent you here on a wild goose chase, it helps your case.'

'There is no case,' said Nightingale. 'I found her hanging there when I went into the house.'

'And if Inspector Hoyle says that he sent you to the house that gives you the reason for being there. Without confirmation from him you're still in the wrong place at the wrong time.'

Nightingale pulled on his cigarette. 'I'm not sure that Robbie would back me up.'

'Abusing the CRO database, was he?'

Nightingale flicked away his cigarette butt. 'Robbie's dead,' he said.

'What happened?'

'RTA,' said Nightingale. 'A stupid, senseless accident. He was on his mobile and he stepped out in front of a taxi.'

'I'm sorry,' said the superintendent. 'Did you tell anyone else that you were coming to Abersoch to see Connie Miller?'

Nightingale nodded. 'My assistant. Jenny McLean.'

'And where is she at the moment?'

'London. Holding the fort.'

'And if I were to telephone this Jenny McLean she would confirm your story, would she?'

'She knew I was coming to Abersoch and why, yes. She helped me track down her address.'

The superintendent frowned. 'Why would she do that?'

'All I had was a first name. Constance. And the town. Abersoch. Jenny helped me track down the address. She's good with databases.'

'And she'll confirm this, will she?'

'I hope so,' said Nightingale. 'I really, really hope so.'

Thomas gestured at the door. 'Okay, let's get back to it.'

4

M ia sipped her caramel latte and stared longingly at
the packet of Rothmans on the table. Coffee and
cigarettes went together like fish and chips, and coffee
never tasted right if she wasn't smoking. She looked out
through the window at the three metal tables and chairs
that had been set up on the pavement. She desperately
wanted a cigarette but it was freezing cold outside and
the weather forecast had been for snow. She hated winter,
especially an English winter. She shivered and looked
over at the customers queuing up to buy coffee. The door
opened and as a cold wind blew into the shop a man
joined the end of the queue. He was in his early thirties,
maybe five years older than her, tall with jet-black hair
and pale white skin. He was wearing a long overcoat that
looked like cashmere and a bright red scarf around his
neck.

She stared out of the window again for a while, and
when she looked back at the queue the man had gone.
She twisted around the other way and saw him sitting in
an armchair by the toilets. He caught her look and smiled.
She flashed him a tight smile and looked away. She picked
up her pack of cigarettes and toyed with it. A grey-haired
old woman sitting at the next table glared at her with

open hostility as if she was daring Mia to light up. Mia scowled at her.

There was a mirror on one wall and she could see the man's reflection. As she watched, he took a coin from his pocket, flipped it into the air and caught it He slapped it down onto the back of his left hand, and then grinned as he looked at it. He put the coin back in his pocket, picked up his coffee mug, and walked over. Mia pretended not to see him.

'Excuse me,' he said. She turned to look at him. 'I just had to come over and say hello.'

'Why?' she asked.

'Fate,' he said. 'My name is Chance.'

'Chance?'

'As in Chance would be a fine thing. May I join you?'

For a moment she thought of saying no, but then he smiled and she waved at the chair on the opposite side of the table. 'It's a free country,' she said.

'Well, it used to be,' he said, and sat down, carefully adjusting the crease of his trousers. 'I didn't get your name.'

'Mia,' she said. 'Is Chance your real name?'

'It's the name I answer to,' he said. He had the most amazingly blue eyes. The blue of the sky on a crisp autumn morning, Mia thought.

'So it's like a nickname?'

'Sort of,' he said.

She sipped her coffee and watched him over the rim of her mug. He had the chiselled good looks of a TV soap star. A doctor in *Holby City*, maybe. She put her mug back down on the table. 'What was that thing you did, with the coin?'

He shrugged as if he didn't know what she was referring to.

'Come on, you know what I mean,' she said. 'You were looking at me and then you tossed a coin and then you came over.'

'And what do you think happened?'

She giggled. 'I think you weren't sure whether or not you wanted to talk to me so you tossed a coin to decide. Am I right?'

He shrugged carelessly. 'Sort of,' he said. 'I'd already decided that I wanted to talk to you, but I let the coin choose whether or not to follow through on what I wanted.'

She frowned. 'That's the same, right?'

'As near as makes no odds,' he said.

'And you do that a lot?' she asked. 'Toss a coin to decide what to do?'

'Not a lot,' he said. 'Always. And not just any old coin.' He put his hand in his pocket and took out a fifty-pence piece. 'This one.'

She held out her hand and he gave it to her. She examined both sides but she couldn't see anything out of the ordinary. 'It's just fifty pence,' she said.

He took it back, made a fist of his hand and kissed the knuckles before putting the coin back in his pocket.

'Are you serious?' she said. 'You let the coin make all your decisions?'

He shrugged again. 'It's more complicated than that, Mia,' he said. 'I give it choices, and it decides whether or not I proceed. That way fate takes responsibility for my actions.'

'So you toss a coin to see if you'll order a latte or a cappuccino?'

'Not a coin. *The* coin. And no, I only ask it to decide on the important things.'

'Like whether or not to talk to me?'

'Sure,' he said. He clinked his coffee mug against hers. 'That was one of the big decisions of my life.'

She laughed and put her hand up to cover her mouth. Her fingernails were painted the same garish pink as her lips. 'You could have just come over,' she said. 'I would have talked to you anyway.'

'You're missing the point,' he said. 'If I'd just walked over, everything that happened would have been my responsibility. But doing it this way, the coin is responsible. Do you see?'

'I think so,' she said. 'But what's special about it? It's just a fifty-pence piece.'

'It's not special,' he said. 'It's just that it has to be consistent. It has to be the same coin every time or it won't work.'

'What won't work?'

Chance sat back in his chair and put his hands behind his neck. 'If I used different coins that would be just luck. What I do has nothing to do with luck, it's all about fate.' He winked. 'So do you live near here, Mia?'

'Just down the road,' she said. 'I always have a coffee here on the way back from Tesco.' She pointed at the supermarket carrier bags at her feet.

He removed his hands from behind his neck and fished the coin out of his pocket. He held it in the flat of his right hand and smiled at her.

'What?' she said.

He flipped the coin, caught it deftly in his right hand and slapped it down onto the back of his left.

'Heads,' she said.

Chance shook his head. 'It's not your call,' he said. He removed his hand. The coin had landed heads side up.

'I was right,' she said, jiggling her shoulders from side to side like an excited child.

Chance smiled and put away the coin. 'Mia, why don't I help you carry your bags home?'

'You want to come home with me?'

'Sure.' He drained his coffee and got to his feet.

'Is that why you tossed the coin? To see whether or not you wanted to go home with me?'

Chance reached down and picked up her bags. 'That's right.'

She laughed and again her hand flew up to cover her mouth. 'You're crazy,' she said.

He grinned. 'Mia, you don't know the half of it,' he said.

'What if it had landed tails?'

'Then I'd have finished my coffee and left.'

She stood up and linked her arm through his. 'It's my lucky day,' she said.

Mia lived in a mansion block in a quiet street ten minutes' walk from the coffee shop. Chance carried her bags of shopping for her and made small talk as they walked, asking about her family, what she liked to watch on television, and where she liked to go of an evening. He listened intently and agreed with everything she said, which Mia took as a good sign. He was different from the type of men who generally tried to chat her up. He was good-looking and well dressed and he seemed genuinely interested in what she thought. It was only when she put the key into the lock of the door to the block that she realised she had spent the entire walk talking about herself. Other than that his name was Chance and he liked to toss a coin, she knew nothing about him. She looked over at him and he flashed her a movie-star smile.

'Okay?' he asked, as if sensing her momentary unease.

She smiled back. 'You're not a serial killer, are you?' she asked.

He nodded. 'Yes,' he said. 'Yes, I am.' His face broke into a grin. 'Mia, you're crazy.'

'I think you're right,' she said. 'It's just that you're too good to be true. I don't know when the last time was that a man offered to carry my bags.'

'It's a pleasure,' he said. 'And you don't have to invite me in. I can take a rain check.'

She opened the door but kept her hand on the key. He was right. She wasn't under any pressure. It was totally her choice and whatever happened was her decision. She didn't usually take strange men back to her home. But then most of the men who approached her were pigs, out for only one thing. Chance was different; there was no doubt about that. He was better looking, better dressed, and was obviously way smarter than anyone she knew. She smiled at him again and he flashed his movie-star smile back at her. Something her mother always said sprang into her mind. Opportunity knocks only once. If she turned him down now, she might never see him again. 'Don't be silly,' she said. 'I've got wine in the fridge. You can help me drink it.'

She walked into the hallway and up the stairs to her first-floor flat. He followed her and waited while she unlocked the door. 'Home sweet home,' she said.

She showed him where the kitchen was and he put the

carrier bags on the counter. She got a bottle of Frascati from the fridge and picked up two glasses. 'White okay?' she asked.

'Great,' he said, taking off his overcoat and scarf and draping them over the back of a chair. 'Why don't I open that for you?'

She gave him the bottle and he picked up a corkscrew then followed her through into the sitting room. There was an LCD television and a leather sofa and an armchair. All the furniture had come with the flat. Chance sat down on the sofa and opened the wine. 'So, what do you do, Mia?' he asked.

She frowned, not understanding the question. 'Do?' she repeated.

'Your job,' he said, stretching out his long legs. 'What do you do for a living?'

'I'm on the social,' she said.

Chance nodded approvingly. 'And you can afford this? It's a nice place.'

'It's covered by housing benefit,' she said. 'The neighbours aren't happy because they have to pay for theirs but I'm entitled, so screw them.'

'Exactly,' he said.

'It's because of the economy, innit?' she said. 'The landlord couldn't find any tenants so he kept cutting the rent, and then it got so cheap the council said they could cover it with housing benefit, so here I am.'

'You get income support?' he asked as he poured wine into the two glasses.

She nodded. 'Disability because of my nerves. A hundred and sixty a week, which isn't bad. Plus another seventy for mobility.'

'And it beats working,' he said. 'You should have kids. You'd get more money and the council will find you a bigger place.'

'I thought of that,' she said, lighting a cigarette. She offered him the pack but he shook his head.

'I bet you did,' he said. He pushed one of the glasses towards her.

She smiled coyly. 'Are you putting yourself forward for the job?' she asked.

'I might just do that,' he said, and flashed her his movie-star smile.

She sipped her wine. 'That coin thing – you're serious?'

He nodded. 'It's not a thing, it's my life.'

'Why? Why do you do it?'

'I told you. So that the coin makes decisions for me. Because if I don't make decisions myself then it all comes down to fate. I believe that everything is pre-ordained and there's no such thing as free will.'

She frowned, unable to follow his train of thought.

'It's only by throwing in an element of randomness that you can gain control of your life,' he continued. 'Everybody should do it. They'd find themselves truly free.' He raised his glass to her. 'Here's to you, Mia. And here's to the coin. Because if it wasn't for the coin, I wouldn't be here with you now.'

'That's true,' she said. She reached over and clinked her glass against his.

They both drank, then Chance stood up and walked over to the window. The street below was lined with cars but there were few pedestrians. He reached for the strings that controlled the blinds and gently closed them. 'I always prefer blinds to curtains, don't you?' he asked.

'I guess so,' she said, flicking ash into a ceramic ashtray in the shape of a lucky clover. She patted the sofa. 'Come and sit down,' she said.

He put his hand into his pocket and took out the fifty-pence coin. He tossed it. And smiled to himself when he saw the way it had landed. He looked up and grinned at her as he put away the coin.

'What?' she said. 'What did you decide?'

He walked towards her. 'It's a secret,' he said.

She laughed. 'You're terrible,' she said. 'You can't let a coin rule your life.'

'Oh yes, I can,' he said. He bent down and kissed her on the top of her head.

'At least give me a hint,' she said. She stubbed out her cigarette and then sat back and held out her hands.

He chuckled as he reached into his pocket 'Let's just say that it's not your lucky day, darling.' His hand re-appeared, holding a cut-throat razor. She opened her mouth to scream but before she had even taken a breath he had slashed the blade across her throat and arterial blood sprayed over the wall.

5

Jenny McLean was tapping away on her computer when Nightingale walked in and tossed his raincoat over the chair by the door. 'I hate the Welsh,' he said.

'That's a bit racist, isn't it?' she said. 'Catherine Zeta-Jones seems quite sweet. And Richard Burton. What an actor.'

'Let me be more specific. Welsh cops. I hate Welsh cops.'

'Yes, I rather gather that you got on the wrong side of Superintendent Thomas. He didn't seem a happy bunny at all on the phone yesterday. I definitely got the impression that you weren't winning friends and influencing people in the valleys.'

Nightingale strode through to his office and picked up the mail that Jenny had left on his desk. 'Any chance of a coffee?'

'I hear and obey, oh master.'

Nightingale dropped down into his high-backed fake-leather chair and swung his feet up onto his desk. He flicked through the mail. Three bills, a threatening letter from the VAT man, a CV from a former soldier who had been injured in Iraq, a mail shot offering him a once-in-a-lifetime opportunity to sign up for an investment seminar where he would learn how to be a millionaire within five years, and a letter from a fitness centre down the road offering him twenty per cent off a year's membership plus the offer of three sessions with a personal trainer.

Jenny carried his mug of coffee over to him and put it on the blotter in front of the computer. As she sat down on the edge of his desk she noticed the plaster on the side of his head. 'What happened?'

Nightingale picked up his mug and sipped his coffee. 'I cut myself shaving.'

'I'm serious, Jack.' She reached out to touch the plaster but Nightingale moved his head away.

'It's nothing,' he said. 'The official report probably says that I head-butted the cop's baton.'

'A policeman hit you? Why?'

'Let's just say that my trip to Wales didn't go as planned,' he said.

'You didn't tell him about the séance, did you?'

'I didn't think that would be a good idea,' said Nightingale. 'He wanted to know what I was doing in her house. I told him that I thought she was my sister but then he tried to pin me down on where I'd got the info from. I figured that telling him my dead partner gave me the intel at a séance probably wouldn't get a sympathetic hearing.'

'But why were the police involved anyway?' she said. 'You were just going to talk to her, right?'

'That was the plan,' he said. 'But she went and spoiled it by killing herself.'

'What?'

'Hanged herself, just before I got there. Didn't Thomas tell you any of this when he called you?'

'He was only interested in why you'd gone to Abersoch. I said you'd been tipped off about your sister and then he asked me about Robbie. I figured that something was up so I told him you knew about Constance, but I said I didn't know who gave you her name.'

'Smart girl.'

'Yeah, well, I called you but your mobile was off.'

'They'd taken my phone off me,' said Nightingale. 'They took bloody everything off me, as it happens. Kept me in a forensic suit all afternoon and I didn't get back to London until after midnight.'

'Why did she kill herself?'

'No idea,' he said. 'There was no note, and according to the cops she wasn't depressed. I got there, the door was open, I went inside, she was hanging from the banisters. And the Welsh cops are adamant that she's not my sister.'

Jenny frowned. 'But she was the only Constance in Abersoch. I checked.'

'Robbie got it wrong, then,' said Nightingale. 'Or somebody was pushing the pointer thing on the Ouija board.'

'There were only the two of us, Jack, and I certainly wasn't pushing.'

'And there'd be no point in me sending myself on a wild goose chase,' said Nightingale.

'So what went wrong? We did everything we were supposed to do with the Ouija board, didn't we? We got through to Robbie and Robbie said your sister was in Abersoch.'

'Strictly speaking, we asked him where my sister was and we got two words. Constance and Abersoch. And that's all we got. Maybe talking to the recently departed isn't an exact science.' He sipped his coffee again. 'Or maybe the cops are wrong. I never knew that I was adopted, right? I was thirty-two years old before I found out that Ainsley Gosling was my real father. He did my adoption in total secrecy and he'd have done my sister's adoption the same way. He hid his trail and he hid it well.' He sighed. 'I'll give it a day or two and go back to talk to her parents. I need to nail it down for sure.' He put his coffee mug back on the desk. 'Much happen while I was away?'

'You had a phone call from that solicitor in Hamdale. Ernest Turtledove.'

Nightingale frowned. Turtledove was the man who had turned his life upside down when he broke the news that William and Irene Nightingale weren't Jack's real parents and that he was actually the son of a Satanist and devil-worshipper, who committed suicide after naming Nightingale as his sole heir. 'What did he want? Is it about the estate?'

'Said he needed to see you. I asked but he wouldn't say what it was about. He said that it was private.'

'I'm not schlepping all the way out to Hamdale on a whim,' said Nightingale. 'Can you get him on the phone for me?'

Jenny went through to her office to make the call. A few minutes later she shouted that Turtledove was on the line.

'Mr Nightingale?' said the solicitor hesitantly, as if he was expecting someone else.

'Yes,' said Nightingale. 'My assistant said that you needed to see me.'

'That's right. Something has come up.'

'What, exactly?'

'I'm afraid I can't go into details over the phone,' said the solicitor. 'I really need to see you in person.'

'You're more than welcome to come to my office, Mr Turtledove.'

The solicitor sighed. 'I don't travel, I'm afraid,' he said. 'My leg, you know. I can't drive, and you know what public transport is like.'

'It's a long trip either way, Mr Turtledove. Can you at least tell me what it is that's so important that you need to see me in person?'

'I have to give you something.'

'Why didn't you give it to me three weeks ago when I first came to see you?'

'Because it has only recently come into my possession,' said the solicitor. 'I do apologise for this, Mr Nightingale, but I have been given strict instructions and I have to follow them.'

'What is it you have to give me?'

'It's an A4 envelope.'

'Why not courier it to me?'

'I really can't, I'm afraid. As I said, I do have strict instructions.'

'This is connected to Ainsley Gosling, I assume?'

'I assume so, too,' said Turtledove. 'Can you be here this afternoon?'

6

Hamdale was just a dot on the map and it wasn't much bigger in real life: a cluster of houses around a thatched pub and a row of shops that would have been out of business if Tesco or Asda opened up within twenty miles. Nightingale left his green MGB in the pub car park and smoked a Marlboro as he walked to Turtledove's office, which was wedged between a post office and cake shop. He stood outside the cake shop as he finished his cigarette. The cakes were works of art, birthday cakes in the shapes of football pitches and teddy bears, layered wedding cakes with ornate icing, cakes shaped like cartoon characters. A sign in the window announced the shop's internet address and the fact that they could do next-day delivery anywhere in the United Kingdom but not Northern Ireland. A pretty brunette in a black and white striped apron smiled at him and Nightingale smiled back. He tossed his cigarette butt into the street and pushed open the door to the solicitor's office. A bell dinged and Turtledove's grey-haired secretary looked up from her old-fashioned electric typewriter.

'Mr Nightingale, Mr Turtledove's expecting you,' she said. 'Would you like a cup of tea?'

'I'm fine, thanks,' he said.

She started to get up but Nightingale waved for her to stay put. 'I know the way,' he said.

He opened the door to Turtledove's inner sanctum. The solicitor was sitting behind a large oak desk piled high with files, all of them tied up with red ribbon. There was no sign of a computer in the office, or of anything that had been manufactured within the last fifty years. There was a single telephone on the desk, a black Bakelite model with a rotary dial, and a rack of fountain pens with two large bottles of Quink ink, one black and one blue.

'Mr Nightingale, so good of you to come,' said Turtledove, pushing himself up out of his high-backed leather chair.

'I just hope it's worth my while,' said Nightingale.

Turtledove extended a wrinkled, liver-spotted hand. It might have been Nightingale's imagination, or poor memory, but the solicitor looked a good ten years older than the last time they'd met. The lines on his face seemed deeper, his eyes more watery and his teeth yellower. He used a wooden walking stick with a brass handle in the shape of a swan's head to steady himself as he shook hands with Nightingale. Even his tweed suit seemed older and shabbier, the elbows almost worn through and the trousers baggy at the knees. 'Please, sit down,' said the solicitor as he limped back around to his chair.

'What do you have for me, Mr Turtledove?' asked Nightingale.

The solicitor lowered himself into his chair with a soft groan. 'I'm afraid I have to ask you for some form of photo identification,' he said.

'You know who I am, Mr Turtledove. I was here just

three weeks ago. I'm Ainsley Gosling's sole heir,
remember?'

'Please, Mr Nightingale, bear with me. I am instructed
to confirm your identity before I give you the envelope.'

'Where did this envelope come from?' asked
Nightingale, pulling his wallet from his trouser pocket.

'From the same law firm that sent me your late father's
will,' said Turtledove.

Nightingale fished out his driving licence and gave it
to the solicitor. Turtledove studied it for a few seconds
and then handed it back. He pulled open the top drawer
of his desk and took out an A4 manila padded envelope.

'I don't understand why you couldn't just post or
courier it to me,' said Nightingale. He took it from the
solicitor. There was a typewritten receipt clipped to one
corner.

'Please sign and date the receipt,' asked Turtledove,
handing Nightingale one of his fountain pens. He sat
back in the chair and steepled his fingers under his chin.
'It wasn't so much your identity that I was asked to
confirm,' he said. 'It was more that I had to check that
you were still . . .' He winced before finishing the sentence.
'. . . alive,' he said. 'My instructions were that I was to
confirm that you were still living and hand you the envelope personally.'

Nightingale signed the receipt and slid it, and the pen,
across the desk towards the solicitor.

'And if I wasn't alive?' said Nightingale. 'What then?'

'Then I was told to put the envelope and the DVD
through a shredder and burn the shreddings.' He frowned.
'Is that what they call the waste that has gone through a
shredder? Shreddings?'

Nightingale was surprised the elderly solicitor even knew what a shredder was. 'I've no idea, Mr Turtledove,' he said. He looked at the padded envelope. 'There must have been a covering letter, because if there wasn't you wouldn't have known about the stipulation that you had to confirm that I was still in the land of the living.'

Turtledove nodded. 'Yes, yes of course, there was a covering letter. Now let me see, where did I put it?' He frowned again and began rearranging the files on his desk. Little puffs of dust burst into the air like miniature explosions and he began to cough. He took a handkerchief from the top pocket of his jacket and coughed into it. Nightingale saw flecks of blood on the white linen before Turtledove slipped the handkerchief back into his pocket.

'Are you all right, Mr Turtledove?' asked Nightingale.

The solicitor forced a smile. 'I'm fine, Mr Nightingale,' he said. 'Just old.' He leaned back in his chair. 'Angela!' he called. 'Come in here, please.' Turtledove gestured with his hand at the door. 'My wife and secretary,' he said.

'Keeping it in the family,' said Nightingale.

'She's a trained book-keeper, and makes the perfect cup of tea,' said Turtledove. 'I'd be lost without her.'

The door opened and Mrs Turtledove looked at her husband over the top of her gold-rimmed spectacles and smiled. 'You yelled?' she said.

'I'm sorry, my love,' said Turtledove. 'The envelope we were sent for Mr Nightingale – I can't find the letter that came with it.'

'I haven't filed it yet, so it should still be in the in tray,' said Mrs Turtledove.

The solicitor began rifling through papers in a wire tray. His wife sighed. 'The other in tray, dear,' she said.

The solicitor pulled a face and started sorting through another stack of papers.

'It was delivered by a courier, was it?' Nightingale asked Mrs Turtledove.

'A motorcycle courier,' she said.

'A local firm?'

'I hadn't seen him before,' said Mrs Turtledove. 'In fact, he didn't take his helmet off and he had a black visor so I don't actually know what he looked like. But it wasn't a firm we've used before, I know that.'

'I don't suppose you remember the name? Of the company?'

'It had courier in it, but I suppose they all do, don't they?'

Nightingale nodded. 'I suppose they do.'

Mr Turtledove produced a sheet of paper and waved it triumphantly. 'Found it,' he said.

'Told you so,' said his wife. She closed the door as Turtledove handed the letter to Nightingale. There was no letterhead, no company name, no address or phone number, and no signature at the bottom. It was type-written and comprised a simple set of instructions, which Mr Turtledove had carried out impeccably.

'I'm assuming that you will be paid for this?'

'The bank in Brighton that handled your late father's finances has already transferred the money to our company account.'

'This is all very irregular, isn't it, Mr Turtledove?'

'Mr Nightingale, nothing about your case has been the least bit regular from the start.' He coughed again and dabbed his lips with his handkerchief.

Nightingale gave the sheet of paper back to the solicitor. 'Would you by any chance know anything about my sister?' he asked.

'Your sister?'

'Gosling had another child two years after I was born. A girl. Like me, she was adopted at birth.'

Turtledove shook his head. 'My only involvement with Mr Gosling has been the administration of his estate and passing on that envelope. I know nothing of any other relative.' He scratched his forehead. 'Not that having a sibling would affect the will, of course. Mr Gosling was quite clear that you are his sole beneficiary.'

'How is the work going on the will?'

'Slowly but surely,' said Turtledove. 'I think it should all be tied up in another month or so.'

'What's the hold-up?' asked Nightingale.

'No hold-up,' said Turtledove. 'These things just take time, that's all.' He gestured at the envelope that Nightingale was holding. 'I do hope that's good news,' he said.

Nightingale scowled. 'Considering what I've been through in the last three weeks, I very much doubt it,' he said.

7

Nightingale pushed open the door to the office, waving the padded envelope that Turtledove had given him. 'Great, you're still here,' he said. 'Got any popcorn?'

Jenny looked up from her computer, frowning quizzically. 'I was just about to go home. How did it go?'

Nightingale slid a DVD out of the envelope. 'If I'm right this is another home movie from my dear departed daddy.'

'That's what Turtledove wanted to give you?' She followed him through to his office and watched as he slotted the DVD into the player.

'Yeah, he said he had only just received it. And here's the kicker – he had to prove that I was alive before he could hand it over.'

Jenny picked up the remote. 'Are you sure about this?'

'Sure about what?'

'That you want to know what's on that DVD?'

'Why wouldn't I?'

'Because if it's anything like the last message, it won't be good news. And maybe you'd be better off not knowing what he's got to say to you.'

Nightingale sat down and lit a Marlboro. 'Press "play", Jenny,' he said.

'Do you ever listen to a word I say?' she said, sitting down on the sofa by the door.

'With bated breath, but if it was important enough for me to drive all the way down to Hamdale for, it's important enough for me to watch, whether or not we've got popcorn.'

'We haven't,' she said. 'But there are some chocolate Hobnobs in my drawer.'

'I'll pass,' he said. He waved at the television. 'Please, the suspense is killing me.'

Jenny pressed 'play' and sat with the remote in both hands as the screen flickered into life.

There was no mistaking the face of the bald elderly man that filled the screen as he adjusted the lens. Ainsley Gosling grunted and took a step back, frowning as he studied the camera. His scalp was dotted with liver spots and scabs, and he was wearing the same crimson dressing gown he'd had on for the first DVD they had watched. Gosling turned his back on the camera and waddled over to his bed, then grunted as he sat down, wrapping the gown around his massive stomach. He was holding an opened bottle of brandy in his left hand.

'This was made at the same time as the other video he sent you,' said Jenny.

'I guess it's a PS,' said Nightingale, flicking ash into the crystal ashtray by his computer terminal.

Gosling took a long pull at his brandy bottle, then wiped his mouth with his sleeve. 'I don't know why I'm doing this,' he said, shaking his head. 'There's no way you can possibly be alive to see this. By now you're burning in Hell and cursing the day you were born.' He took another drink, then held the bottle out in front of him. 'Half empty or half full? What do you think, Jack? Are you an optimist, or a pessimist?' He laughed harshly. 'Not that it matters, not if you're in Hell.' He ran his hand over his scalp. 'So, are you dead or alive, Jack? If you're dead then this is a waste of time and the DVD will have been destroyed. But maybe, just maybe, you managed to find a way to survive.' He leaned forward and stared at the camera with watery eyes. 'Maybe you're a chip off the old block,' he growled. 'Are you, Jack? You've got my genes, have you got my guile? Did you manage to pull a rabbit out of the hat at the last minute?'

'I did, actually,' said Nightingale.

Gosling took another gulp of brandy. 'Okay, if you are watching this, Jack, then you did the impossible. You did what I couldn't do. Somehow you managed to beat Proserpine.' Gosling chuckled. 'Even as I say that, I realise how stupid I sound.' He shook his head. 'I'm rambling. Sorry.' He forced a smile at the camera. 'I've been under a bit of pressure, as you can imagine. Here's what happened. Proserpine gave me knowledge. That was the deal I struck. Access to Satanic secrets in exchange for your soul. She kept her side of the bargain and most of what I achieved in my life stemmed from the deal I did with her.' He took a swig from the bottle. 'Hindsight is a wonderful thing, isn't it?' he continued. 'Of course now I know that everything I have, everything I had, is worthless compared with what I lost. I tried to get out of the deal, I tried to get your soul back, but she wouldn't have it. A deal is a deal, and once done cannot be undone.' He threw the bottle at the wall behind the camera and they heard it smash. Gosling sat on the bed, his head in his hands, then he slowly looked up at the camera again.

'So, Jack, did you find some way of saving your soul?'
He leaned to the side and as he moved his dressing gown
fell open to reveal a huge belly, with skin the colour of
boiled chicken. Gosling sat up again and cradled a shotgun
in his lap. 'You can never win when you do a deal with
the dark side, Jack. I know that now. It's like when you
go into a casino, you know. At the end of the day, the
house always wins.' He laughed again and his paunch
jiggled. Gosling pulled his robe closed with his left hand
and stared up at the ceiling. 'I'm sorry, Jack. I'm so, so
sorry for what I did to you and your sister.'

'It's a bit bloody late for sorry,' muttered Nightingale.

Jenny flashed him a withering look.

'What?' said Nightingale. 'Sorry doesn't come close to
making up for what he did.'

Gosling caressed the stock of the shotgun. 'Okay, so
this is what I need to tell you,' he said. 'Two years after
I did the deal with Proserpine, I summoned another devil.
Frimost. I gave Frimost your sister's soul in exchange for
power over women.' He coughed and his massive belly
wobbled under the robe. 'I got what I wanted, all right.
Got laid by some of the most beautiful women in the
world. Names you'd know, Jack. Names that would make
your eyes pop out of your head. The book I could have
written, the stories I could tell.' He shook his head. 'There
was a catch, of course. There's always a catch. Frimost
gave me the tools to get any woman I wanted, but took
away the passion. Sex became a mechanical function,
nothing more. I could get any woman I wanted but deep
down I didn't really want any of them.' He grinned
savagely, baring his yellow teeth. 'That's what they're good
at, the devils,' he said. 'They give with one hand and they

take with the other.' He put both hands on the shotgun. 'You don't realise that when you go into it, of course. They pull you in, they offer you the world, offer you whatever you want.' He closed his eyes and shook his head. 'I was so, so stupid.'

'For God's sake, get on with it,' hissed Nightingale. 'Tell me whatever it is that you want to tell me.'

Jenny pointed at the screen. 'Jack, give it a rest will you? He's going to kill himself, he's terrified.'

'I don't care,' said Nightingale coldly. 'I hope he's burning in Hell as we speak.' He pointed at the screen. 'This is all his doing, Jenny. Don't expect me to feel sorry for him.'

Gosling opened his eyes. 'I tried to find her, Jack. I moved heaven and earth to find her but . . .' He shook his head and sighed. 'I don't know her name, I don't even know if she's still in the country. I gave her to a man who helped me from time to time. His name was Karl, Karl Wilson.'

Nightingale reached for a pen and scribbled down the name.

'He's dead,' Gosling went on. 'I found that out two years ago.'

Nightingale threw down the pen as Gosling continued to talk. 'He poured petrol over himself and set himself on fire. I don't know why. Maybe he just wanted to end it, or maybe it was Frimost shutting the door, but, whatever the reason, he was dead and he was the only one who knew where she was.' He rubbed his face. 'I don't even know why I'm telling you this, Jack. What's the point? Even if you've managed to save yourself there's nothing you can do for the girl.' He sighed and looked down at the shotgun. 'It's time,' he said. 'It's time for me to do what has to be done.' He moaned. 'Oh God, oh God, I'm so sorry.'

'Tell me something,' said Nightingale. 'Give me something I can use.'

Gosling looked back at the camera, almost as if he had heard Nightingale. 'I spoke to Wilson's son and he allowed me to look through his father's effects but there was nothing there that helped, no clue as to what he'd done with the girl. Knowing Wilson, he probably sold the baby and spent the money on coke. He had a bit of a taste for the old white powder.' He shrugged. 'Maybe you're better off just forgetting her. If you did manage somehow to escape Proserpine, then maybe you should just enjoy your life. She was never your problem, Jack. She was my problem and I have to live with the consequences.' His face was bathed with sweat and he wiped it away with his right hand. 'You need to talk to Alfie Tyler; he'll be able to put you in touch with the Order of Nine Angles. He was my driver for a good many years. Tell Alfie that I sent you. And thank him for getting the first DVD to you. Assuming you got that, it was Alfie who put the envelope in the house. And I'm giving him my Bentley. Tell him to keep it serviced.' Gosling ran a hand over his bald scalp. 'The time thing is messing with my head. I'm here telling you this, but by the time you got the first disc I was dead. I'm deader by now but if you are watching this then you know that everything I said was true. Okay, I'll finish this now. It'll be Alfie who finds my body. I'm leaving him a note explaining what he's to do. He'll make a DVD of the first tape and put it in a safe deposit box for you and leave a key in the house. I'll get him to lodge this second DVD with a law firm in the City. They'll get it to you a few days after your thirty-third birthday.' He smiled ruefully. 'Happy birthday, by the way,' he said.

'Ha bloody ha,' said Nightingale.

'Jack, these are your father's last words to you,' said Jenny.

'He isn't my father.'

'Half of your genes came from him; it's his DNA that made you.'

'That doesn't make him my father,' said Nightingale. He waved his hand at the television screen. 'He used me as a bargaining chip – that's all I was to him. So don't expect me to start crying now because he killed himself.'

Gosling slid off the bed, cradling the shotgun. He waddled over to the camera and his robe fell open again as he groped for the 'stop' button. The last thing Nightingale saw before the screen went blank was an expanse of white, mottled flesh.

'Can you believe that?' said Nightingale. 'He sold his daughter's soul so that he could get laid.'

'That's men for you,' said Jenny.

'I'm serious,' said Nightingale. 'What sort of shit would sell his child's soul for sex?'

Jenny stood up. 'Anyway, he's dead. That's the end of it.'

Nightingale ran a hand through his hair. 'It would have been nice if he'd told me where my sister was.'

'You heard what he said. He doesn't know. Didn't know. If he'd known he'd have told you. But at least we know who he sold her soul to. Frimost. Have you heard that name before?'

Nightingale shook his head. 'We should check in Gosling's library. With all those books on the occult there's bound to be something about Frimost.' He looked at his watch. 'Do you want to come with me?'

'It's your call. You pay my wages. Most months, anyway.'

'Just leave the answering machine on. The run-up to Christmas and New Year is always a quiet time for private detectives. It's after the festive season that the phone starts ringing off the hook.'

8

Nightingale stopped the MGB in front of the gates to Gosling Manor and looked across at Jenny expectantly. 'Can you get the gates?'

'What did your last slave die of?' asked Jenny, climbing out of the car. It was dark and the gates gleamed in the MGB's headlights.

'It wasn't overwork,' said Nightingale. He waited until Jenny had pushed open both gates before driving through. She closed them and got back into the car, shivering and rubbing her hands together.

'Why didn't Gosling install electronic gates?' she asked.

'I get the feeling he didn't have many visitors,' said Nightingale. He put the car in gear and drove along a narrow paved road that curved to the right through thick woodland.

'Who's taking care of the grounds?' asked Jenny.

'No one at the moment. Gosling let all the staff go before he topped himself.'

'You're going to have to get someone in when spring comes,' she said, nodding at the expansive lawns to their left, the grass glistening in the moonlight. 'The grass will need cutting and you can't let woodland take care of itself. It's got to be looked after.'

'I keep forgetting that you're a country girl at heart,' said Nightingale.

'Daddy has three gardeners working full-time,' said Jenny. 'And this place isn't much smaller.'

'I'll have to check the money situation,' said Nightingale. 'But I'm pretty sure I don't have enough to pay for a gardener.'

'There's the money from the books you sold from Gosling's library. You got a stack of cash for them.'

'Yeah, but that's got to go towards the mortgages Gosling took out on the house. Could turn out to be negative equity there, in which case I'm really in trouble.'

'Wasn't there insurance? On Gosling's life. I know he killed himself but most policies pay out if the suicide is a couple of years after the policy is taken out.'

'Turtledove didn't mention any insurance policies, so I guess not,' said Nightingale.

He parked in front of the house, a two-storey mansion, the lower floor built of stone, the upper floor made of weathered bricks, topped by a tiled roof with four massive chimney stacks. To the left of the house was a four-door garage and behind it a large conservatory. In the middle of the parking area stood a huge stone fountain, the centre-piece of which was a weathered stone mermaid surrounded by dolphins and fish.

'Are you going to sell it?'

'I think I'll have to,' he said. 'I can't see myself living out here in the middle of nowhere.' He switched off the engine and climbed out. He lit a cigarette as he looked over at the ivy-covered entrance. 'It'd make a great hotel.'

'You should get an estate agent to value it,' said Jenny, getting out of the car. She looked up at the front. 'It really is a beautiful building. Doesn't seem like the sort of place that a Satanist would call home, does it? Even at night.'

Nightingale chuckled. 'Doesn't look like a haunted house, you mean?'

'It's a family house. You can imagine the kids playing on the lawn, Mum in the drawing room, Dad in the study tying fish flies, the faithful retainer in the kitchen giving a couple of pheasants to the cook.'

Nightingale looked over at her, his cigarette halfway to his lips. 'You are joking, right?'

Jenny shrugged. 'Maybe, maybe not,' she said.

'Who has a cook and a faithful retainer these days?'

Her cheeks flushed and she looked away.

Nightingale grinned. 'Daddy?'

'It's a large house and it needs staff,' said Jenny. 'You'll find that out for yourself. I can't imagine you'll want to be dusting and polishing and cleaning windows.'

'Yeah, but a faithful retainer?'

'Lachie is a gamekeeper, if you must know. Now stop taking the piss, Jack. And let's go inside, it's freezing out here.'

Nightingale fished the key from his raincoat pocket and unlocked the massive oak door. It opened easily and without a sound, despite its bulk. He switched the lights on. The hallway was as big as his office, with wood-panelled walls, a glistening marble floor and a large multi-tiered chandelier that looked like an upside-down crystal wedding cake.

There were three oak doors leading off the hallway, but the entrance to the basement library was concealed within the wooden panelling. Nightingale pulled open the hinged panel and reached inside to flick the light switch.

He stepped aside and waved for Jenny to go ahead. 'Ladies first,' he said.

'Age before beauty,' she said. 'I'll follow you.'

'Scaredy cat,' he laughed, and went down the wooden stairs. Despite Nightingale's levity he could understand Jenny's reservations; there was something decidedly spooky about the basement. It ran the full length of the house and was lined with shelves laden with books. Running down the centre of the basement were two lines of display cases filled with all sorts of occult paraphernalia, from skulls to crystal balls. Nightingale had spent dozens of hours down there but had seen only a fraction of the contents.

Jenny followed him down, keeping a tight grip on the brass banister. 'I still don't understand why he kept all this stuff hidden,' she said. 'There's a perfectly good study and library upstairs.'

'I don't think he wanted his staff knowing what he was up to,' said Nightingale. He walked along to a seating area with two overstuffed red leather Chesterfield sofas and a claw-footed teak coffee table that was piled high with books. He sat down into one of the sofas.

Jenny ran her finger along the back of the other. 'Looks like no one's dusted in years,' she said.

'Are you offering?' asked Nightingale.

'No, I'm not.' She sat down. 'So what's the plan?'

Nightingale waved at the bookshelves behind him. 'I guess we need to find books on devils, see if any of them refer to a Frimost. While we're at it, we should start compiling a list of titles so that I can see which ones I can sell. We've got to sort the wheat from the chaff because some of them are really valuable. That's where most of Gosling's money went, remember?'

'It's going to take forever, Jack. There must be – what, two thousand books here?'

Nightingale shrugged. 'Yeah, give or take.'

'And most of them don't even have titles on their spines.'

'The longest journey starts with a single step,' said Nightingale.

'Did you get that piece of wisdom from a Christmas cracker?'

'From Mrs Ellis at my primary school, as it happens. We don't have to do them all at once.' He put his feet up onto the coffee table. 'What do you think's the best way of doing it?'

'Not sitting on your backside would be a good start,' she replied. 'How about we take a shelf each and work along it? We can write the details down and if either of us spots a book on devils we can flick through it and see if Frimost is mentioned.'

'Sounds like a plan,' said Nightingale. He stood up and went over to a huge oak desk that was piled high with books. He pulled open a drawer and found a couple of unused notepads. There were a dozen or so ballpoint pens in an old pint pot and he took two. 'There we go,' he said, giving Jenny a pen and a pad. 'Race you.'

'You're so competitive,' she said.

Nightingale pointed at the bookcase next to the stairs that led down from the hall. 'Might as well be methodical and start there,' he said. 'I'll take the top shelf, you take the one underneath.'

'I've just had a thought,' said Jenny. 'Have you actually looked for a list yet?'

'A list?'

'With this many books, he must have had some sort of inventory. How else would he know if he already had a particular volume?'

Nightingale nodded thoughtfully. 'Okay, that makes sense. But where would he keep it?'

'That's the question, isn't it?' said Jenny. 'He could have put it on a computer or his BlackBerry, if he had one. Or he could have written the list down in a book. Or filed it away.'

'Or maybe he didn't have a list in the first place.'

'Oh ye of little faith,' she said. 'There isn't a computer down here, is there?'

Nightingale gestured at the far end of the basement. 'There's one down there linked to the CCTV feeds but I'm pretty sure it's just for recording. And I haven't seen a laptop.'

'Have you checked the desk?'

Nightingale shook his head.

'Why don't I go through the desk while you make a start on the books?'

'Go for it,' said Nightingale. He took went over to the bookcase, where he started taking books down. They were mostly leather-bound and dusty but they had all been read and had been annotated in the same cramped handwriting. Passages were underlined and there were exclamation marks and question marks in red ink in the margins.

There didn't appear to be any logic to the order that the books were in. There was a book on plant biology next to a book on Greek mythology, then a first edition of *Lord of the Rings* next to a book on fairies. There were historical books, works of fiction, books of photographs and books written by hand. In turn, Nightingale noted down the title and the author and a number corresponding to its position on the shelf.

A bell rang somewhere upstairs. 'Who's that?' asked Nightingale.

Jenny smiled sarcastically. 'I'm not psychic,' she said.

'Yeah, that was just about the only thing missing from your CV,' said Nightingale. He stood up and walked the length of the basement to where half a dozen LCD screens were fixed to the wall in two banks of three. Nightingale tapped a button on a stainless-steel console in front of the screens and they flickered into life. There was a man in a dark overcoat standing in front of the main door, his hands in his pockets.

'Who is it?' called Jenny.

'The last person I want to see just now,' said Nightingale.

9

Nightingale pulled open the front door. Superintendent Chalmers was standing in the driveway,
his hands in the pockets of his cashmere overcoat. He
looked more like a Conservative politician than a policeman in his dark pinstriped suit and perfectly knotted blue
and cream striped tie. Behind him was a hard-faced
woman in a beige belted raincoat, her hair cut short and
dyed blonde. She was in her early thirties, probably a
detective sergeant, with dark patches under her eyes as
if she hadn't slept well the previous night.

'What are you doing working so late?' asked Nightingale.
'Superintendents don't get paid overtime.'

'Thought I'd check out the new Nightingale residence,' said the superintendent. 'Nice. Very nice. Bit
off the beaten trail, though.' He looked around, nodding
slowly. 'Missed you at the office, couldn't find you at
the flat in Bayswater, so thought I'd check out your
inheritance.'

'How can I help you?' asked Nightingale. He looked
at his watch. 'I've got to get back to London.'

The superintendent ignored the question. 'What are
you going to do when they take away your licence for
drunk-driving? Not very well served by public transport,

are you, and a minicab's going to set you back about a hundred quid from London.'

'That's why you're here, is it? To check up on my drink-driving case? Haven't you got better things to do with your time?'

'I'm just saying. You were over the limit so you'll get a twelve-month ban at least, plus a fine. Of up to five grand and maybe even a few months behind bars.' Chalmers looked up at the roof. 'Must be a ton of lead up there. What's security like out here in the sticks? Surrey Police keep an eye on the place, do they?'

'What do you want?' asked Nightingale. He took out his pack of Marlboro and lit one.

'A bit of respect for a start,' said Chalmers.

Nightingale shook his head. 'I'm not in the Job now, and even when I was I had precious little respect for you. You're on private property and unless you've got some sort of warrant then I'm going to have to ask you to leave.' He blew smoke up at the sky.

'I'm told you inherited this place,' said Chalmers. Nightingale shrugged but didn't reply. 'And the guy who left it to you blew his head off with a shotgun. Is that true?'

'You know it's true,' said Nightingale. 'It's my property now and I want you off it.'

'This Ainsley Gosling was your long-lost father, right?'

'My biological father,' said Nightingale. 'I was adopted at birth.'

'I wish I had a rich father to leave me a big house,' said Chalmers.

Nightingale looked pointedly at his watch. 'I've got things to do,' he said.

'I had a call from my opposite number in Abersoch. Seems you were at another murder scene.'

'It was a suicide,' said Nightingale.

'There seem to be a lot of deaths around you these days,' said Chalmers. 'Your uncle and aunt. Robbie Hoyle. Barry O'Brien, who was driving the cab that ran over Hoyle. And of course good old Simon Underwood, who took a flyer through his office window while you were talking to him.'

Nightingale took a long drag on his cigarette but didn't say anything.

'Your mother killed herself, too, didn't she?'

'My parents died in a car crash years ago.'

'You know what I mean, Nightingale. Your birth mother. Genetic mother. Rebecca Keeley. Whatever you want to call her. She slashed her wrists after you paid her a visit, didn't she? Did you think I wouldn't find out about that?'

'She was a troubled woman,' said Nightingale. 'You can talk to the people at the home.'

'Troubled why?'

'She was on medication, Chalmers. She was a sick woman. Yes, I went to see her, twice, but she wasn't able to say much. I don't think she even knew I was there.'

'Why did she put you up for adoption?'

Nightingale shrugged again. 'I don't know,' he lied. There was no way that he was going to tell Chalmers that Keeley had been forced to give up her new-born baby to fulfil a deal that Ainsley Gosling had made with a demon from Hell.

The superintendent nodded at the hallway. 'Are you alone in there?'

'What do you want, Chalmers?' said Nightingale.

'I want you to tell me who else is in the house with you,' said the superintendent. 'I was wondering if maybe the lovely Miss McLean was there so that we could kill two birds with one stone.'

Nightingale frowned. 'What are you talking about?'

'Is Jenny McLean inside or not?' said the superintendent. 'I'm not pissing about here, Nightingale.'

'Yes, she is. Why?'

'Because we want to talk to her, and to you, about what happened in Battersea.' He sneered at Nightingale with undisguised contempt. 'How stupid do you think we are, Nightingale? Did you think we wouldn't check the CCTV cameras and that we wouldn't find out that you were in the flat when George Harrison took a flyer off his balcony?'

10

The uniformed officer, who looked as if he was barely out of his teens, showed Nightingale into an interview room and asked him if he wanted a tea or a coffee. He asked for a coffee and sat down at the table. Chalmers and the female detective had taken Jenny along to another interview room. After ten minutes the constable reappeared with a cup of canteen coffee.

'You didn't spit in it, did you?' joked Nightingale.

The constable stared at him blankly and sat down opposite him.

'Is this going to take long because I'll need a cigarette break soon,' said Nightingale.

The constable shrugged but didn't say anything. Nightingale looked at his watch but as he did so the door opened and Chalmers walked in holding a clipboard and two blank cassette tapes. Behind him was another detective, who Nightingale recognised. Dan Evans. Evans was a detective inspector in his late thirties, with prematurely greying hair and an expanding waistline that hinted at a fondness for beer.

'It's almost midnight,' said Nightingale. 'Can't this wait until tomorrow?'

'No it can't,' said Chalmers.

'You don't need Jenny here,' said Nightingale.

'I'll be the judge of that,' said the superintendent. He nodded at the constable. 'Off you go, lad, we'll take it from here.'

'Yes, sir,' said the constable, and he hurried out.

Evans took the two tapes from Chalmers, sat down opposite Nightingale and slotted them into the recorder.

'She's just my assistant,' said Nightingale.

'She was at a crime scene,' said Chalmers.

'It wasn't a crime; he jumped,' said Nightingale, but the superintendent held up a hand to silence him.

'Wait for the tape, please.'

Evans pressed 'record' and nodded at the superintendent. Chalmers looked up at the clock on the wall. 'It is now twenty-five minutes past eleven on the evening of December the first. I am Superintendent Ronald Chalmers, interviewing Jack Nightingale.' He looked at Nightingale. 'Please say your name for the tape.'

'Jack Nightingale.'

'And with me is . . .' Chalmers nodded at Evans.

'Detective Inspector Dan Evans,' he said.

'For the tape, can you confirm that I have not been charged or cautioned,' said Nightingale.

'You are here to help us with our enquiries,' said the superintendent. 'But I will now ask Detective Inspector Evans to read the caution to you.'

The inspector went through the caution, even though they all knew that Nightingale knew it by heart.

'But I am free to leave whenever I want?' said Nightingale when the inspector had finished.

The superintendent stared at Nightingale with cold eyes. 'At the moment you're helping us with our enquiries.

If that changes then charges might be forthcoming and in that case we will of course follow PACE to the letter.'

Nightingale nodded. 'And Jenny?'

'The same,' he said.

'So how exactly can I help you?' asked Nightingale.

'On November the twenty-third of this year did you and your assistant, Jenny McLean, go to the residence of George Arthur Harrison in Battersea?'

Nightingale folded his arms and sighed. 'You know I did.'

'Yes or no?'

Nightingale sighed again. 'Yes.'

'And why was that?'

'I wanted to talk to him.'

'About what?'

Nightingale glared at the policeman. 'I just wanted to talk to him.'

'About the death of your parents?'

Nightingale nodded.

'For the tape, please.'

'Yes,' said Nightingale. 'I wanted to talk to him about my parents.'

'Because he was driving the truck that crashed into them?'

'Yes,' said Nightingale.

'Why did you leave it so long to go and talk to him? Your parents died fourteen years ago.'

Nightingale didn't answer.

'Did you hear the question, Mr Nightingale?'

'I don't have an answer to that.'

Chalmers leaned forward. 'You don't know why you suddenly felt the urge to go and see the man who killed your parents?'

'I'd only just found out where he lived,' said Nightingale, even though he knew that wasn't the reason.

'Your parents died fourteen years ago. You went to see the man who killed them less than two weeks ago. I don't see that for someone who was a policeman for as long as you were it would have taken fourteen years to track him down. What made you suddenly want to see him again? Revenge?'

'Harrison didn't mean to kill my parents. It was an accident. An RTA, pure and simple.'

'You believe that?'

'Of course I do. There was an inquest, he wasn't charged with anything. It was a rainy night, my father overtook a car on a blind corner and hit Harrison's truck. It was a stupid accident.'

'So you didn't bear him any ill will?'

Nightingale leaned forward and placed his hands on the table. 'Are you stupid?' he said. 'If I did want him dead I'd hardly have waited fourteen years before throwing him off a balcony. Give me some credit, Chalmers. If I wanted to kill someone I'd be a bit more creative than that.'

'Maybe you lost your temper. Maybe he said something that set you off.'

'We were talking on the balcony and he jumped.'

'Why did he do that?'

Nightingale shrugged. 'I really don't know. We were having a conversation and he jumped.'

'Like Simon Underwood did?'

'Am I helping you with your enquiries into the death of George Harrison or Simon Underwood?' said Nightingale.

'There seems to be a pattern here. You go to talk to people and they die. It happened in Canary Wharf with Simon Underwood, in Abersoch with Constance Miller and in Battersea with George Harrison.'

'What do you want me to say?' asked Nightingale.

'I want the truth,' said Chalmers, leaning forward and interlinking the fingers of both hands as if he was about to pray. 'I want you to tell me what happened. I want you to tell me why George Harrison died. Did you kill him?'

Nightingale's jaw dropped. 'Did I what?'

'Did you push George Harrison off the balcony?'

'Of course not.'

'He just decided to commit suicide while you were there?'

Nightingale nodded. 'That's what happened.'

'And Miss McLean will back you up on that, will she?'

'She was inside the flat. She wasn't on the balcony.'

'So you're saying that she won't be able to back you up?'

'She didn't see me push Harrison off the balcony because that's not what happened.' Nightingale stared scornfully at the superintendent. 'You've got nothing,' he said. 'If you did you would have charged me by now. You know I was there and I'm not denying it, but there'll be no forensic that suggests I did anything but talk to him. Jenny McLean was there and she'll back me up.'

'We'll see about that,' said Chalmers.

'Yes,' said Nightingale. 'We will.' He looked at the clock on the wall. 'Are we done?'

'We're done when I say that we're done,' said the superintendent. 'We have CCTV footage of you arriving at the tower block where Mr Harrison lived. And we have video of you leaving thirty-eight minutes later. So you and Mr Harrison must have had quite a chat before he decided to throw himself off the balcony.'

'He let us in, we went out onto the balcony, we talked for two minutes at most, and then he jumped.'

'Why were you on the balcony?'

Nightingale sighed. 'He wanted some air. And I wanted a smoke. I was just about to light a cigarette when he jumped.'

'Then explain to me why you were in the building for thirty-eight minutes.'

Nightingale rubbed the back of his neck. 'I don't like lifts. We walked up nine flights and we walked down.'

'Why don't you like lifts?'

Nightingale folded his arms. 'I just don't.'

'Fear of heights?'

'It's nothing to do with heights. It's being suspended in a box held up by wires that makes me nervous.'

The superintendent tapped his pen against his clipboard. 'So let's say it takes – what, a minute per floor? Nine floors, nine minutes. Probably a bit faster going down. Let's say a total of sixteen minutes up and down. That leaves twenty-two minutes. You said that you spoke for just two minutes before he went over the balcony. So that leaves twenty minutes to be accounted for. What were you and Miss McLean doing for those twenty minutes?'

Nightingale stared at the superintendent but didn't say anything.

'Are you refusing to answer the question?'

'I'm thinking how best to phrase my answer,' said Nightingale.

'Just tell the truth,' said Chalmers. 'That's all we want. What were you doing for twenty minutes?'

'I was cleaning,' said Nightingale quietly. 'I was cleaning the surfaces that we touched.'

'You were removing forensic evidence,' said the superintendent.

'You could say that, yes.'

'You wiped away your fingerprints. You cleaned everything you had touched, and then you left. Is that correct?'

Nightingale nodded.

'For the tape, please.'

'Yes,' said Nightingale.

'You tampered with a crime scene?'

'It wasn't a crime scene,' said Nightingale.

'So why destroy forensic evidence unless you wanted to hide your guilt?'

'I wanted to avoid this,' said Nightingale. 'I wanted to avoid being given the third degree for something I didn't do. I thought it would be easier just to walk away and not be involved.'

'But you can see how what you did suggests that you had something to hide?'

'I can see that, yes,' admitted Nightingale.

'So why didn't you call nine-nine-nine instead of running away?'

'He fell nine floors,' said Nightingale. 'He was beyond needing the emergency services.'

'The police,' said Chalmers. 'Why didn't you report it to the police?'

Nightingale glared at the superintendent. 'Because I wanted to avoid this.'

'This?'

'Being interrogated as if it was somehow my fault. It wasn't. He jumped of his own accord. I don't know why he did it, but he did, and nothing I did or said afterwards was going to change what had happened.'

'You left a crime scene,' said Chalmers.

'It was a suicide and suicide isn't a crime.'

'But pushing someone to their death most definitely is,' said Chalmers.

'That's not what happened.'

'In which case you should have given the police the opportunity of deciding whether or not a crime had taken place.'

'Are you going to charge me?' asked Nightingale.

'Not right now,' said Chalmers, writing a note on his pad.

Nightingale stood up. 'Then I'm out of here.'

'That's up to you. But this isn't over.'

'It never is with you, Chalmers,' said Nightingale.

11

Nightingale walked out of the police station and lit a cigarette, then phoned a minicab firm. He had smoked half his cigarette when Jenny appeared.

'Well, that was a waste of everybody's time,' she said.

'I'm sorry,' said Nightingale.

'It's not your fault,' said Jenny, buttoning up her coat. 'Just bloody-minded policemen.'

'Who questioned you? The female cop?'

'She was in the room but a uniformed inspector asked the questions. Some guy called Johnson. Do you know him?'

Nightingale shook his head.

'He was an idiot. They were trying this "good cop, bad cop" routine with the woman pretending that she was my new best friend and Johnson threatening me with life behind bars for helping you cover up a murder. Please tell me that all cops aren't as stupid as that?'

Nightingale blew a tight plume of smoke up at the sky. 'It varies,' he said. 'Chalmers isn't stupid but he's got his sights set on me. What did you tell them?'

'I said you pushed Harrison off the balcony and threatened to kill me if I told anyone.' Nightingale's jaw dropped and Jenny grinned and shook her head.

'Don't do that to me,' he said.

'Well, for goodness sake, Jack, what do you think I said?'

'I just hope you told them what happened,' he said. 'Because that's what I did.'

Jenny sighed. 'Please give me some credit,' she said. 'Anyway, if they weren't happy with what we said they wouldn't have let us go, would they?'

'They can't hold us without charging us,' said Nightingale. 'And they don't have enough evidence for that.'

'There you are, then,' she said.

'You told them about cleaning the flat, the fingerprints and all?'

She nodded. 'I figured I had to, right? If they'd looked at the CCTV footage then they must have gone looking for fingerprints and it would have been obvious that the place had been wiped clean. So yeah, I told them.'

Nightingale nodded. 'That's good. At least we're consistent,' he said.

'Do you think that'll be the end of it?'

'I hope so,' said Nightingale. 'But Chalmers will carry on sniffing around, that much I'm sure of. He's already spoken to the Welsh cop so I think I'm going to have more hassle on that front.' He dropped his cigarette butt on the ground and stamped on it.

Jenny nodded at his foot. 'You'd better watch that they don't do you for littering.'

They had to wait for almost an hour before a minicab turned up outside the police station. 'This is outrageous,' said Jenny as she got into the back of the car. 'They picked us up and brought us here so they should bloody well take us back.'

'It doesn't work like that,' said Nightingale as he climbed in and pulled the door shut. 'Lifts home went out with *Dixon of Dock Green*.'

'We should sue them,' said Jenny. 'They didn't arrest us; they just wanted to question us. They should at least have let you drive here in your car.'

'They probably thought I'd do a runner,' said Nightingale.

The driver twisted around in his seat. He was dark-skinned with a heavy beard. 'Where to?' he growled.

Nightingale looked at Jenny. 'Do you want to come back to the house while I pick up the MGB or shall I drop you in Chelsea?'

'I'll go home,' she said. 'You'd be better collecting the car during the day, Jack.' She looked at her wristwatch. 'I thought there were laws about when the police could question people.'

'PACE doesn't apply when you're helping them with their enquiries.'

'Oh that's what we were doing, was it? Why does Chalmers have it in for you?'

Nightingale grimaced. 'He's never liked me, right from the first time we met. Reckons I'm a maverick.'

Jenny laughed. 'Well, he's probably right.'

'Yeah, well, he's a box-ticker; everything has to be done by the book. He won't have it any other way.' He tapped the back of the driver's seat. 'Chelsea, mate,' he said. 'Is it okay to smoke?'

'No smoking,' said the driver.

'Terrific,' said Nightingale. 'Where are you from?'

'Afghanistan,' said the driver, putting the car in gear and driving off.

'I thought they were big smokers in Afghanistan,' said Nightingale.

'This is England,' said the driver. 'No smoking in taxis.'

'So you left Afghanistan because of the Taliban?' asked Jenny.

The driver laughed and slapped his chest with the flat of his hand. 'I am Taliban!' he said proudly. 'I leave my country when the Americans invaded. Americans kill many Taliban. Very dangerous to stay there. So I come to England.'

Nightingale leaned forward. 'Are you saying you got asylum in the UK because you were with the Taliban?'

The driver grinned at Nightingale in the rear-view mirror. 'England is a great country,' he said. 'They give me lawyer, house for me and my family, and easy to get driving licence. Many of my friends are here already. Next month my wife's mother is coming. She will be British citizen also.'

Nightingale looked at Jenny and shook his head in amazement. 'Yeah,' he said. 'England is a great country. Can you believe that?'

Jenny grinned at Nightingale. 'You're going to have to get used to this,' she said. 'When they take away your licence you'll be in cabs all the time.'

'Maybe,' said Nightingale. 'But I've got a plan.'

12

Nightingale took a minicab to Gosling Manor first thing the next day and drove the MGB back to London. It was mid-morning when he got to the office. He put a brown paper bag on Jenny's desk. 'Muffins and croissants,' he said. 'The breakfast of champions.'

Jenny looked up from a stack of printed sheets. 'Did you bring coffee as well?'

'Don't go all gift horse on me,' said Nightingale. 'You know your coffee's much better than their mass-produced stuff.'

She looked inside the bag. 'Banana chocolate chip,' she said. 'My favourite.'

'Glad I can do something right,' he said, leaning against the edge of her desk. 'So what's happening?'

'I've been looking at suicides in Abersoch,' said Jenny.

'Now why on earth would you be doing that?'

'From what you said, there's no doubt that Constance Miller killed herself. But the cops seem determined to pin it on you, right?'

Nightingale nodded. 'Yeah, that was weird. It's as if they wanted it to be murder. They wanted to turn it into something that it wasn't.'

'That's what I thought,' said Jenny, breaking a chunk off one of the muffins and popping it into her mouth.

Nightingale looked over at the coffee-maker and Jenny sighed.

'Coffee, Jack?'

He grinned. 'You really are psychic, aren't you?' As Jenny went over to the coffee-maker he picked up the printed sheets.

Jenny looked over her shoulder. 'I started by Googling suicides in Wales,' she said.

'Why?'

'Do you know how many women have killed themselves in Wales over the past two years?'

Nightingale shrugged. 'It's a pretty depressing place,' he said.

'You are so Welshist,' she said.

'Bollocks – some of my best friends are Welsh. How many?'

'Just over three hundred,' she said. 'Which, considering the size of the population, is about average for the UK.'

'So?'

'So, I've been looking at the suicide rate for the area around Abersoch. And it's way up. Much higher than average.' She took two coffees over to her desk, gave one to Nightingale and sat down.

'I'm listening,' he said.

'Here's the thing. Every year between five and six thousand people kill themselves in the UK. Tends to be more in a recession, fewer when things are going well.'

'Makes sense,' said Nightingale, tapping out a Marlboro.

'Men are more likely than women to kill themselves.' She grinned. 'Probably all that testosterone. So the suicide rate for men is just under seventeen for every hundred thousand. That's about three-quarters of the total. For every one woman who takes her own life, three men do the same.'

'We die younger too,' said Nightingale. 'It really isn't fair.' He lit his cigarette and blew a perfect smoke ring up at the ceiling.

'This is serious, Jack,' said Jenny, leaning forward. 'The national suicide rate for women aged between fifteen and forty-four is the lowest of any group. Fewer than five per hundred thousand. Which means that in Wales, with its population of just under three million, you'd expect fewer than a hundred and fifty women of that age to kill themselves. That's equivalent to three hundred over two years.'

'Which is about right, you said.'

She took the printed sheets from him and fanned them out, then handed one back to him. It was a map with red dots on it. 'Yes, for the country as a whole. But then I looked at the area around Abersoch. Abersoch gets crowded during the summer months but at this time of year it's only locals living there and they number about a thousand. So, statistically, you'd expect fewer than one suicide a year among women. But so far this year there have been three.'

Nightingale nodded thoughtfully as he looked at the map. 'Okay, but suicides sometimes come in clusters. We had a rash of them in south London when I was a cop. Teenager topped herself and posted her suicide note on Facebook; within six months two others had followed suit. There was a bit of a panic on for a while but then it all died down.'

'This is different, Jack,' she said. 'This has been going

on for five years now, at least. That's as far back as I've gone so far.'

'What exactly do you think has been going on?'

She gave him another sheet, this one a map of Wales. Like the first map, it was dotted with red circles. 'I widened the search area to include Caernarfon and a few other towns within an hour's drive of Abersoch. That takes the population up to almost twenty thousand. With a population of that size you might expect one woman a year to commit suicide. Again, it's just between the ages of fifteen and forty-four we're looking at. The suicide rate starts to go up with age after that, obviously.'

'Why obviously?' asked Nightingale.

'Older people get sick, Jack. They get cancer and they have strokes and they get heart disease and a lot decide to end it themselves. People die after being married for years and their spouses can't go on alone.'

Nightingale shivered. 'You're painting a pretty depressing picture of old age.'

'Well, if you know any good points, let me know,' said Jenny. 'Look, if you had two women killing themselves then that could possibly be a statistical variation, but any more than that really should set alarm bells ringing.'

'The suspense is killing me,' said Nightingale. 'How many were there?'

'This year, six. Constance Miller was the sixth. And last year there were five. There were five the year before that. Over the past five years there have been twenty-four suicides when you would have expected five at the most.'

Nightingale took a long pull on his cigarette but didn't say anything.

'I did a cross-check with a similar-sized population

in south Wales,' she said. 'It came in bang in line with expectations.'

'And no one has spotted this?'

She pressed a button on her keyboard. An article from the *Cardiff Mail* flashed up on the screen. 'The local press has run a few stories on it, trying to link the suicides to activity on various social networking sites.'

'What, suicide becomes fashionable so everyone wants to do it? That's what they reckoned was happening in London. The me-too factor. Peer pressure.'

Jenny nodded earnestly. 'That's pretty much how they're playing it, yeah,' she said. 'They ran a couple of articles but then the story just died.'

Nightingale nodded at the screen. 'Why are you so interested in all this?'

'We got her name from the Ouija board. There has to be some reason for that.'

'Coincidence,' said Nightingale.

'You don't believe that,' said Jenny. 'We were trying to talk to Robbie and you were sent to Abersoch and Connie Miller killed herself just as you got there. That can't be a coincidence, and you know it. You were sent there for a reason, Jack.'

'Which was?'

Jenny took a deep breath. 'Okay, this is what I think. What if someone is killing women and making it look like suicide?'

'You mean a serial killer?'

'What better way of hiding your murders than making them look like suicides?'

'And you're saying that whoever it is has killed two dozen women in the last five years?'

'I'm saying it's a possibility, yes.'

'So why aren't the Welsh cops onto it?'

'Maybe they are,' she said. 'Maybe that's why they were so keen to pin Connie Miller's killing on you. You might have been their serial killer.'

'But they don't want to start a panic so they're keeping mum?' said Nightingale. He nodded thoughtfully. 'You could be right.' He took a long pull on his cigarette and blew smoke. 'So why did Robbie tell us to go to Abersoch? Why did he send us to Constance Miller?'

'That's the question, isn't it?' said Jenny.

'It's a hell of a mistake. We ask him where my sister is and he sends me off to a serial killer's latest victim.' He shrugged. 'The more I think about it, the more I wonder if Constance Miller actually is my sister.'

'I thought the Welsh cops ruled that out?'

'Cops are cops,' said Nightingale. 'Most of the time they operate with tunnel vision. Just because they think she's not my sister doesn't mean that's gospel. Until a few weeks ago, I thought Bill and Irene were my biological parents. If someone had ever told me that I was adopted I'd have laughed in their face. Gosling was very good at covering his tracks.' He blew more smoke up at the ceiling. 'I've got to go back to Abersoch.'

'Why?'

'Maybe she is my sister. Maybe the cops are wrong. I have to find out for sure.' He pointed at Jenny's computer. 'Can you go on line and find me a hotel for tonight? I'll go home and pick up some stuff. And see if you can get an address for Constance Miller's parents off the electoral roll.'

Jenny winced. 'Are you sure that's a good idea?'

Nightingale pushed himself off her desk and headed for the door. 'No, but it's the only one I've got at the moment.'

13

It was evening and had been dark for several hours by the time Nightingale arrived in Abersoch. Jenny had booked him into the Riverside Hotel, which was on the banks of the River Soch and a short walk from the harbour. He parked his MGB behind the hotel and carried in his small suitcase. A pretty redhead checked him in and took him to his room.

'Are you here on business?' she asked after she'd shown him how to use the cable TV.

Nightingale looked out of the window. His room was at the front of the hotel and he had a view over the river. 'Sort of,' he said.

'This is the quiet time of the year,' she said. 'We don't get many tourists. But we're full over Christmas and New Year.'

'It's a lovely hotel,' he said, slipping her a five-pound note. 'I heard that there have been a few deaths in the area recently. That's not put people off coming, has it?'

'Deaths?' she frowned. Then her eyes widened. 'Oh you mean the suicides? Did you read about that in London?'

'Yeah, it said the police weren't sure what was going on.'

'The last story I heard was that they'd all been on some

Facebook site or something,' she said. 'There was a woman died on Tuesday, did you know?'

'Really?' said Nightingale, feigning ignorance. 'What happened?'

The redhead shuddered. 'She hanged herself. Connie Miller. She used to drink in our bar sometimes. Vodka tonic, no lemon. Nice woman. We can't believe what happened.'

'Must have been depressed, I guess.'

'I don't think so,' she said. 'They say she tied a washing line to the banister and jumped off the landing.' She shuddered again. 'I could never do anything like that.'

'Me neither,' agreed Nightingale.

'I'd use tablets or something. I couldn't face trying to hang myself. Can you imagine what it must be like?'

'I can't,' said Nightingale, even though he knew exactly what it had been like for Connie Miller. He jumped as the phone rang.

'I'll leave you to it,' said the redhead, and she closed the door behind her as she left.

Nightingale picked up the receiver, frowning because nobody knew that he was in Abersoch.

'Jack, it's me.' It was Jenny. 'I've been ringing your mobile but it keeps going through to voicemail.'

Nightingale fished his phone out of his raincoat pocket and looked at the screen. 'I haven't got a signal,' he said.

'Well, I've got you now,' she said. 'And I've got an address for Connie Miller's parents.' Nightingale picked up a pen. 'Are you sure about this, Jack?'

'Depends what you mean.'

'You're planning to talk to them, right?'

'Sure.' He sat on the bed. There was a copy of the New English Bible on the side table and he picked it up.

'You're thinking of going up to complete strangers and asking them if a Satanist gave them their daughter?'

'Well, I intend to be a bit more tactful than that,' he said. 'I'll play it by ear.'

'Go easy on them, please,' said Jenny. 'They've just lost their daughter.'

'I'll be careful,' said Nightingale. 'Cross my heart. Now give me the address.' Jenny read it out and Nightingale scribbled it down on a sheet of hotel notepaper. 'Don't suppose you'd do me another favour, would you?'

'What, exactly?'

'Would you mind going back to Gosling Manor and getting stuck into the inventory? I really do need to know what books are there.'

'Jack, it's miles from anywhere.'

'The way things are going, I'll never get it done,' he said.

'You're the one who decided to run off to Wales.'

'Pretty please?'

'Jack . . .'

'Pretty please with sugar on top?'

'I'm not sure that I want to be out in the depths of Surrey on my own,' she said. 'And you know how spooky that basement is.'

'Gosling Manor is right out of *Country Homes and Gardens*,' said Nightingale.

'The house is lovely; it's the basement that gives me the heebie-jeebies.'

'What are you, twelve?' laughed Nightingale.

'And let's not forget that your father blew his head off in the master bedroom,' said Jenny.

'So now you're scared of ghosts?'

'It's not a question of being scared.' She sighed. 'Well, maybe it is. Maybe I could ask Barbara to come with me. Would that be okay?'

'Of course. Why wouldn't it be?'

'You might not want a stranger traipsing through your house, that's all.'

'It's my house in name only,' said Nightingale. 'I've no personal attachment to it. And Barbara's not a stranger. She's your psychologist friend who I met last month, yes?'

'Psychiatrist. That's right.'

'Sure, take her along. I'll call you later.'

After he ended the call he went downstairs. The redhead at reception was happy to supply him with a street map of the village and he took it through to the Front Door bar and ordered a Corona and a club sandwich. He took his beer over to a corner table and while he waited for his food he studied the map. Connie Miller's house was a couple of hundred yards from the hotel and her parents lived on the edge of the village.

A young barman with his blond hair tied back in a ponytail brought him his sandwich and Nightingale ate it slowly as he mulled over what he was going to do next. He knew he was taking a risk, a stupid risk at that, and there were a dozen reasons why he should just get into his MGB and drive back to London. But he also knew that he wouldn't be able to rest until he was certain whether or not Connie Miller was his sister.

14

Nightingale took his hands out of his raincoat and lit a cigarette as he stared at Connie Miller's house. From the outside there was no sign that someone had died there. It was like every other house in the road, though it was the only one in total darkness. It was just after eleven o'clock at night and the pavements were deserted. Abersoch wasn't the sort of village where people stayed out late, especially in the middle of winter. A cold wind ruffled his hair and he turned up the collar of his raincoat. The forecast had been for temperatures just above freezing with the threat of snow to come.

He smoked his cigarette as he walked past the house to the end of the street, and then dropped the butt down a drain. He took out a pair of black leather gloves and put them on. The only sound was from the occasional car in the distance. He walked back to the house, not too quickly, not too slowly, looking casually left and right to reassure himself that no one was watching, then opened the gate. He grimaced as the hinges squeaked, then closed it behind him and walked quietly down the paved path that led to the back of the semi-detached house.

He reached the kitchen door and paused. The last time he'd been there the kitchen door was open but this time it was locked. He checked the kitchen window and that was also locked, and when he stood back and looked up he could see that the windows on the first floor were all securely closed. There were French windows leading into the sitting room. He pushed them with his gloved hands. There was some movement but they were locked. He put a hand up against the window and peered inside. There were no signs of any alarm sensors, and no alarm box on the outside of the house.

Nightingale turned around and looked at the garden. At the far end, backing onto a neatly clipped head-high privet hedge, was a wooden garden shed with a pitched bitumen-coated felt roof. He walked down the garden, keeping close to the hedge on his left and watching the house next door. The shed door wasn't locked but, like the front gate, it squeaked as he opened it. There was a petrol mower inside and a selection of old gardening tools, including a spade. He took the spade back to the house and used it to prise open the French windows. He slid back the door and stepped inside. The only sound was his breathing and he made a conscious effort to calm down. He put the spade on the floor and closed the French windows.

He walked across the dining room and opened the door to the hallway. Although he had a small torch in his pocket he didn't use it; he didn't want to risk anyone outside seeing the beam and there was enough moonlight to see by. He stepped into the hallway.

Apart from the stains on the carpet, there was no trace of Connie Miller or her suicide. The shoe that had been at the bottom of the stairs had gone, as had the washing line that she'd used to hang herself. He stood for a while staring up at where he'd first seen her, the body gently swaying in the air. He felt his heart start to race and took a deep breath to steady himself.

He went into the sitting room. It was neat and tidy, with an Ikea futon and an Ikea coffee table and a small television on an Ikea cupboard. Tucked away in one corner was a computer on an Ikea desk. He sat down in front of the computer and switched it on. He took out his mobile. He smiled when he saw that he had a signal and he phoned Jenny. 'I need your help,' he said.

'I'm in bed, Jack.'

'Okay, but I still need your help,' he said. 'I'm sitting at Connie Miller's computer. I want to copy her files and stuff – can you talk me through it?'

Jenny groaned. 'You really are computer illiterate, aren't you?'

'I have other skills,' he said. 'What do I do?'

'What are you going to copy the files onto?'

'I was hoping you'd tell me.'

'Do you have a thumb drive on you?'

Nightingale laughed. 'Yeah, it's in my pocket next to my personal jet pack. Of course I don't have a thumb drive.'

'Okay, look around and see if you can find one. Or recordable DVDs.'

'There're some DVDs next to the keyboard.'

'There you go, then.'

Jenny spent the next fifteen minutes talking him through the process of transferring files from the computer to a DVD. When he had finished he went back into the hallway and slowly climbed the stairs, his gloved hand on the banister. At the top of the stairs were three doors. Nightingale guessed correctly that the room at the front of the house was the main bedroom. He opened it to find a double bed with a black teddy bear propped up against the pillows. On one wall was a framed picture of white horses racing through foaming surf. There were small tables either side of the bed. On one there was a lamp and a Garfield alarm clock, on the other a photograph of a couple in their fifties in a brass frame. Nightingale picked up the photograph. It was probably her parents, he figured. They looked like a nice couple, and the man had his arms protectively around his wife and a proud tilt to his chin as he looked into the camera. 'Do you know why she did it?' Nightingale whispered to the image. 'Do you have any idea why she killed herself?'

He put the photograph back on the bedside table and walked over to the dressing table. He caught sight of his reflection and grinned at himself. 'Jack Nightingale, cat burglar,' he said. 'Where did it all go wrong?'

There were two hairbrushes next to a line of perfume bottles. The larger of the two brushes had several hairs among the bristles. Nightingale took a Ziploc bag from the pocket of his raincoat, slipped the hairbrush into it and sealed it.

He went into the bathroom. It was spotless, the towels neatly folded on a heated rack, hair treatment products in a neat line on a shelf, a tube of toothpaste neatly squeezed at the end. There was an Oral B electric toothbrush slotted into a charger. Nightingale picked it up, pulled off the brush head and put it in a second Ziploc bag. He looked around for a replacement head and found one in a drawer. He slotted it into the handle and put the brush back into the charger. As he looked into the mirror above the wash-basin he caught a glimpse of red letters written across the wall behind him. Nightingale froze, his mouth open in surprise. He stared at the letters, which glistened wetly. They were uneven and irregular as if they had been smeared carelessly across the tiles. His eyes widened as he stared at the single sentence. His mind scrambled to read the back-to-front words in the mirror:

YOUR SISTER IS GOING TO HELL,
JACK NIGHTINGALE.

With his pulse pounding in his ears, he put a gloved hand out to the mirror, touching it gently as he stared at the reflection. He felt the blood drain from his head and for a moment he almost fainted, then he took a deep breath and turned around. The tiles were spotless. Nightingale blinked and shook his head but there was nothing on the wall. He rubbed his face and swallowed. His mouth had gone dry so he bent down and drank from the cold tap and then he went back downstairs, left the house through the French windows and slid them shut. He put the spade back in the shed and closed the door, then walked along the side of the house to the pavement. There was no one around as he walked through the gate and along the street, and he lit a cigarette as he headed back to the hotel.

15

Nightingale had breakfast in the hotel – egg, bacon, sausage, tomato, mushroom, white toast and coffee in the restaurant followed by three cigarettes sitting at a trestle table in the garden – before walking to the house where Connie Miller's parents lived. It was a small brick cottage on the edge of the village, surrounded by tall conifers that swayed in the wind. The sky was grey and overcast and there were half a dozen seagulls hunched together on the roof.

Nightingale walked up to the front door. There was no bell but in the middle of the door there was a weathered iron knocker in the shape of an owl's head with a ring held in its mouth. He knocked and then stood back, looking up at the cottage. The curtains were drawn in the upstairs windows. He knocked again. He heard a dog bark and turned around to see an elderly woman wrapped up in a duffle coat walking a cocker spaniel on a lead. He smiled and nodded as she walked by. He looked at his watch. It was nine o'clock in the morning. There was no car parked in front of the house so it was possible the Millers had already left the house. He knocked again, then took his mobile phone from his raincoat. The phone signal was patchy around the hotel but now he had a full signal. He phoned 118-118. The operator soon had a number for the Millers and Nightingale asked her to put him through. He heard a ringing tone and a second later a faint ringing from inside the house. The call went un-answered and Nightingale cut the connection. He walked over to the garage at the side of the house. The door opened upwards and it wasn't locked. Inside was a dark blue VW Passat.

'Terrific,' muttered Nightingale. He knew he should walk away. He should go back to the hotel, get into his MGB, and drive back to London. He could phone from London and ask any questions he had then, and if no one answered the phone – well, so be it. He had the toothbrush head and the brush with its hairs and that was all he needed to confirm whether or not Connie Miller was his sister. He closed the garage door.

There was a wooden gate at the side of the garage. It opened silently on well-oiled hinges. Nightingale had a sick feeling in the pit of his stomach as he walked down the path, his mind racing. The car in the garage suggested that there was someone at home but, if there was, why wasn't the phone being answered and why did no one react to the knocking? 'Because they're dead' was the thought echoing through his mind. 'They're dead and you're going to find their bodies and the shit is going to hit the fan again.'

Nightingale wanted a cigarette but he knew that it wasn't the time for a smoke. The garden was a neat square of grass with a line of conifers marking a border with another cottage. There was a wooden bird table in one corner with a metal mesh container filled with peanuts. Two blue tits flew away as Nightingale walked over to the kitchen door. 'If it's locked I'm calling it quits,' he whispered to himself. 'I walk away and get the hell out of Dodge.' He put a gloved hand on the knob and turned. The door opened and Nightingale's heart began to pound.

He stepped into the kitchen and carefully closed the door behind him. 'Mr Miller? Mrs Miller? Hello? Is anybody there?'

There was an electric kettle next to the sink and Nightingale touched it with the back of his gloved hand. Even through the leather he could feel that the kettle was hot. His mouth had gone so dry that it hurt when he swallowed. His heart was racing and he took a deep breath and exhaled slowly. He knew that he shouldn't be in the house but he couldn't walk away, not without knowing what, if anything, had happened to the Millers. He moved towards the hall, his Hush Puppies squeaking on the gleaming linoleum.

The hallway was carpeted, a red hexagonal pattern on a blue background, more suited to a pub than a home, and over a small teak table there was a framed painting of the Virgin Mary, whose eyes seemed to follow him as he crept towards the front door. He looked up the stairs, half expecting to see a body hanging there, but there was nothing. There was a door to the left that was ajar. Nightingale pushed it open. 'Mr Miller? Mrs Miller?'

A fire was burning in the grate, which was flanked by two winged armchairs. There was a woman slumped in the armchair on the left. All he could see was the top of her head, light brown hair streaked with grey, and an arm resting on the side of the chair.

'Mrs Miller?' he said. There was no response.

A ginger and white cat was curled up on the sofa by the window and it lifted its head and stared at Nightingale with impassive green eyes. Nightingale wasn't a cat person. He preferred dogs. A dog couldn't hide its true feelings. If it was happy its tail wagged and its eyes sparkled. If it was scared its ears went back and its tail went between its legs. Cats didn't show emotion, though; they just stared and kept their own counsel. Dogs were loyal, too, but cats cared only about their own comfort. When he was still a constable walking a beat Nightingale had been called to a house where an old lady hadn't been seen for more than two weeks. He'd had to break in and he'd found the old woman sprawled across the rug in front of her television. What was left of her. The woman had four cats and they had done what was necessary to survive. They'd started with the soft tissue – her face and thighs – and there wasn't much that was recognisably human by the time Nightingale got there. He'd never forgotten the way the cats had rubbed themselves up against his legs as he'd stared down at the body, mewing and arching their backs. Dogs never ate their owners, no matter how hungry they were. They sat and waited for help or barked to get attention, but that was all.

The cat mewed softly and its tail twitched, then it settled its head on its paws and continued to stare at Nightingale. As he walked towards the fireplace he saw that the woman was wearing purple slippers and one of them had slid off. There was a cup of tea, untouched, on a table at the side of the chair. If she was dead, there didn't appear to have been a struggle.

Nightingale reached out and gently touched the woman's shoulder. That was when she turned to stare up at him in terror and screamed as if she had just been stabbed in the chest.

16

M rs Miller put the cup and saucer on the table at the side of the sofa. 'Milk and no sugar,' she said. She put a plate of chocolate biscuits next to the cup of tea. 'From Marks and Spencer,' she said. 'They do wonderful biscuits.' She sat down in the armchair and smiled at him. 'You must have been so shocked when I screamed.'

Nightingale nodded. 'I thought you were . . .' He shrugged. 'I don't know what I thought.'

Mrs Miller held up her iPod with its in-ear headphones. 'I always listen to music on this,' she said. 'I'm a little bit deaf and I can turn the volume up without annoying the neighbours. They're a marvellous invention.'

'So I hear,' said Nightingale.

'Do you know how many records I have on this?'

Nightingale grinned. 'A lot?'

'I'll say. More than fifty. Fifty albums, and look, it's not much bigger than a box of matches, is it?'

'It's tiny,' agreed Nightingale.

'So I didn't hear you knock and I didn't hear the phone, and when you touched me . . .'

'I am so sorry about that,' said Nightingale. 'But when you didn't answer the door and I saw that the kitchen door wasn't locked, I thought that maybe something had happened to you. I'm just glad that you're okay.'

'And you're a journalist, you said?'

'Freelance,' said Nightingale. He didn't like lying to Mrs Miller but he knew that people were happier talking to reporters than to private investigators. 'I just wanted some background on Connie. For her obituary. What sort of person she was, what sort of life she had, just so that people can appreciate her more. Sometimes a cold news story gives the wrong impression, you know?'

'I still can't believe what happened,' said Mrs Miller. 'I just . . .' She shook her head. 'You never expect . . .' She wiped a tear from her eye with the back of her hand, then reached for a box of tissues and used one to dab at her face.

'I am so sorry about your loss,' said Nightingale.

'I don't know what to do,' she said. 'The doctor gave me some tablets and I keep listening to my music but nothing helps, not really.' She showed him the iPod again. 'Connie gave me this. And put all my records on it. She was always so good with computers.' She dabbed at her eyes. 'Still, I must be strong, right? That's what my husband says.'

'Where is he, Mrs Miller?'

'He's out walking, with the dog. Says it helps him, to keep moving.' She sighed. 'Connie was the perfect daughter, you know? We never had any problems with her. She was a happy baby, she was never any trouble at school, she worked hard and she . . .' Her eyes misted over and she put a hand on her chest. 'I'm sorry,' she said. 'I'm still . . .' She sighed. 'I can't believe it. I can't believe she'd do such a thing.' She pulled another tissue from the box and blew her nose. 'I'm sorry,' she said.

'Was she upset about anything? Depressed?'

Mrs Miller blew her nose. 'I don't think so. If she was, she never said anything to me or to my husband. But then I suppose they don't, do they? People who are depressed bottle it up. I wish she had spoken to me. I don't know why she didn't.'

'What did she do for a living, Mrs Miller?'

'She worked for an estate agent. She was so good at it. She liked dealing with people and everyone liked her. She was always smiling, always happy.' She dabbed at her eyes again.

'What did she do in her free time? Did she have any hobbies?'

'Not really,' said Mrs Miller tearfully. 'She liked the internet. She spent hours on her computer, I think. I used to tease her about it. She told me she had three hundred friends on Facebook and I said that in my whole life I don't think I had more than ten real friends. They're not real friends on Facebook, are they?'

'I don't think so.'

'That's what I said. If she was ever going to find a husband she'd have to find him in the real world, not on the internet.'

'So she didn't have a boyfriend?'

They both looked around at the sound of footsteps in the kitchen. 'Are you expecting someone, Mrs Miller?' whispered Nightingale.

She frowned. 'It's not my husband; he always shouts when he opens the door.'

There was the sound of a chair scraping across lino. Nightingale stood up, motioning for Mrs Miller to keep quiet. He looked around for something to use as a weapon.

There was a brass poker and a matching brush in a stand by the fireplace. He picked up the poker and held it up as he walked on tiptoe towards the kitchen.

He had taken just two steps when someone shouted, 'Now, now, now!' and four uniformed police officers rushed out of the kitchen, screaming and waving batons. Nightingale dropped the poker and raised his hands but the men steamrollered over him, knocking him to the ground.

17

Superintendent Thomas clicked his ballpoint pen as he stared impassively at Nightingale. The detective constable who had sat in on the last interrogation was also sitting across from Nightingale.

'At least this time I get to keep my clothes on,' said Nightingale.

'You think this is funny?' asked the superintendent. 'You think that breaking into a woman's house is funny, do you? I know that in London you punish burglars with a slap on the wrist but here in Wales we take breaking and entering very seriously.'

'I didn't break in,' said Nightingale. 'And you know I didn't. When your men burst in and beat me up I was having tea with Mrs Miller.'

'My men took what steps were necessary to take you into custody.'

'I wasn't arrested and I wasn't informed of my rights, which means custody wasn't an issue. We were having tea together. If your men had bothered to ask her, she'd have told them that I was her guest.'

'You were holding a weapon.'

'A poker. I'd picked up a poker.'

'Which counts as a weapon.'

'We heard a noise in the kitchen. We didn't know who it was.'

'They were uniformed police officers.'

'Yeah, well, we didn't know that when we heard them in the kitchen, did we? We heard a noise, I picked up the poker, then your men charged in and assaulted me.' He sat back in his chair and folded his arms. 'Do your men make a habit of assaulting people for the hell of it?' he asked.

The superintendent clicked his pen again. 'You told her that you were a journalist,' he said quietly.

Nightingale winced. 'A little white lie,' he said. 'I thought she'd be more likely to talk to a journalist than a private detective.'

'And that works, does it?'

Nightingale shrugged. 'Yeah, it does. Especially if you say you're with the local paper.'

'That's misrepresentation and fraud.'

'Not really,' said Nightingale. 'I wasn't trying to con her out of money, I just wanted some information.'

'So you lied?'

'I bent the facts. I didn't think she'd be able to handle the fact that I was the one who found her daughter. It's not as if I was pretending to be a police officer.'

'None the less you broke into her house and lied about your identity.'

'The back door was open.'

'You seem to make a habit of walking into other people's houses, don't you?'

'I've already explained about Connie Miller. And when I wanted to talk to her parents, I knocked on the door. Then I went around to the back of the house and knocked again. I tried the door and it was open.'

'Any normal person wouldn't have tried the door,' said the superintendent. 'Any normal person would have gone away and tried again later.'

'I thought . . .'

'Yes, what did you think? What exactly was going through your mind when you walked uninvited into Mr and Mrs Miller's house?'

Nightingale ran a hand through his hair. 'To be honest, I thought that maybe something had happened. Something bad.'

'Such as?'

Nightingale wanted a cigarette, badly. 'In view of what I found when I went to Connie Miller's house, I was expecting the worst. I thought maybe she was dead. Then I saw her sitting in her armchair and she didn't seem to be moving.'

'She screamed,' said the superintendent. 'Loud enough to wake the dead. A neighbour out walking her dog called us.'

'I surprised her,' said Nightingale. 'She was listening to her iPod. It was all a misunderstanding.'

'Telling her that you were a journalist was a misunderstanding? I think not.'

'I need a cigarette,' said Nightingale. He gestured at the tape recorder. 'Look, the fact that you haven't bothered switching this on suggests you're not going to take this anywhere. You just want to haul me over the coals and I understand that and I consider myself hauled. But we both know that I haven't done anything that merits an ASBO, never mind a court appearance.'

'Why did you come back, Nightingale? Why did you travel right the way across your country and then across mine to lie to a sweet lady who's still grieving over the loss of her only daughter?'

Nightingale stared at the policeman but didn't say anything.

'I'm waiting,' said Thomas.

'What do you expect me to say?'

'The truth would be a good start.'

Nightingale sighed. 'I wanted to know why Connie Miller killed herself.'

'And why would that be any concern of yours? I already told you that she wasn't related to you.'

'Maybe not, but I found her body. We had a connection.'

'And so you went back to London and then decided to come all the way back here because you think that you have a "connection" as you call it.'

'I know there's something not right about her death,' Nightingale said quietly. 'I also know there are more suicides than there should be in this part of the world. Something's going on. You know it and now I know it.' He gestured at the tape recorder. 'You're not switching that on, so I can go, right?'

'What do you know about Connie Miller's death?' asked the superintendent. 'What do you know that you're not telling me?'

'I know that you think there's a serial killer on the loose who's making the murders look like suicides.' It had been a shot in the dark but Nightingale had the satisfaction of seeing the policeman's jaw tighten and his eyes harden. 'Why haven't you gone public?' asked Nightingale. 'Don't people have the right to know what's going on?'

The superintendent clicked his pen several times. The

detective constable turned to look at him and Thomas put the pen down and interlinked his fingers. 'The problem, Nightingale, is that we don't know what's going on. You're right – the suicide rate in north Wales is way above what it should be. But we've no proof yet that there's a serial killer on the loose.'

'But when you found me in Connie Miller's house, you thought it might be me that was behind the deaths?'

'You were the stranger in town and we found you with her still-warm body.'

'But now you know I'm in the clear, you're still looking for the killer.'

'We're not sure that there is a killer.' The superintendent sighed. 'I need a cigarette.'

18

Nightingale offered his pack of Marlboro to Thomas and the superintendent took one. Nightingale slipped a cigarette between his lips, lit it, and then lit the policeman's.

Thomas nodded his thanks, inhaled and blew smoke. He looked at the cigarette and nodded approvingly. 'Marlboro are okay, aren't they?'

'They hit the spot,' said Nightingale. 'You smoke Silk Cut, right?'

'Have done since I was a kid,' said Thomas. 'How long have you been a smoker?'

Nightingale pulled a face. 'Had my first at school but my parents were vehemently anti-smoking so I didn't really start until I was at university.'

'University?' said Thomas. 'Fast-track graduate-entry copper?'

'For my sins,' said Nightingale.

'Never had much stock in that,' said Thomas. 'The best cops are the ones who put in the years on the streets. That's where you learn what matters, not on bloody courses.'

'I walked a beat,' said Nightingale.

'Yeah, but I bet you made sergeant in three years and inspector two years after that.'

Nightingale shrugged. 'That's the way it works,' he said. He blew smoke up into the air. 'I figure you don't get too many serial killers in this neck of the woods.'

'We had one back in 1995,' said Thomas. 'I was a lowly DC then but I was on the case. Guy called Peter Moore killed four men for fun. But you're right – they're few and far between. Of course, we don't know for sure that there's one out there now.'

'Could be a cluster, right?'

'Could be. You get cancer clusters and disappearance clusters, so a suicide cluster is possible.'

'Is there anything about any of the suicides that suggests there was someone else involved?'

Thomas shook his head. 'No forensics, no eyewitnesses.'

'Notes?'

'Sometimes. Not always. It could be that the ones that have notes are genuine suicides.'

Nightingale inhaled, holding the smoke deep in his lungs for several seconds, and then exhaled slowly. 'What about methods? How did the ones who didn't leave notes kill themselves?'

'Hanging, like Connie Miller. Tablets. Slashed wrists.'

'But always in private? No witnesses?'

'Nothing suspicious in that,' said Thomas. 'Women tend to do it quietly. It's men who want to go out in a blaze of glory – throwing themselves in front of trains or smashing up their cars. Women are the gentler sex, God bless them.'

'Mrs Miller said that her daughter didn't go out much.'

'I'm not sure that's true,' said Thomas. 'She wasn't one for the bright lights, but she had plenty of friends. And none of them thought that she was depressed.'

'She was online quite a lot, that's what Mrs Miller said.'

'Who isn't, these days?'

'Did you check her computer?'

Thomas narrowed his eyes. 'You wouldn't be trying to teach your grandmother to suck eggs, would you?'

Nightingale chuckled. 'Wouldn't dare,' he said. 'But she might have been talking to someone on email or on social networking sites, Facebook, MySpace, those sorts of places.'

'There was nothing on her computer that raised any red flags,' said Thomas. 'We checked her emails. And her Facebook page. And we gave the house a going-over. And we spoke to her family, friends and colleagues. They weren't aware of anyone in her life who might have been a danger to her.'

'So the killer, if there is one, is a stranger.'

'Which, statistically, means a white middle-aged male in a low-paid job who wet his bed and set fires and tortured small animals when he was a kid.'

'That's probably half the male population of Wales, right?' Nightingale grinned. 'Joke.'

The superintendent blew smoke. 'What about you? Were you a bed-wetter?'

'I didn't kill Connie Miller,' said Nightingale. 'I live in London; why would I come all the way to Wales to kill? It'd be a hell of a lot easier to do it on my home turf. And a lot easier to hide what I was doing.'

'You might have a reason.'

'Like what? I hate the Welsh, is that it?'

'Who knows?' said Thomas. 'The Yorkshire Ripper went after prostitutes. Harold Shipman murdered pensioners. Maybe you've got a thing about Welsh women. Maybe you were once snubbed by Charlotte Church or Catherine Zeta-Jones. I'm not a profiler, I'm a cop. And at the moment you're the only suspect I've got.'

'Assuming you have a serial killer and not just a statistical variation,' said Nightingale.

'Killer or not, it doesn't explain why you keep breaking into houses in Abersoch.'

'I didn't break in anywhere,' said Nightingale, though he instantly realised that he'd lied. The previous night he'd done exactly that, forcing the French windows of Connie Miller's house. He took a long drag on his cigarette. 'Look, here's what I'd be thinking if it was my case—'

'Which it isn't,' interrupted the superintendent.

'Which it isn't,' agreed Nightingale. 'But if it was, I'd be looking for someone local. Not Abersoch local maybe, but north Wales local. And not someone in her close circle but someone she knew. Possibly through the internet. Someone she trusted enough to let him get close to her.'

'Are you on the internet much?'

Nightingale grinned. 'Me? I'm a Luddite. I've barely mastered my TV remote. Anything I need off the internet, my assistant does it for me.'

'The woman I phoned who backed up your alibi?'

'That's right, Jenny. She's up on all the hi-tech stuff. Me, I don't trust any technology that I can't fix myself. Have you looked under the bonnet of a car recently? You wouldn't know where to start if you had a problem. Most mechanics are lost, too. They need a computer to tell them what's wrong and then they just replace whatever the computer tells them to.'

'Yeah, it's a brave new world, all right,' said the

superintendent. 'Policing is going the same way. These days it's all CCTV and forensics and DNA; no one bothers going around asking questions any more.'

'You seem to be doing all right on the question front,' said Nightingale, flicking ash.

'Because with Connie Miller there're no forensics, no CCTV, just a dead body and you crouched over her with a knife.' The superintendent took a long pull on his cigarette and narrowed his eyes as he stared at Nightingale. 'You ever worked a serial-killer case?' he asked after he'd blown smoke at the ground.

Nightingale shook his head. 'Not a case. But I talked to one once. He was holed up in his house with armed cops outside. I was sent to talk to him. Nasty piece of work. Liked butchering women. Raped them with knives.' Nightingale grimaced. 'Negotiators are trained to empathise but he was impossible to get close to. He was a true sociopath; killing to him was the same as eating and drinking. I spent the best part of three hours talking to him. He only wanted to tell me what he'd done.'

'Like a confession?'

Nightingale shook his head. 'It was more like boasting. He knew what was going to happen and he wanted to share what he'd done with someone. Anyone.'

'And what did happen?'

'He died,' said Nightingale flatly.

'Killed himself?'

'Sort of,' said Nightingale. 'Charged the armed cops with a knife in his hand.'

'Death by cop,' said Thomas. 'Probably best, if he was as evil as you say.'

'He was evil, all right.' Nightingale dropped his

cigarette butt to the ground and stamped on it. 'I can go, right?'

'I guess so,' said Thomas. 'Just do me one favour?'

'What's that?'

Thomas flicked his cigarette away. 'Don't come back to Abersoch.'

'I wasn't planning to.'

'And I'll be talking to Superintendent Chalmers again.'

'I'm sure you will,' said Nightingale.

'And I still think you killed Connie Miller.'

Nightingale nodded. 'I did pick up on that,' he said.

19

When he woke up early on Saturday morning Nightingale thought about going for a run in Hyde Park, but then decided against it in favour of a bacon sandwich, a black coffee, and two cigarettes while he read the *Daily Express*. The main story was about three bank bosses who between them were set to receive bonuses of more than £200 million. Nightingale shook his head in disbelief as he read the story. 'Who the hell did you sell your souls to for a deal like that?' he muttered. Inside the paper was a story about declining attendances in the nation's churches while worship at mosques was up thirty per cent. The Archbishop of Canterbury said that the internet was to blame and that the Church of England would be revamping its website in a bid to win back worshippers. Nightingale put down the paper as he finished his coffee. He couldn't think of any of his close friends who went to church regularly. For marriages and funerals, certainly, but not to worship.

He went through to the hall and took his tatty address book from his raincoat. He flicked through it, looking for Alfie Tyler's number. Nightingale didn't trust phones and rarely stored numbers in his mobile. Phones broke down and SIM cards mysteriously lost their data for no apparent reason, but, in Nightingale's experience, once a number was written down in an address book it tended to stay there.

Tyler answered, his voice thick from sleep. 'Who the hell is this?'

'Jack Nightingale, Alfie. Wakey, wakey, rise and shine.'

'What time is it?'

'Just after nine-thirty.'

Tyler groaned. 'What do you want, Nightingale?'

'Had a late one last night, did you? Out hustling pool?'

'Snooker. And I've got to do something for cash now that I'm no longer gainfully employed.' He groaned and coughed. 'Call me back later, I'm sleeping.'

'Hang on, hang on,' said Nightingale. 'I need a chat. Can I come round?'

'I'm all chatted out,' said Tyler.

'Why don't I come round to your place with a wad of notes and I'll play you for a monkey a game?' said Nightingale. 'We can talk while you beat me.'

Tyler chuckled. 'You're a persistent bastard,' he said. 'Okay, there's a Starbucks on the way. Bring me a large Mocha and two chocolate croissants.'

'You got a sweet tooth, Alfie?'

'Just bring my breakfast and your money and we'll talk,' said Tyler, and he ended the call.

Tyler lived on the outskirts of Bromley in south London. The Saturday morning traffic was light and Nightingale got there just after eleven o'clock. The large black wrought-iron gates that fronted the driveway leading to the six-bedroom, mock-Tudor house, complete with tall chimneys, were locked. Chained and locked with a massive brass padlock. Nightingale frowned as he held the padlock.

The last time he'd visited Tyler the gates hadn't been locked. He looked around for a bell or an intercom but there was no way of announcing his presence. He leaned against his car and lit a cigarette, then took out his mobile phone and called Tyler's number. It rang out, unanswered.

Nightingale cursed and put the phone away, then went back to the gates, wondering whether or not to try climbing over them. They were a good nine feet tall and topped with fleur-de-lys points. He peered through the bars. Tyler's black Bentley was parked in front of the double garage. As Nightingale blew a tight plume of smoke through the gate, the front door opened and Tyler appeared, wearing blue and white striped pyjamas.

Nightingale waved at him. 'Alfie, over here!' he shouted. 'The gates are locked.'

Tyler ran a hand through his hair, walked out of the house and headed towards the garage.

'I've got your Mocha and your croissants!'

Tyler ambled into the garage and reappeared a few seconds later holding a coil of rope.

'Hey, come on! Stop pissing about.'

Tyler showed no signs of having heard Nightingale. He went over to the front door and tied one end of the rope to the door knocker, a large brass lion's head with a thick metal ring gripped in its jaws.

'Alfie! What are you playing at?'

Tyler walked slowly to the Bentley, playing out the length of rope. Nightingale dropped what was left of his cigarette onto the tarmac and ground it with the heel of his shoe. He grabbed the metal gates and shook them. They rattled but the chain held firm.

'Alfie, come on, this isn't funny!'

Tyler stood next to the driver's door of the Bentley and began to fashion the rope into a noose.

Nightingale cursed under his breath. He jammed his right foot against one of the bars and pulled himself up. He managed to get halfway up the gate before he lost his grip and slid down. He took off his raincoat, tossed it onto the bonnet of his MGB and threw himself at the gate. He hauled himself up, gritting his teeth at the pain, his feet scrabbling against the bars, but he didn't have the strength and he slipped back down, tearing his palms. He yelled in frustration as he stared through the bars. Tyler had finished making the noose and he slid it over his head. For a couple of seconds he looked towards the gates but he didn't seem to notice Nightingale standing there.

'Alfie, for God's sake, will you open these bloody gates!' shouted Nightingale.

Tyler opened the door of the Bentley and climbed in. He pulled the door shut but the rope prevented it from closing completely. The engine started and white exhaust billowed around the rear of the car.

'Oh no, please, no . . .' whispered Nightingale.

The engine roared and the car leaped forward. The rope went taut almost immediately but the two-ton Bentley didn't even jerk as it accelerated down the driveway. Nightingale threw himself to the side a second before the car crashed into the gates, Tyler's headless corpse slumped over the wheel, blood still pumping over the walnut dashboard.

20

Superintendent Chalmers sat back in his chair and looked up at the ceiling of the interview room. 'Right, Nightingale, I'm sure you know your rights as well as any ex-copper does, but I have to tell you that you do not have to say anything. But it may harm your defence if you do not mention when questioned something which you later rely on in court. Anything you do say may be given in evidence.'

'Are you going to charge me?' asked Nightingale.

'That remains to be seen,' said Chalmers. There was a manila envelope on the table in front of him.

'So why the caution?'

'You know why,' said Chalmers. 'You've only been off the Force for two years. This questioning might well result in charges being laid, in which case you have to be cautioned prior to the questioning. I'm assuming you haven't completely forgotten the Police and Criminal Evidence Act.'

'I said I'd come here to help you with your enquiries.'

'And we're grateful for that. But we don't know where those enquiries will lead so I have to caution you before we begin. Now, tell me again how Alfie Tyler comes to be sitting behind the wheel of his car minus his head.'

'It was suicide,' said Nightingale. 'I told you. I've told you three times already.' He nodded at the digital tape recorder on the desk. 'It's not my fault you didn't have the machine switched on.'

'Just answer the question, please,' said the superintendent.

Detective Inspector Dan Evans, who was sitting next to Chalmers, sighed, folded his arms and stared at Nightingale with undisguised contempt.

'He tied a rope around his neck, tied the other end to his door knocker and then he drove his car at the gates.'

'Where were you while all this was happening?'

'The other side of the gates. I couldn't get in.'

'And you just stood there and watched, did you?'

'No, I shouted myself hoarse and tried to get over the gates, but they were too high. I was still outside when the cops arrived.'

'So you just let him kill himself, did you?'

'There wasn't time for me to do anything.'

'You were trained as a hostage negotiator. You're used to dealing with suicides. Remember? That was part of your job, talking to people in crisis.'

'I remember,' said Nightingale. 'But he wouldn't talk. He didn't say anything. In fact he didn't seem to notice I was there – he looked like he was in a trance. He just tied the rope around his neck and got into the car.'

'Did you say something to him, something that set him off?'

'Like what?'

'I don't know. Maybe you insulted his mother. Maybe you threatened to expose some dirty dark secret. People don't usually decapitate themselves for no reason.'

Nightingale took his pack of Marlboro out of the pocket of his raincoat.

'You can't smoke in here,' said Chalmers.

'I'm not smoking, I just like feeling the pack,' said Nightingale. 'It's a tactile thing.' He tapped the pack on the table. 'Look, Tyler was expecting me. I called him before I went round and he said he'd see me. We were going to play snooker.'

'Snooker?'

'We'd played before.'

'So it was a social call but rather than play snooker with you he chose to take off his head?'

'I'm as surprised as you, Superintendent.'

'There's no record of Mr Tyler having any mental problems in the past. Though he does have a conviction for GBH.'

'He can handle himself,' said Nightingale. 'I mean, he could. He could handle himself.'

'Broke a few limbs in his time, did Mr Tyler. Did you know that?'

'I'd heard.'

'He was an enforcer for a heavy mob in north London. Broke a few arms and slashed a few faces. Not the sort of guy you'd want to meet in a dark alley. Or any sort of alley, for that matter.'

'I think he'd mellowed,' said Nightingale. 'He was fine with me.'

'And you wanted to talk to him about what, exactly?'

Nightingale tapped the pack of Marlboro against his right temple. He wanted a cigarette, badly. 'He drove my father around. He was a chauffeur slash bodyguard slash dogsbody.'

Chalmers frowned. 'Your father? Which father? William Nightingale or the man who killed himself and left you the big house?'

'Look, it doesn't matter what Alfie Tyler did for my father. It was suicide. It was clearly suicide. I was on the other side of locked gates when it happened. He tied a rope around his neck himself, he started the car himself, and he drove the car at the gates himself. Once he'd killed himself I called three nines and I stayed outside until the cops showed up. This has nothing to do with me.'

Chalmers nodded slowly. 'So you're saying that his death was nothing to do with you?'

'Absolutely nothing to do with me.'

'Nothing at all?'

'That's what I keep telling you.'

Chalmers smiled thinly and picked up the manila envelope. He opened it and took out a crime-scene photograph, the date and time printed across the top. 'Perhaps you can explain this, then,' he said. 'This was how we found his bedroom.'

Nightingale took the photograph. It was a bedroom, presumably Tyler's. A king-sized bed with leopard-print sheets and pillowcases and a large gilt-framed mirror above it. And written across the mirror in brown smears was a sentence that made Nightingale catch his breath:

YOUR SISTER IS GOING TO HELL,
JACK NIGHTINGALE.

21

Chalmers tapped the photograph with his index finger. 'The thing is, Nightingale, you don't have a sister, do you?'

'It's complicated,' said Nightingale.

'According to your personnel file, you were an only child.'

'You've been looking at my file?'

'You're a suspect in several possible murders,' said Chalmers. 'I'm entitled to look at whatever files I want to.'

'I haven't killed anybody,' said Nightingale. 'I want a cigarette.'

'You can smoke when we've finished.'

Nightingale stood up. 'I'm finished now.'

Chalmers got to his feet and glared at Nightingale. 'Sit the hell down, Nightingale. Sit the hell down and answer the questions I put to you.'

Nightingale shook his head. 'I'm out of here.'

'If you don't sit down I will arrest you for destroying evidence at George Harrison's apartment. Then I get to hold you in a cell for twenty-four hours. And if I can find a superintendent to sign off on you then I can add another twelve hours to that.' He smiled cruelly. 'Wait a minute . . . I'm a superintendent, aren't I? So it's an automatic thirty-six hours in a police cell. Is that what you want, Nightingale? All PACE requires is that I give you one main meal and two snacks a day; it doesn't say anything about cigarettes. So are you going to stop being an arse-hole and sit down or do I arrest you?'

Nightingale looked at Chalmers for several seconds, then he shrugged carelessly and sat down.

'Thank you,' said the superintendent. He dropped down onto his chair and linked his fingers. 'Now, this is what I want from you, Nightingale. I want you to agree to give us a DNA sample and your fingerprints. We will cross-check them against the crime scenes we have.'

'You already know I was at George Harrison's apartment. And Connie Miller's house. And I've been inside Alfie Tyler's house.'

Chalmers sighed. 'Please don't start telling me how to do my job,' he said. 'We'll check your samples against Tyler's car and the rope he used to kill himself. And I'll be talking to my opposite number in north Wales. And we'll be going over the Harrison crime scene with a fine toothcomb.'

'You'll be wasting your time.'

'It's my time to waste.' Chalmers slid a sheet of paper across the table to Nightingale. 'Sign this and we'll do what has to be done.'

'Then can I have a cigarette?'

Chalmers gave him a pen. 'Yes, then you can have a bloody cigarette.'

22

Nightingale blew smoke up at the sky. Inspector Evans stared at the ground glumly. 'What's your problem?' asked Nightingale. They were standing outside the police station. A uniformed constable and a community service officer were also on the pavement, smoking with serious faces.

'I had tickets for the Arsenal match today,' he said. 'A bloody box.'

'No way,' said Nightingale.

'I've got a mate who works for Emirates, the airline. He gets seats as a perk, and gave me two for the game today. I was going to take my boy.'

'I'm sorry,' said Nightingale. 'Really.'

Evans pulled a face. 'It's not your fault,' he said. 'Chalmers is a prick. There are others he could have brought in today. But I'm an inspector so he brings me in because inspectors don't get overtime. Plus, he knew I had the tickets.' He shrugged. 'It's no big deal; my brother-in-law's taking my boy.'

'Yeah, well, I'm sorry.'

'No problem.' He jutted his chin out. 'What you did to that paedo, that took guts.'

'Allegedly,' said Nightingale. He dropped his cigarette butt onto the ground and stamped on it.

'That's why you left, right?'

'I wasn't given much of a choice.'

'But they couldn't prove anything, right? You were in the office when he went out through the window?'

'Allegedly,' said Nightingale. 'It's not something I talk about.'

'I can understand that,' said the detective. 'But guys I've spoken to all say the same thing. You did what they'd have wanted to do. He was screwing his daughter, right? Nine years old.'

Nightingale nodded. 'Yeah.'

Two years had passed since little Sophie Underwood had died but he could remember every second as clearly as if it had just happened. He remembered how her voice had changed to a dull monotone and the way she hadn't looked at him as she'd spoken. 'You can't help me,' she'd said. 'No one can help me.' Then she'd kissed her doll on the top of its head and, without making a sound, she'd slid off the balcony and fallen thirteen floors to her death. He shuddered at the memory of the sickening thud her little body had made as it slapped into the tarmac.

'My daughter's eleven,' said Evans. 'If anyone touched her, I'd do them, without even thinking about it.'

'You'd think about it,' said Nightingale, 'but you're right – anyone who touches kids, they deserve anything they get.'

'And the mother knew, right? She knew what the bastard was doing?'

Nightingale nodded. 'She said not but there was no way she couldn't have not known, not with the marks he'd left on her. Anyway, she killed herself, not long after they buried the girl.'

Evans stamped on the ground, trying to keep the circulation moving in his feet. 'Damn it's cold,' he said. 'They reckon snow's on the way.'

'White Christmas,' said Nightingale. 'God rest ye merry gentlemen.' He took out a second cigarette.

Evans pointed at the pack. 'Have you got a spare one?'

Nightingale raised an eyebrow. 'You smoke?'

'Used to,' said Evans. 'Wife made me give up when our boy was born.'

Nightingale tapped out a cigarette and gave it to the detective.

Evans shrugged 'I figure that if I don't actually buy them, I'm not really a smoker.'

'Nice philosophy,' said Nightingale. He lit the man's cigarette and Evans inhaled gratefully. 'Chalmers doesn't really think I'm going around killing people, does he?'

Evans blew a cloud of smoke, and coughed. He patted his chest and grinned shamefacedly. 'He thinks you killed Simon Underwood and that you got away with murder,' he said.

'He's not alone in that,' said Nightingale.

'Yeah, but Chalmers has taken it personally,' said Evans. 'He reckons you've got friends in high places, which is why you weren't charged with Underwood's death.'

Nightingale's eyes narrowed as he pulled on his cigarette. He tried to blow a smoke ring but the wind whipped it away as soon as it left his mouth. 'He does, does he?'

'He has a point, right? You're alone in the office with Underwood and he exits through the window. How many floors up?'

'Twenty,' said Nightingale.

'And the next day you resigned. Chalmers thinks you should have been charged with murder.'

'There was no proof, no CCTV, no evidence.' Nightingale shrugged. 'And no witnesses.'

'Me, I couldn't care less,' said Evans. 'One less paedophile in the world and you won't find me shedding any tears. But Chalmers is gunning for you.'

'He's wasting his time,' said Nightingale. He dropped what was left of his cigarette onto the ground and stood on it. He gestured at the door to the station. 'Come on, let's get this over with. And when we've finished I'm going to need a lift back to Tyler's house to pick up my car.'

'Still driving that MGB? When are you going to get yourself a decent motor?'

'It's a classic.'

'It's an old banger. But yeah, I'll arrange a car to run you back. Just don't tell Chalmers.'

23

Jenny was sitting at her desk reading the *Daily Mail* when Nightingale arrived at the office first thing on Monday morning. 'The wanderer returns,' she said. 'How did it go?'

'Good news, bad news.' Nightingale swung his attaché case onto her desk and clicked the locks. He opened the case and handed her a DVD. 'Here's what I took from Connie's computer. Let me know if there's anything interesting.' He took out two Ziploc bags and put them down in front of her. 'A hairbrush and a toothbrush,' he said. 'Should be DNA there somewhere.'

'Please tell me the back door was open,' she said.

'Best you don't know,' he said. 'Do me a favour and get that off to the lab ASAP. If we have to pay extra for a rush, so be it. I could do with the results yesterday.'

'I'll tell them,' said Jenny. 'They'll want a sample from you too, remember.'

Nightingale grinned and took a sealed tube from the attaché case. 'Did a cheek scrape this morning,' he said, putting the tube next to the two bags.

Jenny spotted a copy of the New English Bible in his case. 'Since when have you been reading the Bible?'

'Thought it might have something I can use,' he said. He smiled ruefully. 'Haven't found anything yet.'

She picked it up and flicked through it, her mouth opening when she saw the hotel stamp inside the front cover. 'You stole this from the hotel?'

'I didn't steal it. It's a Gideon Bible. They give them away.'

'To hotels, Jack.' She dropped it back into his attaché case. 'I can't believe you stole a Bible. You'll burn in Hell, you know that?'

'So I've been told.'

'And what's the bad news? You said good news, bad news.'

'You don't want to know.'

'Jack . . .'

Nightingale sighed, lit a cigarette and told her what had happened at Alfie Tyler's. And how he'd spent most of Saturday in a police cell.

'Is it over?' asked Jenny.

'Probably not,' said Nightingale. 'They took my prints and my DNA and Chalmers is going to try to pin one or all of the deaths on me.'

'But he can't. You didn't kill anyone.'

'I know that and you know that, but Chalmers has the bit between his teeth.' He closed the attaché case and walked through to his office. 'And it's going to get worse before it gets better.'

Jenny followed him into his office and folded her arms as he sat down. 'What happened?' she asked.

'I had another run-in with the Welsh cops,' said Nightingale. 'When I went round to see the parents. It's no biggie but the superintendent will be calling Chalmers again.' He put his hands up when he saw her face fall. 'It'll be okay,' he said. 'I spoke to Mrs Miller and she was fine. She even made me a cup of tea.' He grinned at her. 'Speaking of which . . .'

'And Tyler. Why did he kill himself?'

'Jenny, I've absolutely no idea. I spoke to him on the phone and he was as happy as Larry. Then when I went around to his house it was like he was in a trance.'

'But he definitely killed himself?'

'No doubt about that. I watched him do it.'

Jenny frowned. 'Why didn't you do something?' she asked.

'Don't you start,' said Nightingale. 'You're as bad as Chalmers.'

'He thinks you're involved?'

'I was involved. I was there. But yeah, he's trying to make something of it. He took DNA and they Live-scanned my prints and he'll be looking for forensics. But there won't be any. I didn't go anywhere near the car.' He shrugged. 'It'll blow over. How are we doing, work-wise?'

'A few emails from suspicious spouses wanting to know how much it would cost to prove that their nearest and dearest is fooling around,' she said.

'How long is a piece of string?'

'Exactly what I said,' replied Jenny. 'And one of your regulars has been phoning. Eddie Morris. He's in trouble again and needs your help. He's been charged with burglary but swears blind he didn't do it. Wants you to stand up his alibi.'

'Did you tell him that the cops will do that as part of their investigation? The first thing they'll do is check his alibi.'

'He swears blind he was in a pub in Elephant and

Castle when one of the burglaries happened so he thinks if he can stand that one up then all the charges will disappear. His problem is that the cops spoke to the landlord and the bar staff and no one remembers Eddie being there.'

'So he wants me to track down anyone drinking in the pub who can vouch for him?'

'That's the plan.'

'Sort of pals that Eddie's got, they'll do that anyway whether he was there or not.'

'He swears he didn't do it, Jack. I think he's hoping you might track down a pillar of the community who'll put his hand on a Bible and say that Eddie was in the pub.'

'I'll give him a bell,' said Nightingale. 'If that's all we've got I think I'll take a run by Gosling Manor and get to work on the inventory. Did you go on Friday?'

'Barbara and I were there for about three hours,' she said. She went back into her office and took two notebooks from her desk. 'We've listed about five hundred books.' She gave the notebooks to him.

'You're a star,' said Nightingale, flicking through one.

'Barbara was fascinated,' she said. 'In fact I think she wants to talk to you about borrowing a few volumes, maybe doing a paper on them.'

'On what, exactly?'

'It's better coming from her, but I think she wants to do something about the fact that in the third millennium people actually believe that witchcraft works.'

'Maybe it does,' said Nightingale.

'Or maybe, as the world becomes more technologically sophisticated, people need to hold on to some sort of belief system. I think she wants to do it along the lines of witchcraft moving into the vacuum left by the decline of religion.'

'I'll make sure I order a copy,' said Nightingale.

'It was good of her to help me,' said Jenny. 'It got dark while we were there and I wouldn't have wanted to be there on my own.'

'You see, that's a crazy thing to say. You're in a basement. It doesn't matter if it's day or night outside. It's the same. You have to have the lights on either way.'

'Oh it matters, Jack,' said Jenny. 'Trust me, it matters.'

'What about today? Are you up for helping me?'

'Are you giving me a choice?'

'Well, it's not really in your job description, is it?'

'I don't recall there being much of a job description, actually,' she said. 'Other than being your assistant.'

'I still don't understand why you took the job, what with all the qualifications you've got.'

Jenny shrugged. 'I'm an underachiever,' she said. 'No drive or ambition.'

'You're the smartest person I know,' said Nightingale.

'Thank you, kind sir.'

'Would you drive? I didn't bring the MGB in today.'

'Sure. I'm always happier in a car with airbags anyway.' She went back into her office and switched off her computer. 'What are you going to do with the library once you've finished the inventory?'

'Hopefully sell a big chunk of it,' he said. 'It's not as if I've got any interest in witchcraft or spooky stuff. Gosling paid big bucks for his collection and I'll happily take whatever cash I can get.'

'What's happening about your father's estate?' asked

Jenny. 'When will you know if there's any money coming your way?'

'I'm still waiting to hear from Turtledove. He said we should know something in January. But he wasn't hopeful that there'd be much money coming my way, not with Gosling Manor mortgaged to the hilt. How about a coffee before we head off?'

'Are you offering to make one?'

Nightingale waved at his feet, up on the desk. 'I'm sort of comfortable now, and you're up.' He grinned at her. 'I'll get the next one, promise.'

24

Jenny parked her Audi next to the mermaid fountain in front of Gosling Manor. 'I suppose I'm going to have to get used to driving you around,' she said.

'Why's that?' asked Nightingale as he climbed out of the car.

'Because they take away your driving licence for drink-driving,' she said. 'The only question is how long for.' She picked up a briefcase from the back seat and locked the car doors.

'I wasn't in an accident and I wasn't speeding,' said Nightingale. 'I was barely over the limit.'

'Doesn't matter, these days,' she said, following him to the entrance. 'You might think about getting a full-time driver.'

'I'm not made of money,' said Nightingale. He unlocked the front door. 'Honey, I'm home!' he shouted. His voice echoed around the hallway.

'You really are twelve years old, aren't you?'

'Can you imagine me living here on my own?' he said, holding the door open for her. 'What if I heard a noise in the middle of the night? How long would it take to check every room?'

'That's probably why Gosling put in his CCTV system,'

she said. Nightingale closed the door and followed her over to the section of wood panelling that hid the stairway leading down to the basement. She pulled open the panel and switched on the basement lights. 'Anyway, if you don't want to live here, sell it.'

'Easier said than done,' said Nightingale. 'The bottom's fallen out of the luxury-mansion market ever since Brown went after the bankers.'

'Arabs or Russians, then,' said Jenny. 'They've always got money. This is a beautiful house, Jack. It'd sell.'

They went down the stairs. Jenny put her briefcase on the desk and took out the two notebooks they'd been using to compile the inventory. 'We finished the bookcase by the stairs, and most of the one next to it,' she said. 'I thought I might put them on computer. It'd make it easier to sort through them by subject or author. What do you think?'

'Good idea,' said Nightingale. He lit a cigarette and went over to the desk to get a crystal ashtray. He grinned when he saw the Ouija board beneath it. 'I wondered where that had got to,' he said.

The board was a large square of oak that had cracked across the middle. Two words were printed in silver letters in the top corners, YES on the left and NO on the right, and the letters of the alphabet were embossed in gold in two rows across the middle of the board. Beneath the letters were the numbers zero to nine in a row, and below them the word GOODBYE.

He picked it up and showed it to Jenny. 'You know Parker Brothers still sell Ouija boards as a kids' toy,' he said. 'They even do one that glows in the dark.'

'I didn't know that,' said Jenny, taking off her coat and draping it over the back of one of the sofas.

'Yeah, and actually Ouija is a trademark. Hasbro owns it. Before Parker Brothers made their set, they were just called spirit boards or talking boards.'

'Fascinating,' said Jenny, her voice loaded with sarcasm.

'Do you know where the name Ouija came from?'

'*Oui* is yes in French and *Ja* is yes in German?'

Nightingale grinned. 'That's what a lot of people think, but it's more complicated than that. You know Wicca, right? Witchcraft? Well, the guys who designed the game wanted a spooky name and one of them was talking to some Spanish chap and it turns out that the Spanish pronunciation of Wicca is Ouija. So that's what they went with.'

'I prefer my version,' she said. 'Anyway, since when did you become an expert on Ouija boards?' asked Jenny.

'I've been reading up on it.'

She put her head on one side and narrowed her eyes. 'Did you ask me here because you wanted to work on the inventory, or because you wanted another go at the Ouija board?'

'Jenny . . .'

'I'm serious, Jack. I don't like being played.'

'I swear it hadn't occurred to me until the moment I saw it,' said Nightingale. 'You know me better than that.'

'I thought I did,' she said. 'But recently you've been . . .' She shrugged. 'Forget it.'

'I've been what?' asked Nightingale. 'What do you mean?'

'You're under a lot of pressure, I understand that.'

'It's been a rough few weeks,' agreed Nightingale. He stubbed out his cigarette.

'But just remember that I'm on your side. You don't

need to play games with me. If you want something, just ask.'

'Jenny, I swear . . .'

She held up her hand. 'Okay, I believe you.'

He went to put the board back on the desk, but he stopped and turned back to look at her. 'Do you want to try again?' he asked.

She held his look. 'Do you?'

'Everything we need is here from the last time,' he said. 'Except for the freshly cut flowers and there isn't a florist for miles.'

'There're heathers and stuff in the garden,' said Jenny. 'So you'll do it?'

Jenny sighed. 'Jack, it's up to you. But if we're going to do it I'd be happier if we did it back at my place. We could open a bottle of wine and make a night of it.'

Nightingale could hear the uncertainty in her voice. She was putting a brave face on it but he knew she wasn't happy at the prospect of using the Ouija board again. 'This is where Robbie spoke to us,' he said. 'And alcohol and the Ouija board don't mix. Can you do me a favour and see what plants you can find? The more colourful the better.'

As Jenny headed back upstairs, Nightingale went to a cupboard and took out five blue candles, slotted them into candle holders and spaced them evenly around a circular table, then put the Ouija board in the centre. He lit the candles with his cigarette lighter, then went over to the desk and pulled open one of the drawers. Inside were all the things that he'd needed the first time they'd used the board, including the old planchette, distilled water, herbs and consecrated sea salt.

He put the planchette on the board and poured the

water into a crystal glass, then set out the herbs. He was just standing back to admire his handiwork when Jenny returned, clutching a handful of twigs with orange-brown flowers.

'Do you know what they are?' she asked. 'I'll give you a clue: they're very appropriate.'

Nightingale shook his head. 'Botany was never one of my subjects,' he said.

'What's your degree in again?'

'Economics.'

'Never.'

'What?'

'Economics? You can't even balance your cheque book.'

'There's a big difference between the theoretical and the practical,' he said. 'Ask me something about supply-side economics.'

'Okay. What is it?'

Nightingale grinned. 'It's a macroeconomic theory described by Jude Wanniski in 1975 that basically says that the economy is best served by lowering barriers to producing goods and services, which in turn lowers prices. It's in contrast to Keynesian macroeconomics, which argues that demand is more important than supply.' He winked. 'I got a First.'

'You never cease to amaze me,' she said. 'If you were that good, why did you become a cop?'

Nightingale shrugged. 'It's a long story,' he said. He waved at the board. 'Are you playing for time because you don't want to do this?'

'I'm ready when you are,' she said. She held up the twigs again. 'Witch hazel,' she said. 'How appropriate is that?'

'Brilliant,' said Nightingale, taking the twigs from her. 'Be a sweetie and get the lights, will you?'

As Jenny went up the stairs again, Nightingale put the witch hazel into a crystal vase and placed it on the opposite side of the table to the glass of distilled water. Jenny switched off the lights and came back down into the basement. The flickering candles cast moving shadows over the walls. She sat down at the table next to Nightingale.

'You remember what to do?' asked Nightingale. He sat down and picked up the planchette. It was made of ivory that had yellowed with age.

'How could I forget?' she asked. 'We visualise a white light all around the table.'

'That's right. A protective light, pure white. Keep thinking about the light whatever happens.' Nightingale pinched some sage from a small bowl and sprinkled it over the candles one by one, then he rubbed some on the board and the planchette; finally he sprinkled lavender and salt over the board.

'It's very Jamie Oliver, isn't it?' said Jenny.

Nightingale wagged a finger at her. 'You have to take this seriously,' he said.

'I'm trying,' said Jenny. 'Believe me, I'm trying.'

'Are you ready?'

'As I'll ever be,' she said.

Nightingale nodded. 'Okay.' He took a deep breath before speaking in a low monotone. 'In the name of God, of Jesus Christ, of the Great Brotherhood of Light, of the Archangels Michael, Raphael, Gabriel, Uriel and Ariel, please protect us from the forces of Evil during this session. Let there be nothing but light surrounding this board and its participants and let us only communicate with powers and entities of the light. Protect us, protect this house, the people in this house and let there only be light and nothing but light, Amen.'

'Amen,' repeated Jenny.

Nightingale looked up at the ceiling. 'We're here to talk to Robbie Hoyle,' he said. 'Robbie, are you there? Please, talk to us.'

The planchette twitched under their fingers.

'Robbie, is that you?'

The candle flames simultaneously bent away from the stairs as if a draught was blowing from the door.

'We want to talk to Robbie Hoyle,' said Nightingale, raising his voice. 'Robbie, are you there?'

The planchette scraped across the board and pointed at the word YES.

Nightingale cleared his throat. His mouth had gone suddenly dry.

'Robbie, we need to talk to you about my sister,' he said.

The planchette gradually moved back to its original position.

'Abersoch,' whispered Jenny. 'Ask him why he sent you to Wales.'

Nightingale flashed her a warning look to keep quiet. 'Robbie, this is Jack. I'm here with Jenny. We want to talk to you about my sister. Can you talk to us?'

The planchette slid over to YES again, then moved purposefully back to the middle of the board.

'Robbie, can you tell—' Before Nightingale could finish, the planchette slid purposely upwards and pointed at the letter Y. As soon as it reached the bottom of the Y it jerked to the left and settled on the letter O. Then in quick succession it touched U and R.

'Your,' said Jenny. She shivered and looked around the basement. 'Can you feel a draught?' she asked.

Nightingale nodded. There was a cold breeze blowing from the far end of the basement, even though there were no doors or windows there. The candle flames began to flicker.

Nightingale opened his mouth to speak but, before he could say anything, the planchette started to move again, touching six letters one after the other: S-I-S-T-E-R.

'Your sister,' said Jenny.

Nightingale didn't look at her. The planchette had already started to move again.

I-S. It stopped briefly and then moved on. G-O-I-N-G.

'Is going,' said Jenny. 'Going where?'

Nightingale's eyes widened. He had a sick feeling in the pit of his stomach because he knew without a shadow of a doubt what was coming.

The planchette stayed where it was for several seconds and then it began to move. Nightingale could feel his fingers pressing down on the pointer as if they were trying of their own accord to stop it from moving.

'Jenny, you're not . . .?'

Jenny shook her head fiercely, her eyes fixed on the planchette as it continued to slide across the board.

T-O. It hesitated for a few more seconds, but Nightingale already knew where it was going next. It headed towards the H.

'No!' he said. He took his hand off the planchette but it carried on moving, this time towards the E. 'Leave it, Jenny!' he shouted.

Jenny looked at him, confused.

'Let go of it!' yelled Nightingale.

He reached over and grabbed her arm. He pulled it away and she let go of the planchette. They both stared wide-eyed as it carried on moving. It stopped over the letter E for less than a second and then started to slide towards the L.

'What's happening, Jack?' asked Jenny

Nightingale stood up, grabbed the board and threw it against the wall. As it crashed to the floor, the candles blew out and Jenny screamed.

25

Nightingale reached into his jacket pocket and pulled out his lighter. He flicked it with his thumb and a small flame sputtered into life.

Jenny was sitting on her chair, her hands either side of her face as she stared at him in horror. She jumped out of her chair and grabbed Nightingale's arm. 'Get me out of here,' she said, her voice trembling.

'It's okay,' he said.

'It's not okay!' she shouted. 'Get me out of here now!'

Her outburst stunned him for a moment but then he took her with his left hand and guided her to the stairs. He kept the lighter in his right hand as he went up the stairs with her, but before he had got halfway the flame was burning his thumb and he let it go out. Jenny screamed again and he clicked the lighter despite the pain. The lighter sparked and then the flame flickered, casting shadows over the walls as he pushed her up the stairs ahead of him. She threw open the panel and staggered into the hallway. Nightingale followed her. He put the lighter in his pocket and tried to hold her but she thrust him away.

'What happened down there, Jack?'

Nightingale shrugged but didn't say anything.

'Was that Robbie?' asked Jenny.

'I don't think so.'

'Some other spirit?'

'I don't know, Jenny. Maybe.'

'And you knew what they were saying, didn't you? That's why you tossed the board.'

'It was a message that I've seen before.'

'It spelled out something about your sister, didn't it? Your sister is going to— To what, Jack? What is your sister going to do?'

'Jenny, please . . .'

'To Hell? Is that it? Your sister is going to Hell. Is that what it was trying to say?'

Nightingale nodded.

'And when did you see it before? The messages you told me about before your birthday said you were going to Hell, right? Now they're talking about your sister? Is that it?'

'Now's not the time, Jenny.' He was sweating and he wiped his face with his sleeve.

'Don't shut me out!' she shouted. 'Damn you, Jack. You can't half involve me in this. It's all or nothing. There are no half measures.'

Nightingale sighed. 'I'm sorry.'

'Don't. I want the *truth*, not an apology. I want to know why you tossed the board when you did.'

'Because it wasn't Robbie. He wouldn't have said that. Somebody or something else was using the board.'

'And the wind? Where did that come from? And why did the candles blow out?'

Nightingale put his hands on her shoulders and this time she didn't push him away. He looked into her eyes. 'I don't know, kid. I'm sorry.'

Her eyes burned into his. 'Where did you hear that before? The message?'

Nightingale took his hands off her shoulders and put them in his pockets. 'When I went to see Connie Miller.'

'She wrote it?'

'She said it.'

Jenny frowned. 'You said that she was dead when you got there.'

'That's the thing,' said Nightingale. 'She was.'

Jenny shook her head. 'No,' she said. 'You're not saying what I think you're saying, are you?'

'She was dead but her eyes opened and the words came out.'

Jenny slumped against the panelled wall. Nightingale tried to steady her but she pushed his hands away. 'Don't touch me,' she said.

'It just happened,' he said. 'But I couldn't tell anyone. How could I explain that a dead woman spoke to me? They'd think I was crazy. Or lying.'

'And she said that your sister was going to Hell?'

Nightingale nodded. 'And when I went back the same words were written on her bathroom wall. At least I thought they were. Maybe I imagined it.'

'Why didn't you tell me this before?'

'I couldn't,' he said. 'Not on top of everything that's happened. And deep down, I wondered if it was just my mind playing tricks.' He took a deep breath. 'And Alfie Tyler wrote the same words before he killed himself.'

'How do you know that? You said you were stuck outside the gates.'

'Chalmers showed me a crime-scene photograph.'

'And he did . . . what? He wrote it how? He left a note?'

Nightingale looked uncomfortable. 'Just leave it, Jenny.'

'I can't leave it. This involves me. Chalmers had me in for questioning, remember?'

'Okay, he wrote it across his bedroom mirror. In faeces – shit.'

'I know what faeces are,' she said. 'He used that to write on the mirror?'

Nightingale nodded. 'That's what Chalmers said. And he showed me pictures to back it up.'

'Why would Tyler do that, Jack? Did he even know that you had a sister?'

'I think I mentioned it to him when I first met him. But it was news to him. Gosling hadn't said anything about having children.' He shrugged. 'He could have been lying, of course.'

'But if he wasn't, why would he write that your sister was going to Hell?'

'You're asking the wrong person, Jenny. I've got no idea what's going on. I keep thinking that maybe my mind is playing tricks on me. That maybe I'm imagining things.'

'A crime-scene photograph isn't your mind playing tricks, is it?' She jerked her thumb at the entrance to the basement. 'And we didn't imagine what happened down there. Something was moving the pointer because I'm sure that neither of us was doing it.'

'I know,' he said. 'And whatever it was is still down there.' He took a deep breath. 'We have to go back, Jenny.'

'No bloody way,' she said.

'If we've brought a spirit over it'll stay here until we send it back.'

'Just lock the door and brick it up,' she said. 'We should leave. Now.'

Nightingale put his hands on her shoulders again and looked into her eyes. 'We have to do this, Jenny.' She tried to look away and he shook her gently. 'There're no ifs, buts or maybes. We've opened a portal and we have to close it. There's no telling what else might come through.'

'Which is exactly why I'm not going back down there.'

'It has to be the two of us, kid,' said Nightingale. 'We opened it, we have to close it.'

'Jack, please . . .' She was close to tears.

'I wouldn't ask if it wasn't important,' said Nightingale. 'Believe me, if we don't go down there and finish what we started, we'll be opening up a world of hurt.' He squeezed her shoulders. 'I'll be with you,' he said.

She forced a smile. 'That's supposed to reassure me, is it?'

'Good girl,' said Nightingale.

'You owe me,' she said.

'I know.'

'Big time.'

He put his arm around her and guided her towards the basement.

26

Nightingale kept his hands on Jenny's shoulders as he followed her down the stairs into the bowels of the house

'There's no way we're using the candles,' she said, her voice still shaking.

'The lights are staying on,' promised Nightingale.

'Shouldn't we get a priest to do an exorcism or something?'

'It's not a possession,' said Nightingale. 'I know what to do.'

'How?'

'I read a book.'

When they reached the bottom of the stairs Nightingale led Jenny over to the table and sat her down.

The Ouija board was lying on the floor in front of a display case that was filled with skulls. Nightingale picked it up and took it over to the table. As he put it down, Jenny leaned away from it.

'It can't hurt you,' said Nightingale. A cold wind blew from the far end of the basement making them both shiver. 'Ignore it, Jenny. Where did the planchette go?' he asked, looking around.

Jenny shook her head but didn't answer.

Nightingale bent down and looked under the table but couldn't see it. As he stood up a large globe by a book-covered desk began to slowly turn. He went over to it and placed his hand flat on America. The globe stopped spinning but as soon as he removed his hand it began to turn again.

'Jack, please . . .' said Jenny.

The globe began to turn faster and faster until the continents blurred into a beige mass. There was a thump behind them and Nightingale turned to see a book lying on the floor, its pages flicking by as if they were being rifled by an unseen hand. Another book fell from the top shelf and hit the ground with a dull thud. Then another. And another. Then books began to rain from the shelves, splattering onto the tiled floor.

'Jack!' screamed Jenny.

She stood up but Nightingale pointed at her. 'Stay where you are!' he shouted. 'Stay in the chair!'

A large leather-bound book flew towards Nightingale's face and he ducked. It grazed the back of his head and thudded into the bookcase behind him. As he straight-ened up he saw the planchette next to one of the sofas, and he ran over and grabbed it.

The fluorescent lights overhead began to flicker as Nightingale hurried to the table and sat down next to Jenny. He slapped the ivory planchette onto the board. 'Your hands, Jenny,' he said. 'Put your hands on it.'

Jenny reached out and placed the fingertips of both hands onto the planchette. Nightingale put his hands on top of hers and together they started to move the pointer towards GOODBYE. Nightingale could feel the piece of ivory fighting against them as if it had a life of its own. He grunted and pushed harder.

'It won't move,' Jenny gasped.

Behind them books continued to tumble down from the bookshelves. Cupboard doors were throwing themselves open and then slamming shut, and papers were blowing off the desk and flapping around in the air.

'It will,' said Nightingale. 'Keep pushing.' He looked up at the ceiling. 'In the name of Jesus Christ, I command all human spirits to be bound to the confines of this board. I command all inhuman spirits to go where Jesus Christ tells you to go, for it is HE who commands you.'

One of the fluorescent lights made a popping noise and the tube shattered. Bits of glass tinkled down onto the tiles.

The planchette began to slide over the board, but it took all Nightingale's and Jenny's strength to keep it moving towards GOODBYE.

Nightingale took a deep breath. 'Jenny, you have to say it with me.' Another fluorescent light exploded behind them.

'I don't know the words,' she gasped.

'Just repeat after me,' he said. 'We both have to say it.' He began to recite the prayer again and Jenny followed haltingly. When they reached the end the planchette seemed to give up and they slid it across to GOODBYE. Nightingale sighed. 'Amen,' he said. He nodded at Jenny.

'Amen,' she repeated.

Suddenly there was only silence. Papers fluttered to the ground and the doors of the cupboards remained shut. Nightingale looked over at the globe. It slowed to a stop.

'It's over,' he said. He took his hands off Jenny's. She looked at him fearfully and let go of the planchette. It stayed where it was, obscuring the letter D.

Jenny exhaled and sat back. 'Is that it?' she asked.

Nightingale nodded. 'I think so.'

'Think?'

'It's fine,' he said. 'You can feel it, right? You can feel how the atmosphere has changed.'

Jenny shivered. 'I want to go home,' she said.

27

Nightingale drove Jenny's Audi back to her mews house in Chelsea. She didn't say a word all the way home. Nightingale tried to get her to break her silence but the most he could get out of her was the occasional nod or shake of the head. He walked her to the door and waited until she unlocked it.

'Jenny, I'm sorry,' he said, handing her the car keys.

'It wasn't your fault,' she said, refusing to look at him.

'I shouldn't have asked you to do it.'

She shrugged. 'You couldn't have done it on your own,' she said. 'One person can't work a Ouija board.'

'I had no idea it would turn out the way it did,' he said.

'I know that.'

She stepped across the threshold. For a moment Nightingale thought she was going to invite him in for coffee but then she shook her head and closed the door on him. Nightingale lit a cigarette. He blew a smoke ring up at the moon. He looked back at Jenny's house and saw the bathroom light go on.

Nightingale smoked his cigarette. The bathroom light went off. He was just about to flick the butt away when his mobile rang. He looked at the display and smiled when he saw it was Jenny calling him.

'What are you doing?' she asked.

'Loitering with no intent,' he said.

'There's a pretty serious Neighbourhood Watch around here. If you're not careful someone will call the police.'

'I was just going.'

'Everything's all right, Jack,' she said. 'I'm fine.'

'I really am sorry.'

'You don't have to keep saying that. Do you want me to call you a cab?'

Nightingale looked up at the bedroom windows but couldn't see her. 'I'm okay. I'll pick up a black cab on the King's Road. Look, I'll swing by tomorrow morning, first thing.'

'You don't have to.'

'I want to. Sleep tight. Don't let the bed bugs bite.'

'Idiot.'

The line went dead. Nightingale saluted the bedroom windows, then turned and walked down the mews.

28

Nightingale caught a black cab and was heading back to Bayswater and had the driver drop him close to where he'd parked his MGB. He'd been shocked by what had happened in the basement but had hidden his unease from Jenny because he didn't want to make her more upset than she already was.

He climbed into his car and drove to the cemetery where Robbie Hoyle was buried. He made only one stop on the way – at an off-licence. He parked close to the entrance to the cemetery and switched off the engine of his MGB. It continued to turn over for a couple of seconds before cutting out. He flicked off the lights, picked up the Oddbins carrier bag and walked through the wooden gates. Robbie Hoyle's grave was on the far side of the cemetery, close to a line of conifers that whispered in the cold breeze that was blowing from the north. Nightingale shivered as he stood looking down at the grave.

There was no headstone and there wouldn't be for another eight months or so, until the soil had settled. There was just the earth, and a small wooden cross with Hoyle's name, his date of birth and the day he'd died – run over by a taxi as he crossed the road. The details of his death weren't on the cross, of course, and they wouldn't be on the headstone. They never were. Visitors were happy enough to know the names and dates of the deceased, but no one wanted to be confronted with how they'd died. Robbie Hoyle. Crushed to death under the wheels of a taxi, his spine broken, his spleen ruptured, his lungs filling up with blood as he took his last breath. The words that would be carved into the marble would be less graphic. 'Loving husband and father. He died too young.'

Nightingale took out a Marlboro and lit it. 'Everyone dies too young,' he muttered to himself after he'd blown smoke into the night air. 'Everyone wants just one more day.'

He took the bottle of red wine from the carrier bag and unscrewed the top. 'I know, I know, you hate screw-top bottles, but I don't have a corkscrew in the flat.' He held the label towards the wooden cross. 'It's French, and it was twelve quid, so I reckon it's a good one.' He poured a slug of wine onto the earth and watched it bubble and soak into the soil. He took a drink from the bottle and wiped his mouth with his sleeve. 'Never been a huge wine fan,' said Nightingale. 'But I figured if I bought you a Corona you'd think I was a cheapskate.'

He poured more wine onto the grave then took a long pull on his cigarette, held it for several seconds and let it out slowly, enjoying the feel of the nicotine entering his bloodstream. 'I really thought that was you in the basement, talking to me and Jenny through the Ouija board.' He chuckled. 'How crazy does that sound? I'm talking to a decomposing body about communicating with spirits by using a piece of wood and a chunk of elephant's tusk.'

He took another drink from the bottle and poured some

more over the grave. 'I do wonder if maybe I'm imagining it all, Robbie. What if I'm lying in a bed somewhere, a hospital or an asylum, and all of this is a dream? I tell you, that would explain a lot of the shit that's been happening to me.'

He sighed and stared up at the night sky. 'Jenny told me about some Chinese philosopher, back in the fourth century before Christ, name of Chuang Tzu. He had a dream that he was a butterfly, flying about enjoying himself. Then he woke up. But he couldn't decide if he was Chuang Tzu and he had been dreaming that he was a butterfly, or if he was a butterfly and now he was dreaming that he was Chuang Tzu. That's how I feel now, Robbie, like I'm trapped in a dream. Or a nightmare.'

He blew smoke and poured more wine onto the soil.

'Here's what I don't get, Robbie. I can talk to devils. I can summon them. It's not easy and you have to know what you're doing but it can be done. You draw a magic circle and you do shit with salt and herbs and you say the right words and, Abracadabra, a devil appears. You can talk to them and you can deal with them. So if there are devils, then there are angels. Why can't you call on angels when you need them? My old man left me a library full of books on devil-worship and Satanism and I've not found a single book that tells you how to contact an angel. Why is that? Why can you call up the bad guys but the good guys are ex-directory? And if there are devils, there has to be a Satan, right? That the devils answer to. Lucifer. If there are devils, and I know there are, then Lucifer has to exist. But here's the big one, Robbie. Here's what I really don't get. If there's a Lucifer then there's a God.

But where is He in all this? If all this crap is going on in the world, why isn't He doing something about it?'

He flicked ash on the grave and took a drink from the bottle.

'And how can there be a God, Robbie? How can there be? What sort of God tells people that they shouldn't eat pork, but makes bacon taste so good? What sort of God tells people they shouldn't cut their hair and they should spend their lives covering it with a twenty-foot-long piece of cloth? Or tells people that if they blow up innocent folk on a Tube train they'll spend eternity being serviced by seventy-two black-eyed virgins? I'm not sure I'd want anything to do with any of those Gods.' He poured the rest of the wine over the grave. 'And I sure as hell have nothing but contempt for any God who'd allow you to die the way you died. You were a good cop, Robbie, but you were also a good man, a fair man, and your wife and daughters needed you. There was no reason for you to die. If there was any sort of God, or any sort of justice in the world, you wouldn't be lying in that grave.'

Nightingale put the bottle back into the carrier bag.

'There's no God, Robbie. How can there be? He's as much of a nonsense as Father Christmas and the Tooth Fairy. No rational, intelligent person believes that God created the universe or that He decides who goes to Heaven and who goes to Hell. So if there's no God then there's no devil, and if there's no devil then nothing that's happened to me over the past month makes any sense at all. Unless I'm out of my freaking mind.'

Nightingale looked up at the night sky and blew smoke. 'We did the Ouija board thing again and it went wrong. We had to end the séance by invoking Jesus, but it's just words, right? If there's no God then there's no Jesus. But it worked. So what does that mean? I don't know, Robbie, this whole business is doing my head in.'

Nightingale flicked away his cigarette butt. 'So there you have it, Robbie. I'm as crazy as a coot and the fact that I've come out to tell this to your dead body just goes to show how far gone I am.' He flashed a mock salute at the grave. 'You take care, yeah. I miss you, you bastard.'

Nightingale turned and walked away from the cemetery.

29

Graham Kerr sat back in the armchair, crossed his legs, and relished the moment, the few minutes that stood between life and death, between a happy home and a burned-out shell filled with bodies. Kerr loved fires. He loved the smells and sounds and the feel of the heat, but the nature of his weakness meant that he could never see the fruits of his talent, at least not close up. Instead he had to take his satisfaction in the anticipation of what he was about to do. He rattled the matchbox, smiling at the click-click-click of the matches as they rattled together. Then he slid open the box and inhaled the fragrance of the matches within. The matches, as always, were Swan Vestas. Kerr loved the colours of the box, the red, green and gold, and the feel of the strip of sandpaper along the side. And he could feel himself grow hard at the scraping sound he'd soon be hearing, followed by the hiss as the red phosphorous head burst into life. Kerr shuddered and gasped softly. He took out a match and sniffed it. There was only one thing that smelled better than an unlit match and that was a match that had been used. He teased himself by touching the match head against the striker and twisting it ever so slightly. Kerr had never liked safety matches. They were the poor relation of the match family; they didn't smell as good, they didn't sound as good, and they didn't look as good. He had never used a safety match and he never would.

He looked slowly around the room. His eyes had become accustomed to the darkness and he could see everything. The cabinet filled with poor-quality china and crystal. The sideboard with its framed photographs of the children and grandchildren that they saw twice a year at most. The bag of knitting by the sofa, and the stack of *OK!* and *Hello!* magazines on the coffee table.

Kerr breathed in slowly through his nose, savouring the smells in the room. The lingering scent of the woman's too-sweet perfume, the acrid odour of the man's feet, the smell of overcooked vegetables and stale cooking fat from the kitchen.

They would be dead soon, the husband and wife sleeping upstairs. The smoke would kill them as they slept, long before the fire consumed them. People always died in the fires that Kerr set. That was the point of setting them. And it meant that fire investigators always moved in to examine the aftermath. They wanted to know two things: where the fire had started and what had caused it. Kerr's skill was to provide answers to both those questions in such a way as to eradicate all thoughts of arson from the investigators' minds.

Investigators would first study the site from a distance, then move in towards the site of origin, and then they would begin sifting through the ashes and collecting samples. They knew that fires had a tendency to burn upwards and outwards so they would look for V-shaped patterns on the walls. Air currents helped spread a fire, which rose faster as it got hotter. The nature of the burning material also influenced the speed and direction of the fire. Cloth burned faster than carpet which burned faster than wood. A skilled investigator could look at the colour of burned material and know the temperature it had reached at the height of the fire, and could also make assumptions based on the way objects had been deformed, the patterns left by smoke, and the depth of charring.

By reading the clues correctly, the investigator could determine where the fire had started. That's where many arsonists gave themselves away, Kerr knew. They were so keen to make sure the fire took that they set it in several places, and that was a red flag to any half-decent investigator. As was the use of an accelerant. The most common ways of starting a fire involved the use of petrol, turpentine, diesel and kerosene, but anything inflammable could be used, including alcohol, acetone and any one of a number of solvents. Amateurs assumed that the fire would remove all traces of any accelerant, but Kerr knew better. The investigators took samples and had them analysed in labs that were capable of identifying the tiniest trace of liquid hydrocarbons, and the wrong hydrocarbon in the wrong place meant only one thing: arson. Kerr had set more than fifty fires and killed almost a hundred people, and never once had anyone suspected that his fires were anything other than tragic accidents.

Kerr followed a set of rules he had drawn up at the start of a killing spree that had lasted more than fifteen years. He only ever set a fire in one place. He never took an accelerant with him. Amateurs walked the streets with cans of petrol or bottles of white spirit; Kerr never had anything on him more suspicious than a box of Swan Vestas. That was what made him so good at what he did – he never took anything to a fire, and he never took anything away. Before he even so much as struck a match, he would sit in whatever building he had decided to burn and he would imagine that he was a fire. He would become the flames, growing slowly at first then devouring everything, burning and destroying until there was nothing left but ash.

For Kerr to hide what he'd done, he had to provide a story that the investigators would believe. A house where there was a smoker was the easiest. A burning cigarette dropped onto a sofa next to an ashtray would do the job on its own, even if Kerr didn't help it by fanning the flames with a magazine. Candles were good. All he had to do was light one and place it near a curtain. And electrical appliances were a good choice, especially electric fires; plug-in air fresheners were a godsend; houses with working fireplaces were always easy to burn. If all else failed there was the kitchen, where a left-on oven could be made to look like the source of a house fire.

He put the match back in the box and the box in the chest pocket of his shirt. The matches rattled as the box settled and Kerr quivered with excitement.

The house Kerr was in belonged to a retired couple. Mr and Mrs Wilkinson. They were upstairs, fast asleep. There was a smoke alarm in the hall but Kerr had taken out the battery and placed it in the rubbish bin for the investigator to find. It was Monday, the day that Mrs Wilkinson did her ironing. She did her washing on Sunday afternoon and her ironing the day after, as regular as clockwork. Kerr knew her schedule because he had been watching the house for weeks. He knew the Wilkinsons always went to bed before eleven and that they never locked their kitchen door.

They both read the *Daily Telegraph* and a copy had been left on the sofa. Kerr stood and picked up the paper. He flicked through it. Mr Wilkinson had completed the crossword. He was a smart man, a retired headteacher who played bridge competitively and was a leading member of the local MENSA group.

Mrs Wilkinson kept her ironing board and iron in a cupboard in the kitchen. He went to get them and carried them through into the sitting room. He opened out the board and stood it next to the sofa. That was where Mrs Wilkinson usually did the ironing, so that she could watch the television as she worked. There was a socket behind the sofa and Kerr plugged in the iron. He placed it on the ironing board, checking that the handle was in the correct position because Mrs Wilkinson was left-handed and a smart investigator would know that.

Kerr placed the copy of the *Daily Telegraph* next to the iron, which was clicking quietly as it heated up. Kerr stood back and put his head on one side. Mrs Wilkinson had finished ironing but had gone upstairs without switching the iron off. She was an old lady, absent-minded. Her husband had followed her, and had put the newspaper on the ironing board. Why? Who knew why? It was just one of those things that old people did sometimes.

Kerr took out his box of matches. He looked at the iron and the paper. The iron would get hot, the paper would burn, the paper would fall onto the sofa, that would burn, burning fabric would fall onto the carpet and that would burn and then it would spread to the sideboard and the bookcase and then the room would be an inferno and the hallway would be full of smoke that would quietly suffocate the couple upstairs.

He could have waited for the hot iron to ignite the paper but if he did that he would miss the best part, the part that he enjoyed the most. He took out a match and struck it and then held it close to his face and inhaled the smoke. He smiled and touched the yellow flame against the newspaper. The paper burned quickly. Kerr shook the match to extinguish it before putting it back into the box. He slipped the box into his shirt pocket, then carefully slid the burning newspaper off the ironing board and onto the sofa. He moved a cushion so that it was leaning against the newspaper, then stood back from the flames. He could feel the heat on his face and he basked in it like a cat enjoying the sun.

The flames licked around the cushion and it crackled and burst into flames. Plumes of black smoke spiralled up to the ceiling. Kerr knew that it was time to go but as always the pull of the flames was strong, calling him to stay, to watch, to enjoy. He hardened his heart and walked out of the sitting room. He let himself out of the front door and walked down the path to the street. The nearest house was a hundred yards away and even if the neighbours noticed the fire it would be at least half an hour before the fire engine arrived. By then it would all be over.

Kerr had parked his car a short walk from the Wilkinsons' house. He took one more look back. A yellow light was flickering against the curtains, casting black rippling shadows. Kerr blew the house a kiss and headed for his car.

30

Nightingale drove back to his flat to pick up clean clothes and cleaning supplies, then drove to Gosling Manor on autopilot, barely aware of the twists and turns in the road. Part of him didn't want to go, but he knew there was only one way he could find out who or what had been in the basement. And there was only one person he was sure could help save his sister's soul. The roads were clear and he arrived at the house shortly before ten o'clock. The gates were still open but he closed them after he'd driven through, then parked and smoked a cigarette in the cold night air before heading inside. He switched on the lights and went slowly up the staircase, running his hand along the banister.

Nightingale didn't know much about magic circles or how they worked. He had learned how to construct one and he knew that he was safe only so long as he remained inside its confines, but other than that he knew next to nothing. The circle that he'd used the first time he had summoned Proserpine was still in the master bedroom, but he had a gut feeling that protective circles could only be used once. He figured that they were probably like the gaskets in his beloved MGB. Whenever he took the engine apart, which was at least twice a year, he always installed brand-new gaskets. More often than not the old ones would probably work but experience had taught him that it was better not to take the risk.

All the bedrooms off the upstairs hallway were clean, but Nightingale figured there was clean and there was magic-circle clean so he fetched a bucket and a brush from the kitchen and spent the best part of an hour washing and rewashing the floor of the bedroom next to the one where Ainsley Gosling had ended his life with a shotgun blast.

There was a small bathroom leading off the bedroom and he emptied the dirty water down the toilet, then took off his clothes and stepped into the shower. He used a plastic nail brush to clean under his fingernails and his toenails, and shampooed his hair twice. He worked up a lather with a fresh bar of coal tar soap, rinsed himself off, and then repeated the process. He dried himself with a new, unused towel, then put on fresh clothes. He smiled at his reflection in the mirror above the sink. 'Squeaky clean,' he said.

He'd brought up everything that he needed from the basement in a cardboard box that now stood in the middle of the room. On the top was the box of chalk. He took out a stick and carefully drew a circle about twelve feet in diameter, with the cardboard box in the centre. Picking up the birch branch that he'd taken from the garden he slowly ran it around the chalk mark and then put it back in the box. He used the chalk to draw a pentagram inside the circle, directing two of the five points towards north. Then he drew a triangle around the circle, with the apex pointing north, making sure that there was plenty of room between the two shapes. Any devil summoned to the magic circle would remain trapped between the circle and the triangle. Finally he wrote the letters MI, CH and AEL at the three points of the triangle. Michael. The Archangel. Sworn enemy of Satan and the fallen angels. Michael was the Angel of Death, who, according to the Bible, appeared before every soul at the point of death giving them a last chance to redeem themselves. It was the power of the Archangel that would keep Proserpine trapped within the triangle and keep Nightingale safe inside the pentagram.

He straightened up, then took a small glass bottle from the cardboard box. Consecrated salt water. He removed the stopper and carefully sprinkled the water around the circle. He replaced the stopper, put the bottle back in the box, and took out five church candles. He placed them at the five points of the pentagram, struck a long match and carefully lit them, moving clockwise around the circle. When he'd finished he blew out the match and put it into the box. He'd written a checklist of everything he was supposed to do and he methodically worked through it, ensuring that he hadn't forgotten anything. At the bottom of the list was the Latin phrase that he had to repeat when he wanted Proserpine to appear.

He took a deep breath and exhaled slowly. He desperately wanted a cigarette but smoke was an impurity that would weaken the circle. He wiped his hands on his trousers and then picked up a plastic bag full of herbs. He took a handful and sprinkled it over the candles one by one, again moving clockwise. As the herbs hit the flames they spluttered and sparked and the air was soon thick with cloying fumes. Nightingale took a lead crucible from the box and poured the rest of the herbs into it, then used another long match to ignite them. He took another deep breath and his head started to swim. He felt the strength drain from his legs and his knees began to buckle but he bunched his hands into fists and gritted his teeth, forcing himself to concentrate. He stood in the exact centre of the pentagram and slowly read out the Latin phrase, carefully enunciating every syllable. Then he shouted the final three words: '*Bagahi laca bacabe!*'

The air was so thick with smoke that he could no longer see the walls. The ceiling shimmered and went dark, and then the smoke began to form into a slowly moving vortex. His eyes were watering and he could taste something metallic at the back of his mouth. There was a flash of lightning and the smell of cordite and then the floorboards began to shake.

Space seemed to fold into itself and there was a series of rapid-fire bright flashes. The air went blurry and then suddenly came back into focus and she was standing there, dressed in black with her black and white collie dog standing by her side. Her face was a deathly white, her hair jet black and spiky, her lashes loaded with mascara, black lipstick emphasising her pout. She was wearing a black leather motorcycle jacket with an upside-down silver crucifix on the left lapel and a leering silver skull on the right, tight black jeans with ripped knees and black stiletto heels. Her toenails and fingernails were painted a glossy black to match her eyes.

'Nightingale,' she said. 'I didn't expect to see you again so soon.' Her dog barked and she stroked it behind the ear.

'Good dog,' said Nightingale.

The animal bared its fangs at him. 'Don't tease him,' said Proserpine. 'He doesn't like being teased.'

'Who does?' said Nightingale. 'How're things?'

'Things?'

'Life, or whatever passes for life for a demon from Hell.'

'You wouldn't understand.'

'I've an enquiring mind.'

She sneered at him. 'Trying to explain my existence would be like you explaining quantum physics to a cockroach.'

'When I summon you, where do you come from?'

'The Elsewhere,' she said. 'Somewhere else. Somewhen else. You wouldn't understand.'

'Another dimension?'

She shook her head, almost sadly. 'You use words without any comprehension of their meaning. You have no idea what a dimension is. You know nothing. A blink of an eye ago and you humans thought the world was flat. And then you believed that the sun went around your little planet. Now your brightest minds tell you that the universe was created from nothing and is expanding outwards.'

'And it isn't?'

She laughed and the dog looked up at her and wagged its tail. 'What do you want, Nightingale?'

Nightingale folded his arms 'Help,' he said.

Proserpine laughed again and the walls shook as if the building was in the grip of an earthquake. 'Help?'

'My sister. Ainsley Gosling sold her soul as well as mine.'

Proserpine shrugged. 'So?'

'People keep telling me that she's going to Hell.'

'They're probably right.'

'Tonight I used a Ouija board in the basement. Someone or something gave me the same message.'

'And again, so?'

'I thought it might have been you.'

'Well, you thought wrong. I have no interest in your sister. You're not the centre of my universe, Nightingale. Why would you think I care what happens to you or those close to you?'

'I sort of assumed you saw and heard everything.'

'Well, you sort of assumed wrong. You call me and I'll come to see what you want. But when I'm in the Elsewhere I don't give you a second's thought.'

'I'm hurt.'

'No, you're not, but carry on wasting my time like this and you'll feel pain like you've never felt before.' She folded her arms. 'What do you want? Why did you call me?'

'My sister's soul. Ainsley Gosling sold it to one of your lot. Frimost.'

'Frimost?' repeated Proserpine.

'You know him?'

'By reputation,' she said. 'He's a nasty piece of work.'

Nightingale grinned. 'That's ironic, coming from you.'

Proserpine narrowed her eyes. 'What do you mean, exactly?'

'Well, you're all devils, aren't you? The Fallen. Sending souls to Hell and all that jazz. I guess to an outsider you'd all look like nasty pieces of work. No offence.'

Proserpine roared with laughter and the floor shook. 'None taken,' she said. 'But we're not all the same,

Nightingale. And, if you meddle with Frimost, you'll discover that to your cost.' She put her hands on her hips. 'So what do you want?'

'I want to know how to get my sister's soul back,' said Nightingale. 'I want to know how to deal with Frimost.' He studied Proserpine with unblinking eyes, looking for any hint as to what was going through her mind. As a police negotiator he'd learned that body language and facial expressions were more of a key to what a person was thinking than what came out of their mouths. But Proserpine wasn't human, she was a demon from the bowels of Hell, and her face was as smooth and feature-less as porcelain, her eyes like pools of oil.

'What do you think I am, Nightingale?' she said. 'Phone a friend?'

'I thought we had a connection,' he said. 'I helped you get what you wanted, didn't I?'

She sneered at him. 'We had a deal, Nightingale. That doesn't mean we had a connection.'

Nightingale rubbed the back of his neck. The skin there was soaking wet. 'My sister's an innocent in all this,' he said.

Proserpine grinned. 'There are no innocents, Nightingale. Haven't you heard of Original Sin?'

'Her soul was sold on the day she was born,' said Nightingale. 'It wasn't her choice and she didn't do anything wrong. She didn't do a deal; she has no idea what's coming.'

'Do I care?' The dog growled again and Proserpine patted him on the neck. 'We won't be here long,' she said.

'Actually, that's not true, is it?' said Nightingale.

She looked up at him, her eyes narrow slits. 'What do you mean?'

'According to the rules of the game, if I summon you, you have to stay here for as long as I want you to. And you have to stay in the space between the circle and the triangle. That's right, isn't it?'

Proserpine straightened up and cocked her head to one side. 'So now you're an expert on summoning devils, are you?'

'I just know what I've read,' he said. 'And what I've read says that you're a prisoner until I let you go.'

She nodded slowly, clearly amused.

'What's funny?' he asked.

'*Little Britain*,' she said. 'That always makes me laugh. The fat bald one, what's his name?'

Nightingale shrugged. 'I don't watch much TV these days.'

'You should,' she said. 'Reflects life the way it's lived. And *The Office*. Now that was funny. The place they work in reminds me of Hell.'

'I thought Hell was fire and brimstone.'

'It can be,' she said. 'Do you want a visit?'

'You can take me?'

'Just ask.'

'And you'll bring me back?'

She laughed and this time the floor shuddered as if the house was in the grip of an earthquake. 'I shall miss your sense of humour, Nightingale,' she said.

'When?'

'When you're dead.' She ran her hand through her spiky hair. 'It's time for you to let me go,' she said. 'You keep me any longer and you'll try my patience.'

'You have to stay until I say you can go.'

She folded her arms. 'Really?' she said.

'That's what the books say.'

'You don't want to believe everything you read in books,' she said. 'There's a lot of crap in the Bible, for instance. And don't get me started on the Koran.'

'I just want some advice,' he said. 'Some guidance. Give me that and I'll release you.'

'What if we just wait and see?' she said quietly.

'What do you mean?'

A cunning smile spread slowly across her face. 'You really don't understand the magic circle, do you?' she said.

'It got you here, didn't it?'

'Yes, it did,' she said. 'And you're inside the circle and I'm outside, but which of us is really trapped?'

Nightingale felt something cold run down his spine and he shivered.

'Time is different for me, Nightingale. You measure your fleeting life in seconds and minutes. I measure mine in . . .' She shrugged. 'I don't measure it,' she said. 'Time just is. Time to me is like length, breadth and width. It's just there. It doesn't move the way it does for you.'

Nightingale frowned. 'I don't understand what you mean,' he said.

'Of course you don't,' she said. 'But understand this. I can stand here for a hundred years. A thousand. A million, if necessary. But you? Could you do twenty-four hours in that circle? A week? Could you do a month? Without food or water? And even without food and water how long do you think you can stay there before you lose your mind?' She grinned. 'How about we give it a go?' She dropped her arms to her sides and stared at him impassively.

'This is ridiculous,' said Nightingale.

Proserpine said nothing but continued to stare at him. Her eyes were black and featureless, the irises blending perfectly into the pupils; but there was no reflection in them so it seemed as if they absorbed everything. Her face was a blank mask and he couldn't tell if she was looking at him or through him. He walked around the cardboard box and then faced her again. She hadn't moved, and neither had the dog. It was as if they had frozen.

'You're sulking, is that it?' he asked.

There was no reaction.

'You're just going to stand there and do nothing?'

She stayed where she was, frozen to the spot. Nightingale walked up to her and stared at her across the chalk outline. He held up his right hand and waved it in front of her face. Her eyes continued to stare fixedly ahead and there was no sign that she was even breathing.

He moved his head closer to hers, taking care not to cross the pentagram, but still Proserpine didn't react. He walked back to the centre of the pentagram and stood there watching her. The seconds ticked by. A minute. Two minutes. Nightingale realised that she was right. Time was crawling by and there was no way he could spend hours in the pentagram, never mind days or weeks. And so long as she was in the room, he couldn't step outside the pentagram because then it would all be over. The pentagram wasn't only protection, it was a prison. He looked at the dog. It was completely motionless and the eyes were dull and lifeless. Nightingale stared at the dog, waiting to see if it would blink, but a full minute passed and nothing happened.

He paced slowly around the pentagram. The herbs were still smouldering in the lead crucible. He looked at his watch. Only five minutes had gone by since Proserpine and her dog had stopped moving but it felt like hours. He walked over to her side of the pentagram and took a deep breath. 'Okay, I'm sorry,' he said. 'I apologise.' He put his hand over his heart, fingers splayed. 'I didn't mean to offend you and I've learned my lesson.'

Proserpine smiled. 'That's better,' she said. The dog woofed quietly and its tongue lolled from the side of its mouth.

'I just thought that the spell was what you did if you wanted to converse with a devil.'

'It is, but it's not to be misused. I'm not a dog to be summoned by the jerking of a chain.'

The dog growled and Proserpine bent down and rubbed it behind the ear. 'That's right, honey, no one will ever chain you.' She looked up at Nightingale and smiled. 'So we're done, right?' she said.

'Is there anything I can say or do that would persuade you to help me?'

She straightened up and shrugged her shoulders. 'A deal,' she said. 'You could offer me a deal. That's the only good reason to summon a devil. We're usually summoned by those with a soul to sell.' She licked her lips with the tip of her tongue. 'What about it, Jack Nightingale? Do you want to sell your soul?'

'I've gone to a great deal of trouble to keep it, thanks,' he said.

'An exchange, then?' she said, her voice a throaty whisper. 'Your soul for your sister's?'

'You could do that? Even though her soul isn't promised to you?'

'I can pull strings, Nightingale. So do we have a deal? Your soul for hers? It's no biggie; it would put you back where we started. Your soul was always mine anyway.'

'Only because my father sold it to you before I was born,' he said. 'I was never given a choice in the matter. Now I do have a choice, and I want to keep it.'

'So we're done, then,' said Proserpine. 'Say the words to end this and I'll be on my way.'

'What about a little help?' said Nightingale. 'Some guidance?'

'I'm not an agony aunt. I take souls. You're starting to try my patience, Nightingale.'

Nightingale put up his hands. 'Okay, okay,' he said. 'How about a deal? What would you want to answer a few questions?'

'What are you offering?'

'Proserpine, I have enough trouble buying birthday presents for my secretary, how on earth would I know what you want? I'm guessing that book tokens wouldn't cut it.'

Proserpine threw back her head and laughed. The room shook and the bottle of consecrated salt water fell out of the cardboard box and shattered. The dog's tail swished from side to side as it arched its head to look up at its mistress. The herbs flared in the crucible and a shower of sparks rained down on Nightingale's shoulders. 'You want to buy information from me?' she asked. 'With trinkets?'

'What do you want?' asked Nightingale. 'Tell me what you want and maybe we can do a deal.'

'Is this how you worked when you were a police negotiator, Nightingale? Promise them anything so long as
they come along quietly?'

'If you find out what a person in crisis wants, then
more often than not you can offer them something that
will make their life easier.'

Proserpine's eyes narrowed. 'I'm not in crisis,
Nightingale.'

'No, but I am. Look, I don't know where my sister is
– hell, I don't even know who she is. But I'll do whatever I have to do to find her.'

'I've already told you, I can't help you with that.'

'No, but you can help me get her soul back. Assuming
that I can find her. But I need intel. Intel that you can
supply me with.'

Proserpine studied him with her unblinking black eyes
for several seconds, and then she slowly nodded. 'You
want questions answered?'

'I need to know how to help my sister.'

'From what you've said it sounds as if she's beyond
help.'

'That's what everyone said about me, but I did okay.'

Proserpine smiled slyly. 'Maybe you did. And maybe
you didn't.'

'What does that mean?'

'It's not over until the fat lady sings,' said Proserpine.
'So how about this? For every question of yours that I
answer, you give up ten years of your life.'

Nightingale's jaw dropped. 'What do you mean by "give
up"? You mean I go to prison?'

'I mean you die ten years earlier than you would have
done.'

Nightingale's mouth had gone suddenly dry but he tried not to show his discomfort. 'I'm not keen on that, frankly,' he said.

'Are you sure you want to do this, Nightingale?'

Nightingale ran a hand through his hair. 'Yes,' he said.

'Are you really sure?' pressed Proserpine. 'You don't even know this person. Why does her welfare concern you so much?'

'She's my sister.'

'So?'

'So she's the only family I have. She's blood.'

'And blood isn't worth ten years?' she asked.

'It's a bit steep. What else have you got?'

Proserpine sighed and folded her arms, then cocked her head like a hawk scrutinising potential prey. 'How about this?' she said. 'You want "intel" as you call it. Fine. But for every question of yours that I answer, I'll send someone to kill you.'

Nightingale's brow furrowed. 'Someone or something?'

Proserpine smiled. 'Now you're thinking,' she said. 'Don't worry, they'll be human. Genetically anyway.'

'And they'll try to kill me?'

'Oh they'll be professionals, Nightingale. They won't be playing with you. '

'And what do you get out of it?' he asked. The nicotine craving had returned with a vengeance and he gritted his teeth.

'Entertainment,' she said. 'Amusement. Plus I can use you as a reward.'

'Reward?'

'A treat. Something to show my minions that I care for them. They do so love to serve me. Do you want the deal or not, Nightingale? If not, say the words and I'll be on my way.'

'It's a deal,' he said. 'And you'll answer any question that I ask you?'

A cruel smile spread across her face. 'Yes, Nightingale, I will.' She bit down on her lower lip and watched him.

Nightingale wondered why she was smiling, then realisation hit him like a punch to the solar plexus. He'd asked his first question and she'd answered it. And that stupid slip was going to cost him an attempt on his life. 'Okay,' he said, nodding slowly. 'I see how it works.' He stopped speaking as his mind whirled. He was going to have to be very, very careful because the next words out of his mouth would be a matter of life or death.

31

There was a white VW Golf parked next to Jenny's Audi when Nightingale arrived at her house at eight o'clock the following morning. As he climbed out of his MGB, a middle-aged lady in a fur coat, walking two Yorkshire terriers on leads, wished him a good morning. Nightingale resisted the urge to tug his forelock. He rang Jenny's buzzer and a female voice he didn't recognise said, 'Who is it?' through the speakerphone.

'It's Jack,' he said. 'Jack Nightingale. Is Jenny okay?'

The speakerphone clicked and went quiet. Nightingale heard footsteps and then the door opened. It took him a couple of seconds to recognise the brunette standing in the doorway. Barbara McEvoy was an old friend from Jenny's student days, the psychiatrist that Jenny had taken to Gosling Manor. She smiled at him but her eyes were wary as she stepped back and let Nightingale across the threshold.

Barbara pointed to a door at the end of the hallway. 'Jenny's in the kitchen,' she said, closing the front door as Nightingale headed down the corridor.

Jenny was sitting at a breakfast bar in a pink bathrobe, toying with a bowl of cornflakes. 'You're up early,' she said. Her hair was tied back in a red scrunchy.

Barbara came into the kitchen behind him. 'Ouija boards aren't toys, Jack,' she said. 'They can do a lot of damage.'

'Is that a professional opinion?' asked Nightingale. Barbara was a psychiatrist at one of the larger London hospitals.

'I'm serious, Jack. I've known patients develop all sorts of problems after playing with them.'

'Problems like what?' asked Nightingale.

'Depression. Hallucinations. Schizophrenia, in one case.'

'Come on, Barbara, you're not suggesting that a Ouija board can cause schizophrenia.'

'Of course not, but if someone already has mental-health issues, messing around with the spirit world isn't likely to help.' Barbara poured tea into a mug and handed it to him.

'I'm surprised that you're not accusing us of imagining things.'

Barbara frowned. 'Why do you say that?'

Nightingale sipped his tea. 'Because you're a psychia-trist. I didn't think you'd believe in spirits.'

'I don't,' she said. 'But that doesn't mean that I think Ouija boards aren't dangerous.'

'But Jenny told you what happened?'

'She said that you were playing with the board in the basement and that you got upset and the candles went out. And that you then forced her to go back to finish the séance.'

'The session had to be finished; the spirit had to be banished.'

'Jack, come on, you don't believe in spirits, do you?

You don't really think that you were talking to someone who'd died, do you?'

Nightingale folded his arms and looked across at Jenny. She flashed him a warning look and he realised that she hadn't told her friend everything. She certainly hadn't told Barbara that Nightingale had negotiated with a demon from Hell to save his soul from eternal damnation. 'What do you think happened, Barbara?' he asked quietly

'I think you let your imaginations get the better of you. I think the game went a bit too far and Jenny paid the price.' She put her hands around her mug. 'Ouija boards are a way of getting in touch with thoughts and emotions that are usually suppressed. Most people assume that someone is consciously pushing the glass or the pointer or whatever, but in fact that's often not the case. You might have three or four people around the board and all of them would swear blind that they weren't trying to influence what was happening. And the thing is, they'd probably all be telling the truth.'

'You mean they might be doing it subconsciously?' asked Nightingale.

'Exactly.'

'And why would they do that?'

Barbara shrugged. 'There's a host of reasons,' she said. 'You have to remember that a lot of times people use the Ouija board to try to contact a loved one who's died. So they're under a lot of stress to start with. And often there's something they want to say to that loved one, and something that they want to hear back. So there's an element of wish-fulfilment. That might be as simple as wanting to hear that they're still loved. Plus there's the fear of death, of course.'

'Fear of death?' repeated Nightingale.

'Most people want to believe that death isn't the end,' said Barbara. 'They want to get a message from beyond the grave so the subconscious kicks in and gives them what they want. It's not a harmless game, Jack. Even for consenting adults. Jenny said that you were trying to contact your partner. Robbie?'

Nightingale nodded. 'He died a few weeks ago.'

'And I'm guessing you had unresolved issues with him?'

'Sure,' said Nightingale. Jenny was still keeping her head down, unwilling to look at him. 'I know it was stupid.'

'And the basement of an empty house wasn't the best venue. I mean, the house is lovely, but there is some seriously disturbing stuff in the basement.'

'No argument here,' said Nightingale. Jenny looked up at him and smiled. 'You don't have to come in today,' he said. 'You can hang out here with Barbara.'

She shook her head. 'No, I've got lots to do,' she said. 'I'll get changed.'

'Jack's right,' said Barbara. 'We can try some retail therapy. Karen Millen's got a pre-Christmas sale.'

'Really, I'd rather work.'

'Work rather than shop?' Barbara looked at Nightingale, her eyes narrowing suspiciously. 'You've done some magic thing on her, haven't you? Bent her to your will?'

'I wish,' laughed Nightingale.

32

Nightingale dropped Jenny off at the office and then drove to Camden. He left his MGB on the third floor of a multi-storey car park close to Camden Lock market. The Wicca Woman shop wasn't easy to find unless you were looking for it; it was tucked away in a side street between a store selling exotic bongs and T-shirts promoting cannabis use, and another that specialised in hand-knitted sweaters. A tiny bell tinkled as Nightingale pushed open the door. He smelled lavender and lemon grass and jasmine and he saw an incense stick burning in a pewter holder by an old-fashioned cash register.

Alice Steadman was arranging a display of crystals on a shelf by the window. Her face broke into a smile when she saw him. 'Mr Nightingale, I'm so pleased to see you.' She was in her late sixties, with pointy bird-like features and grey hair tied back in a ponytail. Her skin was wrinkled and almost translucent but her eyes were an emerald green that burned with a fierce intensity. She was dressed all in black: a long silk shirt-dress that reached almost to her knees, a thick leather belt with a silver buckle in the shape of a quarter moon, thick tights and slippers with silver bells on the toes.

'Why's that, Mrs Steadman?'

'Because the last time we met you were asking me about selling souls to the devil. I must admit you had me worried.'

'I was just curious,' said Nightingale. He held up the carrier bag he was holding. 'I brought you a gift.'

She giggled girlishly. 'Oh you shouldn't have. Books? From your collection? Oh let me see.'

Nightingale gave her the carrier bag. Inside were three books that he'd taken from the shelves in the basement of Gosling Manor. They were all old and bound in leather, one was about witchcraft in the Middle Ages and the other two were books of spells, both lavishly illustrated.

Mrs Steadman gasped. 'Oh my goodness,' she said. She looked at him, her eyes wide. 'You can't possibly give these to me, Mr Nightingale. They're far too precious.'

'They're no use to me, Mrs Steadman,' said Nightingale. 'And I'll be selling most of what I have. I just wanted to thank you for all the help you gave me.'

She clasped the books to her chest as if she was afraid that he might change his mind. 'Well, let me at least offer you a cup of tea,' she said.

'You read my mind,' said Nightingale.

Mrs Steadman pulled back a beaded curtain behind the counter. 'Briana, can you take over the shop for me?' she called.

Nightingale heard soft footsteps and then a punk girl with fluorescent pink hair appeared. Like Mrs Steadman she was dressed all in black and she had a chrome stud in her chin, two studs in each eyebrow and a nose ring. She grinned at Mrs Steadman. 'Is this your new boyfriend, then?' she asked in a nasal Essex accent.

'No, Briana, of course not,' said Mrs Steadman, but her cheeks flushed. 'I'm just going to make Mr Nightingale a cup of tea.'

Nightingale followed her through the curtain to a small room where a gas fire was burning, casting flickering shadows across the walls. She put the books on a circular wooden table and waved for Nightingale to sit on one of three wooden chairs. Above the table was a brightly coloured Tiffany lampshade, and on one wall was a flatscreen television tuned to a chat show.

Mrs Steadman picked up a remote and switched off the television. 'I tell Briana that television destroys the brain cells, but she won't listen to me,' she said, going over to a kettle on top of a pale green refrigerator and switching it on. She looked at him over her shoulder. 'Milk and no sugar,' she said.

'You've a good memory,' said Nightingale.

'I'm not senile yet, young man,' she said archly.

'I know that, Mrs Steadman,' he said. He nodded towards the beaded curtain. 'How's business?'

'Better than ever,' she said, spooning PG Tips into a brown ceramic teapot. 'I think the recession means that more people are looking for help.'

'Spells to make money?' asked Nightingale.

'Not just money, but that's obviously an issue. When times are hard people look for answers and Wicca has them in abundance. Wicca helps you to find your place in the natural order of things and helps you to live in harmony with others.'

When the kettle had boiled she poured water into the teapot and carried it over to the table on a tray with two blue and white striped mugs and a matching milk jug. She sat down and poured the tea, then added milk.

'How's your business, Mr Nightingale?' she asked, watching him like an inquisitive bird.

'Ticking over,' said Nightingale. 'I do a lot of divorce work and when times are hard relationships are always stressed.'

Mrs Steadman sipped her tea and studied him over the top of her mug. 'I get the feeling that you didn't come just to give me the books,' she said.

Nightingale smiled. 'You can see right through me, can't you?'

'I'm a good reader of people, that's true.'

'You'd have made a great detective.'

'I'm sure you mean that as a compliment,' she said, putting down her mug. 'So how can I help you?'

Nightingale ran a hand through his hair. 'It's a bit embarrassing, actually.'

'A love potion?'

Nightingale laughed out loud. 'Sadly, no,' he said.

'There's no lady in your life?' she said with a mischievous twinkle in her eyes.

'Mrs Steadman, I didn't come here for help with my love life,' he said. 'It's more practical than that. I'm about to lose my driving licence. I did a silly thing and drove after I'd been drinking.'

'That is silly,' said Mrs Steadman. 'Drinking and driving is very dangerous.'

'I know,' said Nightingale, holding up his hands. 'It was a stupid thing to do. It's no excuse but I was under a lot of stress.'

'So the police caught you, did they?'

Nightingale nodded. 'I was breathalysed and charged

and when it goes to court I'll lose my licence, unless . . .' He left the sentence unfinished.

'Unless you can use magic to help you out of your predicament?'

'When you put it like that it does sound ridiculous, doesn't it?'

She ran her finger around the rim of her mug. 'It's not ridiculous, but it is rather unethical.'

'Sorry, it was a stupid idea,' said Nightingale. 'It's just that I really can't do without my car. Forget I asked.'

Mrs Steadman chuckled. 'You do give up easily, don't you?' she said.

'Now you're sending out mixed signals,' said Nightingale. 'Is there anything that can be done?'

'What exactly is it that you want?' she asked.

Nightingale shrugged. 'Some sort of lucky charm, maybe. Something that would help me win the case.' He threw up his hands. 'I don't know, Mrs Steadman. The more I talk about it, the crazier it sounds.'

'Actually it's not at all crazy,' she said. 'But you'll need more than luck, you'll need something specific. And the more specific the spell, the greater the risk.'

'Why's that?'

'Let's just say that you have to be careful what you wish for.' She sipped her tea. 'I'll give you a spell, Mr Nightingale. Just be careful, that's all.'

'Magic?'

'Yes, magic. But Wicca magic. Even though, strictly speaking, you're asking for something that I suppose is borderline illegal.'

'I had been drinking, that's true,' said Nightingale. 'But I wasn't drunk, and I wasn't a danger to anyone.'

Mrs Steadman held up a delicately boned hand. 'Really, Mr Nightingale, it's not my concern. I know you're a good man.'

'I wish that were true.' He smiled when he saw her face fall and realised she wasn't used to his sense of humour. 'Thank you, Mrs Steadman. Really.'

'You're welcome,' she said. 'It's the least I can do considering the books you've brought me. Now, first you need a red candle. It must be three times as tall as its diameter. And it must be a crimson red, not blood red. You need to be in a darkened room, the darker the better, though moonlight is acceptable. This has to be done at night-time, between midnight and two o'clock. You put a horseshoe around the candle. The open end facing you, the closed end facing north. The shoe must have been worn by a white mare that has yet to foal.'

Nightingale frowned. 'A mare?'

'A mare is a female horse more than three years old. Prior to that she's a filly. You're not an equestrian, are you?'

'I'm more of an internal-combustion aficionado,' he said. 'Where am I going to get a white mare's shoe?'

'I have everything you need in stock,' said Mrs Steadman. 'I have a supplier who runs a riding stable in Wimbledon. Now, you need a piece of virgin parchment, a quill made from a swan's feather and black ink that has been prepared in the Persian way.' She smiled at him. 'And yes, before you ask, I have the ink. And the parchment. And the feather.'

'You're a godsend, Mrs Steadman.'

'Now, you write down what you want on the parchment while you chant these words: "What I want I write here, please take my dream and bring it near, what I want is what I should get, let all my dreams now be met." Then you fold the parchment in half and in half again and hold it over the flame of the candle and let it burn. It must burn completely while it's in your fingers – the more of the parchment that remains, the less likely it is that you'll get the wish granted. Ideally you want it to turn to ashes in your hand. Then you rub the ash between your hands until there is nothing left. And this is important: you mustn't wash your hands until the following night. Until after midnight. If you wash your hands before then, you negate the spell.'

'And that'll work?'

'Of course it'll work, young man. Provided you do exactly as I've said.'

Nightingale sipped his tea. 'If it's as easy as that, why doesn't everyone do it?'

'A lot do,' she said. 'There's more interest than ever in Wicca.'

'But it's not as if it's generally known, is it? That magic can get you off a drunk-driving charge?'

Mrs Steadman chuckled. 'We tend not to advertise,' she said. 'And I doubt that many solicitors would be prepared to suggest magic as an alternative to legal advice.'

'But it will work, right?'

'I would hope so, yes. The proof, as they say, is in the pudding.'

33

J enny was signing for a letter when Nightingale arrived back at the office. A cycle courier in skin-tight black Lycra leggings and a fluorescent green top nodded at him.

'Aren't you cold out there?' asked Nightingale. 'It's brass monkeys.'

'It's fine so long as you keep moving,' said the man. He had a New Zealand accent and sun-bleached hair that suggested he was more at home on a surfboard than pedalling around the streets of London. Jenny handed him back his receipt pad and thanked him.

'It's the DNA results, I had them do a rush job,' said Jenny as the courier headed out. She smiled brightly at him and held up the envelope. 'Do you want to open this or should I as part of my secretarial duties?'

'You go ahead,' he said.

She opened the envelope and took out a sheet of paper. 'And the winner is . . .' She frowned as she read the letter, then looked up. 'I'm sorry, Jack. She's not related to you.'

Nightingale shrugged. 'Nothing to be sorry about, kid,' he said. 'She killed herself, remember. If she's not related to me then my sister's still out there somewhere.'

Jenny reread the letter and then gave it to Nightingale.

'I don't understand this,' she said. 'Why did the Ouija board tell you to go to Abersoch in the first place? What was to be gained by sending you to see a girl who'd just killed herself?'

'I wish I knew,' said Nightingale. 'But I think that pretty much proves it wasn't Robbie talking to us.' He read the letter from the lab. It confirmed that there were no matching sequences in the two DNA samples.

'Well, if it wasn't Robbie, who was it? And who would want to tell you that your sister is going to Hell? Do you think it might be Proserpine?'

Nightingale didn't say anything.

'You look like a kid who's just been caught stealing sweets,' said Jenny.

'I do not.'

'You've been up to something.'

Nightingale held up his hands. 'Guilty as charged,' he said. 'You should have been a cop.'

'What did you do, Jack?'

He sighed. 'I called up Proserpine.'

Jenny's eyes widened. 'You did not!'

'Why ask if you don't believe me? I summoned her, and it isn't her behind the messages. And it wasn't her down in the basement. She said that my sister's soul was nothing to do with her.' He took off his raincoat and hung it on the rack by the door.

'And you believe her?'

'I don't think there's any reason for her to lie. Maybe it's like Barbara said and it's our subconscious at work.'

'You mean we were pushing the planchette? Because I wasn't. Were you?'

'Not deliberately, of course. That's the whole point of

the subconscious, isn't it? It works without you knowing why or how.'

'But at one point it was moving on its own, Jack. And the spinning globe? The books? I didn't tell Barbara about that, but we saw what we saw. Something was down in the basement with us, and it wasn't Robbie. And if it wasn't Robbie last time, maybe it wasn't Robbie before. Which means that someone or something wanted you to go to Abersoch.' She flashed a smile. 'But at least now we know for sure that Connie Miller wasn't your sister.'

'Yeah, Thomas was telling the truth after all,' agreed Nightingale.

'So what are you going to do?' asked Jenny.

'I'm going to find her,' said Nightingale.

'How, exactly?'

Nightingale grinned. 'I've got a plan,' he said. 'I'm a private detective, remember? Finding missing people is what I do.'

'By the way, I looked at the DVD with the files from Connie Miller's computer.'

Nightingale shrugged dismissively. 'You can leave that now. There's no connection to me.'

'Jack, there could be a serial killer out there.'

'That's the police's job.'

'I'm serious, Jack. She spent a lot of time on sites about depression and suicide. And she was getting a lot of email from a guy in Caernarfon. He wanted to meet her. His name's Craig. Caernarfon Craig he calls himself.'

Nightingale frowned. 'The cops should have followed that up.'

'I don't think so. She was using a separate email account that she'd set up just to log on to some of the darker sites.'

'How did you find that out?'

'One of the files you downloaded had her passwords.'

'The cops would have found that, surely?'

'I don't think so. It was tucked away in one of her correspondence files. She was pretty good at covering her tracks. I think she wanted to talk to people without them knowing who she was. There're a lot of weirdos on the internet.'

'Send it to the cops, Jenny. Let them follow it up.'

'And how exactly would I explain away the fact that I've got copies of her personal emails?'

'Okay, what do you want to do?'

She smiled. 'Like you, I've got a plan.'

34

The barista was a Ukrainian teenager with bad acne and he had trouble understanding the girl so it was a full ten minutes after entering the coffee shop that Nightingale finally had his two coffees. He took them to the table where Colin Duggan was whispering into his mobile phone. Duggan pocketed the phone as Nightingale put the coffee mugs on the table and sat down.

'One low-fat latte,' said Nightingale. 'Are you off pubs, then? In the old days it would have been a pint of best in the Rose and Crown.'

Duggan picked up his coffee and sipped it. He was an inspector, the same rank as Nightingale had been when he left the Metropolitan Police. He was completely bald with elf-like ears and a mischievous smile. He was wearing a beige raincoat over a dark suit and had a Burberry scarf around his neck. 'I keep out of them these days,' said Duggan. 'No point in rubbing my nose in it.'

'On the wagon?'

Duggan patted his expanding waistline. 'Diabetes,' he said. 'I can keep it under control by watching what I eat and drink but the doctor says that if I don't get a grip on it now I'll be on medication for the rest of my life.'

'Bloody hell, Colin, you're not even fifty. How can you have diabetes?'

'Forty-six,' said Duggan. 'But it's nothing to do with age. It's the booze and the fish suppers. And the cigarettes. I've given them up too.'

'Smoking doesn't give you diabetes,' said Nightingale. 'Zero calories and they reduce stress. If anything, you'd be better off smoking more.'

Duggan grinned and scratched his fleshy neck. 'Yeah, if it wasn't for lung cancer they'd be the perfect food.'

'I'm not sure how true that cancer thing is,' said Nightingale. 'I've known people who've smoked all their lives and never had so much as a cough. And there are non-smokers who've never even tried a single cigarette who've died of lung cancer.' He patted his chest. 'My lungs are fine. I reckon your genes have a lot to do with it. You either get cancer or you don't; smoking is just one of lots of factors.'

'So you've got good genes, have you?' chuckled Duggan.

'Yeah, that's sort of why I wanted to see you.'

'I knew there'd be something,' said Duggan. 'I haven't seen you since the Sophie Underwood thing.'

Nightingale nodded. 'I know. Sorry.'

'Hell of a thing, that.'

That wasn't how Nightingale thought of what had happened that cold November morning. It wasn't a 'thing'. It was a pivotal moment in his life and Sophie's death had changed him forever. Duggan had been there and had seen the girl fall to her death. Nightingale had been on the balcony of the flat next door, trying to talk her back inside. 'Yeah,' said Nightingale. 'It was.'

'What happened to the father, who'd been fiddling with her – he deserved it.'

'Yeah,' agreed Nightingale.

'Seems like a lifetime ago.'

'It was.'

'I'm back in CID and you're a gumshoe.'

Nightingale chuckled. 'Do they still say that? I thought that went out with Humphrey Bogart and Sam Spade.'

'Guys I work with call you lot much worse than that,' said Duggan. 'The days of cops running checks for you private eyes for the price of a pint are well gone. These days, get caught and you lose your job, your pension, everything.'

Nightingale grimaced. 'That's not good news, Colin.'

Duggan raised his coffee in salute. 'Don't worry, Jack. You've got a lot of friends in the Job, me included. What do you need?'

'I'm trying to track down my sister and I've drawn a blank through all the usual channels,' said Nightingale.

'Never knew you had a sister.'

'Neither did I until recently,' said Nightingale. 'Thing is, she's my half-sister – same father, different mother. And she was adopted on the day she was born. So I don't know her name or her date of birth.'

'You're not making this easy, are you?' said Duggan.

'I was hoping you could run a check on the National DNA database.'

Duggan raised his eyebrows. 'You think she's in the system?'

'I know it's an outside chance but there are five million samples in the database and it's growing at thirty thousand a month. She might have been arrested for something and had a sample taken.' Nightingale sighed. 'I know it's a long shot, Colin, but I don't have anything else.'

'So you want me to run your DNA and see if there's a sibling match?'

Nightingale shook his head. 'No need. Our father's DNA is already in the system. A guy called Ainsley Gosling. He committed suicide last month. Robbie Hoyle checked my DNA against Gosling's a few weeks ago.'

'Why did he do that?' asked Duggan.

'I'd just been told that Gosling was my biological father. I wanted to make sure that he really was.'

'What happened to Robbie was a damn shame,' said Duggan.

'Yeah,' agreed Nightingale. 'It was a bitch.'

'I couldn't get to the funeral. I was up in Liverpool interviewing a guy on remand.' Duggan shook his head. 'What a waste. Just goes to show, right? Enjoy life while you can because none of us knows how long we'll be here.' He sipped his latte. 'Okay, so all I need to do is run Gosling's DNA through the database to check for close matches. Shouldn't be a problem.'

'On the QT, obviously.'

Duggan grinned. 'Obviously,' he said. 'I've a couple of missing-person cases on the books – I'll bury the search in one of those. Probably take me a day or two.'

'You're a star, Colin,' said Nightingale, clinking his mug against Duggan's.

'So what's the story? I didn't know you were adopted.'

Nightingale shrugged. 'Until recently, neither did I.'

'This sister, she was born after you?'

'Yeah, two years after. She'll be thirty-one now.'

'So he gave up two kids for adoption one after the other. That's bloody strange, isn't it?'

'You don't know the half of it, Colin.'

Duggan sipped his coffee. 'What about the birth mother?'

'Different mothers,' said Nightingale. 'Mine's dead; my sister's I don't know about.'

'Must feel strange, suddenly finding out that you have a sister after thirty-odd years. If you do find her you're going to have a hell of a lot to talk about.'

Nightingale nodded but didn't say anything. Duggan was right. Finding his sister would be hard enough, but if he did manage to track her down he was then going to have to explain to her that Ainsley Gosling had sold her soul to a demon from Hell. It wasn't a conversation he was looking forward to.

35

J enny was at her desk peering at her computer screen
when Nightingale walked into the office on Friday
morning. She looked at her watch pointedly.

'I know, it's ten o'clock, but I had a late one last night,'
said Nightingale. He put a memory card on the desk.
'Mr Walters was right – his child bride is fooling around
behind his back.'

'Child bride is a bit harsh,' said Jenny. 'She's twenty-
three.'

'Yeah, and he's fifty-one. That means he was almost
thirty when she was born, which in my book makes him
more than old enough to be her father.'

'You are so judgemental,' sighed Jenny, picking up the
memory card.

'Plus, she's Latvian or Ukrainian, so he probably bought
her off the internet at childbride dot com.'

'Jack, you're terrible.'

'I'm a realist. You've seen the guy. Overweight, face like
the back of a bus, IQ in single figures. She's less than
half his age and fit as a butcher's dog. What did he think
was going to happen?' He looked over her shoulder. There
was a Facebook page on her screen. 'Busy, I see,' he said.

'I've been posting on the sites that Connie Miller visited.

My name is Bronwyn and I'm depressed because I don't have any friends and I hate my job.'

'Bless,' said Nightingale.

'You'd be surprised at how many depressed people there are out there.'

'The phrase "get a life" comes to mind. Of course people are going to be depressed if they sit around on their computer every day.'

'I've come across the guy that Connie was emailing but he hasn't reacted to any of my postings yet.'

'He's probably just another sad bastard thinking about topping himself,' he said. He nodded at the memory card in her hand. 'Let's have a look at what I've got. At least it might help pay the bills.'

Jenny slotted the card into the reader attached to her computer.

'The guy she's with is Roger Pennington. Owns a car dealership in south London and a very nice house in Clapham.'

'Married?'

'Footloose and fancy-free and, if I know anything about Latvian mail-order brides, she'll be divorcing Mr Walters and shacking up with Mr Car Dealership quicker than you can say "serves you right". Make sure you send the bill before she takes him for everything he's got.'

'How did you get so cynical?' asked Jenny. Her fingers played over the keyboard and she called up the pictures and videos that had been stored on the card.

'Ten years as a cop and two years doing this,' said Nightingale. 'It's not as if I see people at their best, is it? Anyway, what are you doing over the weekend?'

'I'm off to the country with Barbara to see Mummy and Daddy,' she said.

'Hunting, shooting and fishing?' He peered at the pictures on the screen.

'Not at the same time, obviously,' she said. 'And it'll be a bit cold for fishing, anyway. You should come down with me one weekend. They'd love to meet you.'

'Mutual,' said Nightingale.

'I'm serious, Jack. They keep asking about you.'

'I'd like to meet them, too. I just think that I'd be a bit out of place, that's all.'

'Nonsense,' she said. 'You'd have no problem getting on with Daddy He's a smoker, too. And he collects classic cars.'

'How rich is your dad, exactly?'

She grinned. 'Very.'

'And his house, it's bigger than Gosling Manor, right?'

'Size isn't everything.'

'How many bedrooms has it got?'

'I don't think we've ever counted,' she laughed. 'Are you telling me you won't visit because their house is bigger than yours?'

'I'm joking,' he said, holding up his hands in surrender. 'I'd love a weekend in the country. I'm not sure about the shooting bit, though.'

'We're slap bang in the middle of the pheasant season. It's a great day out – you really should try it.'

'The shooting, I'm fine with; it's the killing birds bit that I'm not happy about.'

'Daddy has a clay-pigeon shoot as well. You don't have a thing about clay discs, do you?'

'I guess not.'

'Daddy does have a rule that you have to eat anything you shoot and you might find them a bit chewy.' She laughed at the look of surprise on his face, then noticed the dirt on his hands. 'What have you been doing?' she asked. 'Your hands are filthy.'

Nightingale looked at his palms. They were streaked with ash. 'Had a problem with the car,' he lied. He pointed at the screen. 'Can you print out the stills and copy the video onto a DVD?' His mobile phone rang in the pocket of his raincoat and he went to retrieve it.

It was Colin Duggan. 'Jack, how are they hanging?' asked the policeman.

'All good, Colin,' said Nightingale.

'I've got good news and bad news,' said Duggan. 'The good news is that I got a hit on the DNA. A definite sibling. Same father as you but a different mother. She's a thirty-one-year-old woman so the dates are in line with what you were looking for.'

'That's brilliant, Colin.'

'Yeah, but don't get too excited. Wait until you hear who she is.'

36

Nightingale ended the call, went through to his office and sat down. He lit a cigarette and swung his feet up onto the desk.

Jenny got up and followed him. 'What's wrong?' she asked.

Nightingale blew a smoke ring up at the ceiling. 'I know who my sister is. And I know where she is.'

'Jack, that's brilliant. Are you going to see her?'

Nightingale looked pained. 'I'm not sure.'

'There's a problem?'

Nightingale nodded. 'Yeah, there's a problem. A big one.'

'Come on, don't keep me in suspenders.' She grinned. 'How bad can it be?'

'Her name's Robyn. Robyn Reynolds.'

Jenny frowned. 'Where have I heard that name before?'

'Splashed across the tabloids and the evening news,' said Nightingale. 'She's the serial killer they caught two years ago.'

Jenny put her hand over her mouth, her eyes wide. 'No,' she said.

'I'm afraid so.'

'She killed five children, didn't she?'

'Butchered them, Colin said. She's in Rampton now. The loony bin.'

'Oh Jack . . .' groaned Jenny. 'I'm so sorry.'

'You and me both, kid.' He pulled on his cigarette and held the smoke deep in his lungs before letting it out slowly.

'There's no doubt, is there?'

Nightingale shook his head. 'It's a perfect parental match,' he said.

'Is it worth comparing her DNA to yours, to make sure?'

'There's no point, not with us having different mothers.' He sighed. 'There's no doubt, Jenny. My sister's a convicted serial killer.' He forced a smile. 'At least we know where she is. And that she won't be going anywhere for a while.' He flicked ash into the ashtray. 'It's not what I expected, that's for sure.'

'I'll see what there is on the internet,' she said, heading back to her desk.

Nightingale leaned back in his chair and blew smoke rings up at the ceiling. He remembered the Robyn Reynolds case, and the killings she was responsible for. The murders had been front-page news during Nightingale's final three months as a police officer, and Reynolds had been caught shortly after he'd left the Met.

He finished his cigarette and stubbed out the butt in his ashtray. He opened the bottom drawer of his desk and took out the bottle of brandy he kept there for his clients, the ones that needed a stiff drink to deal with bad news. He looked around for a glass but couldn't see one close by. There was a mug by his feet but it had stale coffee in it. He groaned and leaned back in his chair.

Jenny returned with a handful of printed sheets. 'It's a bit early for brandy, isn't it?'

'I feel like a drink.'

'I'll make you a coffee.'

'An alcoholic drink,' he said.

She gave him the sheets and took the bottle from him. 'I'll make you an Irish coffee.'

'It's whiskey in an Irish coffee,' he said. 'Irish whiskey, to be precise. If you use brandy, it's a Parisienne coffee.'

'And if I spit in it, that'll make it an assistant's revenge,' she said, heading over to the coffee-maker. 'Just be grateful for what you get.'

'You wouldn't spit in my coffee,' he said.

'Wouldn't, shouldn't, couldn't,' she said, pouring coffee into a mug.

Nightingale flicked through the sheets he was holding. 'She has her own Wikipedia page?'

'Yeah, but there's not much on it,' she said. She looked over her shoulder. 'Notice the date of birth?'

Nightingale looked at the first sheet. 'November the twenty-seventh. We've got the same birthday.'

'That can't be a coincidence,' said Jenny.

'How does Gosling manage to have two kids born on the same day, two years apart?'

'It's not difficult,' said Jenny. 'He can time the conception and then do a Caesarean if necessary.'

'That's incredibly controlling,' said Nightingale.

'Come on, Jack. He produces kids for no other reason than to sell their souls. Gosling is in total control of everything he does so why would you be surprised that he'd time the births?' She brought over his mug of coffee. 'Maybe there's something significant about November the twenty-seventh.'

'Jimi Hendrix was born on November the twenty-seventh. And Ernie Wise. And Emperor Xiaozong of China.' He grinned. 'In 1127, if you were going to ask.'

'I wasn't,' said Jenny.

'It could just be a coincidence,' said Nightingale. 'Plus we were both adopted but our adoptive parents are shown as our biological parents, so the date of birth could be suspect anyway.' He shrugged. 'Actually, it might be an idea to get a copy of her birth certificate just to check.'

'I'll get one from the General Register Office,' said Jenny.

'There're no pictures of her,' said Nightingale, flicking through the sheets.

'She was never photographed,' said Jenny.

'How can that be? The press always get pictures.'

'I Googled her and there're no pictures anywhere. There's not much detail about what she did, either.'

'She killed five kids. How can there be no details?'

'She pleaded guilty so not much was read out in court. The tabloids went to town, obviously, making her out to be a cross between Myra Hindley and Jack the Ripper, but they're low on details. There were no interviews with her parents, she didn't seem to have any friends, and the police didn't comment.' She nodded at the sheets. 'The newspapers spoke to the detective in charge but he wouldn't say anything other than that he was happy the case had a satisfactory conclusion.'

Nightingale sipped his coffee and frowned. 'There's not much brandy in this.'

'It's half past ten in the morning, Jack.'

'Coffee and brandy and cigarettes – the breakfast of champions.'

'You said that about muffins and croissants.'

Nightingale raised his mug in salute. 'I'm flexible,' he said.

'You're upset, aren't you?'

'That my sister's a serial killer? What do you think?'

'I think you should go and see her.'

Nightingale nodded. 'You're probably right.'

37

Getting to see Robyn Reynolds wasn't as difficult as Nightingale had imagined it would be. Rampton Secure Hospital was just that, a hospital, and so there weren't the same restrictions on visits as there were at high-security prisons. He started phoning the hospital first thing on Monday morning and by Tuesday afternoon had managed to get through to one of the doctors who were treating Robyn Reynolds. The doctor had been sceptical at first but Nightingale emailed him his DNA profile, and after the doctor had compared it to that of Robyn Reynolds he'd phoned back and said that Nightingale could visit on Wednesday afternoon.

It took Nightingale almost three hours to drive up to Nottinghamshire. His MGB didn't have satnav and he'd forgotten to ask Jenny to program the location into his phone, but he'd always had a good sense of direction and he had a road atlas open on the passenger seat, just in case.

Rampton Secure Hospital was actually closer to a village called Woodbeck than it was to Rampton but Nightingale doubted the building would be any less sinister if they changed the name. It was a huge Victorian red-brick edifice that looked as if it had once been a hotel, but the high security wall, CCTV cameras, and bars and mesh over the windows were evidence of its true purpose.

A uniformed security guard checked Nightingale's passport and a printout of the email he'd received from the doctor who was treating Robyn Reynolds. The guard peered at Nightingale through thick-lensed spectacles, handed the documents back and pointed at a car park in the distance. Nightingale parked the MGB and walked to a door with a sign above it that read 'VISITORS' ENTRANCE'.

Rampton might have been a hospital rather than a prison, but the security arrangements were as strict as at any Category A prison. He had to show his passport and email to another uniformed guard, this one sitting behind a window of bulletproof glass. His details were written down on a clipboard and the passport and email were passed back to him through a hatch, along with a visitor's badge on a clip. Nightingale clipped it to his raincoat. A glass door rattled back, allowing Nightingale to walk through into a holding area, where two guards, one male and one female, were waiting for him.

The female guard was in her forties and looked bigger and stronger than her male colleague. Her hair was close-cropped and she had a square jaw with a dimple in the centre of her chin and small piggy eyes and a cruel sneer that suggested she'd like nothing more than to give him a full body-cavity search.

'Hi, I'm a visitor,' said Nightingale, tapping the badge.

'We assumed that,' she said. 'Very few people try to break in.' She smiled and her eyes sparkled. She had a soft voice with a West Country burr, and as her smile broadened she took on the look of a kindly aunt. Nightingale felt suddenly guilty about his first impression of her. The door rattled shut behind him. 'Do you have a mobile phone?' she asked.

Nightingale nodded and took it out. The guard who had given him the badge had moved to another window. The female guard gestured at the window. 'Please give your phone to Mr Walker there, and anything sharp that you have on you. Pens, penknives, ice picks, hatchets, axes, samurai swords . . .'

She was halfway through the list before Nightingale realised that she was joking. 'Right,' he said, 'will do.'

'Ignore Agnes, she's easily amused,' said the woman's colleague. The guard was in his forties, overweight and with a shaved head. There were thick rolls of fat at the back of his neck and he had a double chin that made his head look square. 'We just need to be sure that you don't take in anything that can be used as a weapon.'

'No problem,' said Nightingale. He took out a small Swiss Army knife and passed it and the phone through the hatch to the guard behind the glass. In return the guard gave Nightingale a numbered token.

Agnes gestured at a metal-detector archway and asked Nightingale to walk through it. It beeped and Agnes asked him to take off his belt. The second time through the arch, it remained silent.

As Nightingale put his belt back on the guard behind the glass pressed a button and another glass door rattled back to give Nightingale access to the hospital.

'This way, sir,' said Agnes and she ambled along the corridor, swinging her key chain. At the far end of the corridor was a barred gate and Agnes opened it, waited for

Nightingale to go first, then went through it herself and relocked it.

'Must be a pain, opening and closing doors all day,' said Nightingale.

'You get used to it,' she said. 'So you're here to see Robyn? That's a first.'

'She doesn't get many visitors?'

'You're the only one I've seen,' she said. 'When she first arrived we had half of Fleet Street trying to bribe their way in.'

'Can't be much fun, working in here,' said Nightingale.

'I didn't sign up for the fun,' she said. 'Pays well and there's as much overtime as you want.' She nodded at a door that had a small white plastic sign with a name on it – Dr Rupert Keller – in black letters. 'Your sister is going to Hell, Jack Nightingale.' The West Country accent had gone, replaced by a dull expressionless voice.

'What did you say?'

Agnes frowned. 'I said that this is Dr Keller's office,' she said. She knocked on the door and opened it.

Nightingale stared at the guard as she walked away, wondering if he had misheard her.

'Mr Nightingale?' Dr Keller was sitting at his desk and peering at a computer screen. He stood up and extended his hand. He was in his mid-fifties, with skin so pale that it was almost translucent. Nightingale could see the bluish arteries in the back of the doctor's hand and there was hardly any strength in the man's grip. He was wearing a white coat over a tweed suit and a red wool tie and there were thick-lensed spectacles perched on the end of his nose. 'I thought it might be helpful if we had a chat before you see your sister,' said the doctor, waving for Nightingale to sit on one of two chairs in front of the desk.

'Thanks for arranging the visit,' said Nightingale, sitting down. 'I wasn't sure how easy it would be to get into a secure mental hospital.'

'We like our inmates to keep in touch with their families whenever possible,' said Dr Keller. 'Robyn hasn't had any visitors since she arrived two years ago. But that's not unusual. The sort of crimes that our patients have committed means that friends and relatives tend to keep their distance.' He looked across at his computer screen. 'I was just looking at her file. I see that you were only recently added as next of kin.'

'To be honest, Dr Keller, I only discovered last week that we're related.'

The doctor nodded. 'Yes, I see that,' he said. 'However, the DNA is conclusive so we have no problem listing you as a family member even though it is a little unorthodox. You have the same father, correct?'

Nightingale nodded. 'Same father, different mother. We were both adopted at birth. I was obviously surprised to find out her circumstances.'

Dr Keller smiled, showing uneven teeth. 'I'm sure you were,' he said. 'But if you don't mind me asking, why did you decide to visit Robyn?'

'She's my only family,' said Nightingale. 'My adoptive parents died years ago, so when I discovered that I had a sister, albeit a half-sister, I wanted to make contact. Of course I'd be happier under different circumstances, but we have to deal with the world the way it is, don't we?'

'Unfortunately, yes,' said the doctor.

'Is she okay to talk to?' asked Nightingale.

'She's lucid, and at times she can be charming.'

'But she's sick, right? Otherwise she wouldn't be in here?'

'That's a question that can be answered on many levels,' said the doctor. 'She's one of our more manageable inmates, but, bearing in mind the nature of her crime, she is always handled carefully.'

'In what way?'

'She isn't regarded as a danger to other inmates or staff, but she is regarded as an escape risk.'

'Has she ever tried to escape?' asked Nightingale.

'She's been the perfect inmate – she's polite and deferential and follows the rules,' said Dr Keller. 'But she's a sociopath and as such is perfectly capable of pretending to be cooperative until she is presented with an opportunity either to kill again or to escape.'

'But you're okay for me to see her?'

'Absolutely. Her victims have all been children and she's never shown any hostility to other inmates or to staff here. I've no doubt that if she was never to go near children then she would be perfectly fine.'

'And what is it about children that sets her off?'

The doctor shook his head. 'We have no idea,' he said. 'Two years of intense therapy, both one-on-one and in group situations, have got us nowhere. She refuses to talk about herself.'

'Is that unusual?'

'For someone like Robyn, yes. Obviously our emotionally disturbed inmates have communication problems, and some are so heavily medicated that communication is difficult if not impossible, but Robyn isn't on any medication and she is quite articulate. She simply refuses to open up to us.'

'Why do you think that is?'

The doctor exhaled through pursed lips. 'Hand on heart, I think she knows that she is going to be behind bars for the rest of her life, either in a secure mental facility such as Rampton or, if she is ever found to be sane, then in a high-security prison. If she takes that view then there is nothing to be gained by accepting any treatment that might help her.'

'She'll never be released?'

'It's up to the Home Secretary, but look at what happened with Myra Hindley. And what Robyn did was considerably more –' he struggled to find the right word – 'horrific, I suppose. I doubt that the great British public would ever allow her to be released.'

'But could she be cured? If she cooperated?'

Dr Keller looked pained. 'Again, hand on heart, I don't think so. She's a classic sociopath and there's no magic cure for that. She's not the way she is because of a chemical imbalance or because of something that happened to her in the past. She is simply wired differently to you and me.' He tapped the side of his head. 'She's physically different; her neurones, her neural pathways, they're just different, and nothing is ever going to change that. She butchered young children and never showed any remorse, or any guilt, and I don't think any amount of therapy is going to make a scrap of difference.'

'Like paedophiles,' said Nightingale. 'It's their nature and you can't ever change them.'

The doctor nodded in agreement. 'It's a similar condition,' he said. 'There are ways of controlling the impulses of paedophiles, but basically you are right. Once a paedophile, always a paedophile. Once a sociopath . . .'

He finished the sentence with a shrug. 'We can keep your sister away from society so that she isn't a danger to others, but so far as treatment goes . . .' He shrugged again. 'Let's just say that I don't believe in miracles.'

'Who does, these days?' said Nightingale.

38

A CCTV camera monitored their progress as Dr Keller and Nightingale walked down a long corridor. The walls were painted pale green below waist height and the upper half was cream. There were fluorescent lights set into the ceiling, shielded by wire mesh.

'Prior to 2001 we were administered by the Home Office, along with Broadmoor and Ashworth special hospitals,' said Dr Keller. 'But since 2001 we've been part of the Nottinghamshire Healthcare NHS trust. So, strictly speaking, we are a hospital. But all NHS regions can avail themselves of our high-security service, making us a dumping ground for problem patients around the country.'

'But they're all insane, right? That's why they're here?'

Dr Keller laughed. 'That's the way the media portrays us, but it's not as simple as that. We do have a large number of patients with mental-health issues, that goes without saying. But we also care for patients who are deaf or have learning disabilities but have to be placed in a high-security setting. And of course we do have a Dangerous and Severe Personality Disorder Unit, which is where we're going now.'

'That's where my sister is?'

'She was convicted of five horrendous murders, Mr Nightingale. Where else would she be?' He unlocked another barred gate and they went through. 'That's not to say that all our patients have been through the criminal justice system. About a quarter haven't been convicted of anything but have been detained under the Mental Health Act.' He stopped in front of a door. 'This is our visiting area,' he said. 'There has to be a guard present at all times, I'm afraid. But the guard is there for security reasons and won't be eavesdropping.'

He pushed open the door to reveal a room with several tables, each with four chairs that were bolted to the floor. At the far end of the room were two vending machines, one filled with snacks and chocolate, the other for dispensing drinks.

'Please take a seat and I'll have your sister brought in,' he said. As Nightingale sat down, Dr Keller took a transceiver from the pocket of his white coat and spoke into it. He then walked over to the table where Nightingale was sitting. 'She's on her way. I'll ask the guard to bring you back to my office when you're done. I'd be interested to hear how you got on.'

Dr Keller left the room and it was almost fifteen minutes before the door opened and a female guard appeared.

'Mr Nightingale?' she said. She was in her thirties with close-cropped black hair and a fierce stare.

'That's me,' said Nightingale.

The guard stepped to the side and a woman walked in. Nightingale wasn't expecting to see a family resemblance but he was still taken aback by how small she was. Barely five feet tall. She was wearing a baggy grey polo-neck sweater, dark blue Adidas tracksuit bottoms and red

Converse tennis shoes. She didn't look up as she walked over to the table and all he could see of her face was a slightly pointed chin and pale lips. Her hair was dyed blonde but the roots were chestnut brown. Nightingale realised her hair was pretty much the same colour as his own.

She sat down and clasped her hands together, keeping her head down so that he was faced with a wall of blonde hair. The guard walked over to the vending machines and stood there with her arms folded.

Nightingale leaned forward. 'Did Dr Keller tell you who I am?' he asked, his voice a low whisper.

Robyn said nothing. She stared down at the table, breathing through her mouth.

'He told you I'm your brother? My name's Jack.'

'Bollocks,' she whispered.

'It's true. They wouldn't have let me in otherwise.'

She continued to stare at the table, breathing heavily. Her hands were still clasped together, the fingernails bitten to the quick.

'Robyn?'

She flinched as if she'd been struck but still refused to look at him.

'I'm your brother, Robyn.'

For several seconds she didn't react and for a moment he thought she hadn't heard him, then she slowly raised her head. 'No way,' she said.

'Way. Big way.'

She looked up. Her eyes were dark brown, so dark that the irises were almost black. Her eyebrows were thin, as if they'd been carefully plucked. 'What do you mean, big way? That doesn't mean anything.'

'I'm guessing it means the opposite of no way. I'm your brother.'

'I was an only child.'

'We have the same father. There's no doubt. I checked your DNA.'

'How did you get my DNA?'

'It's on file. Everyone who's been arrested is in the system. There's no doubt, Robyn.'

'If you're my brother, why didn't my parents tell me?'

'Because they didn't know.'

She sat back in her chair, folded her arms and scowled at him. 'You're full of shit,' she said. 'How could they be your parents and not know?'

'Because you were adopted, Robyn. You were adopted and so was I. Our father was a man called Ainsley Gosling. He killed himself a few weeks ago.'

'I wasn't adopted,' she said flatly.

'You were. On the day of your birth. That's what happened to me. I was adopted by Bill and Irene Nightingale.'

'So you're Jack Nightingale?'

Nightingale nodded.

'And our father is Ainsley Gosling?'

Nightingale nodded again.

She sneered at him. 'This is a joke, right?'

'It's deadly serious.'

'No, you don't get it,' she said. 'Our father was Gosling, you're Nightingale and I'm Robyn. What's with the bird thing?'

'I don't know,' said Nightingale. 'Coincidence maybe.'

'There are no coincidences,' said Robyn emphatically. 'Everything is connected.'

'That's a philosophy all right,' said Nightingale. 'But I don't think there's a reason we've all ended up with birds' names.'

'I bet you're wrong,' she said. 'And, if it's true, why did this Gosling have us both adopted? And why did he put us with different families?'

'That's where it gets complicated,' said Nightingale. 'But can I ask you something first?'

Robyn shrugged. 'Sure.'

'Your parents. Do you still see them?'

'After what I did?' She snorted contemptuously. 'They wanted nothing to do with me.'

'But they're still alive?'

'Allegedly.'

Nightingale grinned.

'What's so funny?' she snapped.

'I say that a lot,' said Nightingale.

'Say what?'

'Allegedly.'

'Yeah?'

Nightingale nodded and retrieved his pack of Marlboro from his raincoat pocket. 'Can we smoke in here?'

Robyn shook her head. 'They say we're a hospital and not a prison so we can't smoke. Some of the inmates went to the High Court a few years ago to fight it but they lost.' She smiled slyly. 'But rules are meant to be broken, right?' She looked over at the guard. 'Miss Boyle, would it be all right if my brother and I have a cigarette?'

The guard wagged a finger at her. 'It's against the rules, Robyn, you know that.'

'Oh come on, Miss Boyle. You think we don't know that you sneak into the Ladies for a quick smoke in the afternoon? Go one, one smoker to another. Pretty please.'

The guard laughed and shook her head. 'You're a bad girl, Robyn. Go on, then, just the one. But if anyone comes in I'll have to put you on report.'

'Thanks, Miss Boyle,' said Robyn. She winked at Nightingale. 'They're okay in here really,' she said.

Nightingale chuckled, tapped out a cigarette for her and one for himself. He took out his lighter and lit them both, then he offered the pack to the guard but she waved him away.

'More than my job's worth,' she said. 'But thanks anyway.'

Nightingale put the packet away. 'That was nice of her,' he said quietly. 'She didn't have to do that.'

'We're all human beings trying to get through life as best we can, Jack,' said Robyn. She blew a perfect smoke ring up at the ceiling. 'What about your parents?' she asked.

'Dead,' said Nightingale. 'Car crash while I was at university.'

'University? You a smart guy, Jack?'

He grinned. 'Allegedly.' He took a long drag on his cigarette. 'Was it because of the court case that your parents cut you off?'

Robyn shook her said. 'The rot had set in long before then,' she said.

'What was the problem? Were you a difficult kid?'

'I wasn't the problem,' she said, and shook her head again. 'My mum was all right; my dad was a bastard.'

'Bastard in what way?'

She scowled. 'Screwed me on my sixteenth birthday, – does that count?'

'Yeah, that counts.'

'At least he waited until I was legal,' said Robyn. 'Did me on my sixteenth birthday while Mum was at the shops, and tried again two days later. I stuck a knife in him and got on a train to London.' She shivered and took a long pull on her cigarette. 'I guess me being adopted explains a lot. Wasn't incest, wasn't paedophilia; it was plain old rape.'

'You never suspected they weren't your real parents?'

She shook her head fiercely. 'I used to dream that I was really a princess and that my parents were the king and queen of some faraway country and that one day they would come for me, but that's not how it turned out.' She flicked ash onto the floor. 'I don't suppose my genetic father was a king, was he?'

'Not exactly, no,' said Nightingale.

'So who was he, this Ainsley Gosling?'

'It's a long story, Robyn.'

She laughed harshly. 'Jack, time is the one thing I have plenty of right now.'

39

Robyn sat back, her hands on the table. 'You are shit-ting me,' she said. 'You're trying to run some sort of con on me.' She looked over at the guard, who was still leaning against the drinks vending machine, out of earshot. 'I can't believe they let you in here.'

'It's God's truth,' said Nightingale, leaning towards her. 'Though I guess that's not exactly appropriate under the circumstances.'

'Have you got any money on you? Any coins?'

'Sure.'

She gestured at the vending machines. 'Get me a coffee. Black. No sugar.'

'That's how I take mine,' said Nightingale.

'That's how half the population drink it,' she said scorn-fully. 'It doesn't mean we're joined at the hip.'

She glared at him as he got up from the table. He slotted a pound coin into the machine and pressed the button for black coffee. He asked the guard if she wanted one but she shook her head.

'I wouldn't say no to a Kit-Kat, though.'

'Who would?' asked Nightingale. He gave her the Kit-Kat and then got a second coffee. Robyn was still glaring at him when he carried them back to the table.

'You're running some sort of long con,' she said as he sat down. 'You're setting me up for something.'

'Robyn, you're serving five life sentences and everything you own would fit in a supermarket carrier bag. Why would I be conning you?'

She leaned forward and stared at him. 'My biological father was a Satanist and he left you a huge mansion in Surrey?'

'That's the gist of it, yes.'

'Why didn't he leave me anything? I mean, a big house wouldn't be much use to me in here but I could do with a few quid.'

'He didn't know where you were or who your adoptive parents were,' said Nightingale. 'He tried to find you but couldn't. I only tracked you down because I had access to the national DNA database.'

'And he worshipped the devil?' She sneered and shook her head. 'Maybe that's where the crazy gene came from.' She sipped her coffee and grimaced. 'You know one of the things I miss most about being in here?'

Nightingale raised his plastic cup. 'Decent coffee?'

She grinned. 'Bloody right. It's horrible, isn't it?'

'I've had better,' agreed Nightingale. 'A lot better.'

Robyn put her chin in her hands. 'Why are you really here, Jack? Is there something else you want to tell me?'

Nightingale blew smoke up at the ceiling as he wondered how much he should tell her. She seemed rational enough but he wasn't sure if that was an act or not. He shrugged. 'I thought we should meet. That's all.'

'Are you worried that you might be crazy?'

'Why do you say that?'

'Because I'm in an asylum. And if you're right and we share the same DNA then maybe you're crazy, too. Because this whole Satanism devil-worship thing does suggest that you might have the odd screw loose.'

'I hadn't thought of it that way.'

'Liar,' she said. 'I can see it in your eyes that you're lying. How do I know the whole thing's not a lie? How do I know this isn't some stupid therapy that Keller wants to try on me?'

'Like I said, I don't gain anything by lying to you. Have you got a few million quid tucked away that no one knows about?'

'I wish.'

'So try to trust me on this. We're siblings. Same father, different mothers.'

She rubbed her face. 'Do you know who our mothers are? Our birth mothers?'

'I met mine,' said Nightingale. 'I don't know who yours was.'

'How did you find her?'

'Through Gosling's records. I traced her to a nursing home.'

'Can you do the same and track down my mother? My birth mother?'

'I'll try,' said Nightingale. He sipped his coffee. It was bitter and tasted of chemicals. 'Can I ask you something, Robyn?'

She shrugged. 'I guess,' she said. 'Seeing as how you're my long-lost brother.'

He looked at her with slightly narrowed eyes. 'What they said you did . . . to those kids. Did you do it?'

'I'm in here, aren't I?'

'There are plenty of innocent people in prison. That's why they have appeals.'

'What do you want me to say? That it's all a terrible misunderstanding? That I'm innocent and there's been a miscarriage of justice?'

'Something like that, yeah.'

She grinned, jutting her chin up and wrinkling her nose. 'Sorry to disappoint you,' she said. 'But yeah, I did it. Killed them, all five of them.' She paused. 'Allegedly.'

40

Dr Keller slowly stirred his tea and nodded at the plate of biscuits in front of Nightingale. 'Please, help yourself,' he said.

Nightingale picked up a custard cream and dipped it into his tea. 'She doesn't seem like a killer,' he said.

The doctor continued to stir his tea. 'Sociopaths are adept at concealing their true natures,' he said. 'Every emotion they display is learned behaviour. They have no true emotions but if they are smart they learn to mimic them.'

'They act, is that what you mean? They pretend to be happy or sad or angry?'

Dr Keller nodded. He put his spoon on the saucer so carefully that it made no sound. 'In a nutshell, yes.'

'She seems so normal. Even made a few jokes.'

'Don't get me wrong,' said Dr Keller. 'I'm not suggesting that she's a danger to you or to anyone else in this institution. But she is insane. I can assure you of that.'

'Why do you say that? She looks and sounds normal, so how do you, as a professional, come to the conclusion that she's mad?'

Dr Keller chuckled quietly. 'Mr Nightingale, we would never put it as crassly as that.'

'But that's what you mean, isn't it? You're saying she's as mad as a hatter despite the outward appearance.'

'She killed five children, Mr Nightingale. And she has expressed absolutely no remorse.'

Nightingale put his biscuit into his mouth, chewed and swallowed.

'Did she talk to you about the killings?' asked the doctor.

'Only to admit that she'd done it.'

'No explanation, no asking for understanding or forgiveness?'

Nightingale shook his head. 'Just said that she'd killed them.'

'That, right there, is textbook sociopathic behaviour,' said the doctor. 'A normal person would be full of guilt and remorse. Or would at least offer up some sort of explanation for their actions. But Robyn tells us as little as she apparently told you. Yes, she did it, she killed those five children, but she won't say one word about what drove her to it.'

'And that's par for the course?'

'I'd say that it applies to a third of the inmates here, yes. She has therapy sessions, one on one with medical staff, and group sessions with other inmates present, and, while she's pleasant and sociable, she never opens up.'

'But it's not denial, is it? If it was denial she would be saying that she didn't do it, right?'

'Correct,' said Dr Keller. He sipped his tea, watching Nightingale over the top of his cup.

'Earlier, you said there was no cure.'

'That's right. She's hard-wired as a sociopath and nothing we can do can change that. There's no operation that will alter the way she thinks, and there's no miracle drug that we can use. She is what she is, I'm afraid.'

'So she'll never be released?'

'I would think it highly doubtful,' said the doctor.

Nightingale picked up another custard cream and dunked it into his tea. 'I know this is going to sound stupid, but there's no doubt that she did it, is there?'

Dr Keller's eyes narrowed. 'What do you mean?' he asked.

'Well, the thing is that, because she pleaded guilty, there wasn't a lot of information released to the court. She pleaded guilty to five murders and received five life sentences. But there were no details of what she did or how she did it. Her legal team didn't speak in mitigation, so the media only got the bare facts.'

'And you think there might have been a miscarriage of justice?' Dr Keller shook his head. 'First of all, she pleaded guilty. Second of all, she continues to admit her guilt. And third of all . . .' He leaned forward. 'I've seen the files, Mr Nightingale. I know what she did and, considering the circumstances under which she was arrested, I can assure you there is no doubt as to her guilt.'

'Red-handed?'

'Literally. She was awash in the boy's blood.'

'She used a knife – that was in the papers.'

'She gutted him like a pig,' said the doctor. 'But first she slit his throat so deeply that his head was almost severed.'

'Fingerprints? DNA?'

'The knife was in her hand when the police turned up. And as I said, she was covered in his blood.'

'How did the cops know where she was?' asked Nightingale.

'That I don't know,' said the doctor. 'But they found her with the body. Covered in blood, holding the knife.'

'And the other killings?'

'All children. All gutted. And she confessed to the lot.'

'But never said why she did it?'

Dr Keller shook his head. 'Not a word.'

Nightingale took his pack of Marlboro out of his raincoat pocket, but put it away when he saw the look of disapproval on the doctor's face. 'This is going to sound a little off the wall, but was there any sort of occult slant to the killings?'

Dr Keller frowned. 'I don't follow you.'

Nightingale shrugged. 'Pentagrams, Satanic ritual, witchcraft symbols.'

'You're wondering if the devil made her do it?'

Nightingale shrugged again. 'Killing five kids. It sort of sounds like human sacrifice, doesn't it?'

'It sounds like the actions of a serial killer.'

'But it's unusual for serial killers to kill kids, isn't it? Especially female serial killers. If there are kids involved then there's usually a sexual motive, right?'

Dr Keller nodded hesitantly. 'Well, yes, I suppose so. Child killers are generally middle-aged males and more often than not the killings follow on from sexual activity, either as a way of heightening sensations or through fear of being caught.'

'And in my sister's case there was no evidence of sexual assault?'

'None at all,' agreed Dr Keller.

'So, if there was a reason, maybe in her mind she might have been sacrificing them. And the fact that she used a knife, that suggests a ritual, doesn't it?'

'I doubt that your sister would have had access to a firearm, so that really only leaves knives, strangulation or beating with a blunt object,' said the doctor. 'I'm not sure that the knife is significant.'

'Knives are personal, and planned,' said Nightingale. 'She must have taken the knife in advance, which means she must have had a reason for killing the children. She wasn't acting on impulse or out of anger. She planned it.'

'You seem to know a lot about murder,' said the doctor.

'I was a policeman, in a former life.'

'A detective?'

Nightingale shook his head. 'Firearms officer, but I was also a negotiator. I did a fair amount of psychology as part of my training.'

'Well, what you say is true, except that your sister is a sociopath so the general rules don't always apply. She might simply have killed because she wanted to, and the normal constraints that would prevent you or me from killing weren't there to stop her. She had the impulse to kill and she followed it. You and I and the rest of what we call normal people don't act on our violent impulses. We learn to control them. That mechanism is missing from the psyche of a sociopath. Killing, to them, can be a natural impulse equivalent to eating or defecating.'

'But going back to my original question, there was nothing vaguely Satanic about what she did?'

Dr Keller pursed his lips and shook his head. 'If anything, it was the opposite.'

'What do you mean?'

'Her last victim. Timmy Robertson. She killed him in a church. On an altar, I believe.'

41

'So you didn't tell her?' asked Jenny, deftly picking up a prawn with her chopsticks and dipping it into a small dish of hot sauce. 'You went all that way and you still didn't tell her that Gosling sold her soul and yours? And that on her thirty-third birthday it's so long and good night?'

Nightingale shrugged. He tried to pick up a piece of beef but the oyster sauce made it slippery and it fell onto the white paper tablecloth to add to the dozen or so food stains that proved testimony to his lack of chopstick skills. 'You chose Chinese just because you know I can't handle these things, didn't you?'

They were eating in a restaurant close to Jenny's mews house, one of her favourites. Nightingale had hit heavy traffic on the way back from Nottinghamshire and phoned her on his mobile to tell her that he'd be late and to arrange to see her for dinner.

'I chose Chinese because I offered to buy you dinner and because I like Cantonese food,' said Jenny. She smiled brightly. 'I can get you a fork if you want.'

'I'll struggle on,' said Nightingale.

'Don't think I didn't notice that you changed the subject. Why didn't you tell her that a devil was coming to claim her soul on her thirty-third birthday? That Gosling had traded her soul and that there's nothing she can do about it?'

Nightingale sighed. 'How could I tell her, Jenny? She looked at me like I was crazy when I told her that I was her half-brother. And even after I'd told her about the DNA evidence she was doubtful. If I'd told her that Gosling had sold her soul to a devil before she was born she'd have had me thrown out. Or committed. Can you imagine what the doctors would have done if they'd known? They'd have put me in a jacket with long sleeves before you could say "paranoid schizophrenic".'

An elderly waitress dressed in black Chinese pyjamas brought a steel bowl of bok choi in garlic sauce over to the table. She spoke to Jenny in guttural Chinese and Jenny answered. The old woman cackled and walked away, as bow-legged as an elderly mariner.

'You were talking about me, weren't you?' asked Nightingale, trying unsuccessfully to pick up another piece of beef.

'She asked me if you were my new boyfriend and I said I'd rather crawl across broken glass than go on a date with you.' She popped a piece of chicken into her mouth. 'It sounds better in Cantonese.'

'New boyfriend?' said Nightingale. 'What happened to the last one?'

Jenny jabbed her chopsticks at him. 'My love life is a closed book to you, Jack Nightingale, and it's going to stay that way. And you've changed the subject again.'

'I thought the conversation had just progressed,' said Nightingale. 'Moved on.'

'I know what progressed means,' said Jenny.

'I was using repetition for emphasis,' said Nightingale.

'No, you were using it to distract me,' she laughed. 'And it's not working.'

Nightingale sipped his Tsingtao beer. 'My sister's in an insane asylum,' he said. 'They call it a secure mental facility but it's an asylum. I'm not sure that telling her that her soul has been promised to a demon from Hell is actually going to help her.'

'If it's true, she has the right to know.'

Nightingale's eyes narrowed. 'If it's true? What do you mean?'

'Don't get all defensive, Jack,' she said.

'No, I want to know what you mean.'

'Jack, please . . .'

'You do believe me, don't you?'

'Of course I do.'

'Look at me, Jenny.' He leaned towards her. 'I'm serious, look at me. I'm having enough trouble convincing myself that this is actually happening. If you don't believe me, then I might just have to accept that I'm going crazy.'

She looked into his eyes and smiled. 'I believe you, Jack. Hand on heart, scout's honour, cross my heart and hope to die, by all that's holy, blah blah blah. I believe you.'

He smiled. 'Thank you.'

'It was a slip of the tongue. But it's the fact that I do believe you that makes me so sure she has the right to know. If it was nonsense then it wouldn't matter either way.'

'Suppose I tell her and it pushes her over the edge?' asked Nightingale.

'She killed five kids,' said Jenny. 'That boat has pretty much sailed.'

'Okay, but I tell her and then what? She's locked up; there's nothing she can do. She's going to spend two years sitting in a cell knowing that she's going to Hell.' He sipped his beer again.

'So she's better off spending that time in ignorance?'

'What can I do?' He put down his chopsticks. 'Look, I don't want to tell her what the problem is until I can offer her a solution. It's as simple and as complicated as that. And at the moment I don't have anything approaching a solution.'

'But you've got a plan, right? You've always got a plan.'

'I'm going to talk to the detective who ran her case,' said Nightingale. 'I'll take it from there. He's already said he'll see me tomorrow.'

'That's not much of a plan, is it?'

Nightingale shrugged. 'Honey, right now it's all I've got.'

When they'd finished, the elderly waitress brought over a white plate with two Chinese cookies and the bill. Jenny slid the bill out from under the cookies and pushed the plate towards Nightingale.

'I'll pass,' he said.

'Chicken,' said Jenny, taking one of the cookies and crushing it with her fingers. She fished out a small slip of paper, read it, smiled, and held it out to him. 'He who knows he has enough is rich.'

'Bit sexist,' said Nightingale. 'There's an even-money chance that a woman's going to be reading it.'

'You're such a spoilsport.' She held out the plate for him.

Nightingale shifted uncomfortably in his chair. 'I don't think it's a good idea,' he said. 'Tempting fate.'

'What do you mean?'

'I've been getting enough shitty messages from beyond

the grave recently. I can do without one in my fortune cookie.' He nodded at the plate. 'You open it for me. As part of your secretarial duties.'

'I think it's bad luck to open someone else's fortune,' she said.

'Jenny, bad luck is the only sort of luck I've been having lately,' he said. 'I don't think you opening my cookie is going to make it any worse.'

'Suit yourself,' she said. She cracked open the cookie and looked at the fortune inside. Her eyes widened and she sat back in her chair. 'Oh my God,' she gasped, putting a hand up to her mouth.

'What?' said Nightingale, leaning forward. 'What does it say?'

'It's horrible,' she said, shaking her head. 'It's so, so horrible . . .'

'Jenny, show me,' said Nightingale, holding out his hand.

Jenny's face broke into a grin. 'You're so bloody gullible sometimes,' she said, waving the fortune in his face. 'You need to relax.' She held it with both hands and read it to him. 'Your life will be happy and peaceful.' She laughed. 'I think this one's mine.' She gave it to Nightingale and he shook his head as he read it.

'I'd settle for happy and peaceful,' he said. 'Who writes these things?'

Jenny shrugged. 'They're supposed to make you feel good,' she said. 'If you feel good you'll come back to the restaurant. Positive reinforcement.' She put three twenty-pound notes onto the plate.

'At least let's split it,' said Nightingale, reaching for his wallet.

'I said I'd buy you dinner,' said Jenny. The old waitress

came over and Jenny told her that she should keep the change. As they headed for the door, a young Chinese man with gelled hair and a single diamond earring handed Jenny her coat and helped her on with it.

A small Chinese girl, who barely reached Nightingale's shoulder, gave him his raincoat. He smiled at her but she stared stonily at him, her eyes as dark as polished coal. 'Your sister is going to Hell, Jack Nightingale,' she said, her voice flat and robotic.

'What?' said Nightingale. 'What did you say?'

The girl's face creased into a smile showing grey teeth and receding gums. 'I say hope see you again,' she said.

Jenny put a hand on his arm. 'What's wrong?' she asked.

'Nothing,' said Nightingale. 'But I'm not hopeful about that happy and peaceful forecast.'

42

Bernie Maplethorpe laughed and slapped the bar with the palm of his hand. 'That's funny, Chance, that's a bloody hoot,' he said. 'Where did you hear that?'

'On the internet,' said Chance. He nodded at the beer pumps. 'Do you want another pint?'

'Why don't we toss for it?' said Maplethorpe. 'You can use your magic fifty-pence piece.'

'It's not magic, Bernie,' said Chance.

'You said it made decisions for you.'

'It chooses,' said Chance. 'There's a difference. I give it two choices, and fate decides the outcome.' He clapped Bernie on the back. 'Anyway, I'm done for the night. Do you want a lift home?'

'You're driving?'

'You're starting to sound like my wife,' said Chance. 'What have I had, three pints? That's nothing.'

'It puts you over the limit,' said Bernie.

'Now you're definitely starting to sound like the missus,' laughed Chance. 'I'll take it easy and I'll stick to the back roads.' He slid off the bar stool. 'Now do you want a lift or not?'

'Yeah, go on.'

Bernie headed out of the pub with his new-found

friend. Chance took his keys from his pocket and clicked the fob. The lights of a black Range Rover flashed.

'Bloody hell, mate, that's a flash motor,' said Bernie. 'What did you say you do for a living?'

'I didn't,' said Chance, opening the car door and climbing in. 'I wheel and deal, duck and dive, anything that makes a quick buck.'

'How much would a car like this cost?' asked Bernie, getting in and settling into the buttery-soft leather seat.

'A lot,' said Chance. He grinned across at Bernie. 'But I nicked it.'

'You did not.'

'Won it in a poker game,' said Chance, starting the engine.

Bernie laughed. 'I'm never sure when you're joking and when you're not,' he said.

'You can't take life too seriously, Bernie, that's what I always say.'

Ten minutes later Chance brought the car to a stop outside Bernie's neat three-bedroom semi.

'Do you want to come and meet the wife?' asked Bernie. 'I've beer in the fridge.'

Chance took his fifty-pence coin from his pocket and tossed it. It came up heads. 'Yeah, why not?' he said.

'You're serious? You let the coin decide whether or not to come in for a beer?'

Chance nodded. 'You should try it, Bernie. It's liberating.' He climbed out of the Range Rover.

The two men walked together up the path to the house. Bernie unlocked the door. 'Honey, it's me,' he called. 'I've brought a friend with me.'

A young woman with permed hair and square-framed glasses appeared from the sitting room. She was over-weight and wearing a denim dress that was at least two sizes too small for her. She had a face that was almost square, with several double chins, and flabby forearms that wobbled as she walked down the hallway.

'This is Maggie, my better half,' said Bernie, hugging her. 'Maggie, this is Chance.'

'Have you been getting my husband drunk?' asked Maggie in a strident Belfast accent.

Chance flashed her a disarming smile. 'I don't think he needed any help,' he said. His smile widened. 'He's not drunk, Maggie. Two beers, that's all we had.'

'But now we're home and dry I'll crack open a couple of cans,' said Bernie, heading for the kitchen. 'Take a seat, Chance.'

'Bernie, your dinner's in the oven,' whined his wife. She sighed theatrically. 'He always does this to me. Says he'll be home and then stays in the pub.'

'It was my fault, Maggie,' said Chance. 'I'm sorry. I'll just head off.'

'Don't you dare,' said Bernie, returning with two cans of Harp lager. He tossed one to Chance. 'You've got time for a beer. You can tell Maggie the joke about the two Arabs and the camel.' He put his arm around Chance's shoulders and ushered him into the sitting room.

There were two grubby sofas either side of a cheap wooden coffee table piled high with celebrity magazines and mail-order catalogues. Bernie pushed Chance down onto one sofa and dropped onto the other.

Maggie pushed her husband to the side and sat down

next to him. 'What sort of name is Chance, anyway?' she said, squinting at him through her glasses.

Chance smiled amiably. 'It's more of a nickname.' He put his can of lager onto the coffee table, took out his fifty-pence coin, kissed it softly, then tossed it into the air. He caught it with his right hand and slapped it down onto the back of his left, then took his right hand away and smiled again.

'What's he doing?' Maggie asked her husband.

'He uses the coin to make decisions,' explained Bernie.

'He what?' Maggie frowned. 'What sort of decisions?'

Chance was already getting to his feet. He had the coin in his left hand and he reached into his jacket with his right.

'Are you going, mate?' asked Bernie. He grinned at his wife. 'The coin probably told him it was bedtime.'

Chance's right hand appeared, holding a cut-throat razor. He flicked it open and then smoothly slid it across Bernie's throat. For a second there was just a thin red line across the skin and then blood spurted right and left as his mouth dropped open in surprise. The can of lager fell from his hands and rolled across the carpet. His hands went slowly up to his neck, bathed in glistening blood, but they barely reached his chest before he slumped back on the sofa.

Maggie stared at her dying husband, her eyes wide open. Her whole body was juddering as if she was in the grip of an electric shock.

Chance smiled at her. 'Do you feel lucky, Maggie?' he asked.

She frowned in confusion. Her mouth moved but no words came out. A deep groan came from somewhere deep in Bernie's chest and then he went still. Blood continued to pour from the gaping wound in his neck and it pooled in his lap.

Chance winked and tossed the coin high in the air.

Later, as he stood in the shower washing off the blood of Bernie Maplethorpe and his tiresome wife, Chance felt the water go suddenly scalding hot. He yelped and jumped out of the shower and then yelped again when he saw the girl and her dog standing in the doorway. He bowed his head and covered his private parts with his hands. 'Mistress Proserpine,' he said.

'I can see your coin is still coming up heads,' said Proserpine. 'You made a right mess downstairs.'

'The coin guides me, Mistress Proserpine,' he said. 'I am always grateful for your gift.'

'I need you to do something for me, Chance.'

'Anything, Mistress Proserpine,' he said, going down on one knee. 'My life is yours.'

'And your soul,' she said. 'Let's not forget your soul.'

43

Alistair Sutton was an old-school detective, a big man in a worn suit, with bleary eyes and the pained expression that came from having been lied to more times than he'd ever be able to recall. He smiled without warmth as he shook Nightingale's hand and asked for a vodka and tonic before Nightingale had even offered him a drink. The chief inspector had agreed to meet Nightingale in the Cape of Good Hope pub, next to the Albany Street police station, close to Regent's Park. It was a modern brick-built public house, surrounded by council flats and close to the Royal College of Physicians. It was, thought Nightingale, the perfect community for twenty-first-century Britain. The unemployed and workshy could get drunk, have a punch-up, get medical treatment and be taken to the cells without ever leaving the street.

Sutton had kept him waiting for more than an hour. 'Murder case,' he said by way of apology. 'Five Asians hacked a black teenager to death in an alley.'

'Racial?' asked Nightingale, waving a ten-pound note at a barmaid who was busy texting on her iPhone.

'Drugs,' said the detective. 'Turf war. We'll get them, we always do; but for every one we put away there're half a dozen waiting to take their place.' He scowled. 'The way of the world. This country's going to Hell in a hand-basket.'

Nightingale managed to attract the barmaid's eye and ordered the drinks. 'Do you want to sit?' he asked the detective.

'With my feet, damned right I do,' said Sutton. He ambled over to a bench seat in the corner by a fruit machine and stretched out his legs.

Nightingale paid for the drinks and carried them over to the table. He sat down opposite Sutton. 'We never met, did we?' asked Nightingale. 'In the Job?'

'No, but I heard of you, obviously,' said Sutton. 'Truth be told, that's the only reason I agreed to see you. I'm not one for sharing intel with private eyes. These days they take away your pension any chance they can. But what you did to that paedo – you did what a lot of us wish we could do.'

Nightingale sipped his beer. 'Yeah, well, it cost me my job,' he said.

'The Job's not what it was,' said Sutton. 'Now it's all about ticking the right boxes and meeting targets. It's bugger all to do with putting away villains. Not that there are many real villains around any more. Most of the crime is done by drug-fuelled sociopaths.' He shrugged. 'You've caught me on a bad day,' he said.

Nightingale raised his glass in salute. 'How many years have you put in?'

'Twenty-seven,' said Sutton. 'I can go with a full pension in three and I probably will. I've already put out a few feelers and I can probably go into the British Transport Police at the same rank, get my pension and a bloody good salary on top.'

'I thought you were fed up with the Job?'

'I am, but I do that for five years, maybe ten, and I'll be set for life. Two pensions, a big lump sum and me and the missus will be off to New Zealand.'

'Have you got family there?'

Sutton shook his head. 'No,' he said, 'but it's the furthest place from this shit hole that we can find.' He drained his glass, put it down on the table and looked at Nightingale expectantly.

'Another?' asked Nightingale.

'You read my mind. Make it a double this time. I don't plan on going back to the factory.'

Nightingale went to the bar and fetched the detective a double vodka and tonic. When he got back to the table he sat down next to Sutton. 'So, Robyn Reynolds. I went to see her yesterday.'

'Yeah, you said when you phoned. What's your interest?'

'She's my sister.'

Sutton's jaw dropped. 'Bullshit,' he said. 'She was an only child.'

'She was adopted. At birth.'

Sutton scratched his chin. 'No. We went right through the family history. John and Rachael Reynolds were her parents, but they pretty much disowned her when they discovered what she'd done.' He frowned. 'You went to see her?'

Nightingale nodded. 'In Rampton.'

'They let you in? Why would they do that?'

'I had the right DNA,' said Nightingale. 'I am her brother. Half-brother, anyway.'

Sutton squinted at Nightingale as he sipped his drink. 'How's that possible?' he said as he put down his glass.

'We have the same father. Different mothers but the same father. And we were both adopted at birth. I went to Bill and Irene Nightingale; two years later she went to her family.'

'If you were adopted at birth the records would have been sealed,' said the detective. 'How did you track her down?'

'Her DNA was taken when she was arrested, and it came up when I had them run my father's DNA through the national database looking for a parental match.'

'Clever,' said Sutton. 'But Reynolds is thirty-one and you're . . .?'

'Thirty-three,' said Nightingale. 'Turned thirty-three two weeks ago.'

'So why wait until now to track down your long-lost sister?'

Nightingale shrugged. 'I'm not sure. I guess I just wanted to know if I had any family. My adoptive parents died a few years back, and my aunt and uncle passed away recently.'

'You must have been a bit put out to discover she was a serial killer,' said Sutton. He swirled the ice cubes around his drink with his finger. 'Right bloody shock that must have been.'

'The month I've been having, it was par for the course. I have to say, though, that she didn't seem that disturbed.'

'Hopefully they keep her doped up,' said the detective. 'She was an evil bitch.' He put up his hand. 'I know she's your sister and all but she killed five kids. Butchered them.' He shuddered. 'I try not to think about what she did, you know?'

Nightingale nodded. 'I saw what was in the news-papers but there wasn't much detail released in court.'

'Yeah, the CPS took the view that because she was pleading guilty there was no point in being too graphic. They reckoned the parents had been through enough. Very few people actually know what that bitch did.'

'She used a knife, right?'

'And her hands. She ripped them apart.'

'Did she ever say why she did it?'

Sutton shook his head. 'She said not one word about the killings,' he said. 'She'd chat about the TV, the weather, the news, politics, about anything under the sun. But as soon as we went anywhere near the kids and what she did to them, she clammed up.'

'But there was no doubt, right? No doubt that she did it?'

Sutton narrowed his eyes. 'Is that what this is about? You're planning some sort of appeal? Trying to get her out of there? Because I'll tell you now, that's not going to happen. She's as guilty as sin.'

Nightingale put up his hands. 'That's the last thing on my mind,' he said. 'Up until three weeks ago, I didn't even know that I had a sister. But I spent some time with her and she seemed . . .' He struggled to find the right words.

'Coherent?' suggested the detective. 'Plausible? Well-balanced?'

'She's acting?'

'She's a sociopath,' said Sutton. 'A stone-cold killer.' He leaned forward. 'You want to know what she did? She gutted them. She cut their throats and then she gutted them from neck to groin. And then she pulled out the organs and rearranged them around the body. Real Jack the Ripper stuff. Guts around the feet, folded out the lungs like wings, smeared blood everywhere. That's how they found her, over Timmy's body. She abducted him from school, took him to St Mary's church in Clapham, and butchered him.'

'Inside the church?'

Sutton frowned. 'Why the hell does that matter?'

'It doesn't. I'm just trying to get a feel for what happened.'

'She butchered a nine-year-old boy. End of story. Case closed.'

'I'm not trying to undo the work that you did,' said Nightingale. 'And I'm not trying to screw up your case.'

'It's unscrewupable,' said Sutton.

'Exactly,' said Nightingale. 'I just wanted a chat, just to put it into perspective. She's all the family I've got left.'

'What was she like with you?'

'Like you said, plausible and coherent. Look, the details of what she did, the details that weren't in the papers . . .'

'The chief super wanted to hold them back because he was worried about copycats.'

'So the MO was the same in all five cases?'

Sutton nodded. 'The bodies were mutilated in the same way. According to the pathologist, the same knife was probably used in all five killings and the wounds matched the knife they caught her with. All the kids were killed in churches, but we held that back.'

'All the experts who spoke to her reckoned she was insane?'

Sutton laughed sarcastically. 'Her sanity was never

an issue. There are some crimes that are so horrific . . .'
He shook his head. 'She butchered kids, Jack. There's no
crime worse than that. And anyone who does it is crazy.
There was nothing she could say that would ever excuse
or explain what she did.'

'But she didn't even try?'

Sutton shrugged. 'What possible reason could she give
for murdering five children?'

'None,' said Nightingale.

'Exactly,' said Sutton. He drained his glass and slammed
it down on the table. 'Make it another double,' he said.

44

Jenny walked into Nightingale's office carrying a mug of coffee. He had taken the top drawer from his desk and emptied the contents over the floor. He was down on his knees rooting through the papers, notebooks and cigarette lighters and muttering to himself.

'What are you looking for?' she asked, putting the mug down next to his computer terminal.

Nightingale sat back on his heels. 'Remember the money that I got from Joshua Wainwright last time?'

'Two million euros? I'm not likely to forget that.'

'Yeah, well, Wainwright gave me a copy of the receipt with his phone number on it. Now I can't find the bloody thing.'

'I filed it,' she said. 'With the rest of the company receipts.'

'Are you serious?' he said. He could see from the look on her face that she was. 'Your efficiency never ceases to amaze me,' he said. He began to refill the desk drawer.

Jenny went back to her office and retrieved the receipt from the filing cabinet by her desk. She photocopied it, returned the original to its file and gave the copy to Nightingale. 'Are you going to see him again?'

'Yeah, thought I'd show him the list of what we've found so far and have a chat. Kill two birds.' He nodded at a printout on his desk. 'There're a couple of hundred books there and with any luck he'll want to buy a few.' He sipped his coffee. 'We could do with some cash, right? What with me still having to pay the mortgage on Gosling Manor and all.'

'We're owed more than two thousand pounds from clients but that's about it,' she said. 'We've lost a lot of work with you concentrating on your sister.'

'It's got to be done, Jenny,' said Nightingale, leaning back in his chair. 'If I don't help her, who will?'

'Was the cop any use last night?'

'Yeah, he was okay. He said he'd try to get an address for her parents.'

'And then what?'

'I'll pay them a visit.'

Jenny perched on the edge of Nightingale's desk. 'Jack, are you sure that's a good idea?'

'They might know something,' said Nightingale.

'What do you think they might know?'

'Maybe they met Gosling. Maybe he told them what he'd done.'

Jenny looked pained.

'I'll wear my kid gloves. Softly softly.' He put down his coffee mug. 'I've got to follow up any lead I can. No one else gives a toss about her, Jenny. They've put her in an asylum and thrown away the key.'

'Because she killed kids, Jack.' She shuddered. 'I can't think of anything worse, can you? Killing kids?'

Nightingale sighed. 'I can't argue with you,' he said.

'Because you know I'm right.'

Nightingale threw up his hands. 'What do you think I should do? Walk away?'

'Would that be so bad?'

'She's my sister.'

'She's your half-sister, a woman that you've met once in your life, who decided of her own volition to murder innocents. And you want to do what? Save her soul? Jack, if there's any justice in the world she'll burn in Hell for what she's done.' She stood up, her eyes blazing. 'Her soul is damned anyway; you're just whistling in the wind.'

Nightingale reached for his cigarettes.

'You know they're a crutch,' she said. 'Whenever you're faced with something that makes you feel uncomfortable, you smoke.'

Nightingale tapped out a cigarette, slid it between his lips and lit it. 'I smoke because I like to smoke,' he said. 'Anyway, this isn't about me smoking. It's about me wanting to help my sister.' He threw up his hands. 'I know that you're talking a lot of sense, I know that there's probably nothing I can do to help her, but I have to try.'

'Why, Jack?'

Nightingale groaned. 'I don't know what you want me to say. She's my sister. That's the only answer I can give you.'

'She's killed children,' said Jenny flatly.

'And she's behind bars for that. Okay, it's a hospital and not a prison, but she's still locked up. But what's going to happen to her soul, that's different. Gosling put her in that position, he did a deal for her soul, and now she's all on her own. She has no idea what she's up against. if I don't help her then who will? She's my sister, Jenny. The only family I've got. And I'm all she's got.'

'You keep saying that, but she's not really your sister, in the same way that Gosling wasn't really your father.'

'We share the same DNA. That means we're related.'

'But up until three weeks ago you hadn't heard of either of them,' said Jenny. 'Family isn't about DNA, Jack. It's about growing up together; it's about connections, a shared history. You keep telling me that Bill and Irene Nightingale were your real parents, even though you know your DNA came from Gosling and your birth mother. Rebecca Keeley.'

'Gosling paid Keeley twenty thousand pounds to have me and she gave me up the day that I was born, so I don't think that qualifies her for maternal privileges. And the fact that Gosling sold my soul to a devil negates any dead daddy feelings I might ever have had.'

'Exactly,' said Jenny. 'They're not family.'

'But my sister's different. None of this is her fault. Gosling did to her exactly what he did to me. She can't help herself but maybe I can.'

'How? How do you expect to help a killer locked up in a secure mental hospital?'

Nightingale flicked ash into the ashtray at his side. 'I didn't say I know what to do, just that I have to do something.' He groaned. 'Jenny, you wouldn't understand, you're an only child.'

Jenny's jaw dropped. 'What?'

'You don't have any siblings, so you wouldn't understand.'

'Jack, I've got a brother. Five years older than me.'

Nightingale grimaced. 'Sorry,' he said. 'I didn't know.'

'The reason you don't know is because you've never asked,' she said.

'I'm sorry. Really.'

Jenny folded her arms. 'Here's a question for you. How many Jack Nightingales does it take to screw in a light bulb?'

Nightingale looked out of the window and didn't reply.

'Just the one,' continued Jenny. 'He holds up the bloody bulb and waits for the world to revolve around him.'

Nightingale held up his hands. 'You're right. I can be a bit self-centred at times.'

'Self-obsessed,' she said. 'Which is another way of saying that you don't care about anyone other than yourself. That's why I don't understand this sudden urge to save a woman that you barely know.'

He shrugged. 'I don't understand it myself, Jenny. I just know that I have to try. She's all I have.' He grinned at her. 'Present company excepted.'

45

Joshua Wainwright said that he was passing through the UK on Sunday afternoon on his way to Switzerland. Nightingale arrived at Biggin Hill airport in Kent just after three-thirty and already the sky was darkening. He showed his driving licence to a bored security guard, who checked his name against a list on a clipboard. The guard pointed towards a car park next to a large glass-sided building. 'You can park over there,' he said. 'Go through into reception and they'll tell you where the jet is.' The guard raised the barrier so that Nightingale could drive his MGB through.

Inside the general aviation terminal an equally bored receptionist pointed towards Wainwright's Gulfstream jet, parked in front of a hangar. 'Mr Wainwright's plane will be leaving within the hour,' she said.

'I know, it's all a bit rushed,' said Nightingale. 'He's a regular visitor, right?'

'At least once a month,' she said. 'Usually at the weekend.'

'Beats flying economy, doesn't it?'

'You've got that right,' said the receptionist.

'How much would Wainwright's plane cost, do you think?'

The receptionist wrinkled her nose. 'It's a Gulfstream

G550,' she said. 'Anywhere between forty-five and seventy million dollars.'

Nightingale whistled. 'It's a different world, isn't it?' he said. 'Think how many years you'd have to work to earn that much money.'

'Years? Lifetimes, more like. It's a funny old world, innit? Most of us are working all the hours God sends to make ends meet but there are people flying around in private planes and living the life of Riley.'

'Who was Riley, anyway?'

The woman shrugged. 'Probably a banker,' she said. 'Those bastards, they run the economy into the ground and then us taxpayers pay to bail them out.' She jerked a thumb at Wainwright's jet. 'He's not a banker, is he?'

Nightingale shook his head. 'Nah, I don't think so.' He smiled at her and went outside. The lights were on in the cockpit of the Gulfstream and Nightingale saw two pilots deep in conversation. There was a set of steps leading up to the open hatch and Nightingale climbed them slowly. As he got to the top, a blonde stewardess with waist-length shampoo-commercial hair appeared. She was wearing a stylish grey suit and blood-red high-heeled shoes.

'Mr Nightingale?' she said.

'That's me,' said Nightingale.

She showed him into the cabin. Joshua Wainwright took a foot-long Cuban cigar from his mouth and grinned when he saw Nightingale.

'Jack, how the hell are you?' he asked in his mid-Western drawl. He had a New York Yankees baseball cap on his head and a thick gold chain around his neck from which dangled a fist-sized letter J that looked as if it was solid

gold. Wainwright swung his feet off a white leather foot-
stool, stood up and shook hands with Nightingale. He
was a couple of inches shorter than Nightingale with skin
as black as strong coffee and the muscular upper arms
of a man who either lifted a lot of weights or injected
steroids. From the strength of Wainwright's grip,
Nightingale figured it was the former.

'All good,' said Nightingale.

Behind Wainwright was another model-pretty flight
attendant in a grey suit, this one a brunette with razor-
sharp cheekbones and piercing blue eyes. She smiled at
Nightingale as if he was judging a beauty pageant and
she was a front-runner.

'Drink, Jack?' asked Wainwright.

'I'm driving,' said Nightingale.

Wainwright waved him to one of the leather seats. He
sat down and flicked cigar ash into a massive crystal
ashtray. His face was smooth and unlined and Nightingale
would have been hard pushed to put his age at more than
twenty-five. 'Just the one?'

Nightingale grinned. 'A Corona would be good,' he
said. 'If you don't mind me drinking a Mexican beer?'

'Hey, what they did at the Alamo is old news,' said
Wainwright. 'You can't spend your life looking back. It's
like the whole slavery thing. You've got to move on.'

'You don't look like someone who's been held back on
any front,' said Nightingale.

'That's the truth,' agreed Wainwright. He sucked on
his cigar and then blew smoke at the ceiling. 'I was glad
to get your call, Jack. The last time we met I was a bit
worried.'

'Because?'

'Because you were talking about Gosling selling your soul.'

Nightingale shrugged. 'All's well that ends well,' he said. 'Anyway, I'm still here.'

'Glad to hear it,' said the American.

Nightingale took a computer printout from his jacket pocket and gave it to the American. 'My secretary's been through about five hundred of the books in my late father's library,' he said. 'We haven't bothered with anything that looked like it was mass-produced – I figured if there'd been substantial print runs you'd already have them. This list is the old stuff, leather-bound, antique. Some of them are hundreds of years old.'

The blonde stewardess handed Nightingale a bottle of Corona with a sliver of lime in the neck. He smiled his thanks and pushed the lime down into the bottle.

Wainwright sucked on his cigar as he studied the list. He raised his eyebrows. 'This one, De Lamiis. It's a first edition it says here.'

'Then that'll be right,' said Nightingale. 'My assistant is thorough.'

'It says published in 1489, but there were two editions that year, both marked as firsts. It's the woodcuts that I'm interested in.' Wainwright looked up from the printout. 'You need to check if there are small upturned crosses in the bottom corners, left or right. If the crosses are there you can name your own price.'

'If they're not?'

'Then it's just a book,' said the American. He jabbed his cigar at Nightingale. 'The woodcuts of the first edition are a little bit special. There are seals in there that have never been published before or since.'

'Seals as in stamps?'

'Satanic seals,' said Wainwright, nodding. 'Secret insignia. There were only a hundred copies published with the special woodcuts but then the author came under pressure from the Vatican to remove them. Which he did.'

'I'll check as soon as I get back.'

'I'm serious, Jack. If you've got the right edition, I'll give you this plane. And the girls.'

The two stewardesses beamed at Nightingale as if they were happy to be included in the deal.

Wainwright went back to scrutinising the list while Nightingale sipped his beer.

'Have you seen the copy of *Daemonologie*?' said Wainwright, tapping the list. 'Do you know what state it's in?'

Nightingale shook his head. 'I haven't seen that one. My secretary did most of the books.'

'If it's pristine then I'll buy it,' he said. 'The copy I have is pretty shabby. You know King James the Sixth of Scotland wrote it, right?'

'I didn't know that.'

'Yeah, at the end of the sixteenth century. Not much of real use in it, but it's worth owning. I'll pay top dollar.'

'I'm sure you will,' said Nightingale.

Wainwright picked up a Mont Blanc pen from a side table and put ticks next to a dozen or so of the titles. 'You've got two books here by Aleister Crowley,' he said. '*Magick Book 4* and *Liber Al Vel Legis, The Book of the Law*. I'll have them both. But what I really want is a diary of his. He's rumoured to have written one during the last five years of his life and it's believed that one of his followers published a very limited edition after he died.

A dozen copies at most were printed and distributed to his closest friends and members of his coven. The presses used to print the book were destroyed and the typesetter is supposed to have killed himself. No one knows where the twelve copies are or who has them.'

'I'll have a look in the basement,' said Nightingale. 'Any idea what it's called?'

'It might not even have a title,' said Wainwright. 'It would have been published in 1948, that's all I can tell you. But I have to warn you: if you do come across a copy, you mustn't sell it.'

Nightingale laughed. 'To anyone other than you, you mean?'

'To anyone,' said Wainwright. 'The rumour is that if a copy was ever sold, the buyer and the seller would both die.'

'It's cursed, you mean?'

'It's not really a curse. The book itself is fine, and ownership is quite safe. But if a copy is sold for money . . .' He shrugged.

'You believe that?'

'I know that Aleister Crowley was one of the most powerful Satanists who ever lived,' said Wainwright. 'And his closest followers were only one step behind him.'

'And a book can be cursed?'

'Anything can be cursed,' said Wainwright. 'I'm serious about this, Jack. If you do find a copy don't try to sell it. Come to me and we'll work out a deal.'

'A deal?' Nightingale grinned. 'You're not after my soul, are you?'

'A deal for the diary – one that doesn't involve a financial transaction,' said the American. He handed the list back to Nightingale and put down the pen. 'Let me know when I can see those and I'll come along with cash. And I need you to keep an eye out for another book. It's called *The Lemegeton*. Or *The Lesser Key of Solomon*. First published in the seventeenth century. But I need to know about the binding. The binding is as important as the content.'

Nightingale nodded and put the list away. 'Can I ask you a question?' he asked.

Wainwright picked up a crystal tumbler filled with whiskey and ice. 'Can't promise I'll answer, but go ahead.'

'You're rich, right?'

'Not as rich as Bill Gates or Warren Buffet, or that Mexican who heads the rich list, but I do okay for a black guy.'

'But you weren't born rich, were you? You don't come from money.'

'Made every cent myself.' He raised his glass to Nightingale. 'Started from nothing. Less than nothing. Father ran off before I was born, mother did laundry to try to make ends meet and failed miserably. Had no money to pay for any sort of education. Had to do what I had to do to survive.'

Nightingale nodded and tapped the neck of his bottle against his temple. 'That's one hell of a jump. From there to here.'

'And I'm guessing you want to know how much is down to my specialist knowledge of the occult?'

'You got me,' said Nightingale. He took a long drink from his bottle, his eyes never leaving Wainwright's face. 'Is everything you've achieved the result of a deal you did with . . .' He grinned and shook his head. 'I feel stupid even asking,' he said. 'We're sitting in a Gulfstream jet and I'm talking about something that would have had us burned at the stake in the Middle Ages.'

'Actually, if you'd gone around telling people that you could sit in a metal bird and fly from here to America in six hours they'd probably have burned you as a witch anyway,' said Wainwright. 'Much of the technology we take for granted in the twenty-first century would have had you put to death or committed to an asylum back then.'

'But what we're talking about is the exact opposite, isn't it?' said Nightingale. 'You're saying that you can do a deal with a devil and get rich. And if you went around saying that, you'd be treated as an idiot or fitted for a straitjacket.'

'I'm not saying anything of the sort,' laughed Wainwright. 'You're the one who's doing all the talking at the moment.'

'But you're not contradicting me, are you?'

Wainwright chuckled. 'There's the cop in you coming out,' he said.

'I'm sorry,' said Nightingale, settling back in his seat. 'Old habits die hard.'

'Nah, I see where you're coming from,' said the American. 'This is all new territory for you and you want as much information as you can get. But there's a limit to what I can tell you. There's an element of non-disclosure involved, you have to understand that. The true believers don't shout it from the rooftops because they've a vested interest in keeping the knowledge to themselves. And the principals, well, they've always preferred to work in the shadows.'

'The greatest trick the devil ever pulled was to convince the world that he doesn't exist,' said Nightingale.

'That's the truth,' agreed Wainwright.

'Because if there's a devil, then there's a God. You can't have one without the other. So if the world believed in the devil then it would also have to believe in God. And given the choice, most people would side with God.'

Wainwright laughed out loud. 'You believe that? You believe that people are inherently good? Look around you, Jack. Look how people treat each other. Whether they're Christians or Muslims or non-believers, they rape and kill and lie and steal. Do you think they would behave any differently if they truly believed there was a God?'

'I'm having trouble with the devil thing,' sighed Nightingale.

'You and the whole Catholic church,' said Wainwright.

'I mean, understanding what it means. You've summoned devils, right?'

'That's not the sort of thing you ask,' said the American. 'You've heard of the sanctity of the confessional, haven't you?'

'Sure.'

'Well, this is sort of the opposite.'

'But you have, right?'

'Jack, please. I've already told you that there's a non-disclosure agreement. Even if I wanted to tell you, I couldn't. Just leave it at that.'

'Okay, what about this: there are devils, lots of devils – three billion, right?'

Wainwright frowned. 'Who told you that?'

'It was in Sebastian Mitchell's diary. "There are sixty-six princes under the devil, each commanding six thousand six hundred and sixty-six legions. And each legion is made up of six thousand six hundred and sixty-six devils.'''

'Too many sixes,' said Wainwright. 'You sure that was in his diary?'

'I got it second-hand,' said Nightingale. 'My secretary was reading it. It was in reverse Latin.'

'Well, someone screwed up,' said Wainwright. He sipped his whiskey. 'There are only six hundred and sixty-six legions. That makes the total number just over a hundred and thirty-three million.'

'That's still a big number,' said Nightingale.

'Hellishly big,' said Wainwright. He grinned and raised his glass.

'So how do you know which one to summon?'

Wainwright shrugged. 'Word gets around,' he said.

'Can you do a deal with any of them?'

'You wouldn't bother with the rank and file,' said the American. 'There's not much they can deliver. And the princes probably wouldn't bother with you. You'd be better off going for the heads of the legions or their number twos.'

'And who's at the top of the tree? Satan?'

'Lucifer, yes,' said Wainwright. 'Directly below him would be Beelzebuth, a prince, and Astaroth, a grand duke. Beelzebuth and Astaroth are pretty much level in the hierarchy but they'd both probably argue otherwise.'

'And you can summon them?'

Wainwright laughed, a harsh bark that echoed around the cabin. 'You really are a lamb to the slaughter aren't you, Jack?'

'I'm just curious.'

'Yeah, well, you know what curiosity did to the cat.'

Wainwright took another sip of his whiskey, then nodded slowly. 'You can summon all three of them, but it would be the equivalent of opening the door to a nuclear reactor. You couldn't cope with the power. It would blow you away.'

'But they do appear sometimes?'

'If they want to appear, they can choose their form. But if you summon them, they come as they are. And you really wouldn't want any of the big three appearing in their true form. And even if you were able to bear being in their presence, they'd be hell to deal with.' He smiled. 'No pun intended.'

'But a strong Satanist, someone who knew what he was doing, he could?'

'Someone who knew what he was doing wouldn't even attempt it. Even the best, even someone like your late father, wouldn't go any higher than the six subordinates of the three rulers, and even then they'd be taking a risk.' He took a long drag on his cigar. 'You don't mess around with these guys, Jack. Any sign of weakness, any hint that you're not completely in control of the situation, and they'll rip out your heart.'

'Six subordinates, you said.'

'Subordinates, or they're sometimes called inferiors. The three main ones would report to Lucifer. There's Satanachia, he's commander-in-chief of the Satanic Army, and Aglaliarept, he's a commander too. Lucifuge Rofocale functions as a politician, a sort of prime minister, but without elections, of course. All power flows down from Lucifer. But Lucifuge Rofocale has dominion over the wealth of the world and negotiates when there is conflict between the rulers.'

Nightingale smiled ruefully. 'That's what I was, in a previous life,' he said.

'A negotiator?'

'Police negotiator. I was the guy called into sieges, hostage situations, suicides, that sort of thing.' He sipped his beer before asking his next question. 'This Lucifuge Rofocale. How would I summon him?'

'Why would you want to?'

'I've got a plan,' he said. 'And he's a crucial part of it.'

Wainwright shook his head. 'He's way above my pay grade,' he said. 'I wouldn't know where to start. You have to know his character, and by that I mean the symbol that represents him. It has to be written on a special parchment and the ceremony is complicated. I doubt that there're a dozen people in the world who would know how to summon him. And even if you did know how, if you tried it you'd be signing your own death warrant.'

'Even if I was inside the pentagram?'

'The pentagram is part of the protection but it's not the be-all and end-all,' said Wainwright. 'You don't have the experience. Or the power. And, frankly, neither do I.' Wainwright sucked on his cigar and studied Nightingale with unblinking brown eyes. 'Look, Jack, I like you. Plus you've got access to books that I'd love to have in my collection. So I'm happy to help you, if I can.' He tapped ash into the ashtray by his elbow. 'Tell me your situation,' he said. 'Think of me as a priest and this jet as the confessional, if that helps.'

'Interesting analogy,' said Nightingale.

'I'm telling you that you can trust me,' said Wainwright.

Nightingale nodded slowly. 'I appreciate that, Joshua,' he said.

'Call me Josh. And I'm serious.'

Nightingale sipped his Corona. 'Okay, here's the thing,' he said. 'Gosling gave me away when I was born, and he did the same thing with my sister. He gave her up for adoption and he sold her soul to a devil. Frimost.'

'So he wanted power over women, then. It's almost a cliché.'

'There's an added wrinkle,' said Nightingale. 'She's a serial killer. She kills kids. Or at least she did kill kids. She's behind bars now.'

Wainwright's cigar froze on the way to his lips. 'You don't do things by half, do you?' he drawled.

'It does get messier by the day,' said Nightingale.

'How old is she, your sister?'

'Thirty-one,' said Nightingale.

'So she's got two years. I'm assuming that Gosling did the same deal as he did with your soul, right?'

'That's right. It all goes tits up on her thirty-third birthday.'

There's nothing you can do to save her, you know that?'

'There are always options,' said Nightingale. 'Room for manoeuvre.'

Wainwright frowned as he sat back in his seat. 'Once a soul is sold and the person bears the mark, there's nothing that can be done. I told you that before.' His raised his glass to his lips but then his eyes slowly widened. 'You found the mark, didn't you? On yourself?'

Nightingale nodded. 'Yep.'

'But you're still here.'

'Like I said, there's always room for manoeuvre.'

'You escaped Proserpine?'

'Not escaped, exactly. But she's off my back. For the time being, anyway.'

Wainwright raised his eyebrows. 'You're full of surprises,' he said.

'I'm on a steep learning curve,' said Nightingale. He leaned forward, his arms resting on his knees as he held his beer bottle with both hands. 'The last time we spoke you said that my father was part of a sect that practised human sacrifice.'

'The Order of Nine Angles, yes.'

'My father said I should talk to them. They were connected to my sister's adoption and he said they might be able to help me.'

Wainwright exhaled through pursed lips. 'They're dangerous people, Jack.'

'I guessed as much,' said Nightingale. 'The human sacrifice was the clue.'

Wainwright chuckled. 'I know you were a cop, and I know you're a smart guy, but these people are at the sharp end of Satanism. The cutting edge. And they don't stay there by talking to strangers.'

'Understood,' said Nightingale. 'And I appreciate the warning. But I need to talk to one of the members.'

Wainwright ran a hand through his hair and crossed his legs. He was wearing cowboy boots made from grey and white snakeskin with silver spurs that jangled when they moved. 'These people won't open up to strangers,' he said. 'Especially strangers who used to be cops.'

Nightingale grinned. 'I'll be careful,' he said.

Wainwright lowered his voice. 'And I wouldn't want anyone to know who pointed you in their direction.'

'Like you said, this is a confessional.'

Wainwright nodded slowly. 'There's a man by the name of Marcus Fairchild. He's a lawyer in the City. He's in the Order, has been for more than twenty years. But be very, very careful, Jack.'

'Have you met him?'

Wainwright shook his head. 'I only know of him by reputation. He's very well connected, both in the real world and beyond.'

'Thanks,' said Nightingale.

'I'm not sure that you should be thanking me,' said the American.

The cockpit door opened and a middle-aged man in a starched white shirt with gold and black epaulettes emerged, holding a plastic bottle of Evian water. 'Excuse me, Mr Wainwright, but we'll have to start rolling if we're to get our slot,' he said.

'No problem, Don,' said Wainwright. He shrugged at Nightingale. 'Unless you want to come skiing, you're going to have to deplane,' he said.

Nightingale stood up and shook the American's hand. 'When are you back in England?'

'If all goes well in Switzerland, probably Christmas Eve. Next Friday.'

'I'll try to get back to you before then about the books,' promised Nightingale.

The Gulfstream's jets kicked into life and the plane vibrated as Nightingale hurried down the stairs to the tarmac.

46

Nightingale drove home to Bayswater, left his MGB in its spot in the local multi-storey car park and walked around the corner to his favourite Indian restaurant in Queensway. The owner, Maneesh, had his takeaway ready for him.

'Chicken tikka masala, aloo gobi, pilau rice and two popadoms,' he said, handing over the carrier bag. 'You are a predictable man, Mr Nightingale.'

'I know what I like, Maneesh,' he said.

'But we have a large menu, and a chef who has won awards. You should be more adventurous.'

'Maybe next time,' promised Nightingale. 'How are your boys?' Maneesh had two sons, one a final-year medical student, the other a bond trader in the City.

'Both working too hard to give me grandchildren,' said Maneesh. 'I've told them if they don't find wives within the year I'll take them to Bangladesh and force them to marry at gunpoint.'

'Bangladeshi girls are damn pretty,' said Nightingale.

'I could introduce you, Mr Nightingale,' said Maneesh. 'You're too good-looking a man to be single.'

Nightingale laughed. 'And you're too much of a

sweet-talker to be taken seriously,' he said. He paid for his takeaway and left, still laughing.

Even though it was almost eight o'clock the streets were still busy. The area of Bayswater where he lived was never quiet, the shops and restaurants never seemed to close and there was a constant buzz of conversation and argument in a plethora of languages. On the three-minute walk from the restaurant to his second-floor flat in Inverness Terrace he heard Arabic, French, Chinese, Serbian and Greek and another three or four that he couldn't identify. He passed a Nigerian in a long white robe, a gaggle of Muslim women swathed from head to foot in black, a Rastafarian with waist-length dreadlocks, two furiously arguing middle-aged Turkish men who looked as if they were close to blows, and half a dozen Japanese tourists who were studying an upside-down map of the city. Bayswater was never boring and Nightingale loved the fact that he could buy cuisine from two dozen different countries without straying far from his flat.

He waited until he'd put his food out on the coffee table and opened a bottle of Corona before phoning Colin Duggan and asking him to run a check on Marcus Fairchild.

'It's eight o'clock at night and it's Sunday – don't you ever stop working?' asked the detective.

'I wanted to strike while the iron was hot.'

'Are you eating?'

'Curry,' said Nightingale.

'You need a wife and kids, Jack. You've been on your own too long.'

'Remind me again how many times you've been married, Colin?' asked Nightingale.

'It's true, a policeman's life is not a happy one,' said Duggan. 'This Fairchild, have you got a date of birth?'

'Just the name. And he's a lawyer in the City.'

'Oh that Marcus Fairchild,' said Duggan.

'You know him?'

'I know of him, sure,' said Duggan. 'Don't you? Human-rights lawyer. He's the guy they used to call when Cherie Blair was busy. Human-rights cases and libel too. Does the odd high-profile criminal case pro bono. Generally on the side of the underdog and a real pain in the arse. Don't think he's ever lost a case.'

'Interesting,' said Nightingale.

'Not much point in doing a CRO check on him,' said Duggan. 'If he was ever in trouble with the law it'd be all over the papers. What's your interest?'

'It's personal,' said Nightingale. 'Can you see if you can get an address, car registration, the basics. And see if there's any intel at all that suggests he might be shady.'

Duggan laughed. 'Shady? Marcus Fairchild? You should Google him, Jack.'

'I will when I get to the office, mate. But I'm serious. Can you sniff around and see if there's anything about him that's not kosher?'

'Do you want to give me a clue?'

'Anything that doesn't seem right,' said Nightingale. 'I don't have anything specific.'

'I'll see what there is,' said Duggan. 'But I'd be surprised if there's anything. It'd be like finding out the Queen had been done for shoplifting.'

Nightingale ended the call and then phoned Jenny, but

her mobile went straight through to voicemail. He left a message asking her to call him and then went back to his curry. He spent the evening watching an episode of *Midsomer Murders* in which a portly John Nettles wandered around a picturesque village asking aged gentlemen where they were on the night of the fifteenth and if they had bludgeoned a gay antiques dealer to death. It bore, he knew, no relation to the real world. Even before the advent of DNA, the vast majority of murders were solved within twenty-four hours. Death at the hands of a stranger was rare. Nine times out of ten victims died at the hands of spouses, relatives or neighbours. And in most cases either the perpetrator was caught in the act or they gave themselves up to the police. In the rare cases where a victim didn't know their assailant, the murderer almost certainly had a criminal record and would be in the system. Only once in a blue moon would detectives go around knocking on doors and looking for clues.

Jenny rang back just as Nettles had gathered the most likely suspects in the church hall. 'What's wrong?' she asked before he could say anything.

'What do you mean?' he asked.

'It's Sunday, Jack. You said you wanted me to call you, so I thought something had happened.'

'I just wanted a chat.'

'A chat?'

'See how you were. How the family were.'

'We're all fine. We've just finished dinner, as it happens.'

'Yeah? Me too.'

'Curry?'

'How did you know?'

'It's Sunday night. Chicken tikka masala?'

'I really am that predictable, aren't I?'

'I'm afraid so. What did you do today?'

'I went to see Wainwright. Flying visit. He gave me a shopping list of books that he wanted.'

'That's good news.'

'I figured I'd have a root through the basement tomorrow morning.'

'Good luck with that,' she said.

'Is there any way I could persuade you to give me a hand?'

'In the basement?'

'Just for a few hours.'

'You are joking, right?'

'No funny business, I promise. We'll leave the lights on. It was the Ouija board that caused the problems last time. And I won't be doing that again.'

'Jack . . .'

'Please, Jenny. I'll pick you up and I'll bring breakfast. Coffee and croissants.'

She sighed. 'Banana choc-chip muffins. Two.'

'Deal,' he said.

'Any falling books or cold winds and I'm out of there like a bat out of hell.'

'You and me both,' said Nightingale.

47

Nightingale arrived outside Jenny's house at eight o'clock the next morning. He parked behind her Audi and rang her doorbell. She opened the door wearing a white Aran sweater and faded blue jeans. 'You're bright and early,' she said.

Nightingale held up a brown paper bag. 'A low-fat latte and two banana choc-chip muffins,' he said.

'I think I let you off lightly,' she said.

'And a croissant.'

She waved for him to go through to the kitchen and followed him down the hallway. 'So Wainwright is up for more books?'

'Definitely.'

He put the bag down on the counter and took out her latte and the Americano he'd bought for himself. She gave him a plate for the muffins and croissant and then sat down at the kitchen table. He sat down opposite her and sipped his coffee.

'What are you doing for Christmas?' asked Jenny.

'When is it?'

'Are you serious? How can you not know when Christmas is? Saturday. This coming Saturday. What plans have you got?'

Nightingale shrugged. 'Same as usual,' he said.

'Stuck in front of the TV with a microwaved dinner and a bottle of Corona?'

'You make it sound more fun than it is.' He raised his cup of coffee to her. 'Don't worry about me – I'm not into Christmas in a big way.'

'Why don't you come to the country and have Christmas with my parents?'

'Christmas is for families, kid,' he said. 'I don't think your parents will want me intruding.'

'You don't know Mummy and Daddy,' she said. 'It's practically open house over the holidays. My brother's away in Shanghai but there're half a dozen people coming already. And Mummy and Daddy keep asking after you. I've been working for you for over a year and they've never met you. They're starting to wonder if you actually exist.'

'I'm starting to wonder that myself,' said Nightingale. 'Okay, I'd love to come. What should I get them?'

'A bottle of wine would be fine. Or, if you really want to impress Daddy, get him a decent bottle of Scotch. I'm going down on Friday, assuming that you're not going to make me work on Christmas Eve. Why not come with me?'

'Okay, it's a date,' he said.

'No, it's not a date,' said Jenny. 'It's me taking pity on a sad man who thinks that chicken tikka masala is suitable fare for Christmas.'

Nightingale ran a finger around the lip of his coffee cup. 'I've never understood why you stay with me. You're way overqualified, I don't pay you enough and I smoke too much.'

'You've got your good points, Jack.'

'Yeah, but if I have they're few and far between. Whatever the reason, I'm glad you're working for me and I'll try not to be so self-absorbed in future.'

She raised her latte in salute. 'You're not so bad,' she said. 'And your heart's in the right place.' She picked up a muffin and popped a piece into her mouth.

Nightingale took a folded sheet of paper from his jacket and put it on the table. 'Wainwright gave me his shopping list,' he said. 'He's marked the ones that he wants and given me a few other titles he wants me to look out for.'

'That'd be great for our cash flow,' she said. 'Assuming there's anything left after you've paid the mortgage. Have you heard from the lawyer about your father's estate?'

Nightingale shook his head. 'I'll give him a call after New Year if he doesn't get in touch soon.' He sipped his coffee again. 'Remember Mitchell's diary?'

She nodded. 'How could I forget it?'

'The number of devils in Hell, remember that? You said there were three billion.'

'I think so, yeah.'

'Well, Wainwright said that it's much less than that. Still millions, but not three billion.'

'So Mitchell got it wrong?'

'It sounds like it. You know, I'd really like another look at that diary.'

'Why?'

'To check if he was wrong on the number of devils. And also to see what else is in there. It explained how to summon Proserpine. There might be other demons mentioned.'

'Yeah, well, last time I had the bloody thing men with guns took it away from me, if you remember.'

'I know. I'm sorry.'

'I think it's best that you let sleeping dogs lie. Mitchell got his diary back. That's the end of it.'

'Mitchell's dead,' said Nightingale. 'I'm guessing it's still in his house in Wivenhoe.'

Jenny rubbed the left side of her head as if she was getting a headache. 'Jack, please tell me you're not thinking what I think you're thinking.'

'What are you thinking?'

'I'm thinking that you're thinking about breaking and entering, and I'm thinking that if you are thinking that then it's a very, very bad idea.'

'Mitchell's not there any more. The house will probably be empty.'

'Empty or not, it'd still be breaking and entering. Forget it, Jack. Bad things happen when you break into houses. And by you I mean you.'

Nightingale's mobile rang. He didn't recognise the number but he took the call while Jenny devoured the rest of the chocolate muffin. It was Alistair Sutton.

'You were asking about her parents,' said the detective, getting straight to the point. 'I've got an address if you want it.'

'You're a star,' said Nightingale, reaching for a pen.

'Just don't tell anyone where you got it from,' said Sutton. 'They pretty much went into hiding when their daughter was arrested. They changed their names after the court case – they're now known as Adrian and Sandra Monkton.' The detective gave Nightingale an address in Slough and Nightingale wrote it down on a sheet of paper.

'Have you got a phone number?'

'They're not listed. We did have a mobile but that's been disconnected.'

'I owe you one,' said Nightingale.

'Put it on the tab,' said Sutton. 'If you're like most of the PIs I know, it won't be the last time you ask me for something.' He ended the call.

'What?' asked Jenny, breaking a piece off the second muffin.

'What do you mean?' asked Nightingale.

'You've got that look.'

'What look?'

'The look that says you're onto something. Or somebody.'

'My sister's adoptive parents. The ones that took her from Gosling. They live in Slough.'

'Somebody has to, I suppose.'

'So do you fancy a trip?'

'To Slough?'

Nightingale nodded.

'No.'

'Come on.'

'You said you wanted to sort out the books in the basement.'

'That can wait. Come on, it'll be fun.'

'Driving to Slough to see the adoptive parents of a serial killer? In what universe would that be considered fun?'

'I'll pay you overtime.'

'You'll pay me to go to Slough?' she asked.

'Sure.'

'Why?'

'Because I don't want to go on my own.' He stood up. 'I'll buy you dinner.'

'In Slough?'

'When we get back to London.'

'Can I choose the restaurant?'

'Within limits,' said Nightingale. 'Do we have a deal?'

Jenny grinned. 'Yes, we do,' she said.

'Great,' said Nightingale. 'We'll take your car.'

48

Jenny brought her Audi to a halt across the road from the bungalow. The curtains were open and there was a Renault saloon parked in the driveway.

'Looks like they're in,' said Nightingale.

'What are you going to say to them?' Jenny asked.

Nightingale shrugged. 'I don't know,' he said. 'I'll probably wing it.' He pulled his pack of Marlboro from his raincoat pocket.

'Not in the car,' she said.

'It's a non-smoking car?'

'Jack . . .'

'I was joking,' said Nightingale. He opened the door and climbed out. He lit a cigarette as Jenny got out of the car and locked it. Nightingale blew smoke up at the sullen grey sky. 'I want to know if they knew Gosling, or if they got my sister through an intermediary. And if there was an intermediary, I need to know who it was.'

'And if there wasn't?'

'Then I want to know if Gosling said anything to them.'

'Like what?'

Nightingale took a long drag on his cigarette, held it deep in his lungs, and then exhaled slowly. 'That's where the winging it comes in. It's like any good interrogation:

you go where it takes you. If you go in with a fixed line of questioning you can miss the point.'

'They're not going to want to talk to you, you know that?'

'They might. I'm her brother, remember?'

'The brother of the woman who murdered five children,' said Jenny. 'Remember?'

'I'm sensing a lot of negativity,' said Nightingale. 'Does this mean that you don't want to come with me?'

'Jack, I wouldn't miss it for the world,' she said. She nodded at the house. 'I'm looking forward to seeing the master at work.'

'Watch and learn,' said Nightingale, flicking what was left of his cigarette into the road. 'Watch and learn.'

Jenny followed Nightingale to the front door and watched as he pressed the doorbell. There was a buzzing sound inside the house.

Nightingale stamped his feet on the doorstep. 'It's bloody cold, isn't it? he said, his breath feathering in the air.

'They're saying it might snow over the next few days.' Nightingale grinned. 'So much for global warming.' He pressed the doorbell again. 'Come on, come on,' he muttered. 'We're not Jehovah's Witnesses.' He pressed the doorbell again and kept his finger on it.

'Jack!' said Jenny, jabbing him in the ribs. 'You can't do that.'

'If they're not in, it doesn't matter; if they are in, they shouldn't be ignoring us.'

'I said we should have called first. At least we'd have known they were in.'

Nightingale took his finger off the doorbell. He pushed the door but it was locked.

'Jack, you can't do that.'

Nightingale grinned. 'Just checking,' he said. He stepped back from the house and sighed through pursed lips. 'Let's have a look around the back.'

'Let's not,' said Jenny.

'Just a look,' said Nightingale. 'What harm can it do?'

49

The rear garden was meticulously laid out with a perfect square of lawn leading onto two rockeries laden with ferns and, beyond them, a vegetable patch and a small creosoted shed with a tarred roof. Nightingale reached for the handle of the kitchen door.

'Jack, this is so wrong,' said Jenny, folding her arms and shivering.

He turned to look at her. 'I'm just checking to see if it's locked,' he said. 'It's a Neighbourhood Watch thing.'

'It's a breaking-and-entering thing,' she said.

'Jenny, I haven't broken anything,' he said. He reached into his raincoat and pulled out a pair of black leather gloves.

'Why do you need gloves?' asked Jenny.

'It's cold.'

'So you won't leave fingerprints. Because you know that what we're doing is wrong.'

'Do you have any?'

She glared at him. 'No, Jack, I left my burgling gloves at home,' she said, frostily.

'We're not burgling. We're visiting,' said Nightingale. He twisted the door handle and pushed it. 'Anyway, the door's open.'

'Jack!'

'It's okay,' said Nightingale. He leaned into the kitchen. 'Mr Monkton!' he called. 'Mrs Monkton? Is anybody there?'

'If there was, they'd have answered the doorbell,' said Jenny. 'Let's go, Jack.'

Nightingale stepped into the kitchen. There were dirty dishes in the sink and two coffee mugs sitting by a chrome kettle. He took off one of his gloves and gingerly touched the kettle with his knuckles. It was warm but not hot. Instant coffee had been spooned into both mugs.

Jenny stood on the threshold. 'Jack, this is wrong on so many levels,' she said. 'You don't know these people. You can't just walk into their house. And . . .'

'And what?'

She gritted her teeth. 'You make me so bloody angry sometimes,' she hissed.

'What's wrong?' he asked, putting his glove back on.

'Damn you, Jack. We rang the bell, they're not here – let's just go.'

'You're scared, aren't you?'

'I'm scared that I'm going to be arrested for burglary.'

'It's only burglary if we steal something,' said Nightingale. 'But that's not what's worrying you, is it?'

'Please, Jack, let's just go.'

'The kettle's warm, the back door was unlocked. I know what you're thinking, Jenny.'

'Then you know why we have to go,' she said.

'If they're dead, we have to know.'

Jenny closed her eyes. 'Why did you have to go and say that?' she whispered.

'Because that's what you're thinking. I went to see my

aunt and uncle and they were dead. I went to Abersoch and the woman there was dead. You think they're dead too.'

She opened her eyes and shivered. 'I don't want to know if they're dead or not. I don't care. I just want to go.'

'If something's happened, I want to know,' said Nightingale quietly.

'We can read about it in the paper,' she said. 'We don't have to go inside.'

'You can wait in the car. You don't have to be here.' He walked across the kitchen to a door that led to the hallway. He opened it. 'Mr Monkton!' he shouted. 'Are you in? Mrs Monkton? Hello? My name's Jack Nightingale and I'm here about your daughter!'

'If they could answer, they would have done by now,' said Jenny.

Nightingale walked down the hall. The front door was at the far end. To the right of the door was a wooden table with a telephone on it. 'Mr Monkton! Hello?'

The carpet was red with streaks in the pile as if it had only just been vacuumed. There were two doors leading off the hall to the right and two to the left. All were closed.

Jenny called to him from the kitchen. 'Jack, are you okay?'

Nightingale didn't reply. He wasn't okay. He knew she was right, that the best thing was to leave the house and never come back. The Monktons wouldn't have left the house with the back door unlocked, and if they were alive they would have answered when he rang the bell. He opened the first door to his right. It was a bedroom with a pine double bed and a matching wardrobe and dressing table. The room looked as if it had never been slept in, and there was nothing personal in it, no trinkets or books or photographs. Nightingale realised it was probably the guest bedroom and that the Monktons didn't have many guests. He closed the door.

The door opposite opened into another bedroom. From where he was standing Nightingale could see that the duvet was rumpled and there was an open book and a pair of reading glasses on one bedside table and a box of tissues and an asthma inhaler on the other.

'Mr Monkton! Hello!' shouted Nightingale, pushing the door wider.

There was a door next to a double-fronted wardrobe facing the bed and Nightingale could hear running water.

Jenny came up behind him and put a hand on his shoulder. 'What's wrong?'

'There's someone in the shower,' he said.

She tried to pull him away from the door. 'We can't stay,' she hissed. 'They'll have a heart attack if they come out of the bathroom and see us standing here.'

'They can't both be in the shower,' said Nightingale.

'You don't know that,' she said. 'But that's not the point. We should wait outside and keep ringing the bell.'

'Stay here,' said Nightingale. 'Let me check the rest of the house.'

'Jack!' whispered Jenny, but he was already heading down the hall.

The door at the end of the hall opened into a large sitting room. In one corner a television set was showing a chat show with the sound muted. On a table next to the sofa was a packet of cigarettes and an ashtray in which there were three lipstick-smeared butts. Nightingale smiled. Mrs Monkton was obviously the smoker in the family. To his left was a fireplace with a modern mantel-piece. There was a framed wedding photograph next to a vase of dried flowers. Nightingale walked over to the fireplace and picked up the picture. The man was tall and looked like a young Sean Connery in a dark blue suit with large lapels; the woman, who barely came up to his shoulders, was plump with a cheeky smile and long blonde hair. He put the picture back. It was the only photograph in the room.

There were shelves lined with books to the right of the fireplace. The top two shelves were filled with books on military history, the lower three contained romances and books of crossword puzzles and Sudoku.

A car alarm burst into life in the road outside and Nightingale walked over to the window but before he could see anything he heard Jenny scream in terror.

50

Nightingale ran down the hall, his heart pounding. Jenny was standing in the bedroom, looking through into the bathroom, her hands either side of her face.

'What is it?' asked Nightingale.

Jenny took a step back and pointed at the bathroom with her right hand. The colour had drained from her face and her eyes were wide and staring.

Nightingale put his arm around her. He could feel her trembling. 'Jenny?'

She opened her mouth but no words came out. Nightingale reached forward with his left hand and gently pushed the bathroom door.

Mrs Monkton was on her knees by the bath. Her head was underwater, her blonde hair floating on the surface, rippling in the waves caused by the two rivers of water pouring from the taps. The water had turned red but Nightingale couldn't see where the blood was coming from. He guided Jenny over to the bed and sat her down. She stared at him with unseeing eyes.

Nightingale went back to the bathroom. The red water was edging up to the top of the bath and he moved to turn off the taps, but froze as he saw the body sitting on the toilet.

It was Mr Monkton, some forty years older than in the wedding photograph on the mantelpiece and a great deal deader. There was a gaping wound in his throat and a curtain of blood that glistened wetly across the green pullover that he was wearing. His right hand dangled at his side and below it on the tiled floor was a carving knife, the blade smeared with blood.

'Jack?' said Jenny from the bedroom.

'It's okay, stay where you are,' he said.

He turned off the taps just as water cascaded over the edge of the bath and pooled on the floor. As he straightened up he looked into the shower cubicle. Across the side of the cubicle, written in bloody capital letters, were eight words:

YOUR SISTER IS GOING TO HELL,
JACK NIGHTINGALE.

He took a step back, slipped on the wet tiles, and fell against the wall. He lost his balance and fell to the floor, where he lay cursing. As he picked himself up he found himself looking at the murdered man's face. The eyes were open and the upper lip was curled back in a snarl.

Nightingale stood up, wiping his gloves on his raincoat. He went back into the bedroom, where Jenny was still sitting on the bed, her hands covering her mouth.

'Easy, honey,' he said. 'It's okay.'

'How is this okay, Jack?' she whispered. 'How is this even close to okay?'

'Let's get out of here,' he said.

'We can't. We have to call the police.'

'And say that I've been at yet another murder-suicide?'

said Nightingale. 'That's one can of worms I don't want opened.' Jenny began to shake and Nightingale sat down and held her tightly. 'You're in shock,' he said.

'Damn right I'm in shock,' she hissed. She frowned. 'What do you mean, murder-suicide?'

Nightingale nodded at the bathroom door. 'The husband's in there. He slit his own throat. I guess he killed his wife and then topped himself.'

'What?'

Nightingale stood up and held out his hand. 'Let's go, Jenny. We can talk about this somewhere else. You were right – we shouldn't be here. Come on.'

'We have to tell someone,' said Jenny.

'Look, remember what happened when the cops got me for the woman in Abersoch? And my aunt and uncle? This is going to be the last straw.'

'Why's this happening, Jack?' asked Jenny.

Nightingale sat down on the bed again. 'I don't know,' he said.

'Your uncle killed your aunt and then killed himself. And now your sister's father has done the same damn thing. That can't be a coincidence.'

'I guess not.' Nightingale wanted a cigarette but he knew it wouldn't be a good idea to smoke in the Monktons' house.

'You don't have to guess,' she said. 'Someone didn't want you to talk to them. Someone or something.'

'We have to go, Jenny.'

Jenny shook her head. 'No, this time we have to face up to what's happened. We should call the police and tell them everything.'

'They won't believe anything we tell them,' said

Nightingale. 'There are just too many bodies piling up. We have to leave and we have to leave now. This is nothing to do with us.'

Jenny glared at him. 'It's everything to do with us,' she said. 'They're dead because you came to see them.'

'You don't know that,' said Nightingale, though even as the words left his mouth he knew she was right. Somehow someone had known he was coming – why else would the message be on the shower cubicle?

'If we stay, the cops are going to think it was me, Jenny.'

'I was with you. The police'll be able to tell when they died and I'll be able to say you were with me when it happened.'

'But that'll take time and they'll keep us both locked up until they know for sure, and even then they'll add it to the long list of things they think I did. We don't need the hassle. Trust me. I used to be a cop, I know how they work. They go for the easy option and that's what I am. The easy bloody option.' He put his face up close to hers. 'Jenny, we have to get away from here. Now. Okay?'

She nodded slowly. There were tears in her eyes. 'Okay,' she said. She stood up and headed for the door but Nightingale stayed where he was. 'Are you coming?' she asked.

'Wait for me in the car, kid,' he said.

'What are you doing?'

'I just want a quick look around,' he said.

'Jack, there are dead bodies in the bathroom.'

'If I don't do it now, I'll never get the chance,' said Nightingale. 'Once the bodies are discovered the cops will be all over the place. Did you touch anything?'

'Why?'

'Fingerprints. I'll have to wipe down anything you touched.'

'Jack . . .'

'Did you touch anything?'

She shook her head and wiped her eyes.

Nightingale pointed at the door. 'I won't be long, I promise,' he said. 'Get in the car but don't start the engine.'

Jenny went out and Nightingale hurried to the kitchen and grabbed a roll of kitchen towel. He wiped clean anything that Jenny might have touched and wiped the bloody letters off the shower cubicle, then went through to the sitting room. He stood in the middle of the room, his hands on his hips as he consciously slowed down his breathing. He wasn't sure what it was he wanted, but knew that somewhere among their belongings there must be something that would give him a clue to what had happened to their adopted daughter.

The chat show was still on the television. Nightingale picked up the remote and turned the set off. He looked at the wedding photograph on the mantelpiece. There were no pictures of their daughter anywhere in the house. He thought back to his own home, when he was a child. There had been at least a dozen photographs of Nightingale around the house, mainly school portraits, and several albums his mother used to bring out to show visitors. Nightingale had always been embarrassed by the albums and the way that his mother had fussed over them, but now he had them in a drawer in his bedroom. Although he rarely looked at them, he was happy they were there because, as the years passed and his memories faded, he knew he would always have the pictures. Robyn's parents had removed all signs that they had a daughter. But

Nightingale was sure that they wouldn't have thrown them away.

He went over to the sideboard and pulled open the top drawer. It was full of receipts, instruction manuals and bank statements. The second drawer, however, contained a large photograph album with a Van Gogh painting of sunflowers on the front. Nightingale took it out and opened it. The first dozen or so pages were filled with family photographs, with Robyn the centre of attention. Robyn as a baby, as a toddler, as a gawky teenager. The last photograph was of Robyn standing next to a white Vauxhall Astra.

Nightingale took the album with him as he left the house. He closed the front door and joined Jenny in the Audi. 'Are you okay to drive?' he asked.

She turned to look at him. 'Doesn't it affect you, seeing that?'

'Of course it does. But there's nothing we can do to help them. They're dead. Nothing we do is going to change that.'

'And you're not going to call the police?'

'Jenny, do you want to spend another day being grilled by Chalmers and his sidekick? Because that's what'll happen if we tell anybody.' He nodded at the road ahead. 'Just drive.'

51

Nightingale was sitting at his desk flicking through the Robyn Reynolds album when he heard the office door open. A few minutes later Jenny walked into his room. She looked tired and she groaned as she sat down on one of the chairs facing his desk. 'I almost didn't come in today,' she said.

'You could have taken the day off.'

'How could I stay at home with all this going on?' she said. 'There was nothing in the papers about the bodies in the house.'

'It'll take time for them to be found.'

'You could make an anonymous phone call.'

'They always trace them, Jenny. Best to let things take their course.'

She sighed. She'd tied her hair back in a ponytail and her eyes were red as if she had been crying. 'I've been thinking about your sister.'

'Me too.'

'No, I mean I've been thinking that you should just drop it. Drop the whole thing. She's a child killer. She's in a secure mental institution. Whether or not Gosling sold her soul to a devil doesn't seem to matter one way or another.'

Nightingale frowned at her. 'How can you say that?'

'Jack, it seems to me that after what she's done, one way or another she's going to Hell. I don't see it makes any difference if she goes because Gosling did a deal with this Frimost or because she's turned into a monster.'

'She's not a monster, Jenny,' whispered Nightingale. 'I've met her and I can tell you that she's not a monster.'

'She's killed children,' said Jenny. 'More than that, she butchered them.'

'Have you thought that maybe she turned out that way because of what Gosling did to her? That maybe it's because he sold her soul that she became what she is?'

'Gosling sold your soul but you didn't turn into a child killer.'

'I hear what you're saying,' said Nightingale.

'But you're still going to try to help her, aren't you?'

Nightingale smiled thinly and nodded. 'She's my flesh and blood.'

'So was Gosling, and look at what he did to you.'

'She's all I've got.'

'Thanks for that.'

Nightingale groaned. 'I didn't mean it like that, kid. I meant she's the only family I've got.' He grinned. 'Any chance of a coffee?'

'You can do penance for your insensitivity by making coffee for me for a change. For the rest of the week.'

'It's only Tuesday.'

'Only three days, then. Milk. One sugar.'

Nightingale walked over to the coffee maker and stubbed out his cigarette. 'You're a hard taskmaster, Jenny McLean,' he said. 'But I've no idea what I'd do without you. How's Bronwyn getting on, by the way?'

'Caernarfon Craig got in touch. But so far it's just chit-chat. He keeps asking for personal details, like my house and car, but I'm keeping it vague. Most of the time we talk about how we'd do it if we decided to end it all. He sends me links to sites where they talk about all the weird and wonderful ways that people use to kill themselves.'

'Has he asked to meet you?'

'Not yet.'

'Be careful.'

'I'm not stupid. Besides, he only knows me as Bronwyn.'

'So what's your plan? You're just going to toy with him online?'

'No, I'm chatting away and hopefully he'll let slip something that identifies him.'

'Sounds like a plan. Just be careful.'

'Look who's talking,' said Jenny. 'If there's anyone who needs to tread carefully, it's you.'

52

Nightingale nodded at the two men in suits standing by the one-armed bandit in the corner of the pub. They had both put their briefcases on the floor and balanced stacks of pound coins on top of the machine. 'What about those two, Eddie?' he asked.

Eddie Morris shook his head. 'Nah, I don't think so.' He took a gulp of lager.

'Go easy on the old amber nectar,' said Nightingale. 'This could take a long time and increasing your alcohol intake won't help your facial-recognition faculties.'

Morris frowned, his glass inches from his mouth. 'What?'

'If you're pissed as a fart you're not going to recognise anyone,' said Nightingale.

They were in a pub a short walk from Elephant and Castle Tube station. It was where Morris had said he was on the evening that a house in Islington had been burgled. The police didn't believe his story and after spending two hours looking in vain for anyone who remembered Morris, Nightingale was starting to think that perhaps they were right. The landlord had said he didn't remember Morris, and so had the three members of staff, two of whom had been behind the bar the night that Morris claimed to have been there. But Morris was insisting that he was innocent and Nightingale was prepared to give him the benefit of the doubt, for a while longer at least.

'I can handle my beer,' said Morris. He nodded at the bottle of Corona that Nightingale was holding. 'You used to be a bit of a drinker, as I remember.'

'Yeah, I've slowed down a bit,' said Nightingale. 'Got caught over the limit; my case is up soon.'

Morris grimaced sympathetically. 'They don't mess about these days,' he said. 'They take away your licence, and worse.' He chuckled. 'That'd be a laugh, wouldn't it, if we were both inside?'

'Bloody hilarious,' scowled Nightingale. 'But I've got a plan. Listen, you're not winding me up here, are you, Eddie?'

'What do you mean?'

'This alibi business. I don't want to find out that you're wasting my time.'

'My time and my money,' said Morris. 'You're not doing this for free, are you?'

'I'm just saying that if you did it, you might be better off simply admitting it.'

'What do you want me to do, cross my heart and hope to die? Three weeks ago, I was in here drinking. And while I was drinking in here that teacher and her husband were burgled in Islington. I can't have been in two places at once, can I? Stands to reason.'

'But the teacher identified you, right?'

'She saw the guy from the back as he was running away. She picked me out of the line-up but I reckon she had help, if you get my drift. I'm sure the cops showed her my picture. I wasn't there, Jack. I swear, on my mother's life.'

'Last I heard, you were an orphan, same as me.'

'It's an expression,' said Morris. 'That Islington burglary wasn't down to me.'

'What about the others? They're charging you with more than a dozen, right? Same MO. Did you do any of them?'

Morris grinned. 'Best you don't go there, Jack,' he said. 'But they're the ones putting all their eggs in one basket. If I can duck the Islington job, the whole case falls. That's what my lawyer says, anyway.'

'I hope you're right,' said Nightingale. He nodded at a grizzled old man in a worn sheepskin jacket who had just come in through the door, holding several copies of the *Big Issue*. He had a long grey beard and a bushy moustache and cheeks that were flecked with broken veins. 'Him?'

Morris made a fist of his right hand. 'Yes!' he hissed. 'Tried to sell me his comic and I told him where to shove it.'

Nightingale waved the old man over to where they were standing at the bar. They could smell the man's body odour before he got within six feet of them and by the time he stood in front of them, grinning toothlessly, they had to fight the urge to retch.

He held out a copy of the magazine. '*Big Issue,*' he said.

Nightingale fished a two-pound coin from his pocket and gave it to the man. 'Quick question for you, mate,' he said, taking a magazine. 'Do you recognise my friend here?'

The old man screwed up his eyes as if he was looking into the sun. 'Him?' He shook his head. 'Nah.'

Nightingale gave him a second coin. 'Have a better look, mate,' he said. 'Three weeks ago. About this time. Standing right here, he was.'

The old man pocketed the coin, stared at Morris, then

shook his head emphatically. 'Nah.' He started to turn away but Nightingale grabbed his arm.

'Are you sure?'

The old man put his face close to Nightingale's. His rancid breath made Nightingale's stomach churn but he kept on smiling. 'If you give me a tenner, I'll say I did,' he growled.

'That's not what I'm after,' said Nightingale. He looked across at Morris. 'You sure?'

'A thousand per cent,' said Morris. He jabbed a finger at the old man's face. 'You tried to sell me a copy and I told you to sod off.'

'You and a hundred others,' said the old man. He coughed and a wave of foul-smelling breath washed over Nightingale and Morris. 'See now, if you'd given me a fiver I might have remembered you.'

The landlord, a balding man in his fifties with a boxer's nose, appeared at the bar. He pointed a warning finger at the old man. 'You, out!' he shouted. 'I've told you before. If you want to sell it, sell it outside.'

The old man cursed and walked away, clutching his magazines to his chest.

'He's not even homeless, that one,' said the landlord. 'He's shacked up with a woman on benefits down the road. Any money he gets he spends on booze.'

'Good for business, then,' said Nightingale.

'He doesn't buy it here,' said the landlord contemptuously. 'Goes straight to the off-licence.' He walked away to serve a group of businessmen.

'This is a bloody nonsense,' said Morris. He took a long pull on his pint and wiped his mouth with the back of his hand.

'Give it time,' said Nightingale.

'The cops have already been in,' said Morris.

'They'd have come in during the daytime and showed your picture to the staff,' said Nightingale. 'They'd have needed to clear overtime for an evening visit and I doubt they think you're important enough for that. People are creatures of habit for the most part. There are mid-week drinkers, weekend drinkers, daytime drinkers and evening drinkers. If someone was in here the Tuesday night you were here, they might well be in tonight. And they're more likely to recognise you in the flesh than from a photograph.'

'Maybe,' said Morris. 'But I saw that old geezer and he didn't remember me.'

'I doubt that he'd remember his own name,' said Nightingale.

'If we don't find someone to confirm I was here, they'll put me away.'

'Don't worry.'

'That's easy for you to say, Jack. You're not the one they'll send down.'

'There're worse things than prison, Eddie,' said Nightingale. He raised his bottle of Corona. 'Relax. This is only Plan A.'

'What's Plan B?'

'Let's wait and see how Plan A works out.'

Two women walked into the pub and went to the far end of the bar. One had shoulder-length blonde hair, and the other a chestnut bob. Both had long coats and were carrying battered leather briefcases. Morris frowned as he looked over at them.

'Recognise them?' asked Nightingale.

'The blonde, I think,' said Morris. He scratched his chin. 'Yeah, I'm pretty sure I asked her if she wanted a drink.'

'Pretty sure? What's with you, Eddie? Are you getting early Alzheimer's?'

'I'd had a few drinks so my memory's hazy,' said Morris. He wagged his finger at the blonde. 'No, I'm sure. She was here.'

'Don't suppose you can remember her name?'

Morris shrugged. 'I don't think we got that far,' he said.

Nightingale put down his drink 'All right, you stay put.'

He walked over to the two women. A barman was giving them two large glasses of wine.

'Hello, ladies,' said Nightingale.

The brunette looked him up and down and smiled. 'Hello, yourself.'

'The name's Jack,' he said. 'I know this is going to sound corny, but do you come here often?'

The blonde raised her eyebrows and the brunette chuckled. 'Does that line ever work?' asked the blonde. She was in her late thirties, with crow's feet starting to spread around her eyes and the beginnings of a double chin, but her green eyes sparkled like a teenager's.

'It's not a line,' said Nightingale. 'I really want to know. Specifically, three weeks ago.'

The blonde looked over Nightingale's shoulder and saw Morris staring at them. Her face fell. 'You're not with him, are you?'

'Why?' asked Nightingale. 'Do you know him?'

She nodded. 'He came on to me. Three weeks ago. As subtle as a freight train.' She looked across at her friend. 'You know what he said? "Get your coat, you've pulled."'

Like a bloody teenager.' She put up her hand. 'If he's with you, I think you'd better just go now.'

'I'm helping him out, that's all,' said Nightingale. 'Three weeks ago today, right? About this time?'

'I didn't exactly write it down in my Filofax, but I'm in here every Tuesday after work. Girls' night out.'

'Ladies, you don't know how happy that makes me,' said Nightingale. 'Do you mind me asking where it is you work?'

'I don't mind because, if I tell you, you'll almost certainly stop bothering me.' She sipped her white wine and watched him with amused eyes. 'I'm with the Crown Prosecution Service,' she said.

Nightingale grinned. 'This gets better and better,' he said. He took out his wallet. 'I'd like to buy you two ladies a drink. Whatever you fancy.'

The blonde winked at her friend. 'Champagne?' she said.

The friend nodded enthusiastically. 'Bollinger?'

'You read my mind.' She looked expectantly at Nightingale.

Nightingale waved his credit card at the barman. 'Bottle of Bollinger,' he said. 'And a receipt.'

When Nightingale left the pub with Morris an hour later, he had the woman's business card in his wallet and the satisfying warm feeling of a job well done.

'You're a star, Jack,' said Morris, slapping him on the back. 'An absolute star. If you need anything, just ask.'

Nightingale put his hand on the man's shoulder and gripped tightly. 'Funny you should say that, Eddie,' he said. 'There is something you can do for me.'

53

Nightingale drove his MGB up to a set of wrought-iron gates set into a ten-foot-high brick wall. It was a few minutes after eight o'clock in the morning and the sun had only just decided to put in an appearance.

'Is this it?' asked Morris. Nightingale nodded. 'I have to say, Jack, that when I said I'd do anything for you I didn't mean breaking and entering. And I didn't expect you to have me up at sparrow's fart.'

'I'm pretty sure the house is empty,' said Nightingale.

'Yeah, well, it's still breaking and entering.'

'You're as bad as my assistant. Eddie, the guy who lived there is dead. And even if he wasn't, he wouldn't have gone running to the cops.'

'Who was he?'

'A rich nutter,' said Nightingale.

'How did he die?'

'Why does that matter?'

'I just want to know what I'm getting into,' said Morris, patting the sports bag on his lap. 'You sure about this?'

'I'm sure the guy's dead. And I'm pretty sure that without him to pay the bills his security team will have moved out.'

Morris stiffened. 'You didn't say anything about a security team.'

'It's not a problem,' said Nightingale. He climbed out of the MGB. 'He was a bit paranoid, that's all. Anyway, he's dead. I just need you to get me into the house.'

Morris got out of the car and stretched. 'Not much room in these MGBs, is there?'

'It's a classic,' said Nightingale, patting the roof.

'It's a bloody matchbox, that's what it is.' He gestured at the driveway. 'You sure there's no one in there?'

Nightingale walked over to the high black-metal gates. He rattled them. They were locked. He went over to the intercom set into the wall and pressed the buzzer. There was no answer so he pressed it again, this time for almost a minute. 'If there was anyone in there, they'd be telling me to go away, wouldn't they?'

'There's CCTV,' said Morris, pointing at a camera covering the approach to the gates.

'There's lots of CCTV,' said Nightingale. 'But that's not a problem if there's no one in there to look at the monitors.'

'You sure his alarm isn't connected to the local cop shop? Or a monitoring centre?'

'Like I said, he was paranoid. He wouldn't want outsiders coming round.' He lit a cigarette and inhaled deeply, then blew smoke. 'Okay, Eddie, I need you to get in there and let me in. Then you can push off and leave me to it.'

'Push off where?' said Morris. 'We're out in the bloody sticks.'

'Then you can wait here and I'll drive you back to civilisation,' he said.

Morris looked at the gates, then along the wall. 'How am I supposed to get over that?'

Nightingale blew a smoke ring that was quickly whipped away by the wind. 'Bloody hell, Eddie, you're the house-breaker,' he said. 'Allegedly.'

'I don't fancy the gates,' said Morris. 'Give me a leg up over the wall. But away from the CCTV. I hate those things.'

54

Nightingale smoked two cigarettes after he had helped Morris over the wall. He was thinking about lighting a third when his mobile phone rang. It was Morris. 'Please don't tell me you've done a runner, Eddie,' said Nightingale.

'Press the buzzer again,' said Morris.

Nightingale went over to the gate and pressed the button.

'Who is it?' said Morris over the intercom.

'Don't screw around, Eddie,' said Nightingale.

There was a buzzing sound from the gates and then a loud click and they opened. Nightingale got back into the MGB and drove along the curving driveway towards a three-storey modernist cube of glass and concrete. He parked in front of the flight of white marble steps that led up to a gleaming white double-height door.

Morris opened the door and bowed to Nightingale. 'Welcome, m'lord,' he said. 'Would m'lord care for tea in the conservatory?'

'Any problems?' asked Nightingale as he got out of the car.

'Easy peasy, lemon squeezy,' said Morris. 'The alarm's

self-contained but they'd left the manufacturer's override on it. Most people do.'

'How did you get in?'

'Kitchen door,' said Morris. 'Did the lock so no one will know we've been here.' He gestured up at a CCTV camera aimed at the front door. 'The cameras are off.'

'Thanks, Eddie. Do you want to push off or wait in the car?'

'I'll hang around the house,' said Morris, stepping back into the hallway.

Nightingale jogged up the steps, his raincoat flapping behind him. 'You're not thinking about taking anything, are you?' he said.

'I just fancy a look,' said Morris. 'It's right out of one of those posh-homes magazines, isn't it?'

'It's one hell of a house,' agreed Nightingale. 'But we're leaving it exactly the way we found it. No helping yourself to a little souvenir.'

He looked around the white-marbled hallway.

Morris pointed at one of two stainless-steel CCTV cameras covering the hall. 'He really had a thing about cameras, didn't he?'

'Like I said, he was paranoid.'

'Yeah, well, just because you're paranoid doesn't mean that they're not out to get you. What was he scared of?'

'Dunno,' lied Nightingale.

'Because there're more of them cameras inside the house than outside. That's just plain weird.'

'The guy who lived here was weird,' agreed Nightingale. 'How did he die?'

'Like I said, it doesn't matter.'

Morris looked up at a glass feature light hanging from

the centre of the ceiling. It looked like a waterfall that had been frozen in mid-flow. 'Nice,' he said. 'Could get a fair few bob for that.'

'Don't even think about it, Eddie,' said Nightingale. He walked across the hallway towards a jet-black door with a glossy white handle. 'He was through this way.' He opened the door and walked into a long room that over-looked the gardens at the back of the house. The walls and ceiling were white and the floor was the same white marble as in the hallway, though in the centre of the room a pentagram had been set into the floor with black stone. Within the pentagram there was a hospital bed and a green leather armchair with an oxygen tank next to it.

'Now that's just weird,' said Morris. 'He was Jewish, was he?'

'Jewish?'

Morris pointed at the pentagram. 'Star of David. That's a Jewish thing. Mate of mine wears one on a chain around his neck.'

'It's not a Star of David,' said Nightingale. 'If anything, it's the opposite.' He unlocked the French windows, which led out onto a stone-flagged patio. A cold wind blew in from the garden, ruffling his hair.

'What do you mean?'

'Forget it,' said Nightingale. He walked out onto the patio and looked across the well-tended lawns. He frowned as he stared at the flagstones, then he took out his cigarettes and lit one. The last time he'd been at the house he'd drawn a pentagram on the flagstones but now there was no trace of it. It was as if he'd never been there.

Morris joined him on the patio. Nightingale pointed at

the CCTV camera mounted on the rear wall of the house. 'I wonder if there's a recorder at the other end of that?'

'Bound to be,' said Morris. 'They'll all feed to one central location. It'll be linked to a recording system.'

'Think you can find it?'

Morris grinned. 'Does the Pope shit in the woods?' He went back into the house and Nightingale followed him.

There were six identical black doors leading off the hallway. One led to a kitchen, another opened into a storage room, and a third led to a small library lined with books. There was a circular oak table in the middle of the room, with books stacked on it.

'Eddie, go and see if you can find where the CCTV feeds go to.'

'No sooner done than said,' said Morris. He went back to the hallway as Nightingale rummaged through the books.

The diary he was looking for was bound in red leather, the colour of congealed blood. It wasn't on the table but after ten minutes of working his way along the bookshelves he found it wedged between a book on exorcism and another on mythological creatures. He pulled it out and flicked through the yellowing pages, which were covered in handwritten reverse-Latin script with scribbled illustrations.

'Jack!'

Nightingale tucked the book under his arm. 'What?'

'Found it!' shouted Morris. 'Upstairs!'

55

M orris had found the security room on the top floor, at the end of a corridor off which there were half a dozen bedrooms. It wasn't difficult to find as it had the word SECURITY in large capital letters on the door. There was a bank of monitors on one wall and on a table in front of them were a keyboard, three telephones and a MacBook laptop computer. There was a black leather swivel chair pushed close to the table and behind it a stainless-steel bunk bed. To the right was another door leading to a bathroom.

'You were right – the CCTV system has been switched off,' said Morris. 'State-of-the-art system, must have cost thousands.'

'Yeah, Mitchell wasn't short of a bob or two,' said Nightingale. He sat down in the swivel chair and put the diary on the table. 'Can you show me how it works?'

'What is it you want?' asked Morris, leaning over him and switching on the laptop.

'I want to see what was recorded on November the twenty-seventh.'

'Shouldn't be difficult,' said Morris. He flicked on a switch and the monitors flickered into life. Views of the interior and exterior of the house filled the monitors. 'That's the live feed.'

The centre monitor was larger than the rest and it was the main computer screen. By moving the cursor across a panel Morris could change the camera input to any of the monitors, and show up to sixteen inputs on any one screen. He quickly filled all four of the surveillance monitors, which meant that he had the views from sixty-four cameras and almost all were inside the house. One of the screens showed the back of the chair and the monitors.

Nightingale twisted around in his seat. He couldn't see a CCTV camera but there was a stainless-steel light fitting on the wall. 'Sneaky,' he said.

Morris's fingers played across the keyboard and a menu appeared on the main monitor. 'Okay, there we go,' he said. He pointed at the monitor. 'There're the dates; you scroll to the one you want and click on it.' He moved the cursor to 27 November and a second menu filled the screen. 'Those are all the feeds, by number, and the times. You choose a feed and then click on the time. It's all digital so it should be quick. What part of the house are you interested in?'

'I'll do it,' said Nightingale. 'You wait in the car.'

Morris picked up the diary and flicked through it. 'What's this?' he said. 'It doesn't make sense.'

'It's mirror writing,' said Nightingale. 'You have to hold it in front of a mirror to read it.'

'Why would anyone bother to write like that?'

'I told you, he was a nutter. No offence, Eddie, but will you piss off and leave me to it?'

Morris put down the diary and headed for the door.

'And don't think about pinching anything,' warned Nightingale. 'I'm going to pat you down before we leave.'

'I hear you,' said Morris.

'Yeah, well, hear and obey,' said Nightingale.

As Morris left the room, Nightingale tapped on the keyboard and scrolled down to 26 November. He clicked on the feed for the camera covering the patio. A view of the flagstones filled the main screen. According to the digital timer running along the bottom of the screen it was the view at midday. He pecked at the keyboard and the timecode clicked to 23.59.50 on 26 November. Nightingale saw himself sitting in the centre of a pentagram, with candles burning at the five points of the star within the circle. The wind was ruffling his hair and he was holding a book in his lap. Nightingale smiled to himself. At least he hadn't imagined the pentagram. He looked around for some way of boosting the volume but realised that the cameras probably didn't have microphones attached, so there were pictures but no sound. Not that it mattered – he knew exactly what had been said.

The recorded Nightingale stopped reading, closed the book and stared out over the lawn.

Nightingale leaned back in his chair, waiting for Proserpine and her dog to appear on screen. The timecode clicked over to 00.00.00 and the date from 26 November to 27 November. Nightingale frowned. Proserpine had appeared at exactly midnight. So where was she?

The recorded Nightingale got to his feet and opened the book. He began reading aloud from it. Nightingale leaned forward, peering at the screen. Where was Proserpine? Why wasn't she there? She had appeared at midnight and Nightingale had started to read from the book, so why wasn't she on the screen?

Nightingale stared at the digits of the timecode: 00.00.45. Another second clicked by. And another.

'This isn't what happened,' Nightingale muttered to himself. 'She was there. I know she was there.'

Nightingale continued to stare at the recording. Nothing was happening. The timer at the bottom was ticking off the seconds but the Nightingale on screen just stood there, alone. There was no Proserpine. No dog. And no Mitchell being sent to burn in Hell.

56

Jenny was sitting on a stool at the bar and talking into her mobile phone when Nightingale walked in. The wine bar was just off the King's Road, close to her mews house. She put her phone away and waved at him as he went over to her. 'What was so important it couldn't wait until tomorrow?' she asked.

'Can't I see my favourite assistant for a social drink?' he said, sliding onto the stool next to her and putting a Tesco carrier bag on the bar.

'Your only assistant,' she corrected. 'So you're not after anything?'

'Well, maybe just a little something,' he said. 'But we can chit-chat as well.' He smiled at the barmaid, a plump blonde girl in her early twenties wearing a Bristol University sweatshirt, and ordered a vodka and Coke. 'What do you want?' Nightingale asked Jenny.

'I want you not to drink,' she said. 'You're driving, remember?'

'How do you know?'

'I saw your car on the way here. It's a green MGB, Jack. Pretty distinctive.'

'Okay, it's a fair cop. So what do you want to drink?'

'My usual.'

Nightingale winked at the barmaid.

'Make the vodka a double,' he said. 'And a glass of your finest Pinot Grigio for my date. Shaken not stirred.'

'I'm not his date,' Jenny said to the barmaid. 'I'm so not his date. And make his vodka a single. He's driving.'

'A single it is,' said the barmaid. 'And on the date front, you could do worse.' She went to get their drinks.

'Did you pay her to say that?' asked Jenny.

'Let's just say she's a member of my fan club, shall we?'

'Let's not,' said Jenny. 'Do you want to eat?'

'I can eat,' said Nightingale. 'I could even buy you dinner.'

'You're definitely going to ask me a favour,' she said. 'You're as transparent as a Harvey Nicks shop window. I'll grab us a table.'

Nightingale nodded at the carrier bag. 'Take that for me, will you? I'll bring the drinks.'

Nightingale joined her with their drinks a couple of minutes later and dropped his raincoat over the back of his chair. 'She's got a degree in chemical engineering,' he said as he sat down.

'And very large breasts,' said Jenny.

'Didn't notice,' said Nightingale.

'Has she joined your fan club?'

'Is there one?'

'Probably not.' She raised her glass of wine to him. 'Cheers,' she said.

Nightingale clinked his glass against hers. 'Down the hatch.'

'When did you start drinking vodka and Coke? You always drink Corona.'

'Not always.' He patted his stomach. 'It's better for the waistline.'

'I think you'll find there're more calories in a vodka and Coke, especially a double vodka and Coke, than a bottle of beer.' She flashed him a tight smile. 'It's not about the calories, is it?'

He grinned and took a long pull on his drink, then smacked his lips. 'Okay, it tastes good, and it's a quicker way of getting alcohol into the system.'

'What's wrong, Jack?'

'Nothing,' he said. 'Or everything. I'm not sure.' He opened the carrier bag and took out Mitchell's diary.

'Where did you get that from?' she asked.

'Best you don't know,' he said.

'You went back to the house? Jack, please don't tell me that you've been breaking and entering?'

'Strictly speaking, it wasn't me that did the breaking but I did help with the entering.'

Jenny shook her head reproachfully. 'You're going to end up in prison if you carry on like this.'

'I hardly think Sebastian Mitchell is going to press charges,' he said. He grinned. 'Mind you, Hell is probably full of lawyers. What do you think?'

'I think you need to get a grip,' she said. 'You can't keep going into people's houses like this.'

'We need that diary,' said Nightingale. 'And I couldn't see any other way of getting it.'

'The end justifies the means? That's no excuse, Jack.' She held up the diary. 'And now you've passed it on to me, which makes me in receipt of stolen goods. That's a criminal offence, Jack.'

'Jenny, sweetheart . . .'

'Don't "sweetheart" me, Jack Nightingale. It's one thing for you to go around breaking the law, but it's something else when you drag me into it.'

Nightingale put up his hands in surrender. 'Okay, okay, I'm sorry,' he said. 'But let's not forget that Mitchell sent his goons to get it from you. At gunpoint. We found it in Gosling's basement, remember? And possession is nine-tenths of the law.'

'That's a fallacy,' she said. 'Possession has nothing to do with ownership. Your father stole it from Mitchell.'

'That's what Mitchell said. We don't know that it's true.' He reached over and squeezed her hand. 'I'm just saying it's a grey area. Sebastian Mitchell and Ainsley Gosling were as bad as each other. All I want is a look-see at that diary to know if there's anything in it that can help my sister. You can't blame me for that. Besides, they're both dead anyway.'

She held his look for several seconds, then nodded slowly. 'Okay,' she said.

'Are you sure? I don't want you angry at me.'

She took her hand away. 'I'm not angry, Jack,' she said. 'I'm just a bit . . . apprehensive. About what's happening to you.'

'You and me both, kid,' said Nightingale. He sat back and ran a hand over his face. 'It's been a funny few weeks.' He sipped his drink. 'You do believe me, don't you?'

'About what?'

'What happened at Mitchell's house. On my birthday.'

'Of course I believe you. Why would you lie about something like that?'

'I wasn't lying,' he said. 'But there's something strange going on.'

'Spit it out, Jack. What's wrong?'

Nightingale sighed. 'I told you what happened. How Proserpine appeared at midnight and Mitchell left his pentagram and she killed him?'

'Dragged him kicking and screaming into the bowels of Hell is how you described it.'

'And that's exactly how I remember it,' said Nightingale. 'Except . . .'

'Except what?'

Nightingale picked up his vodka and Coke and finished it. 'Let me get another drink and I'll tell you,' he said.

57

When Nightingale had finished telling her what he'd seen on the CCTV footage in Mitchell's house, he picked up his glass and toasted her. 'So what do you think?'

She ran her fingertip around the rim of her glass. 'How am I supposed to answer that?' she said. 'Nothing that's happened over the past few weeks makes any sense, not really. It's like the whole world has turned upside down for us but for everyone else life just carries on as normal.' Jenny sipped her wine, then put down her glass. 'I don't think you imagined it,' she said. 'I know that's what you think I'm thinking.'

'I wouldn't blame you.'

'Just because the CCTV didn't show Proserpine, doesn't mean that she wasn't there.' She leaned towards him. 'I believe you, Jack.'

'I know you do. But there was a hell of a lot of video of me just standing there with a blank look on my face.' He shrugged. 'Maybe it was all in my head. Maybe I imagined the whole thing.'

'You're not a man given to making things up, Jack. I know that much about you.'

'You didn't see the video, Jenny. There was just me,

standing on the patio. But that's not what happened. At least, it's not what I remember happening. She was there. Mitchell came out through the French windows and she . . . she did something. He was frozen to the ground and then she sent him to Hell. Mitchell's people tried to stop her. And her dog, it became this . . . this thing. This three-headed dog-thing.'

Jenny chuckled. 'You see, if you were making it up you'd come up with something better than that.'

'The dog-thing killed Mitchell's men. But there were no bodies. No nothing.'

'You don't take drugs, do you?'

'Of course not.'

'And you're not prone to hallucinations, are you?'

Nightingale shook his head.

'So no, I don't think you made it up and I don't think you imagined it. I think it's more likely that something was done to the video. Either by Mitchell's people or by Proserpine. Someone who didn't want people to know what happened.'

Nightingale swirled the ice cubes around his glass. 'Just so long as you don't think I'm going mad.' He drained his glass. 'Another?'

'You said one drink, Jack. You've had two already.'

'One more won't hurt. It's not as if I'm driving far, is it?'

'Jack . . .'

'Okay, okay. I'll have a Coke.' He stood up and kissed her on the cheek. 'I don't know what I'd do without you.'

'Carry on like this and pretty soon you'll be finding out,' she said.

Nightingale winked at her and headed for the bar.

58

Nightingale walked Jenny home and then went to get his MGB, which he'd parked in a side road not far from her house. When he reached his car he cursed as he saw that the nearside rear tyre was flat. He opened the boot, dropped in the carrier bag, and started unscrewing the spare tyre. Headlights illuminated the rear of the MGB and Nightingale turned to see a black Range Rover coming down the road towards him.

The car slowed and then stopped. Nightingale shielded his eyes against the blinding lights. He heard a door open and close and then saw a figure walk in front of the Range Rover. 'Flat tyre, yeah?' said a voice.

'Yeah,' said Nightingale.

'Do you need a hand?'

'I'm okay,' said Nightingale. 'It's not my first flat.'

The man was tall, a little over six feet. He was about Nightingale's age with jet-black hair and skin that was ghostly pale. He was wearing a long black overcoat and had a bright red scarf around his neck.

The man stuck out a gloved hand. 'The name's Chance,' he said.

'Jack,' said Nightingale, shaking the hand.

Chance nodded at the flat tyre. 'Happened to me last

week. Bloody nail. Still don't know if it was an accident or if someone did it deliberately. Come on, I'll help. You get out the spare and I'll start getting the wheel off. Have you got a torque wrench and a jack, Jack?' He grinned. 'That's funny. A jack, Jack.'

'Former boy scout, always prepared,' said Nightingale. He took a wrench from the tool kit in the boot and gave it to Chance. 'Loosen the nuts first,' said Nightingale. 'Then I'll raise her up.'

'No problem,' said Chance.

As Nightingale pulled the wheel out of the boot, Chance put the torque wrench on one of the nuts and forced it counter-clockwise. He grunted but then grinned as it moved. 'I don't know my own strength,' he said. He loosened the rest of the nuts then stood up, swinging the wrench. 'There you go,' he said.

He moved out of the way to give Nightingale room to work. Nightingale continued to turn the handle of the jack. As he concentrated on the task at hand he hardly noticed Chance step closer. Something slammed against the side of his head and Nightingale slumped to the road. He groaned and rolled over onto his back. Chance dropped the wrench and it clattered on the ground next to Nightingale. Nightingale blinked as he tried to focus, but the man standing above him was a blur. He tried to speak but his mouth refused to work.

Chance reached into his coat pocket and pulled out a cut-throat razor. He flicked out the blade and it glinted in the Range Rover's headlights. He drew back his hand but then hesitated. He put the razor on the roof of the MGB and put his hand in his pocket.

'Proserpine sent you?' croaked Nightingale.

Chance put his foot on the middle of Nightingale's chest. 'Hush,' he said. He tossed a coin into the air, caught it and slapped it down onto the back of his left hand. He removed his right hand and his forehead creased into a frown. 'No way,' he said. He glared down at Nightingale. 'You are one lucky son of a bitch,' he said. His face hardened. 'Best out of three? Why not?' He tossed the coin up into the air again.

Nightingale groped for the wrench. He was still dazed from the blow but his fingers found the cold metal and he picked it up. Chance was looking at the spinning coin, his eyes wide, and he didn't see Nightingale draw back his hand and smash the wrench against his knee. He screamed in pain as the kneecap cracked.

Nightingale rolled over and came up on all fours as Chance howled. Chance grabbed the razor and lashed out with it but Nightingale managed to block it with the wrench. He got to his feet as Chance raised the razor again but Nightingale caught him with a quick kick to the groin. Chance yelped like a dog and Nightingale smashed the wrench down on his wrist. He heard bones break and the razor fell from Chance's nerveless fingers. Nightingale lifted the wrench and backhanded it across Chance's face. Blood spurted from his nose and he fell backwards, unconscious before he hit the ground.

The blip of a police siren made Nightingale look round. He hadn't heard the police car drive down the road behind him. He slowly raised his hands as the car doors opened and two heavily built uniformed officers climbed out.

'Put down the weapon!' one of them shouted.

'It's a torque wrench,' said Nightingale.

'I don't care if it's a bloody cotton bud, drop it now,'

said the officer, taking his baton from its holster and flicking it open.

Nightingale dropped the wrench, keeping his hands high in the air. He nodded at Chance, who was lying motionless in the road. 'He started it,' he said.

59

Nightingale sipped his cup of canteen coffee and grimaced. The police had left him in the interview room for the best part of three hours and had only opened the door once, to give him the coffee and a stale cheese sandwich. He'd taken the fact that they hadn't put him in a cell as a good sign.

The door opened and he recognised a familiar face. Superintendent Chalmers. He was wearing full uniform and carrying a clipboard. 'Get your feet off the table,' said Chalmers, closing the door.

'Why, are you going to charge me with putting my feet on the table? I didn't realise that was an offence.'

Chalmers slapped Nightingale's Hush Puppies with his clipboard. 'Act your bloody age,' he said.

Nightingale took his feet off the table. 'They had no right to bring me in,' he said. 'I'm the victim in this.'

'You told the officers at the scene that you were attacked.'

'My tyre was flat. He stopped to help me change it. Then he hit me with a wrench and pulled out a razor.'

'But he's the one who ended up unconscious in the road.'

'We struggled.' He pointed at the back of his head.

A doctor had put in three stitches and given him Paracetamol for his headache. 'I didn't do this to myself, Chalmers.'

'And you didn't say anything to provoke him?'

'I was on my knees working the jack,' said Nightingale.

Chalmers nodded slowly. 'You were lucky this time, Nightingale,' he said.

'That's funny because I don't feel lucky.' He touched the stitches on the back of his head.

'The man who attacked you. His name is Eric Marshall.'

'He told me his name was Chance.'

'Yeah, well, we went around to Marshall's house and found a diary that he's been keeping. It looks as if he's responsible for a dozen or so unsolved murders over the past five years. One of them is a case I worked on a few years ago. There are details in the diary that only the killer would know.'

'You're joking.'

'Do I look like a stand-up comedian, Nightingale? Seems he had a thing going with a coin. Heads you die, tails you live – something like that. Did you see him toss a coin?'

'I was stunned,' lied Nightingale.

'Yeah, well, apparently he let the coin decide whether his victims lived or died. Looks like he slashed your tyre, by the way. Which suggests he was targeting you.'

'I never met him before tonight,' said Nightingale.

'You sure? Never crossed paths with him while you were in the Job? Or did some private case on him?'

'I'm sure,' said Nightingale. 'So you've got him, then? Done and dusted?'

'There's blood on the razor. Two types. We're doing

DNA analysis now and we'll cross-check with murder cases, but the diary alone will put him away.'

'So I'm a hero?'

'No, Nightingale, you're an arsehole. But unfortunately I can't arrest you for that.' He jerked his thumb at the door. 'Now get the hell out of my station before I change my mind.'

60

Jenny was sitting at her desk reading through a stack of printed sheets when Nightingale walked into the office just before midday. 'I got your message,' she said. 'Something wrong at Gosling Manor?'

'Nah, I was looking for a book,' he said. He held up a Sainsbury's carrier bag. 'Found it, too. The Yank wants it and he's in town tomorrow'

'Christmas Eve?'

'That's what he said.'

'Great, the money should come in handy.'

'Not necessarily,' he said. 'There's some sort of curse attached to it.' He took off his raincoat and hung it on the back of the door.

'What do you mean?'

'If you sell it you die. That sort of curse.'

'Well, don't go swapping it for a handful of magic beans, that's all. We don't have much in the way of cash and Christmas is always the quiet time of the year.'

Nightingale looked down at the sheets she was studying. 'What's this?' he asked.

'Mitchell's diary,' she said. 'The one you took from his house. Took as in stole, of course.'

'But it's not mirror writing. I mean, it's still nonsense but it's the right way round.'

'It's not nonsense, it's Latin,' she said. 'I started doing that thing with the mirror but then I had a brainwave. I scanned all the pages into the computer and then used Photoshop to flip it.'

'Smart girl.'

'If I was smart I'd have thought of doing it sooner,' said Jenny.

'Any mention of Frimost? Or Lucifuge Rofocale?'

'Not yet,' she said. 'It'll take me some time to work my way through it. I've sorted out the mirror image but it's still in Latin and my Latin is a bit rusty.'

'Yeah, well, mine's non-existent.'

'What happened to your head?' asked Jenny, noticing the stitches in his scalp for the first time. 'That's not from when you got hit in Wales, is it?'

'I was attacked,' said Nightingale.

'When?'

'Last night. After I'd walked you home.'

'What happened?'

'Nothing.'

'It's clearly not nothing, Jack. What happened?'

Nightingale smiled 'Guy wanted to give me a shave.'

She narrowed her eyes. 'Don't mess around, Jack. Spill the beans.'

'I tell you what – if you make me a coffee I'll tell you the whole story.'

Jenny raised an eyebrow. 'Did you forget our deal?'

'Was it signed in blood?'

'It was a promise to make me coffee for the rest of the week,' she said. 'And I'm holding you to it.'

Nightingale made them both coffee and they went through to his office. 'I was attacked by a serial killer,' said Nightingale. 'Tried to slit my throat but I came off best.'

'What?'

'He did one of my tyres then offered to help me change the wheel, and then he pulled a knife.' He grinned. 'Turns out he's got form. Chalmers is on the case.'

'Why would he attack you? You don't know him?'

'Complete stranger,' said Nightingale.

'What about the Welsh serial killer? Could it be him?'

Nightingale shook his head. 'This guy wasn't interested in making it look like suicide,' he said. 'He kept a diary, apparently. Detailing his murders. And Chalmers didn't say anything about them being in Wales.' Nightingale sipped his coffee. 'I've got a feeling that Proserpine is behind it.'

'Why?' Nightingale looked away and Jenny sighed. 'Not again. What are you not telling me this time?'

'I sort of did a deal with her.'

'What sort of deal?'

'It sounds crazy,' he said. 'Until last night I wasn't sure that I believed it myself.'

'Everything that's happened over the past few weeks is crazy; one more thing isn't going to worry me. What did you do, Jack?'

Nightingale lit a cigarette before he answered. He needed the nicotine but he also needed time to think. 'Proserpine gave me the information I needed, but there was a price. For every question she answered, she said she'd send someone to kill me.'

Jenny folded her arms. 'She what?'

'That was the deal. By the time I'd finished, she said she'd send three killers after me.'

'She answered three questions?'

Nightingale looked pained. 'Not really. Two. Well, three, but one of them wasn't helpful.' He took another sip of coffee. 'You had to have been there. She's cunning.'

'She's a demon from Hell, Jack, of course she's cunning. What did she say?'

'She told me about a devil called Sugart. He's on a par with Frimost. If I play it right, I can set them against each other.'

'How does that help?'

He shrugged. 'It's complicated.'

'Don't you think you should have told me this before?'

'This whole devil thing, I'm not sure what I believe and what I don't.'

'But, after last night, you know she means it? She's going to have you killed?'

Nightingale gingerly touched the wound on his scalp. 'The bang on the head shows she's serious,' he said. 'One down, two to go.'

'It's not funny,' said Jenny.

'I'm just trying to lighten the moment.'

'Yeah, well, you're failing miserably.' She sighed and went back into her office.

Nightingale took out his wallet and found the receipt on which Joshua Wainwright had written his mobile phone number. He tapped out the number and the American answered almost immediately.

'How're things, Jack?' he said.

'Are you psychic?' asked Nightingale. 'How did you know it was me?'

Wainwright laughed. 'Caller ID,' he said. 'Technology, not witchcraft.'

'I didn't give you my number,' said Nightingale.

'I stored it last time you called,' said Wainwright. 'You sound mighty suspicious, Jack. Someone giving you a hard time?'

'No more than usual,' said Nightingale. 'Where are you?'

'Here and there,' said the American. 'What's up?'

'That diary you wanted. The special one. I found it.'

'You did, huh? You remember what I said?'

'About not selling? Sure. Hardly likely to forget something like that. I thought you'd want to see it straight away. You said you might be in London this week.'

'Darn tooting I'd like it. I'll be in the Ritz tomorrow. Come round, but you'll have to ask for Bert Whistler.'

'Bert Whistler?'

'Low profile,' said Wainwright. 'So what do you want for it?'

'Why do you think I want something?'

Wainwright chuckled. 'Maybe I am psychic, after all,' he said. 'But I figure that if you can't sell it then you'll have come up with a trade. A barter. A quid pro quo.'

'You're right,' said Nightingale. 'But all I want is some information. Advice.'

'I'll see you at the Ritz,' said Wainwright. 'I should be there by noon. We can talk then.'

Nightingale ended the call and went through to Jenny's office. 'Wainwright's in London tomorrow and I'm going to take the books round to him.'

'Jack, tomorrow's Christmas Eve.'

'I don't think Satanists are big on Christmas.'

She shook her head in exasperation. 'You know what I mean. We're going to my parents tomorrow. Remember? I'm driving you to Norfolk in the morning.'

Nightingale groaned. 'I'm sorry,' he said. 'Completely slipped my mind.'

'Yeah, I can see how high up I am on your list of priorities,' she said.

'It's not that,' said Nightingale. 'It's just . . .'

'That there are more important things on your mind,' she said. 'I understand.'

'He'll be at the Ritz. I'll drop off the books and then I'll drive up myself. I'll be there in the afternoon. It's no biggie.' The look of disappointment stayed on her face. 'Jenny, I've already bought your dad a bottle of eighteen-year-old Laphroaig and some lemongrass shower gel for your mum.'

'Shower gel?'

'I'm not good at buying gifts for women,' said Nightingale. 'But the salesgirl said that it makes your skin go all tingly, so that's got to be good, right?'

'Okay, but you'd better be there, Jack. I told them you were coming.'

'I won't let you down, I promise.'

61

Nightingale arrived at the Ritz Hotel at noon. He unbuttoned his raincoat as he walked across the marble floor towards the reception desk, swinging his Sainsbury's carrier bag.

The receptionist was a man in his mid-thirties with a fifty-pound haircut and a made-to-measure suit that was probably worth as much as Nightingale's MGB. He smiled professionally at Nightingale and tapped in the name Whistler on a discreetly hidden keyboard. 'Who shall I say is here to see him?'

'Tell him it's his mother,' said Nightingale.

The receptionist frowned.

'Whistler's mother,' said Nightingale. 'It's a joke.' The receptionist continued to stare impassively at him and Nightingale flashed back to when he was at school, explaining to a teacher why he had a packet of Marlboro and a box of matches in his schoolbag. 'Then again, maybe it isn't,' he said. 'Nightingale. Jack Nightingale.'

The smile reappeared and the receptionist tapped again on the keyboard. 'Mr Whistler hasn't checked in yet.'

'He was supposed to be here at twelve,' said Nightingale.

'That's our understanding too, sir, but, as I said, he's yet to arrive. Would you like to leave a message?'

'I'll wait,' said Nightingale. 'Do me a favour and leave a message that I'm in reception.'

Nightingale left the receptionist typing away and walked over to an armchair. He sat down and waited. From where he was sitting he could see the main door and all of the reception area, but an hour passed and there was no sign of the American. He called Wainwright's mobile phone but it just rang out and didn't go through to voicemail. At one o'clock he went back to the desk and spoke to another receptionist, this one a pretty blonde girl. She confirmed that Wainwright still hadn't checked in.

Nightingale sat down again and continued waiting. It was another hour before a man in a black suit, crisp white shirt and black tie appeared in front of him. He had a head that was completely shaved and a small scar under his left ear. At first Nightingale thought he was a hotel employee but then he spotted a discreet clear-plastic earpiece.

'Mr Nightingale?' he said, in a soft American accent.

'That's me.'

'Mr Wainwright will see you now,' he said.

'I didn't see him come in,' said Nightingale.

'Mr Wainwright uses a private entrance,' said the man. 'He prefers it that way.'

Nightingale stood up as the man headed for the lifts. 'What floor are we going to?' he asked.

'Sixth,' said the man.

'Room six six six, by any chance?'

The man frowned and shook his head. 'Six three two,' he said. 'He always stays in the same suite.'

'I know this is going to sound crazy, but can we use the stairs?'

'Absolutely,' said the man. 'I'm no fan of elevators myself.'

They took the stairs to the sixth floor and then Nightingale followed the man along a plush corridor. The door to Wainwright's suite was opened by a gorgeous blonde in a tight-fitting suit the skirt of which ended a good ten inches above her knees. 'Good afternoon, Mr Nightingale,' she said. 'Do come in. Mr Wainwright is expecting you.' She had an Afrikaans accent and the bluest eyes that Nightingale had ever seen.

She took him through to a sitting room where Wainwright was sprawled on a sofa reading a copy of the *Wall Street Journal*. He was wearing a blue denim shirt, black 501 jeans and a pair of gleaming lizard-skin cowboy boots.

'Jack, good to see you,' said the American. He stood up, shook hands with Nightingale and then waved him to an armchair before sitting down again. 'Sorry I'm late. I had a thing at Westminster and the guy I was there to see was tied up with your PM.'

Nightingale gave Wainwright the carrier bag and sat down.

The American opened the bag and took out a leather-bound book. His eyes widened. 'This is . . . indescribable,' said Wainwright. He looked up at Nightingale. 'Do you know what this is, Jack?'

'Aleister Crowley's diary,' said Nightingale. He looked around but didn't see an ashtray. 'Is it okay to smoke in here?'

'They block-book the suite for me all year round,' said Wainwright. 'We can set fire to the place if we want.' He held up the book. 'This isn't just his diary. It's not just a first edition. It's a bound proof copy, with his corrections in ink. He held these pages and made corrections to them, corrections which were then made before the book proper was printed.'

'But it's still cursed?' said Nightingale. He lit a cigarette.

'I didn't say it was cursed. I just said that whenever a copy was sold, the buyer and the seller died.'

'That suggests a curse, doesn't it?'

'Not in the strict sense of what is usually meant by a curse,' said the American. 'Anyway, curse or no curse, this is beyond price, Jack. This is . . .'

'Priceless?' Nightingale finished for him.

'I don't know what to say to you,' said Wainwright. 'I had no idea that you'd be bringing me this. It's . . .' He shook his head, lost for words.

'Bearing in mind what happens to those who sell it, I want you to accept it as a gift. With my compliments.'

'I accept, of course,' said Wainwright, holding the volume against his chest. 'And I'll be forever in your debt, Jack. Ask and you shall receive.' He grinned. 'Except for cold hard cash, of course.' Wainwright swung his feet up onto an antique coffee table. 'On the phone you said you wanted help with something.'

'That's right,' said Nightingale. 'I need to talk to Lucifuge Rofocale. The devil you said was Lucifer's negotiator.'

Wainwright's jaw dropped. 'Say what?'

'I need to know how to summon him. I have to talk to him.'

'Jack . . .'

He nodded at the book. 'You've got what you wanted; all I'm asking is that you give me what I want.'

'I thought I explained how dangerous it can be to summon the upper echelons.'

'Duly noted.'

'You don't have the experience. Or the power. I'm pretty darn good at it but I don't have the power to call Lucifuge Rofocale, and even if I did, I wouldn't. One slip, one sign of weakness and . . . puff! You'd be ashes. Or worse.' He held up the book he was holding. 'Crowley? Maybe he could have done it, at the height of his powers. But he was one of the greatest Satanists of the last century. You, Jack, what are you? A disgraced cop turned private eye.'

'The "disgraced" label is a bit harsh, Josh.'

Wainwright smiled apologetically. 'I'm sorry. I didn't mean to bite your head off, but I like you, Jack. I really do. And I wouldn't want you to get sucked into something that could only end badly.'

'I don't have much of a choice,' said Nightingale. 'I need to resolve the situation with my sister, and he's the only one who can do that.'

'You want to do a deal with Lucifuge Rofocale?'

'Not exactly. I just want to talk to him. Do you know how?'

Wainwright shook his head. 'He's way out of my league.'

Nightingale pulled a face. 'That's a pity,' he said.

'Well, not necessarily.' Wainwright held up the book. 'If anyone knew how to call up Lucifuge Rofocale, it was Aleister Crowley. The answer's almost certainly here.' He flicked through the pages, a thoughtful frown on his face, while Nightingale sat and smoked. Eventually Wainwright grinned and stabbed at a page. 'There you are.'

Nightingale stood up, walked across to the American and looked over his shoulder.

'This is what you have to do,' said Wainwright. 'But you have to follow his instructions to the letter. The letter, Jack.'

'I understand.'

'Are you sure that you do? Because one mistake, one slip, would mean certain death.'

Nightingale blew a smoke ring towards the ornate ceiling. 'Everyone dies eventually, Josh,' he said.

'True,' said the American. 'But not everyone burns in Hell for all eternity.'

62

Jenny had programmed the address of her parents' house into his phone's GPS system so Nightingale had no problems finding it. It was called Edmund House and it was signposted off the main road. Black railings bordered the estate and he drove onto the property and stopped outside a stone building with leaded windows. He smiled as he saw that it was much smaller than Gosling Manor. He was just about to climb out of his MGB when a uniformed security guard appeared and Nightingale realised that the building was the gatehouse.

'Jack Nightingale,' he said. 'I'm here to see the McLeans.'

'Yes, sir,' said the guard, a heavy-set man in his fifties. 'Just follow the road and park anywhere to the left of the main house.'

He was talking into a transceiver as Nightingale drove off. The driveway curved to the left and bordered a lake that was several hundred yards across. Then the road bent to the right and the MGB crested a small hill to reveal the house for the first time. Nightingale stopped the car and sat looking at it, shaking his head in wonder. It wasn't a house, it wasn't a mansion – it was a stately home that would give Buckingham Palace a run for its money. It was a severe building, grey stone and dark grey slated roof, the main entrance flanked by Corinthian pillars that went up two storeys. He counted a dozen chimneys, with wisps of smoke coming from half of them.

To the left of the house was a line of expensive cars. A black Bentley, a red Ferrari, four Range Rovers, a 7-Series BMW, a large Mercedes and Jenny's Audi. Nightingale eased the car forward and drove towards the house. The closer he got the more immense it looked and he realised it must be at least five times as large as Gosling Manor.

He parked his car next to the Ferrari. As he was taking his suitcase out of the boot a liveried footman hurried over.

'I'll get that for you, sir,' he said, in a broad Norfolk accent.

Nightingale let the man carry his case and followed him up a flight of steps to the double-height front door and into a huge hallway, where the walls were covered in gilt-framed works of art. A butler, slightly overweight and with a receding hairline was waiting for them. He nodded at Nightingale.

'Dinner has already started, sir,' said the butler. 'You're to go straight to the dining room unless you want to freshen up first.'

'I'll go straight in,' said Nightingale. He took off his raincoat and gave it to the man holding his case.

'Simon will put your things in your room, sir, and I'll show you in. Please follow me.'

The butler strode down a wood-panelled corridor to a set of double oak doors, which he opened with a flourish. 'Mr Nightingale has arrived,' he said. He stepped to the side to allow Nightingale through, and then closed the doors behind him.

The dining room was panelled in a light wood with French windows overlooking the rear gardens. The table was set for ten, with three large silver candelabra and gleaming silverware. The guests had just finished their soup and a waitress in a black and white uniform was collecting the dishes. Jenny had twisted around in her chair and was smiling at him. He winked at her.

Sitting at one end of the table was a big man with an expensive tan and short curly hair. He was in his mid fifties and was wearing a charcoal-grey suit over a black silk shirt buttoned at the neck. He stood up and walked over to Nightingale, his arm outstretched. 'James McLean,' he said. 'I'm so pleased to finally meet you, Jack. We were starting to worry that you might not actually exist.'

Nightingale shook McLean's hand. 'Oh I'm real enough,' he said.

The man had a strong grip and his hand easily enveloped Nightingale's. There was a gold Rolex watch on his wrist, and a simple gold band on his wedding finger.

'We're just about to start our main course and the chef hates it if we keep him waiting – but he's allowed to be temperamental because his last restaurant had two Michelin stars – so let me introduce everyone very quickly,' said McLean, putting a hand on Nightingale's shoulder. 'The lovely lady at the head of the table is my wife, Melissa.'

Melissa McLean, a few years younger than her husband, and pretty with the slightly softened angular features of a former model, was wearing a red dress cut low enough to show just a hint of cleavage. There was a large diamond pendant around her neck and matching stones hanging from her ears. More diamonds glinted on her fingers when she waved at Nightingale.

'Next to her on the far side of the table is Marc Allen, next to him is Lesley Smith, and if she seems familiar it's because she's on Channel 4 most nights.'

Allen and Smith nodded and smiled. Smith mouthed 'Hello'.

'You're sitting between Lesley and Sally, she's Marc's wife. Sally's the brains of the Allen family, and the beauty.'

Allen raised his glass. 'Cheers, James.' He was in his late forties, overweight, with several chins and drooping eyelids. His wife was much younger; she was pretty and, like Mrs McLean, was bedecked with expensive jewellery.

'Opposite Sally is Wendy Bushell, who does a lot of work with George Soros.'

Bushell was in her sixties, with shoulder-length grey hair and no make-up but when she smiled it was to reveal a gleaming smile that could only have come from dentures or implants.

'Next to Wendy is Danny, Lesley's husband.'

Like McLean, Danny Smith was a big man and still fit, with a shock of chestnut hair that was only just starting to grey at the temples. He was wearing a black silk jacket that glistened in the candlelight. He raised his glass to Nightingale.

'Next to Danny is your hardworking and underpaid assistant, or at least that's how she describes herself.'

'Daddy!' exclaimed Jenny. She hurried over to Nightingale and gave him a peck on the cheek. She was wearing a short black dress and had a thin gold chain around her neck that he hadn't seen before. 'I thought you weren't coming,' she said.

'I got tied up at the Ritz,' said Nightingale.

'My favourite hotel,' said the final guest at the table, a man in his late fifties. He had a mane of grey hair combed back and a square chin with a dimple in the centre. A pair of delicate half-moon glasses nestled on a pug nose that was flecked with broken blood vessels.

'Be careful what you say around this one, Jack,' said McLean. 'He's one of the best lawyers in England and he loves to argue at the dining table as much as he does in court.'

The grey-haired man raised his hand in greeting. 'Marcus Fairchild, at your service,' he said.

63

It was the best Beef Wellington that Nightingale had ever tasted. That's what he told James McLean, and it was the truth, but then it was actually the only Beef Wellington he'd tasted. In fact the pâté around the beef was too salty for Nightingale's taste and he'd never been a fan of pastry. But he ate and smiled and made small talk with the TV presenter on his left and Sally Allen on his right, who actually was as smart as she was pretty but was clearly only with her husband for the money. His mind wasn't on the conversation, or the food; all he could think about was that the man sitting across the table from him was Marcus Fairchild, the Satanist lawyer that Joshua Wainwright had warned him about.

Fairchild was sitting between Jenny and her mother and had them both entranced with whatever stories he was telling them. The lawyer kept his voice low and Nightingale couldn't hear what he was saying but every now and again there were peals of laughter from their end of the table.

McLean extolled the virtues of the wine, which he said was a vintage Nuits-Saint-Georges that he bought by the case, but as Nightingale sipped and swallowed he barely tasted it. Why was Marcus Fairchild in the house? How did he know James McLean? And why was Jenny clearly so relaxed in his company?

The waitress cleared away the plates and Nightingale took out his packet of Marlboro. He saw a look of concern flash across Jenny's face and she waggled her finger at him across the table. Before Nightingale could say anything, Mr McLean leaned over towards him.

'I'm sorry, Jack, but we're very much a non-smoking house,' he said. 'However, if you fancy a cigarette before pudding there's a terrace off the study with a few nice planter chairs.' He nodded at the double doors. 'Back down the corridor, second door on the left.'

Nightingale thanked him and stood up. He had been craving a cigarette and it would give him a chance to have a quiet word with Jenny. He tried to catch her eye as he headed for the doors but she was deep in conversation with Fairchild again and didn't look up.

He headed for the study. It was a comfortable man's room lined with leather-bound books, with a massive Victorian globe next to the fireplace. On the mantelpiece were half a dozen plaques in recognition of McLean's charitable work. Nightingale took a cigarette from the packet and reached for his lighter. Above the fireplace were several framed degrees and certificates, including a Law Degree from Oxford and a Masters from Yale. He went over to one of the bookcases, half expecting to see the sort of volumes that were in the basement of Gosling Manor, but instead he found an eclectic mix of thrillers, autobiographies, science and reference books.

The study door opened and Nightingale turned around. 'About time,' he said, but it wasn't Jenny standing in the doorway, it was Fairchild.

'Don't even think about lighting up in here, or Melissa will have your guts for garters,' said the lawyer affably. He walked behind Nightingale and opened the French windows. On a stone terrace were four teak planter chairs facing the garden. Hidden spotlights illuminated a dozen or more trees and a large white octagonal gazebo. Fairchild sat down in one of the chairs and took out a leather cigar case. He offered it to Nightingale. 'They're Cuban. Rolled on the thigh of a dusky virgin,' he said. He scratched at his right ear. There were tufts of grey hair sprouting from it, Nightingale noticed.

'Female, I hope,' said Nightingale, sitting down on one of the other chairs. He held up his packet of Marlboro. 'I'll stick with my fags.'

'Ah, you're a cowboy at heart,' said Fairchild. He chuckled and used a silver cigar cutter to neatly clip off the end of his cigar. 'I'm just glad there's at least one other smoker,' he said, lighting his cigar with a match. 'Shame on James for banishing us from the house. Especially when he's fond of the odd cigar himself.' He grinned. 'Mind you, gives a chance for the men to talk, of course.'

Nightingale lit his cigarette and tried blowing a smoke ring, but the wind whipped it away. 'I don't mind being sent outside in the summer, but in the winter you could catch your death,' he said.

'You know, I prefer to smoke outside in the cold,' said Fairchild. 'I don't know about cigarettes but cigars never taste as good in the warm.'

The two men sat in silence for a couple of minutes, enjoying their respective smokes.

'Your sister is going to Hell, Jack Nightingale,' said Fairchild quietly.

Nightingale turned to look at him. Fairchild was holding his cigar at chin level and was watching Nightingale with amused eyes.

'What did you say?'

'I said your sister is going to Hell. That's what everyone has been telling you, isn't it?'

'What?' said Nightingale, stunned.

'What's wrong, Jack? You going deaf?' Fairchild laughed and took a slight drag on his cigar. He didn't inhale, just held the smoke in his mouth and then let it ease through his lips. 'Jenny said you'd been getting messages about your sister. Robyn Reynolds.'

Nightingale shook his head, trying to clear his thoughts. 'Why did she tell you that?' he asked.

'Was it a secret?' Fairchild shrugged. 'I'm sure it wasn't, not considering my involvement in the case.'

'You've got me totally confused,' said Nightingale. 'What do you know about Robyn?'

'I represented her in court,' said Fairchild. 'Didn't Jenny tell you?'

'I think it must have slipped her mind,' said Nightingale.

'She was asking me about famous cases I'd worked on over the years and I mentioned Reynolds. Could have knocked me down with a feather when she said you were related.'

'Half-related,' said Nightingale. 'She's my half-sister. Same father, different mother. Up until a few weeks ago I didn't even know I had a sister.'

'I was her barrister,' said Fairchild. 'She was on Legal Aid but I did it pro bono. Didn't feel that she was getting a decent show.'

'I thought you specialised in human-rights cases?'

'I'm a jack of all trades,' said Fairchild. 'Hired gun; have brief will travel. And there's nothing like the thrill of a good criminal case, no matter which side you're on.'

'She pleaded guilty, right?'

'Yes, but there's guilty and there's guilty. Just because you plead guilty doesn't mean you don't need decent representation.' He sucked on his cigar. 'The stuff about her going to Hell. What's that about?' he said quietly.

'I don't know,' said Nightingale. 'She's been on my mind a lot lately and when it's happened I've only half heard it. How did that come up in conversation with Jenny?'

'I think I mentioned that the tabloids at the time were saying that she should burn in Hell and Jenny said someone had said that to you.'

Nightingale shrugged and tried to look unconcerned. 'Like I said, I was probably imagining it.'

'I thought perhaps members of the public were making their views known,' said the lawyer. He blew a cloud of smoke over the garden. 'There was a lot of ill-feeling at the time, if you recall. A lot of people would have hanged her, given the chance.'

'You were convinced that she was guilty?'

'No question of it,' said Fairchild. 'Open and shut. But there were suggestions that her father abused her.'

'Did that come out in court?'

The lawyer shook his head. 'She wouldn't let me. I have to say, I wish I'd known then that she had been adopted. It would have been useful.'

'We were both adopted at birth,' said Nightingale. 'I don't think that alone would have turned her into a killer.'

'I suppose you're right,' said Fairchild. He smiled at Nightingale. 'Besides, you turned out all right.'

They heard footsteps behind them and turned to see Jenny standing by the French windows. 'Pudding is served,' she said. 'Mummy requires your presence in the dining room.'

Fairchild groaned as he pushed himself up out of the planter chair. 'Banoffee pie?' he said. He stubbed out his cigar in an ashtray.

Jenny laughed. 'Absolutely.'

Fairchild patted his stomach. 'Your cook will be the death of me,' he said. 'I always leave here weighing a good ten pounds more than when I arrived.'

Jenny linked arms with him. 'Come on, Jack,' she said.

Banoffee pie was the last thing Nightingale wanted just then. What he wanted more than anything was to ask Jenny why she was so close to Marcus Fairchild and to ask Marcus Fairchild whether he really did belong to a sect that promoted human sacrifice. He couldn't ask either question, of course, so he just smiled, extinguished his cigarette, and followed them back to the dining room.

64

Nightingale didn't get a chance to talk to Jenny on her own until late at night, when everyone was heading for bed, except for Jenny's father and Fairchild, who had gone out onto the terrace for a last cigar. She took him upstairs to show him his bedroom.

'Why didn't you tell me about Fairchild?' he asked her as they walked down a corridor that seemed to stretch to infinity.

She frowned. 'What do you mean?'

'He represented my sister in court. How could you not tell me?'

'I didn't know until this evening,' said Jenny. 'You got whisked into dinner as soon as you arrived and I didn't want to say anything in front of anybody.'

'And you told him about the messages? About my sister going to Hell?'

'I didn't tell him about Alfie Tyler or Connie Miller, obviously.'

'Obviously.'

'Jack, what's wrong?'

Nightingale fought the urge to snap at her. He took a deep breath and rubbed the back of his neck. 'I don't think you should have said anything.'

'He was her lawyer. He knows her. He might be able to help. That's what I thought. It came up in conversation, before you arrived. I wanted to tell you but we went straight into dinner and then after dinner you went outside with him for a smoke.'

'I get that, but why would you tell him that people were telling me that she was going to Hell? Why's that of any concern to him?'

'He said that Robyn was disturbed a lot of the time. Unbalanced. He was asking about you, how you had reacted when you found out that she was your sister.' She stopped in front of one of the doors. 'This is yours,' she said. 'It's the green room. Very restful.'

'Yeah, I need restful,' said Nightingale. 'You told him that I'd been hearing voices, didn't you?'

'It wasn't like that,' said Jenny. She put a hand on his shoulder. 'Jack, I'm on your side, you know that. Marcus was chatting away and he got me talking. That's what he does, right? He's a barrister. He gets people to open up, to reveal themselves.' She took her hand away and folded her arms. 'I'm not explaining this very well, am I?'

'No, you're not,' he said. 'That was personal, Jenny. And he's a stranger.'

'He's an old friend of Daddy's,' she said. 'I've known him for years. He's not a stranger. Of course I wouldn't have said anything to a stranger. But he's Uncle Marcus. I've called him uncle for as long as I can remember.'

'Did you tell him about the Ouija board?'

'Of course not.'

'You say "of course not", but I don't understand why you said anything about my sister in the first place.'

'Why is that so important, Jack? What's the problem?'

Nightingale opened the bedroom door and motioned for Jenny to follow him inside. She was right – it was restful, with pale green walls, a dark green carpet, and a large mahogany four-poster bed with fern-patterned linen. A fire was burning in a slate fireplace and there was a chocolate mint and a small posy of flowers on one of the pillows. Nightingale closed the door. 'There's something I didn't tell you,' he said. 'Something that Wainwright told me when I went to see him at Biggin Hill. About Fairchild.' Nightingale wiped his face with his hand and it came away wet with sweat. 'He's a Satanist. A devil-worshipper.'

'Nonsense.'

'I'm not making this up, Jenny. He's a member of the Order of Nine Angles. And they believe in human sacrifice.'

'Jack, why are you saying this? It can't possibly be true.'

'That's what Wainwright told me.'

'Then he's lying.'

'Why would he lie about something like that?'

'People lie, Jack. You were a policeman so you know that people rarely tell the truth.'

'I asked Wainwright for the name of someone in the Order of Nine Angles because that was the group that Gosling belonged to. He gave me Fairchild's name.'

'Why didn't you tell me this before?'

'Why should I? I didn't know that he was a friend of your father's. Or that he'd acted for my sister.' He took out his cigarettes. 'This is a mess.' He put a cigarette between his lips.

'Not in the house, Jack,' said Jenny, putting a hand on his arm. 'Mummy will freak out.'

'How will she know?' He pointed at the fireplace. 'There's a fire in the room.'

'She can smell tobacco smoke a mile away, Jack. Please.'

'What if I open a window?'

Jenny sighed. 'Okay, but make sure all the smoke goes out.'

Nightingale went over to the window and opened it. In the distance were two tennis courts, one grass and the other with an orange synthetic surface. Both had a light dusting of frost.

Nightingale shivered and lit the cigarette. 'What's Mummy got against smokers anyway?' he asked. He took a long drag and then leaned out of the window and blew smoke.

'She used to be one,' said Jenny. 'She gave up about six years ago.'

'The zeal of the convert,' said Nightingale. 'They're the worst.'

'I'm sorry,' said Jenny.

'About Mummy?'

Jenny forced a smile. 'About talking to Fairchild. I can't explain why I told him as much as I did.'

'Maybe he hypnotised you,' said Nightingale, only half joking.

'Maybe,' said Jenny. 'He does have a way of looking right at you when he talks to you.'

'Who mentioned my sister first?' asked Nightingale.

'He did.'

'Are you sure?'

Jenny nodded. 'I haven't seen him for a couple of years and I was asking him about his cases. He mentioned he'd represented a serial killer. Then he said it was Robyn Reynolds. That's when I said that you were her brother.'

Nightingale blew smoke through the window. 'This is just plain weird,' he said.

'As opposed to everything else that's happened over the past four weeks?'

'Something's going on, Jenny. This can't be a co-incidence. Wainwright gives me Fairchild's name. Then I come to your parents' house and here he is, large as life and twice as whatever. Then it turns out he represented my sister the serial killer.' He rubbed the bridge of his nose. 'This is giving me a headache.'

'It could just be that, a coincidence.' Nightingale could hear the uncertainty in her voice.

'Which bit? Fairchild being on my sister's legal team? Or him being a Satanist like my dear-departed father?' He took a long pull on his cigarette, then blew smoke out through the open window. 'I don't get what's happening here. I really don't.'

'I've known him for years, Jack. He's not a bad person.'

'Not according to Joshua Wainwright. He says that Fairchild belongs to the Order of Nine Angles. Have you any idea what they do?' Jenny shook her head. 'They kill people,' he said quietly. 'Now do you see? How can that be a coincidence? Marcus Fairchild is in a cult that kills people and he helps my sister plead guilty to the murder of five children.' Nightingale stubbed out his cigarette on the window ledge, then closed the window. 'Why's he here, Jenny?'

'He's one of Daddy's oldest friends.'

Nightingale took the cigarette butt through to the en-suite bathroom and flushed it away. He shrugged. 'I don't know what to think,' he said. He looked at his watch. It was just after midnight. 'Let's talk about it tomorrow. Cold light of day and all that.'

'You know we're all going shooting after breakfast? Shooting on Christmas Day is a family tradition.'

'So I gathered.'

'It'll be fun.'

'I hope so,' said Nightingale.

65

When Nightingale went down to breakfast on Christmas morning, Jenny and her father were already in the dining room, with Marc and Sally Allen and Wendy Bushell. Everyone was casually dressed. Jenny's father was wearing a red sweater with green Christmas trees across the front. Food was laid out in silver serving dishes – scrambled and fried eggs, bacon, sausages, baked beans, tomatoes, grilled kippers and kedgeree – along with fresh fruit and a selection of cereals.

'Help yourself, Jack,' said Jenny. 'They'll get you toast from the kitchen if you want it.'

Jack was carrying three wrapped presents. He handed one to Jenny. 'Merry Christmas,' he said.

'Jack, you didn't have to get me anything,' she said. 'You really shouldn't have.'

'Wait until you've opened it,' he said. 'I'm terrible at gifts.' He handed a wrapped box to McLean. 'I think I'm on safer ground with this one,' he said. 'And this one's for Melissa.' He put the present on the table.

'Really, Jack, you didn't have to.' McLean pulled off the wrapping and beamed when he saw the Laphroaig box. 'Good choice, Jack,' he said. 'Thanks.'

A uniformed maid appeared and asked if Nightingale

wanted tea or coffee. He asked for coffee and then filled his plate. 'I don't suppose you fancy adopting me,' Nightingale said to McLean. 'I am an orphan, you know.'

Jenny finished unwrapping her present and held up a Louis Vuitton shoulder bag. 'Thank you, Jack. It's lovely.'

'I've kept the receipt if you want to change it.'

'It's perfect, thank you.' The maid appeared with a pot of coffee and two toast racks, one full of white toast and the other wholemeal. She placed the toast on the table and poured coffee for Nightingale.

McLean looked over at Nightingale as he buttered a slice of toast. 'Jenny tells me you're a decent shot, Jack,' he said.

Nightingale raised an eyebrow at Jenny. 'She did, did she?' He took a sip of coffee. 'I'm afraid shotguns aren't my thing. I'm happier with an MP5 and a Glock.'

'I'm not sure how sporting it would be to shoot pheasants with an MP5,' said Allen.

'You know, the birds would have more of a chance against a carbine,' said Nightingale. 'A nine-millimetre bullet is relatively small, but the spread from a shotgun at fifty feet would be – what, six feet? Eight?'

'It's not as bad as that,' said McLean. 'The general rule of thumb is that shot spreads about an inch for every yard it travels. So if you were shooting at a bird fifty feet away the spread would be about one and a half feet. I have to say, that would be pushing it, Jack. I wouldn't want to be shooting at a bird more than thirty feet away.'

'I would guess Jack is more used to sawn-off shotguns than Purdeys,' said Marcus Fairchild. Nightingale looked up in surprise. He hadn't heard the lawyer come into room. Fairchild bent down over the server containing kippers and smelled them appreciatively. He was wearing a dark blue pullover, baggy blue jeans and Timberland boots and looked more like a building site labourer than a City lawyer. 'The spread of a sawn-off is about one inch per foot travelled,' he said.

'Come on, Marcus,' said Sally Allen. 'How would you know something like that?'

Fairchild picked up a plate and used silver tongs to take two kippers. 'It was a case at the Old Bailey a few years back,' he said. 'I was defending an armed robber who'd been charged with attempted murder. He was twenty-five feet away from the woman when he pulled the trigger.'

'He shot a woman?' said Allen. 'He shot a woman at point-blank range and you defended him?'

Fairchild waved a languid hand in the air. 'First, anyone is entitled to the best defence they can get.' He smiled. 'Or at least, the best defence they can afford. And this chap had a lot of money hidden away. And second, the point we made was that twenty-five feet isn't point-blank range. Far from it. The shot would have spread out over more than two feet and almost certainly wouldn't have been fatal. My client was something of an expert with a sawn-off so we argued that there was no intention to kill.'

'He got off?' asked Allen.

'Three years, out in just under two,' said Fairchild. 'My client was not dissatisfied.'

'I remember the case,' said Nightingale. 'The cashier was in a wheelchair, right?'

'I'm afraid so, yes,' said Fairchild, deftly filleting a kipper with a surgeon's skill. 'She was unlucky.'

'I'm not sure how much luck comes into it,' said

Nightingale. 'Your client was a career criminal and she was a cashier. He pointed a shotgun at her and pulled the trigger. He made a calculated decision. Luck is something out of our control.'

'Agreed,' said Fairchild.

'Do you think two years was a fair punishment, for what he did?'

Fairchild laughed harshly; the sound was like the bark of an attack dog. 'Fair?' he said. 'We're talking about the law. The law isn't fair. If it was fair there'd be no need for lawyers.'

Mrs McLean breezed in and picked up a glass of orange juice. 'Not shop talk again, Marcus. You have been told about that.'

Fairchild held up his knife and fork. 'I plead guilty, m'lord, and throw myself on the mercy of the court.'

'My fault, I'm afraid,' said Allen. 'I put him in the witness box.'

Mrs McLean looked at her watch. 'The beaters will be gathering in about thirty minutes,' she said.

'It'll give me time to show Jack my Purdeys,' said Jenny.

'You've got your own shotgun?'

'Guns,' she said. 'Daddy got me a pair for my eighteenth birthday.'

'Made to measure,' said McLean. 'But she barely uses them.'

Jenny pushed back her chair and stood up. 'Come on, Jack. You can give me your professional opinion.'

66

The gunroom was at the back of the house. There was a keypad by the metal door and Jenny tapped in a four-digit code before pulling it open. At the far end of the room were metal cabinets and the walls on either side were lined with racked shotguns behind thick wire mesh.

'Bloody hell, Jenny, you could start a small war with this lot.'

'Daddy has a loads of friends who like to shoot and he stores their guns for them. But most of these belong to him. Some of them are antiques. There's one somewhere that King George the Fifth used in December 1913, when he shot over a thousand birds on one day.'

'Now that's just overkill,' said Nightingale.

'One of them was a gift from the Duke of Edinburgh.'

'He's shot here?'

'Several times. And Lord Rothschild and his son, Nat. I think Daddy was sort of hoping that Nat and I might hit it off.'

'No spark?'

Jenny grinned. 'Definitely no spark.' She pointed at one of the guns. 'That was the one from Prince Phillip. It's more than two hundred years old.'

'You'd have thought he'd have run to a new one,' said Nightingale.

Jenny patted him on the back. 'I forgot – you're not much of a Royalist, are you?'

'I think the French had the right idea, pretty much.'

'Well, don't let Mummy or Daddy hear you say that, even in jest.'

She fished a key from the pocket of her jeans and unlocked one of the mesh panels. She took out a shotgun, opened it to check that the breech was clear, then handed it to Nightingale. Nightingale wasn't familiar with sporting guns but he could appreciate the quality, and the beauty, of the weapon. As a serving officer with SO19 he had spent thousands of hours with an MP5 or a Glock in his hands, but he'd never thought of either as anything more than a utilitarian tool. The gun he was holding was a work of art. The stock was gleaming wood that had been polished to perfection, the barrels were silky smooth and flawless, and the engraving was intricate and quite beautiful. He looked closely at the design and he smiled.

'Cats?'

'Not just cats. A particular cat. Rollo, the cat I had when I was a teenager.'

Nightingale broke the gun open, then closed it again and sighted down the twin barrels.

Jenny took its twin from the rack.

'You don't mind shooting birds?' he asked.

'They're bred for it, Jack. And believe me they're well looked after. Some of them are so fat they can barely fly.'

'Makes them better targets, I suppose,' he said.

Mrs McLean appeared at the door to the gunroom.

'Everyone's ready for the off,' she said. She was wearing a waterproof Barbour jacket and a tartan headscarf. 'And Jack, thank you so much for the shower gel. So thoughtful. And Bulgari is one of my favourite brands.'

Jenny shouldered the shotgun she was holding. 'Can you take that one for me?' she asked Nightingale.

'You're going to use them?'

Jenny laughed. 'Of course. They're not for decoration, pretty as they are.'

They walked together down the hall and out through the main entrance to where three Land Rovers were lined up, mud-splattered workhorses that didn't appear to have been washed in months.

'Jenny, you, Jack and Marcus go with Lachie, okay?' said Mrs McLean.

A white-bearded man in tweed plus fours was standing by one of the Land Rovers and Jenny rushed over to him. 'Lachie!' she yelped and hugged him and then kissed him on a whiskery cheek. 'Merry Christmas!'

'And Merry Christmas to you, young lady,' he said in a deep Scottish accent that suggested a life in the Highlands.

'How's Angela?'

'Her leg's playing up again and she's as grumpy as always, but what can you do? She's my wife and, as much as I'd love to have her put down, the law's agin it.'

Jenny laughed and introduced the gamekeeper to Nightingale. 'This is Lachie Kennedy,' she said. 'He's been at the house since before I was born. He worked for the family who sold the house to Daddy.'

Nightingale shook hands with the man. He was in his late sixties but he had a strong grip and he looked

Nightingale straight in the eyes as if getting the measure of him. 'You'll be the private detective from London that Jenny's always talking about?'

'I don't know what I'd do without her,' he said.

Lachie kept a tight grip on Nightingale's hand and brought his face closer. 'You take good care of her, laddie. Do you hear me?'

'Loud and clear,' said Nightingale.

'London can be a hard city at the best of times and I wouldn't want anything to happen to her,' he said. 'Apple of my eye.' He winked at Nightingale. 'Now you get in the back with Mr Fairchild so that the young lady can ride with me.'

'What do I do with this?' said Nightingale, holding up the shotgun.

'Just keep hold of it,' said Jenny.

As Jenny and Lachie got into the front of the Land Rover, Nightingale climbed into the back. Fairchild came out of the house with a battered leather gun case under his arm. He climbed into the back next to Nightingale. The gamekeeper started the engine, revved it, and then headed down the driveway.

'Okay to smoke, Lachie?' asked Fairchild.

'Only if you give me one of your Cubans,' growled the gamekeeper.

Fairchild laughed and held out a cigar. 'It's a deal,' he said.

Lachie slid the cigar inside his jacket while Fairchild lit his.

'So I'm told this is your first time at a shoot,' said Lachie, glancing over his shoulder at Nightingale.

'First time with birds, yes.'

'It'll be a driven shoot because not everyone's experienced,' said the gamekeeper. 'There'll be ten guns in all. You'll be standing about fifty paces apart and the beaters will come through the woodland so absolutely no firing towards the trees. You can load yourself or we can supply a loader, that's up to you. We have pickers-up and dogs from the village and I've got Poppy and Daisy in the back.'

The two springer spaniels in the rear of the Land Rover both barked as if they knew that Lachie was talking about them.

'How many birds do you have, Lachie?' asked Fairchild, winding down the window and blowing blue smoke through the gap. He had his gun case between his legs.

'Two thousand, ready to go,' said the gamekeeper. He turned off the driveway and drove along a rough track that meandered towards woodland in the far distance.

'Two hundred for each gun? That's a lot,' said Nightingale.

'They won't all fly, and the newcomers will have sore shoulders after the first dozen or so shots,' said Lachie.

'All the more for me,' said Fairchild.

'You do this often?' asked Nightingale.

'Every weekend, right through the season, from October the first to February the first. Rarely miss a weekend, even if I've a big case on.'

'I'm guessing you don't eat everything you kill,' said Nightingale.

Fairchild laughed. 'No, but somebody does,' he said. 'Everything I shoot gets eaten eventually.'

'That's the way it goes, sir,' said Lachie. 'Any that the guests don't want are offered to the villagers and any left over after that get sold to a butcher's in Norwich.'

Lachie pulled up near to a table covered with a red and white checked cloth on which were pots of coffee, mugs and foil-wrapped packages. 'Bacon sandwiches,' said Jenny. 'Daddy always gets hungry when he shoots.' There were half a dozen young men standing by the table munching on sandwiches and tossing the occasional titbit to three black Labradors. 'The lads are from the village,' said Jenny. 'They work as loaders and pickers-up.'

They climbed out of the Land Rover as the two other vehicles arrived. Lachie made a quick call on his mobile phone and then went over to talk to McLean, who had put on a heavy jacket and a flat cap and was carrying a weighty gun case.

McLean opened the case, took out a shotgun and broke it over his arm. 'All right, everybody, the beaters are in place. Five minutes to go. Lachie will put you at your stations – he's in charge. Protective glasses and ear protectors are available but it's your choice as to whether or not you wear them.'

Lachie took the group across the grass and showed them where to stand. Jenny was on Nightingale's right and Fairchild on his left. They both had leather bags filled with cartridges.

'I'll load for you, if you like,' Lachie said to Nightingale. 'Give you a bit of free advice too, if you want.'

'I'm still not sure if I'm going to be shooting,' said Nightingale.

'Let's see how it goes.' His mobile rang and he took the call, then waved over at McLean. 'Everyone's in position, sir!' he shouted.

'Well done, Lachie,' said McLean, shouldering his shotgun. 'Let's go.'

67

Nightingale lit a cigarette and watched the hundredth bird of the morning get blown out of the sky with a whoop of triumph from Marcus Fairchild, who had taken to shooting while keeping his cigar clamped between his teeth. Fairchild had two teenagers loading for him and they could barely keep up with his rate of fire.

Over to his right, Jenny was taking a more sedate approach, loading her own gun and taking time between each shot. She smiled over at him and waved. He waved back.

'You sure you don't want to shoot, sir?' asked Lachie, standing at his shoulder. He was holding Jenny's Purdey over his arm. There were two cartridges in the breech but Nightingale had yet to fire the weapon.

'Really, I'm not a big fan of shooting birds,' said Nightingale.

'They're bred for it,' said the gamekeeper. 'We hatch them, we rear them, we feed and we water them. They have a happier life than if they were in the wild.'

'Even so . . .' said Nightingale. 'It seems a bit mismatched.'

'Mismatched?' said Lachie, frowning. 'What do you mean?'

Two more birds fell to the ground close by. One was flapping around, badly injured, its feathers drenched in blood.

'They're not shooting back,' said Nightingale. 'That's seems a bit unfair, don't you think?'

Lachie snapped the shotgun shut and kept the barrels pointing at the ground. 'Fairness doesn't enter into it, sir. They're birds.'

'They are indeed,' said Nightingale. 'But then so am I, in name anyway.' He blew smoke up into the air and the wind whipped it away.

Fairchild was shooting like a machine, with a shot every three seconds.

'And this is one fine gun,' said Lachie. 'Handmade for Miss McLean. Do you have any idea how much a pair of made-to-measure Purdeys costs?'

'A lot.'

Lachie chuckled. 'Aye, a hell of a lot. Be a shame to bring it out and not fire it.' He held the shotgun out to Nightingale.

Nightingale shook his head. 'You have a go, Lachie,' he said. 'Show me how it's done.'

Lachie's eyes hardened, and then went blank. 'Your sister's going to Hell, Jack Nightingale,' he said, his voice flat and lifeless. Then in one smooth motion he swung the shotgun around so that the barrels were pointing under his chin and pulled the trigger with the thumb of his right hand. Nightingale fell back into the mud as Lachie's head exploded into a shower of blood, brain and bone fragments.

68

Nightingale lay on his back, his ears ringing Fairchild appeared, standing over him and looking down. 'My God, man, what happened?' he asked. He held out his hand and pulled Nightingale to his feet. There was blood on Nightingale's raincoat. 'Are you hurt?'

Nightingale shook his head. One by one the guns fell silent though pheasants still flapped overhead.

Marc Allen and Danny Smith were staring down at Lachie's body. McLean had his arms outstretched and was telling Sally Allen and Wendy Bushell to go back to the Land Rovers, while Jenny's mother was hugging Lesley Smith.

McLean shouted over to the boys who had been loading for Fairchild. 'Rob, Peter, go and tell the beaters to stop. Be quick now.' The two teenagers hurried towards the woodland.

Jenny was standing, frozen to the spot, but then she jerked as if she had been stung and ran over to where Lachie lay in the mud. She screamed when she saw that his face had been blown away. Allen put his arm around her and led her a short distance away from the body. Tears were streaming down her face.

McLean strode over, his gun broken over his arm. 'What the hell happened, Jack?' he asked.

'He did it himself,' said Nightingale. 'With Jenny's gun.'

'Nonsense,' snapped McLean. 'Lachie was far too experienced to do something like that. Who was holding the gun?'

'He was. He just . . . I don't know. It happened so quickly. He was talking to me and then . . .'

'Accidents happen,' said McLean.

'It wasn't a bloody accident,' said Nightingale. 'He turned the gun on himself.' He pointed at the shotgun, which was lying across the gamekeeper's ankles. 'How else do you think that got there?'

McLean went over to look at the body. Nightingale glanced around for his cigarette. It was lying in a pool of mud so he took out his pack of Marlboro and lit a new one.

Fairchild joined McLean and the two men stood staring down.

'Did you see what happened?' McLean asked the lawyer.

Marcus shook his head. 'I was too busy watching the birds,' he said.

'This is a nightmare,' said McLean. He walked back to Nightingale, reaching inside his jacket. He pulled out a silver hip flask, unscrewed the top and drank. He offered it to Nightingale, but Nightingale shook his head. Jenny walked over and took the flask from her father without saying anything.

'He was just talking to me, then he put the gun under his chin and pulled the trigger,' said Nightingale.

'What did he say?' asked McLean.

Nightingale looked across at Jenny and saw the look

of panic in her eyes, the flask still close to her lips. 'He was asking me if I wanted to shoot and I said that I was happy just watching,' he said. Jenny took another swig from the flask before her father reached over and took it from her. 'That's all he said before he . . .' Nightingale left the sentence unfinished.

'What do we do, Jack?' asked McLean, putting the flask away. 'You were a policeman. Do we call nine nine nine? Do we ask for an ambulance?' He took a deep breath and exhaled. 'You know, this is the first time I've seen a violent death.' He grimaced. 'Not that I saw it. I heard it. I mean . . .'

'Yeah, I know what you mean,' said Nightingale. 'You should move everyone away from the body. You can call the local police and tell them there's been a suicide. They'll inform the coroner.'

'We just leave him there?' said McLean. 'Can't we cover him up?'

'Best not to,' said Nightingale. 'Once the police see the scene as it is they'll confirm it was suicide. As will the coroner. Then you can get an undertaker to come. His wife's at home, right? Angela?'

McLean nodded. 'Their cottage is on the edge of the estate. I'll go and tell her myself.' He ran a hand over his face. 'She'll be devastated. My God, Jack, how do I tell her?'

Nightingale shrugged, not knowing what to say.

'I'll get Melissa to come with me,' said McLean.

'Where are the nearest police?' asked Nightingale.

'There's a local bobby in the next village. I'm not sure if he'll be working on Christmas Day.' Jenny came over to her father and put her arms around him. He hugged her.

'Call him anyway,' said Nightingale. 'If he's not available

then there'll be a message saying who is. It's not a matter for the emergency services.'

'And no ambulance?'

Nightingale shook his head. 'They won't be able to touch the body until the coroner has pronounced death and the cops have examined the scene. And by then there's no point in taking it to hospital.'

'I'll call an undertaker, let them know what's happening,' said McLean. 'Thanks, Jack. Lucky you were around.'

McLean hugged Jenny again and then went over to the shooters who were still standing by Lachie's body.

Jenny sighed. 'What do you think, Jack? Do you think he was lucky you were around?'

'Jenny . . .'

'What did he say? What did he say before he killed himself?'

'Not here,' said Nightingale.

'What do you mean, not here?'

Nightingale flashed a warning look towards the rest of the shooting party, who were gathered together in a group about twenty feet away from the body.

'Don't use them as an excuse,' she hissed.

Nightingale walked away, drawing on his cigarette. She hurried after him. 'He said what you think he said,' he muttered.

'I've known Lachie since I was born, Jack. He wouldn't kill himself.'

'He just did.' He looked across at her. 'What do you think, Jenny? Do you think I killed him?'

'Of course not,' she said. 'But it wasn't Lachie's decision. Something made him do it.'

'Something? Or someone?'

'I don't know. But whatever it was that forced Lachie to do what he did, it's come to my family's home, Jack. It's come here.'

Nightingale took a lungful of smoke and then exhaled slowly. 'What do you want me to do, Jenny?'

She shook her head. 'Something. Anything. Jack. It could be my mother next. Or my father.'

'Or you?' said Nightingale quietly.

'Yes, Jack. Or me.' She glared at him. 'Damn you, Jack, you have to do something about this.'

'What? What can I do?'

'Something. You have to make this stop. Lachie didn't know you from Adam, but whoever or whatever is after you doesn't care. They'll kill anybody, just to . . .'

'Just to what, Jenny? What does anyone gain by him giving me a message and blowing his head off?'

'That's what you have to find out.'

'How?'

'I don't know, Jack. But you have to get this sorted. We can't go on like this.'

69

Nightingale left Edmund House first thing on Boxing Day. Jenny had insisted that he ate breakfast, though he had no appetite. She'd asked him to stay for at least one more day but Nightingale knew he had to go. She had been right when she said that people were dying because of his sister, and until he did something they would continue to die.

Two uniformed policemen had arrived in a car from Norwich about thirty minutes after McLean had made his phone call. They took a cursory look at the body and then phoned the coroner, who arrived within the hour, pronounced Lachie dead and said he was satisfied the death was a suicide and that there would be no need for a post-mortem. McLean phoned a local firm of under-takers and by early afternoon the body had been taken away.

The shoot was abandoned and most of the guests remained in their rooms during the afternoon. There was a forced frivolity at dinner but by ten o'clock most of the guests had called it a night. No one mentioned Lachie or what had happened to him.

Jenny's mother and father had been in the dining room when they'd eaten breakfast so Nightingale didn't get a chance to tell her what he planned to do, but he phoned her as soon as he got back to his flat in Bayswater.

'I want to know whether my sister killed those children or not.'

'What's that got to do with what's happening?' she asked.

'I think I have a way to save her soul and get her out of Rampton, but first I need to know.'

'She confessed, remember?'

'Something's not right. Proserpine didn't know what Robyn had done.'

'So?'

'So maybe my sister didn't kill those kids. If she was a serial killer, wouldn't Proserpine know?'

'How the hell would I know, Jack? How would anyone know what they know?'

'I'm just saying that maybe my sister didn't kill those kids.'

'She was found beside one of the bodies with a knife in her hand and she confessed.'

'Yeah, well, I've been found beside a body with a knife in my hand and I'm not a serial killer.'

'That was different, Jack.'

'Maybe it is and maybe it isn't,' said Nightingale. 'And maybe she only thinks she killed them.'

'She's in a mental hospital being studied by expert psychiatrists. Don't you think they'd have found out if she was delusional? What am I saying? She's probably in there because she's delusional.'

'She pleaded guilty and was sentenced,' said Nightingale. 'They're not interested in finding out whether or not she's guilty; they just want to cure her if they can.'

'And what are you saying? That she didn't do it but somehow thinks she did?'

'I want to try to get her to remember,' said Nightingale.

'And just how are you going to do that?'

'I was hoping that your friend Barbara might help.'

'Hypnotic regression? Is that what you're thinking of trying?'

'It might work. And, even if it doesn't, Barbara would get one hell of a paper out of it.'

'It won't be any good as evidence,' said Jenny.

'It's not about evidence. It's about me knowing whether or not she did it. Can you be a sweetie and text me her number?'

'You're going to call her today? Boxing Day?'

'Strike while the iron's hot, that's my motto.'

'No, your motto is that everyone has to stop whatever they're doing when Jack Nightingale needs something. Just try to show her some consideration, Jack.'

Nightingale ended the call and went over to his sitting-room window. He stared down at the street below. Three questions. Three killers. One had already tried and he didn't know when the other two would attack, or where, or who they would be. Nightingale wasn't fearful; he'd been threatened many times while he was a police officer. But he was apprehensive and he didn't like having to keep looking over his shoulder.

He took out his pack of Marlboro and lit a cigarette. A young black couple walked down Inverness Terrace, arm in arm. They stopped and kissed under his window and Nightingale turned away, not wanting to intrude on their romance. His mobile beeped and he looked at the screen. He jumped when he saw the message:

YOUR SISTER IS GOING TO HELL, JACK NIGHTINGALE.

The phone slipped from his fingers and fell to the carpet, then bounced under the coffee table. Nightingale cursed and got down on his knees to retrieve it. He sat back on his heels and checked the screen. It was Barbara's phone number, and a smiley face.

70

Nightingale phoned Rampton Secure Hospital first thing on Monday morning and spoke to Dr Keller, who was surprisingly amenable to Barbara visiting Nightingale's sister.

'Barbara McEvoy? I've read some of her work,' the doctor said. 'How do you know her?'

'Friend of a friend,' said Nightingale. 'I told her about Robyn and she said she'd be interested in meeting her. I think she thought there might be a paper in it for one of the scientific journals.'

'I've been thinking of using some sort of hypnotherapy myself, but frankly it's not my field and there isn't enough money in my budget to bring anyone in.'

'Dr McEvoy said she'd do it pro bono,' said Nightingale. He was bending the truth because he hadn't discussed a fee with Barbara, but it sealed the deal and Dr Keller said they could visit anytime on Tuesday.

They arrived at the hospital just after eleven o'clock in the morning. 'It's an imposing building, isn't it?' said Barbara, as she parked her VW. She'd made it a condition of going that they went in her car not his. 'The Victorians really knew how to do public buildings, didn't they?'

'It gives me the willies,' said Nightingale. 'Same with prisons. I always have this nagging fear that they're not going to let me out.'

'Sounds like a guilty conscience,' said Barbara, getting out of the car.

'I think it's more an irrational fear,' said Nightingale. He flipped up the collar of his raincoat as a few flecks of snow landed on his shoulders.

'Like the way you don't like lifts?'

'Jenny told you, huh?'

'We could talk about it some time,' said Barbara. 'Nail down if it's the heights or the enclosed spaces that are worrying you.'

'It's neither. It's lifts,' said Nightingale.

'Safest form of transport on the planet,' said Barbara.

'That's only because of the elevator conspiracy.'

Barbara wagged her finger at him. 'I'd be very careful about talking like that when we're inside,' she said. 'Just in case.'

Dr Keller was waiting to meet them when they walked out of the holding area. He smiled broadly as he shook hands with Barbara. 'I'm so pleased to meet you, Dr McEvoy,' he said. He had taken off his white coat and was wearing a tweed jacket with scuffed leather patches on the elbows and a green and black checked flannel shirt with a brown knitted tie.

'Barbara, please,' she said.

Dr Keller shook hands so energetically that his spectacles slid down his nose. He pushed them back up and shook hands with Nightingale. 'You've heard about what happened to Robyn's parents?'

Nightingale feigned ignorance and shook his head.

'The father drowned his wife in the bath and then cut his own throat. Horrible business.'

'Robyn's been told, has she?'

Dr Keller nodded. 'The police were here last week.'

'How did she take it?'

'It's hard to tell with Robyn. She's very good at disguising her emotions, those emotions that she has.'

'Did the police say anything, about what had happened?' asked Nightingale.

'Just that it was a murder-suicide and that Robyn had to be informed. They asked me if I'd do it.'

'And she was okay?'

'She seemed to be, yes. You have to remember that after she was arrested her parents cut off all contact. She was dead to them and I think it was reciprocated.' He rubbed his hands together. 'Anyway, to the matter in hand.' He smiled ingratiatingly at Barbara. 'I wasn't sure where you'd want to do it,' he said.

'Somewhere quiet, preferably,' said Barbara. 'And it's generally best if the subject can lie down.'

'A sofa?'

'A sofa would be perfect,' said Barbara.

'That's what I thought,' said Dr Keller. 'I don't have a sofa in my office but I've arranged to borrow a colleague's.'

He took them along a corridor and up a flight of stairs to another corridor. The office was halfway down. Dr Keller knocked on the door and opened it, then had a quick look to make sure that it was empty before ushering them in. The office was lined with books and files and there was a coffee table piled high with psychiatric journals. The window was covered with thick wire mesh and barred, and underneath it was a red three-seater sofa.

Dr Keller looked at his watch. 'It's a bank holiday and Dr Muller is away today so you can use her office as long as you want,' he said. 'How long do you think it will take?'

'Two hours is generally long enough for a session,' said Barbara, putting her briefcase on the coffee table. She opened it and took out a small digital recorder.

Dr Keller took her coat and hung it on the back of the door. He had a small transceiver clipped to his belt and he used it to tell the hospital's control centre that they were to send Robyn Reynolds to Dr Muller's office. Five minutes later there was the crackle of a radio in the corridor followed by a knock at the door. Dr Keller opened it. Robyn was there, flanked by two uniformed guards, both female. She was wearing the same grey polo-neck sweater and red Converse tennis shoes as the last time Nightingale had seen her, with baggy blue jeans.

She smiled at Nightingale. 'Can't keep away, can you?' she said.

Nightingale wasn't sure how to greet her. A handshake seemed too formal and he didn't know her well enough to hug her. She seemed to have the same problem. She took a step towards him and then smiled awkwardly and shrugged.

'I'm sorry about your parents,' he said. 'Your adoptive parents.'

'I'm not,' she said. 'Do I care that they're dead?' She shook her head emphatically. 'I couldn't care less, and that's God's own truth.' She smiled brightly. 'So how was your Christmas?'

'Not good, actually,' he said. 'Yours?'

'Every day is pretty much the same in here,' she said. 'I was sort of expecting a card.'

'Sorry,' said Nightingale. He introduced Barbara. 'Did Dr Keller tell you what we want to do?'

'Hypnotise me to get me to give up smoking?' She laughed. 'Joke.'

'It's not really hypnosis,' said Barbara. 'It's more about putting you in a deep state of relaxation so that you can remember what happened to you.'

'Maybe I don't want to remember,' she said.

'That's true,' said Barbara.

Dr Keller thanked the two guards. 'We'll have to stay outside the door,' said one.

'I understand,' said Dr Keller. 'Mr Nightingale and I will be waiting in my office so please show Dr McEvoy there when she's finished.'

'Robyn, why don't you sit on the sofa and relax?' said Barbara.

'Are you going to be swinging a watch or something?' asked Robyn as she sat down.

Barbara smiled. 'It's not like that, Robyn,' she said. 'I'm just going to talk to you.' She picked up the recorder and pulled a chair over so that it was next to the sofa. 'Gentlemen, if you could leave us ladies alone,' she said.

Dr Keller took Nightingale back to his office. He explained that he had rounds to do and left him alone with a copy of the *Daily Telegraph* and a cup of coffee for an hour and a half, then came back and made small talk until there was a knock at the door. It was Barbara.

'All done,' she said.

'How did it go?' asked Dr Keller.

'It was interesting,' said Barbara. 'I think it would

probably be best if I have the session transcribed and send it to you.'

Dr Keller pushed his spectacles higher up his nose with the forefinger of his right hand. 'Would you like some tea? We could have a brief chat.'

Barbara looked at her watch. 'We really have to get back to London,' she said. 'Maybe next time.' She extended her hand and Dr Keller shook it, less energetically than when they'd first met.

He walked them back to the exit and waved as they left the holding area.

As they walked out of the main door Barbara put her head close to Nightingale's ear. 'You are bloody well not going to believe this,' she whispered.

71

Nightingale carried the two glasses over to the corner table where Barbara was fiddling with her digital voice recorder. 'White wine spritzer,' he said, putting the glass down in front of her. He sat down and raised his glass to her. The barmaid had started pouring his Corona beer into a glass before he could say anything, even though in his experience it always tasted better straight from the bottle. Barbara ignored him and concentrated on the recorder so Nightingale shrugged and sipped his beer.

'The first hour or so was mainly about putting her at ease,' she said. 'It was quite hard to get her under. It was as if she was blocking me.'

'She didn't want to be hypnotised?'

Barbara shook her head. 'No, she wasn't fighting me. It was as if there was already some sort of hypnotic control at work. I had to override that before I could get her down to a lower level.'

'Someone else had hypnotised her before?'

'That's what I think. And that's a big problem because we'll have to differentiate between the real memories she has and those that are the result of suggestion.'

'I don't follow you,' said Nightingale.

'Listen to this, first,' she said. She looked at the screen

on the side of the recorder. 'Okay, this is where we were after eighty minutes,' she said. 'I'd taken her back to the church where she was found with the dead boy.' She looked around to make sure that there was no one else within earshot. A middle-aged couple were tucking into Shepherd's pie at the next table. Barbara opened her briefcase and took out a pair of earphones. 'Use these. We don't want to scare the natives,' she said. She plugged them into the recorder.

Nightingale slotted the earphones into his ears and pressed 'play'. It started mid-conversation and it took him a couple of seconds to realise that it was his sister speaking.

'It's dark and I can hear the engine.'

'Why is it dark, Robyn?'

'There's something over my eyes.'

'What? A blindfold?'

'A bag. It's cloth and I can breathe but it's hot. I feel dizzy.'

'Are you dizzy because of the bag over your head?'

'I'm not sure. It's hard to think. It's like I'm drunk.'

'But you haven't been drinking?'

'I don't think so. I can't remember.'

'Try to remember,' said Barbara.

Nightingale sipped his beer and settled back in his chair. Barbara was watching him. 'Okay?' she mouthed. Nightingale nodded.

'I haven't had anything to drink but I think they gave me an injection. In my leg.'

'Why do you think that, Robyn?'

'Something hurt me. Like a pinprick. Then my leg went numb.'

'Okay, now tell me what happens when the van stops.'

'I can hear voices outside then the doors open and they take me out. My feet crunch on gravel. I slip but they're holding onto me so that I won't fall. It's cold and it's raining.'

'You've still got the bag over your head?'

'Yes.'

'What happens next, Robyn?'

'I can hear a door opening. I'm not walking on gravel any more. There's something hard under my feet. I'm inside. I can hear people around me. A lot of people. They're muttering, like they're praying.'

Nightingale picked up his glass and took another sip as he listened. He had a bad feeling in the pit of his stomach as he was fairly sure he knew what was coming next.

'Can you hear what they're saying, Robyn?'

'Yes, but it's not English. I don't know what it is.'

It's Latin, thought Nightingale. That's why she can't understand them.

'What's happening now, Robyn?' asked Barbara.

'A door – there's a door closing. A big wooden door, it sounds like.'

A church door, thought Nightingale. A church in Clapham.

'Talk me through it, Robyn,' said Barbara. 'Keep telling me what's happening.'

'They're making me walk forward. They're holding me by the arms. And the chatting is getting louder, like a buzzing in my ears. Something's happening to my hood. They're taking it off.'

'That's good, Robyn. Tell me what you see.'

'People,' said Robyn. 'Lots of people. They're wearing

black clothes. No, not clothes. Like cloaks with hoods. Long cloaks. I can't see if they're men or women because the hoods hide their faces.'

Nightingale looked over at Barbara. She was watching him intently. He nodded at her and she nodded back.

'I'm in front of an altar,' said Robyn. 'But there isn't a cross there. It's covered with a white sheet. Oh my God.'

'What?' said Barbara. 'What is it, Robyn? What have you seen?'

'A boy. They've got a boy. Who is he? Why's he here?'

Timmy Robertson, thought Nightingale. Little Timmy Robertson.

'They're putting him on the altar and holding him down. He's struggling but one of them has put their hand over his mouth. No, no, no!'

'What, Robyn? What's happening?'

'A knife. One of them has a knife. No, please don't. He's just a boy. Don't! No!'

Nightingale's stomach lurched and then Robyn screamed so loudly that he winced. He pressed the 'stop' button and took the earphones out. 'They murdered the boy,' he said. 'They murdered him in front of her.'

Barbara nodded. 'Assuming that she's telling the truth.'

Nightingale frowned. 'Why would she lie?'

'It's not about lying,' said Barbara. 'It's more mis-remembering. That's why hypnotic regression has to be done by experts. In the wrong hands it's a dangerous tool because it can produce false memories, memories that aren't real but feel real to the subject.' Barbara gestured at the recorder. 'Listen to the end,' she said. 'There's more.'

72

Nightingale put the earphones back in and pressed 'play'. Robyn's voice echoed in his ears.

'There's so much blood,' she said. 'There's blood everywhere. I don't want to look.'

'Breathe deeply, Robyn. Nice and deeply. Everything is okay and you're safe. You're just remembering what happened. No one can hurt you. Do you understand?'

'Yes,' said Robyn.

'Can you breathe deeply for a while, and feel your heart slow down?'

There was silence for several seconds.

'Are you okay now?' asked Barbara.

'I'm okay,' replied Robyn.

'Tell me what you can see,' said Barbara. 'Imagine you are watching it on a television screen. Can you do that? You're not really there; you're watching it on television. Do you understand?'

'I understand,' said Robyn.

'So tell me what you can see.'

'The blood is dripping onto the floor. I can see the boy's eyes and they're wide open but he must be dead because there's so much blood. Everyone is moving closer and they're talking but I can't understand what they're saying. One of them is touching the blood and holding up his hand.'

'Is it a man or a woman?'

'I can't see because they all have hoods over their faces. No, it's a man. His hands are big. Now he's touching someone else on the head, putting blood on them.'

'What do you mean, Robyn? He's marking their forehead with blood? Is that what he's doing?'

'Yes,' said Robyn. 'Now he's doing it to someone else. To all of them. Now they've all got blood on their foreheads.'

'Where are you, Robyn?'

'In the middle of the church, facing the altar. There's someone on either side of me, holding me. Now the man is putting his hand in the boy's blood again.'

Nightingale heard his sister breathing loudly, fast and hard.

'Relax, Robyn, no one can hear you,' said Barbara. 'Stay calm. Deep breaths.'

Robyn's breathing steadied.

'Now, Robyn, tell me what's happening.'

'The man is putting blood on my face. He's saying something but the words don't make any sense and his voice is deep, like I'm hearing it through water. He's putting his face really close to mine but I still can't understand what he's saying.'

'You're doing very well, Robyn. Keep calm. Nothing can happen to you. You're safe. Now tell me what's happening.'

'They're moving me towards the altar. My legs feel so heavy and I can't feel my arms. I just want to sleep.'

'Why are they taking you to the altar?'

'I don't know. Some of the people are leaving. There're just the ones holding me and the man with the blood. He's got a knife now.'

'Is it the knife he used to kill the child?'

'Yes. I think so.'

'Is there blood on the knife?'

'Yes. Yes there is.'

'All right, Robyn, well done. We're almost finished. Tell me what's happening now.'

'They're putting something in my hand.'

'What? What is it, Robyn?'

'The knife. Oh my God, it's the knife. Oh my God.' The words were tumbling over each other.

'Robyn, it's okay. Go back to looking at the television screen. You're not there but you can see everything. You're quite safe.'

'I'm scared.'

'There's no need to be scared, Robyn. Everything's fine. I'm here with you. Take deep breaths. We're going to stop soon. Just a few more minutes. Now, what's happening? Is the knife still in your hand?'

'Yes.'

'So tell me what's happening, Robyn. Tell me what you can see.'

'I'm on the altar. Next to the boy. His blood is all over me. It's still warm. There's so much of it. And I'm so tired. I just want to sleep.'

'What about the man, is he still there?'

'He's talking to me. He's staring at me and talking to me and I just want to sleep.'

'All right, Robyn. We're going to stop soon. Just one more thing. This man, can you see his face?'

'Yes,' whispered Robyn.

'Describe him to me,' said Barbara.

'He's as old as my father. Almost sixty, I think. He has long grey hair and his nose is red, as if he drinks too much. And hair in his ears. I told him he should use clippers.'

'Told him? What do you mean, you told him?'

'I said he should clip the hairs in his ears.'

'When did you tell him?'

'When he came to see me.'

Nightingale frowned, not understanding what he was hearing. She had been held in the van with a hood over her head, so she hadn't been able to say anything to anyone. When had she had a conversation with the man?

'Robyn, do you know this man?' asked Barbara. 'Do you know his name?'

'Yes,' said Robyn.

'Who is he?' asked Barbara.

'Marcus,' said Robyn. 'Marcus Fairchild.'

73

'That's impossible,' said Jenny, pressing the 'stop' button. 'There's been a mistake. Some sort of horrible mistake.' She picked up her glass of white wine and drained it. They were sitting around the table in her kitchen. 'Marcus couldn't . . .' She reached for the bottle of Pinot Grigio and refilled her glass.

'Steady,' said Nightingale.

'Steady?' hissed Jenny. 'This from the man who reaches for a bottle whenever he's under any pressure?' She gulped down more wine as Nightingale raised his hands in surrender.

'Jenny, as I said to Jack, there is a possibility that this is some sort of false memory.'

'Bloody right it is,' said Jenny.

'But I have to say, based on my clinical experience, she's relating events that she believes actually happened.'

'Barbara, what are you saying? You know Marcus. Do you really believe . . .' She closed her eyes and grunted in frustration.

Barbara reached over and put her hand on Jenny's. 'It's Robyn describing what she believes happened to her. Don't get angry at me.'

'I'm not,' said Jenny. 'I'm not angry. I'm just frustrated

because Marcus Fairchild couldn't possibly have done something like that. I've known him since I was a kid. He's known Daddy for donkey's years. Now you're saying that he killed a boy in some sort of ritual ceremony and then framed Jack's sister.'

'You don't always know a person as much as you think,' said Nightingale. 'Most serial killers have parents, or siblings, spouses or children. And usually the family has absolutely no idea what they've been up to.'

'He's not a killer,' said Jenny. 'He wouldn't kill anyone, let alone a child.'

'I'm not saying he is. I'm just saying that if he was, he'd hardly be likely to let you know his true nature.'

'That's the same thing,' said Jenny. 'You think that he murdered that boy and framed your sister. And what about the other children she murdered? Are you saying he killed them, too?'

Nightingale pointed at the recorder. 'It's not me saying anything,' he said. 'It's Robyn who was there. She saw it.'

'She thinks she saw it,' corrected Barbara. 'She's telling us what she remembers, but she might be mis-remembering. We've a lot of work to do before we know for sure one way or another.'

'How do you know that your sister's not making this up?' asked Jenny. 'Maybe she sees this as a way of getting out.'

'That's not going to happen anytime soon,' said Barbara. 'Memories released by hypnotic regression aren't evidence.'

'But the evidence that there is could all have been planted on her,' said Nightingale. 'And if what she's now remembering is true then clearly Fairchild framed her.'

'You can't take this seriously,' said Jenny, exasperated. 'She's in an insane asylum, for God's sake.'

'Secure mental hospital,' said Barbara.

'Yeah, a rose by any other name,' said Jenny. 'Rampton's a nut-house and she's a nut. Courts don't convict serial killers by mistake.'

'They didn't convict her, Jenny,' said Nightingale. 'She pleaded guilty. And the thing is, I think she believes she did it. She's not in there shouting that she's innocent, is she?'

Jenny didn't answer and folded her arms defensively.

Nightingale looked across at Barbara. 'What she said while she was under, does she remember it now? Now that she's awake?'

'She was never asleep,' said Barbara. 'She wasn't in a trance; she was just in a very relaxed state. It was being so relaxed that allowed the memory to come to the surface. But after the session, the memory will go back to where it was. After several sessions she might start to remember properly, but at the moment it's more like a dream than a memory.'

'So she still thinks she killed those children?'

'I didn't ask her,' said Barbara.

'This is ridiculous,' said Jenny. 'Why would anyone admit to murders they didn't commit?'

'Maybe she was hypnotised into believing she did it,' said Nightingale.

'By Marcus, is that what you're saying? First he's a killer and now he's a magician.'

'Jenny, I know you don't want to believe this, but you can't ignore it just because Fairchild is a family friend.'

'I've known Marcus for years; you met your sister for

the first time two weeks ago. Why should I believe her over him?'

'You heard her. Do you think she's making it up?'

Jenny put her hands around her wine glass. 'I think she's in a mental hospital for a reason,' she said. 'I don't see how you can believe anything that she says.'

Nightingale stood up. 'I need some fresh air,' he said.

'Whenever you say that the first thing you do is light a cigarette,' said Jenny.

'I meant that maybe you need some fresh air,' he said. 'I'll get out of your hair.' He patted her on the shoulder. 'You sleep on it. We'll talk it through tomorrow.' He smiled at Barbara. 'Take care of her, yeah?'

'Always.'

74

Nightingale was surprised to find the office door unlocked when he arrived on Wednesday morning, and was even more surprised to find Jenny sitting at her desk. 'I didn't think you were coming in until the New Year,' he said.

'I was bored at home,' she said. 'And I wanted an early start on your receipts for the taxman.'

He looked at her computer screen and smiled. 'And to play on Facebook,' he said.

'I'm checking Bronwyn's Facebook page,' she said.

'Any joy?'

'Sixteen people I've never heard of want to be my friends,' she said.

'It's your sunny disposition,' he said, sitting down on the edge of her desk. 'Are you okay?'

Jenny shrugged. 'I'm confused more than anything. About what happened to Lachie. About what happened to you. The whole thing.'

'You're probably in shock, you know that?'

'Post traumatic stress disorder, is that what you mean? I'm fine, Jack.'

'Do you want to talk about it?'

She laughed. 'To you? And that would help me how?'

'I was going to suggest you talk it through with Barbara.'

Jenny sighed. 'Maybe you're right,' she said. 'But I can't tell her everything, can I? She'll think I'm crazy.'

'What happened to Lachie, you could talk that through with her.' He held up his hands. 'It was just a thought. But whatever you decide, let me know when Lachie's funeral is. I'd like to go.'

'Okay. And, speaking of funerals, I had a phone call from someone telling me that your aunt and uncle's funeral is this afternoon.' She gave him a piece of paper on which she'd written the name of a church.

'Who phoned?'

'It was a woman. She didn't say. I assumed she was from the undertakers. She had all the details.'

Nightingale looked at the note and nodded. 'It's the church where my parents are buried,' he said. 'Up in Manchester.'

'Are you going?'

'It's a bit short notice,' he said, looking at his watch. 'And they say it's going to snow. I don't fancy driving the MGB in the snow.'

'I'll come with you,' she said. 'We can take the Audi. They're your aunt and uncle, Jack. You should be there.'

He looked at the note again. 'We'll have to leave in a couple of hours to get there in time.'

'No problem,' said Jenny. 'There's not much work on.' She gestured at her computer. 'And Caernarfon Craig's gone quiet.'

Nightingale rubbed his chin thoughtfully. 'A visit to a church couldn't hurt, could it?'

75

The outside of the church was old, with ivy-covered stone walls and a moss-spotted slate roof. There were modern touches, though, including wire mesh over the windows, anti-climbing paint on the drain-pipes and a CCTV camera covering the main entrance. At some point the interior had been modernised on a budget, with cheap pine pews and a carpet that was already wearing thin in places. There was only one other person sitting in the pews, a middle-aged woman at the front on the right, curly ginger hair tucked behind her ears.

'Not much of a turnout,' muttered Nightingale. He turned to look at Jenny but she had vanished, then he realised that she was kneeling down, crossing herself. 'What are you doing?' he whispered.

'It's a church, Jack. This is what you do.' She stood up. 'Come on, sit down.'

They moved to the left and sat down. Directly in front of them were two wooden coffins, plain varnished teak with imitation brass handles. There was a small wreath of white flowers on top of each.

'I guess they didn't have many relatives?' whispered Jenny.

'Linda's side of the family are mainly out in Australia,' said Nightingale. 'And they never had kids.'

A young vicar in black vestments walked out of a side door and strode up to the pulpit The service was mercifully short: a sermon and two prayers and it was over.

The vicar came over and introduced himself with a handshake that was as soft as an old woman's and then hurried away. As Nightingale and Jenny headed out of the church, the ginger-haired woman who had been sitting at the front walked over. She wearing a fawn belted raincoat and carrying a black leather shoulder bag.

'Are you Jack Nightingale?' she asked.

'In the flesh,' said Nightingale. 'Are you a friend of my aunt and uncle's?'

The woman shook her head and took a small black wallet from her coat pocket. She flipped it open and flashed her warrant card. 'Detective Sergeant Janet Bethel,' she said. 'Greater Manchester Police.'

'So you're not a family friend, then?' said Nightingale.

'I was the investigating officer,' she said, ignoring his attempt at sarcasm and putting the card away. 'Not that there was much to investigate. I wish all my cases were as clear-cut.' She grimaced. 'I'm sorry, I didn't mean to sound so callous. It's been a rough few weeks.'

'It's not a problem,' said Nightingale. 'I know what it's like.'

'Of course – you were in the Job, weren't you?'

'In the Met. In another life.'

'And you found the bodies?'

'That's right. I'm surprised we haven't met before. I spoke to the uniforms at the scene but no one from CID ever followed up.'

'My boss didn't see the need,' said Bethel. 'It was a clear case of murder-suicide. Her blood all over the axe, along with his fingerprints and DNA; blood spatter all over him, fibres from the rope on his hands, the rope that he'd used to hang himself with. You didn't have to watch much *CSI* to work out what happened. I said it was my case but really all I did was sign off on the paperwork.'

'So, forgive me for asking, but why are you here?' asked Nightingale.

'It's just something I do,' said the detective.

'Nothing to do with the case?'

'Like I said, the case is closed,' said Bethel. 'I just feel . . . it's difficult to say. The fact that I'm the investigating officer means there's a connection, and the funeral is part of that.' She forced a smile. 'It sounds crazy, I know.'

'No, it doesn't,' said Jenny. 'I think it's a lovely thing to do. It shows that you care. And in this day and age that's a rare quality.' She held out her hand. 'Jenny McLean,' she said. 'I'm afraid Jack isn't great with the social graces.' They shook hands.

'I thought there'd be more people here,' said Nightingale, looking back at the church. 'I mean, I know Uncle Tommy didn't have any family other than me and Linda's family is mainly in Australia, but even so . . .'

'I asked the vicar about that,' said Bethel. 'They were well liked in the area and several of the parishioners had asked when the funeral was, but they all backed off when they found out it was a joint funeral. I think they were a bit loath to be saying prayers for your uncle, after what he did.' She looked at her wristwatch, a cheap black Casio. 'I must be going,' she said. 'The boss never likes me to be long at these things.'

'Well, thank you for coming, anyway,' said Nightingale.

'No problem,' said Bethel. 'You're going back to London?'

Nightingale nodded. 'There's not much to keep me here,' he said. 'Do you know what's happening to the house and everything?'

'It's messy,' she said. 'They both had wills but she died first so everything passed to him. And I gather his will left everything to her. I don't think he expected to outlive her. The lawyers will work it out, I'm sure, after they've taken their cut. Why don't you give me your card and I'll call you if anything crops up?' Nightingale fished a business card out of his wallet and gave it to her. She took it and thanked him. 'And I'm sorry about your loss,' she said.

Nightingale and Jenny watched the detective walk away down the path. 'She's nice,' said Jenny.

'I suppose so, for a cop.'

'You were a cop.'

'Yeah, that's how I know that most cops aren't nice. There's only one reason I know that a cop would go to a victim's funeral.'

'In case the killer turns up.' She laughed at the look of surprise on his face. 'Come on, Jack, I watch *CSI*. Everyone knows that.'

'But in this case they know Uncle Tommy did it. So why is she here?'

'Maybe she wanted to meet the famous Jack Nightingale.'

'Notorious rather than famous,' he said. 'But maybe you're right.' He ran a hand through his hair. 'Do you wanna grab a coffee before we head back?'

'Just so long as you don't expect me to make it for you,' she said, smiling sweetly.

Nightingale phoned Dr Keller on the way back to London and asked if he could visit his sister on Thursday. The psychiatrist said that he wouldn't be working but that he was more than happy for Nightingale to visit. He asked Nightingale when he'd be able to see a transcript of Barbara's hypnotic-regression session and Nightingale said that she was still working on it.

He arrived at Rampton Hospital at midday with a large Harrods carrier bag. A guard held out his hand for the bag before allowing Nightingale to walk through the metal detector, then took it over to a steel table.

'Just some things for my sister,' said Nightingale. 'Dr Keller said that it was okay.'

'It's not up to the medical staff what comes in here,' said the guard. He tipped the contents of the bag out onto the table. 'The inmates are here because they're dangerous; they can cause mayhem with a crayon.'

'That's okay, because I didn't bring her any crayons.'

The guard scowled at Nightingale and held up a box of chalk. 'What's this, then?'

'That's chalk. Chalk and crayons are as different as chalk and cheese.' He smiled brightly. 'Her doctor said it was okay. She wants to do some drawing and he figured it would be part of her therapy.'

The guard opened the box and took out a stick of white chalk. He stared impassively as he broke it in half. 'Your sister doesn't need therapy,' he growled. 'She needs the death penalty.' He closed the box and put it back into the carrier bag, then picked up a small cloth bag and untied the piece of string around the neck. 'What's this?' he asked.

'Salt,' said Nightingale. 'Minus the iodine. There's a chance she's allergic to the iodine so we thought we'd try her on de-iodised.'

The guard retied the bag and put it with the chalk. He picked up a small linen pillow. 'What's this for?' he asked.

'It's a herb pillow, to help her sleep,' said Nightingale. 'Dr Keller said it was okay.'

'What sort of herbs?'

Nightingale shrugged. 'There's rosemary and lavender, I think. I'm not sure. I got it from a herbalist.'

'We get a lot of people trying to smuggle drugs in here,' said the guard. 'I'm going to have to get a dog.'

'A dog?'

'A sniffer dog.' The guard called the hospital's security centre on his transceiver and requested a drugs dog at the visitor's entrance, then continued examining the contents of the carrier bag.

Nightingale pointed at two plastic bottles of Evian water. 'She was complaining about the taste of the water in here.'

'There's nothing wrong with it,' said the guard, checking the seals.

'She said it tasted of chlorine.'

There were five white candles in the bag. The guard examined them and looked at Nightingale quizzically.

'Aromatherapy,' said Nightingale. 'The herbalist said they might help relax her.'

The guard sniffed one. 'Can't smell anything,' he said.

'They've got to be burning,' said Nightingale.

The guard nodded and put everything except the pillow back into the carrier bag. 'You'll have to wait for the dog,' he said and nodded at a chair. 'Have a seat; it might take a while.'

Nightingale knew that it was pointless to argue. He sat for twenty minutes until another guard appeared with a German Shepherd, which refused to take any interest at all in the pillow.

When Agnes, the female guard who had accompanied him on his first visit, came to meet him, Nightingale was finally allowed out of the holding area.

'You know that Dr Keller isn't here today?' she asked as she walked down the corridor with him, swinging her keys back and forth.

'That's right,' said Nightingale. 'I'm just here for a chat, to see how she is.'

'She seems happier since you started visiting,' she said.

'How did she react to the death of her parents?'

Agnes shrugged. 'Water off a duck's back,' she said. 'Psychopaths can be like that. They don't react to things the same way that you or I do.'

They reached the door to the visitor's room.

'Can I see her on her own, just so I can have some privacy?' asked Nightingale.

'No can do, I'm sorry,' said Agnes, unlocking the door. 'But there'll be just me and I'll keep well away. There has to be a guard in the room at all times. There are safety issues.'

'I'm her brother,' said Nightingale.

She opened the door and let him go through first. 'That's as may be,' she said. 'But we had a woman who bit her daughter's nose clean off a few years back. She might well be your sister but she's also a psychopath and the medical condition takes precedence, I'm afraid.' She nodded at the tables. 'You make yourself comfortable and I'll go and get her.'

Nightingale sat down and put the carrier bag on the table. Ten minutes later Agnes returned with Robyn. This time she was wearing grey stretch pants, a pink sweatshirt with GAP across the chest and white Reeboks.

'Hi, big brother,' she said, sitting down opposite him.

'How've you been, Robyn?'

'I'm okay,' she said. 'What is this, twice in one week?'

Agnes walked over to the vending machines and studied the contents.

Nightingale leaned forward and lowered his voice. 'I wanted to talk to you.'

'About what?'

'About getting you out of here.'

'I'm not appealing,' said Robyn, folding her arms. 'I'm not going back into court.'

'It's not appealing,' said Nightingale. 'That's not what I had in mind.' He put his hand on the carrier bag. 'I want you to do something much more creative than that.'

'I killed those kids and I deserve to be here.'

'No, you didn't.'

'How do you know?'

Nightingale linked his fingers on the table. 'Do you remember killing the children?'

'Yes,' she said.

'Think, Robyn. Do you actually remember doing it? Do you remember the knife going in, the blood flowing, the way the eyes go blank at the moment of death?'

Robyn swallowed. 'Why are you doing this?' she whispered.

'Because I don't think you did it, Robyn. I don't think you killed those children and I don't think you deserve to be here. Which is why I want to help you to get out.' He looked over at Agnes. The guard was sitting down and reading a newspaper. Nightingale took Barbara's digital recorder from his coat pocket and put it in front of Robyn. The earphones were already plugged in. 'Listen to this,' he said. 'It's what happened during the session you had with Barbara.'

Robyn continued to stare at Nightingale as she reached for the earphones.

77

Robyn looked increasingly confused as she listened to the recording. Deep creases cut across her forehead and at one point she leaned forward and put her head in her hands. Nightingale looked over at Agnes but the guard seemed to be engrossed in her newspaper.

Eventually Robyn sat back and took out the earphones. The blood had drained from her face. 'It was Marcus Fairchild,' she said, her voice a hoarse whisper.

'Yes,' said Nightingale.

'He said he was my friend. He said he'd represent me for no money because he wanted to help me.' She reached over and grabbed Nightingale's hands. 'He lied to me, Jack. He framed me.'

'That's what it looks like.'

'Why would he do that?' Her nails dug into his flesh.

'Maybe they needed somebody to take the blame.'

'They? Who do you mean?'

'He's a member of a group that kills children. Sacrifices them. By setting you up, it would bring any police investigation to an end.'

'But why did I believe that I'd done it?'

'I think he managed to hypnotise you. He planted false

memories in your head, and once you thought you had done it you pleaded guilty and that was that.'

She finally released her grip on his hands and sat back, folding her arms and rocking backwards and forwards.

'Why me? Why did that bastard pick on me? What did I ever do to him?'

Nightingale took a deep breath. 'I think it has something to do with Ainsley Gosling,' he said. 'He was a member of the same group as Fairchild. It's possible that Fairchild found out that you were Gosling's daughter.'

'So my own father sold me out?'

'I don't think so, Robyn. I'm pretty sure that Gosling didn't know where you were. He lost touch with you after you were adopted. But Fairchild could have found out. Maybe there was bad blood between Fairchild and Gosling. I don't know. I wish I had the answers for you.'

'What do I do now, Jack?' She nodded at the recorder. 'You're going to give that to the police, right?'

'I'm not sure that'll help.'

'You have to get me out of here. I didn't do it. I know now that I didn't do it.'

'Unfortunately you said you did and you can't just take it back.'

Robyn pointed at the recorder. 'But that's proof, isn't it? It's proof that I didn't do it.'

'No, it's not proof,' said Nightingale. 'At least not proof that a court will accept. Why would a court believe your new memory over what you said in court?'

'We can tell them that Fairchild hypnotised me.'

'We can't prove that, Robyn. And he's certainly not going to confess, is he? Who do you think they'll believe?

You, a convicted child killer, or Marcus Fairchild, a top City lawyer?'

'So what are you saying? I rot here for the rest of my life for something I didn't do?'

Nightingale shook his head. 'No. I've got a plan.'

'Tell me.'

Nightingale took a deep breath. 'What I'm going to tell you will sound crazy.'

'Any crazier than what I just heard? I don't think so.'

'You understand what happened? Marcus Fairchild is a Satanist. The children were killed in a Satanic ceremony.'

'For what? Why kill children?'

'I don't know,' said Nightingale.

'You don't know much, do you?' she said, her voice loaded with bitterness.

'I know how to get you out of here,' said Nightingale quietly.

'I'm listening.'

78

Nightingale finished speaking and sat back. Robyn stared at him, her eyes wide in disbelief.

'You're mad,' she said. 'You are stark raving mad.'

'Every word I've told you is the truth,' said Nightingale quietly.

'Ainsley Gosling sold my soul to the devil before I was born?'

'To a devil. Yes.'

'A devil? How many devils are there?'

'A lot.'

'What do you mean, a lot?'

'Millions or billions, it depends who you talk to. It's the truth, Robyn. I know it's hard to believe. But the fact that Marcus Fairchild killed those children and had you put away for it shows that there are dark forces at work that most people never even dream about. If someone else had told me this two months ago, I'd have called them crazy too.'

'You know, I'm starting to think that you should be in here with me. Maybe crazy runs in the family.'

'You may be right. But, the way I see it, doing something crazy is the only chance you've got of getting out of here, and of saving your soul.'

'You believe in souls, do you?'

Nightingale stared at her for several seconds, then he nodded slowly. 'I'm starting to, yes.'

'And how exactly are you proposing that I do this?'

'Okay,' said Nightingale. 'This is how it works. There are three superior devils in Hell. Lucifer, Beelzebuth and Astaroth. They're the heavy hitters. Below them are six subordinates. And below them are seventeen ministers.'

'What are you talking about?' said Robyn.

'I'm talking about doing a deal that will get you out of here,' said Nightingale. 'With one of the seventeen ministers. His name is Sugart.'

'Would you listen to yourself? That's a plan? To do a deal with one of Satan's ministers?' She sat back in her chair and folded her arms. 'You know, Jack, there are murderers in here who are a hell of a lot less crazy than you sound right now.'

'You don't deserve to be in here. If you want to get out you're going to have to fight fire with fire.'

'So I do a deal with the devil? Do you realise how crazy that sounds?'

'A devil, not the devil.' Nightingale opened the carrier bag. 'You have to do this, Robyn.'

'This doesn't make sense.'

'None of this makes any sense. Look at me, Robyn. Please, look at me.' He waited until she was looking into his eyes, then he reached over and held her hands. 'I need you to trust me. I can't tell you everything because if I do it'll ruin it, but I swear on my soul, I swear on everything that I hold dear, on all that's holy, that I only want what's best for you. And I swear that if you don't do this, you'll regret it for the rest of your life.'

Robyn tried to pull her fingers away but he held her tightly. 'You don't know me,' she whispered.

'You're my sister,' he said. 'You're the only family I've got left. I wouldn't do anything to hurt you.'

'And on the basis of you being the big brother, the big half-brother that I have met only twice in thirty-one years, I'm supposed to do a deal with the spawn of Satan?'

'He's not a spawn. He's more of a subordinate.'

'Have you heard yourself?'

'Please, Robyn. Do this for me.' He forced a smile. 'It'll make up for all the birthdays and Christmases that you missed. You owe me a lifetime of presents.'

'You didn't get me any presents, either.'

'This is my present to you,' he said. 'Getting you out of here.'

'And how do I do this deal with this devil?'

'I'll tell you how. And when. And you have to do exactly what I say and when I say.'

'It's not a sex thing, is it?'

'No.'

'I don't have to dance naked around an oak tree or anything like that? Because they don't let me out.'

'You can do it in your cell,' said Nightingale. He couldn't tell if she was joking or not.

'They don't call them cells here. They call them rooms.'

'Your room will be fine. It doesn't matter where you do the ritual. What matters is that you do it right and you do it at the right time. It has to be done at midnight on New Year's Eve. Literally as the clock strikes twelve. The timing is important and so is what you say. You have to follow my instructions to the letter. It's your only hope of getting out of here.'

'Why can't we just get another lawyer?'

'Because no one is going to believe us. Do you want to stay here for the rest of your life?'

Robyn shook her head slowly. 'No,' she whispered.

'You're only in here because Fairchild made you believe that you killed those children. But what's done is done. This is your only chance to get out.'

'How do you know it'll work?'

Nightingale swallowed. His mouth had gone dry. 'Because I've already done it,' he said. 'I called up Proserpine and I did a deal with her. It works, Robyn. The fact that I'm here talking to you and not burning in the fires of Hell is proof of that.'

'But how can you prove that my soul has been promised to a devil?'

'There is one way,' he said. 'Anyone whose soul has been sold has a mark. A pentagram. Somewhere on their body. It can be tiny or in somewhere inaccessible, but there has to be a mark.'

Robyn's right hand jerked up to touch the right side of her head, just above her ear.

'You've got it, haven't you?' said Nightingale. 'You've got the mark?'

'It's a birthmark,' she said. 'It's tiny. You can hardly see it.'

'That's your proof, Robyn,' he said. 'The pentagram is the proof.'

'It's a birthmark,' she whispered. She continued to stare into his eyes for several seconds, then she nodded slowly. 'Okay,' she said. 'Tell me what to do.'

79

A n hour later Nightingale walked out of the hospital. Jenny was waiting for him in her Audi. 'How did it go?' she asked.

'She'll do it.' He climbed into the car. 'She doesn't really believe it'll work but she said she'll give it a try.'

Jenny started the engine. 'Now what?'

Nightingale sighed. 'Now we wait for New Year's Eve.'

About twenty minutes after they left the hospital, Jenny drove past a modern brick church with a tall steeple and a sign outside that announced that coffee and biscuits were served every morning at ten.

'Stop here, will you?' Nightingale asked Jenny.

'Here?' she said, looking over at him.

'There,' said Nightingale, jerking a thumb at the church.

'If you need the toilet, we'll stop at a filling station.'

'The church, Jenny. Please.'

Jenny braked, flicked on her indicator and did a quick U-turn. 'What's going on, Jack?' she asked as she drove back to the church.

'I'm going to give God one last chance,' he said.

Her jaw dropped. 'You're what?'

'Eyes on the road, kid,' said Nightingale.

She brought the Audi to a stop next to the entrance to the churchyard. 'What did you say?'

Nightingale shrugged. 'I just want a one-to-one with the big guy upstairs.'

'You're worrying me now,' she said.

'That's the crazy thing about all this, don't you see?' said Nightingale. 'Summoning devils is okay, but anyone who talks about having a conversation with God has a screw loose, right?'

'It's not as simple as that.'

'But I'm right, aren't I? No one really ever has a conversation with God, do they? And if anyone claimed they did, we'd think that they were crazy.'

'The Pope probably talks to God.'

'Probably?'

'You know what I mean. The religious leaders must believe that they hear the voice of God, or they couldn't do what they do. But I don't think that you can just walk into church and have a one-to-one. It doesn't work like that.'

'There's prayer.'

'Yes, there's prayer. If you said you were going in there to pray then I'd say good on you. But that's not what you said. Please, Jack, stop messing around. Let's go back to London.'

'Just humour me,' said Nightingale, opening the passenger door. 'I'll be ten minutes.' He climbed out of the Audi and walked towards the church.

There was a sign by the door announcing that the church was St Mary's and giving the times of the services. A dozen or so candles were burning against one wall and Nightingale lit one and put a one-pound coin into a wooden donation box. It was freezing cold and as he walked towards a large crucifix on the far wall his breath feathered around him. The floor was tiled in grey slate and the pews were oak; there was a large modern stone font in one corner. He looked around but there was no one else in the church.

The crucifix was almost three foot tall and on it was a figure of Jesus, long-haired and dark-eyed, his face tranquil as if being crucified was no big thing. Nightingale knelt down in front of the crucifix and crossed himself.

'I haven't been here much, other than for funerals, so this is the first time I've been able to have a private chat,' he said. He smiled amiably. 'There's been a lot going on.'

His knees began to ache and he sat back on his heels. 'This position hurts like hell,' he said, 'but I guess yours hurts more. I'm going to stand, if that's okay with you.'

Nightingale got to his feet and put his hands in his pockets, then shrugged and took them out. 'I suppose it's you I have to talk to, right? There are no statues of God, just of Jesus and Mary. I've never understood that. It's God that's being worshipped but there are no statues of him, no pictures. Why is that?'

He looked at the Jesus figure and nodded expectantly.

'Oh right, you don't talk back, do you?' He folded his arms. 'Okay, here's the thing,' he said. 'My sister's behind bars, and I want to get her out. She's in a hospital not a prison but the doors are locked and no one'll be giving us a key. She's inside for killing five kids but she didn't do it. Now, there's a devil who's the bee's knees for getting people out of prison. Name of Sugart. Nasty piece of work by all accounts but at the moment he's the only hope I've got.'

As Nightingale began to pace up and down in front of the crucifix he continued talking. 'I've been reading the Bible a bit recently. Trying to get a handle on what's been happening to me. Came across a story about Peter, when he was thrown into prison by Herod. Herod had James, John's brother, put to the sword and figured he'd send Peter the same way. So he threw him in prison and had him guarded by sixteen soldiers, night and day, until he could bring him to trial. Every hour of the day and night Peter was chained to two of the guards. Escape-proof, right? Except the night before his trial, an angel of the Lord appeared. The angel shone a light in Peter's cell and woke him up. As he woke, the chains fell off. All the guards were asleep and the angel led Peter out of prison. He took him to the city's iron gate, opened it, and Peter was free.'

Nightingale stopped pacing, looked up at the crucifix and held his hands out to his sides, palms up. 'So how about it? How about doing the same for my sister? She's an innocent in all this. The guy who set her up is a fan of your opposition. Why not put some balance in the universe? Why not set my sister free? The devil put her behind bars so why can't you get her out?'

He stared at the crucifix for several seconds, then sighed and put his hands into the pockets of his raincoat. 'And that's the thing, isn't it? You pray for a miracle, and you don't get one. You ask for a sign, and no sign's forthcoming. But if I draw a pentagram and say the right words then I get can to talk to devils, and do deals with them. Why can't I call your guys? Why are there tons of books telling me how to summon devils and not one that tells me how to call up an angel?'

Off in the distance he heard a police siren, and a few seconds later the sound of a helicopter high overhead.

'How about a sign? How about just a sign that you're there and listening to me?' Nightingale took out his packet of Marlboro. 'I hear smoking's not allowed in churches, is that right?' He grinned up at the crucifix. 'Shall I put that down as "no comment"?' He tapped out a cigarette and held it out between the first and second fingers of his right hand. 'How about lighting it with a bolt from above? That's easy, right? A flash of lightning and I've got my proof.' Nightingale looked at the cigarette. 'Yes? No?' He shook his head. 'Why is it so bloody difficult? Why can I summon devils but not angels? Why are the bad guys so keen to appear but your lot stay in the shadows? Are you scared? Are you not here, is that it? Has God left the building? Did his only son go with him? Are we in such a bloody mess that you've washed your hands of us?'

Nightingale took out his lighter and lit the cigarette. He stared at the crucifix as he blew a cloud of smoke. A grey haze spread across the feet of the crucified Jesus, then dispersed.

'Well, it's been nice talking to you,' said Nightingale. 'We must do this again some time.' He turned and walked away, his shoes squeaking on the tiled floor.

Nightingale got to Gosling Manor just as it was getting dark on New Year's Eve. Jenny had wanted to go with him but he had insisted on going alone. He brought with him a black rubbish bag filled with cloths, brushes and bleach, and a box full of supplies from the Wicca Woman store. He spent almost two hours cleaning one of the bedrooms, then he went down into the basement and sat down on one of the sofas, smoking cigarettes and preparing himself for what lay ahead.

At eleven o'clock he went back upstairs and filled a bath with warm water, washed himself thoroughly, emptied and refilled it and washed again. He used a brand new plastic nailbrush to clean under his fingernails and toenails, then climbed out of the bath and brushed his teeth for a full five minutes.

He dried himself on a brand-new towel and dressed in clean clothes. He went to the bedroom, knelt down and then began drawing the protective pentagram on the floorboards.

Robyn stood up and looked at the pentagram and triangle that she'd drawn on the floor. She compared it with the diagram that Nightingale had given her. It looked the same. She looked at her watch. It was five minutes to midnight. On the table by the bed she had placed one of the bottles of Evian water and the salt. She mixed them in a beaker which she took with her as she stepped into the pentagram. She slowly sprinkled the salt-water mixture around the edge of the circle and then used a cigarette lighter to light the five candles that she'd placed at the five points of the pentagram.

She looked at her watch again. Three minutes to go. Her heart was pounding and she took a deep breath. Her face was bathed in sweat and she wiped her forehead with her sleeve. What she was doing made no sense, but she had promised Nightingale that she would go through with it. She didn't believe in devils, or angels, or God. So far as Robyn was concerned, people were born, they lived and they died. There was no Heaven and no Hell, just life, and in her heart of hearts she was sure that what she was doing was a waste of time. But Jack Nightingale clearly cared about her, and as he was the only relative she had she would do it for him.

The minute hand on her watch clicked towards twelve. 'Happy New Year,' she muttered, and knelt down to pick up a handful of herbs that she'd taken from the pillow Nightingale had given her. She held it over the candle in front of her and let the herbs trickle through her fingers. They spluttered and sparked and the air was filled with cloying smoke that made her eyes sting. Nightingale had warned her about the smoke and she had covered the smoke detector in the middle of the ceiling with a plastic bag. She dropped a lighted match into a bowl of herbs in the centre of the pentagram and coughed as thick grey smoke mushroomed around her.

She reached into the back pocket of her jeans and took out the piece of paper that contained the phrases she had to read out. Nightingale had said that they were in Latin and it didn't matter what the words meant; all that mattered was that she said the words out loud. She began to speak, syllable by syllable. Her words echoed around the room. The smoke grew thicker and she held the piece of paper closer to her face and blinked. She fought the urge to cough and said the last three words at the top of her voice: '*Bagahi laca bacabe!*'

The smoke began to whirl around her, spinning faster and faster as if she was at the centre of a tornado. The candle flames bent over and her hair whipped around her head. Faster and faster went the smoke, whistling by her ears. She felt the wind tug at her clothes and for a second she almost lost her balance, but she held her arms out to her sides and steadied herself.

Something dark began to form in the smoke, something big, something that swayed from side to side as it solidified, something that wasn't human. Robyn was gripped by an almost irresistible urge to turn to her bed and hide under the covers but Nightingale's warning rang in her ears. No matter what happened, no matter what she heard or saw, she had to stay within the pentagram.

82

Nightingale finished speaking and he stared through the acrid smoke wondering what form Frimost would take. He hadn't been able to find any descriptions of what the devil looked like, never mind a drawing or illustration. And he hadn't wanted to ask Proserpine because every question meant another attack on his life. She had told him about Sugart and how to summon Sugart and Frimost, and that was all.

There was a blinding flash of light and a deep rumbling sound, the air shimmered, folded in on itself and crackled, and then Frimost was standing outside the pentagram. He was black and massively obese, just five feet tall but twice as wide, with a dozen or so chins, thick tubes of fat around his midriff and rolls of fat around his ankles.

Frimost was wearing a brightly coloured man-dress, red and green with splashes of gold, and a pillbox hat of the same material. Around his neck was a gold chain from which hung half a dozen small skulls that looked like the skulls of monkeys or small children. Nightingale tried not to look at them. Frimost was holding a wooden stick with a gold tip on the bottom and a handle that appeared to have been formed from a human shoulder blade. He grunted and banged the stick on the floor, three times. The walls of the room juddered with each blow.

'Who has summoned me?' he asked, in a deep, booming voice.

'My name is Nightingale. You are Frimost? The devil who gives men power over women?'

'What is it you want?' asked Frimost icily. 'Why have you summoned me?'

'To do a deal.'

Frimost looked at him with contempt. 'So you want what I have to offer,' he said. 'You want sex; you want women to desire you. Like all men, you yearn to have your urges satisfied.' He laughed and his body rippled like jelly. 'I can help you, Nightingale. I can give you what you seek. For a price, of course.'

'That's not why I summoned you,' said Nightingale.

'Then what? Do not waste my time, Nightingale. I bore easily.'

'What I have to say won't take long,' said Nightingale. 'I want to do a deal for my sister's soul.'

83

Robyn gasped and covered her face with her hands. She wanted to run but she knew that the door was locked, and Nightingale had drummed into her that under no circumstances should she leave the pentagram. She closed her eyes and mumbled the Lord's Prayer to herself, then something began to laugh, a deep throaty rumble that made her stomach tingle. She squinted through her fingers.

It wasn't human but Robyn didn't know what it was. It was tall, so tall that its head almost touched the ceiling. It was covered in scales and a forked tongue kept flicking from its mouth; the eyes that scrutinised her were reptilian but it stood upright on two legs and it was wearing clothes that looked as if they were made from steel mesh. It was breathing slowly and each time it exhaled she could smell something fetid that burned the back of her mouth and made her want to gag. It moved its head slowly as it looked around the room, then it bent its neck to stare down at her. It opened its mouth, revealing a shark's mouth with row upon row of triangular teeth.

Robyn crouched down, trying to make herself as small as possible. The stench got worse and she threw up, vomit spraying over the floor in front of her. Her heart was racing and she forced herself to breathe slowly. The thing stood facing her, watching her with slanted, yellow, unblinking eyes. Her mind was whirling and she tried to concentrate on what Nightingale had said to her. It was important to address it by name at the first opportunity and to maintain eye contact. And he'd said that on no account should she show fear; but that was easier said than done because the thing standing in front of her could kill her with one blow or bite.

She stood up, fighting the urge to vomit again. 'You are Sugart, and I have summoned you,' she said. She could hear the uncertainty in her voice but she clenched her fists tightly and stared into its yellow eyes.

Sugart looked slowly around the room again, and then back at her. Its chest rose and fell and its foul breath made eddies in the smoky air.

'What is it you want?' asked Sugart. Its voice was low and menacing and seemed to come from deep within its chest.

'I want to get out of here.'

84

Nightingale stared at Frimost as he spoke, choosing his words carefully. 'A man called Ainsley Gosling sold you a soul thirty-one years ago. The soul of his then-unborn daughter. In exchange for her soul, you gave him power over women.'

Frimost nodded thoughtfully. 'That may be so.'

'You don't remember?'

'Many souls are promised to me. Many men want what I have to offer.' He banged his stick on the ground. 'I grow impatient, Nightingale. Get to the point.'

'Her name is Robyn Reynolds now. In two years' time, on her thirty-third birthday, you will claim her soul. I want to get it back for her.'

Frimost laughed and his whole body juddered and shook, from his double chins to the rolls of fat around his ankles. Even after he stopped laughing his flesh continued to slop around his body. 'A deal is a deal, and once done it cannot be undone,' he said.

'Well, that's not strictly speaking true, is it?' said Nightingale. 'Deals can be renegotiated.'

'Only if both parties are willing. And in this case I'm not. I have been promised the soul of Robyn Reynolds and in two years' time her soul will be mine. The deal was done and there is no going back on it.'

'But the deal wasn't with my sister. It was with our father.'

'It makes no difference. A parent can sell an unborn soul up until the moment of birth. You are wasting your time, Nightingale. And more to the point, you are wasting mine.'

'What if there was something else that you wanted? Something that I could offer you in exchange?'

Frimost looked at Nightingale, his eyes narrowing. 'What did you have in mind?'

'That would be up to you,' said Nightingale.

'Would you be prepared to put your soul on the table?' asked Frimost quietly. 'Your soul for hers?'

85

Sugart reached out a claw towards the pentagram, as if testing it. Robyn took an involuntary step backwards then froze as she saw that she was right up against the chalk outline of the pentagram. She forced herself to move back into the centre of the circle. Sugart's chest juddered and a grating rumble resonated from its chest. It was laughing, she realised. It was laughing at her.

'How did you know how to call me?' asked Sugart.

'I asked around,' said Robyn. 'Does it matter?'

Sugart shuffled to the side and cocked its head as it stared at the pentagram. 'You have practised the dark arts before?'

Robyn shook her head. 'I've never needed to. But I'm at the end of my tether now and I can't think of anything else to do.'

'I am your last resort?'

'Yes.'

Sugart smiled. 'My favourite customer.' The tongue flicked out. It was several feet long, grey and slimy, and moved as if it had a life of its own.

'Is that what I am? A customer?'

'I can give you what you want. Your freedom. You will have to pay a price for it. That makes you a customer.'

'So you can do it? You can help me escape?'

'Of course. But are you prepared to pay the price?'

'What price?'

'You know what the price is. If you didn't know, you wouldn't have summoned me.'

'My soul?'

'Yes. Your soul.'

'What if I don't believe that I have a soul?'

'Your belief is neither here nor there. All that I require is for you to offer it to me in exchange for what you want.' The tongue flicked out and just as quickly vanished back into Sugart's mouth.

'I want to get out of here,' said Robyn. 'I want to go far away and I want a new life.'

'Agreed,' said Sugart.

'And I want to never be found, never brought back to this place. I want to keep my freedom.'

'Agreed.'

'You can do that? You can really do that?'

Sugart's face twisted into what passed for a grin. 'If I can't hold up my end of the bargain, what would be the point of all this?'

Robyn ran a hand through her hair. 'Do I have to do something? Sign something?'

'You mean, sign a parchment with your own blood?' Sugart threw back his head and laughed. 'That isn't how it works, Robyn. You tell me what you want, I tell you the price, and if you agree to the price then the deal is done and there is no going back. Your word is your bond.'

Robyn folded her arms. It had gone icy cold in the room and her breath formed clouds around her mouth. 'Then let's do it,' she said.

'You understand there is no going back, and a deal once done cannot be rescinded?'

'I understand.'

Sugart nodded and his reptilian tongue flicked out. 'It is done,' he said.

The smoke rippled and there was a deep rumbling noise that vibrated through Robyn's internal organs, and then Sugart was gone.

Robyn put her hands on her hips and looked around the room. 'Now what?' she said.

86

Frimost rolled his head around, pushing his chin against the rolls of fat around his neck. His face was dripping with sweat and it glistened in the candlelight. 'I am waiting, Nightingale,' he said. 'Your soul for your sister's. That's a deal I can work with.'

Nightingale stared at Frimost for several seconds. 'No,' he said eventually.

'So you want to save your sister, but not at the expense of yourself?'

Nightingale grimaced. 'I went to a lot of trouble to keep my soul. I'm not prepared to give it up now.'

Frimost shook his head. 'You have nothing else I want. So say the words and let me go.'

'If I change my mind about my soul, can we deal?'

'Perhaps,' said Frimost.

'I'll get back to you,' said Nightingale.

'I wouldn't leave it too long.'

'Why? Do I have a sell-by date?'

Frimost laughed and the walls shook. Small puffs of dust rose up from between the gaps in the floorboards. 'You'll find out, soon enough,' he said. 'Now say the words and have done with it.'

Nightingale sprinkled herbs over the smouldering

crucible and wrinkled his nose as the pungent fumes assailed his nostrils. '*Ite in pace ad loca vestra et pax sit inter vos redituri ad mecum vos invocavero, in nomine Patris et Filii et Spiritus Sancti, Amen.*'

Frimost began to laugh again, then there was a flash of light and an ear-splitting crack and he was gone.

'Nice talking to you, Frimost,' Nightingale muttered. He took out his cigarettes and lit one. He blew smoke and looked at his watch. If everything had gone to plan, Robyn should just have finished her conversation with Sugart. If she hadn't, then it had all been for nothing. All he could do now was wait. And hope.

87

Nightingale got home just after two o'clock in the morning. He called Jenny to tell her that everything was okay, then he showered and fell into bed, exhausted. He woke at ten and made himself a bacon sandwich and a cup of coffee, and spent the rest of the morning watching television. At just after midday Jenny phoned and asked him if he'd heard anything and he said that he hadn't.

'I've been checking the internet and Sky News and there's no word of any escape from Rampton,' she said.

'I'm assuming they'll phone me if she does get out because I'm down as next of kin,' said Nightingale. 'What about your Welshman? Caernarfon Craig?'

'He's emailing me through Facebook again, fishing for personal stuff, but I'm still ducking and diving,' she said. 'I've logged onto some of the suicide sites that he's told me about. There're a lot of very depressed people out there, Jack.'

'State the economy's in, I'm not surprised. But you be careful, Jenny. If this guy is behind the Welsh deaths then you could be playing with fire.'

'I know what I'm doing,' she said. 'I'm copying everything he's sent me and once I can identify him I'll pass it all onto the cops.'

She ended the call and Nightingale showered again, then shaved and changed into a clean denim shirt and jeans, made himself another mug of coffee and lay on the sofa watching television. At some point he must have fallen asleep because he was woken by the sound of his door intercom buzzing. He went to answer it.

'Open the bloody door, Nightingale, or by the hair on my chinny-chin-chin I'll blow the thing down.' It was Superintendent Chalmers.

'What do you want?' asked Nightingale.

'I want you to open the door now. If you don't there are two big men here who're going to kick it in.'

'Big men? Are you trying to scare me, Chalmers? Because it's not working.'

'I've got a warrant, Nightingale. And I'm counting down from ten.'

'Yeah, using all your fingers, I'll bet.'

'One way or the other we're coming in, Nightingale.'

Nightingale pressed the button to open the downstairs door. He switched off the television and then opened his front door. Chalmers was wearing a dark raincoat and a sour expression as he clumped up the stairs followed by two uniformed officers.

'Where's the warrant?' asked Nightingale.

Chalmers handed Nightingale an envelope and pushed him to the side. He walked into the sitting room and looked around while the uniforms checked Nightingale's bedroom.

'Nothing here, sir,' shouted one.

'Check the bathroom,' said Chalmers. 'Count the bloody toothbrushes.'

'What are you looking for?' asked Nightingale.

Chalmers gestured at the envelope. 'Not what,' he said. 'Who. It's in the warrant. Your sister.'

'Robyn?'

'How many sisters do you have?'

'She's in Rampton.'

Chalmers sneered at him. 'Not as of today, she isn't,' he said.

'She escaped?'

'No one knows what happened,' said Chalmers. 'Her room was checked this morning and she wasn't there. But she'd left a whole lot of weird stuff behind.'

'So what's that got to do with me?' asked Nightingale.

The superintendent pointed a finger at Nightingale's face. 'See, there's a funny thing. Most people would have asked what sort of weird stuff. But not you.'

'Okay, I'll humour you. What weird stuff?'

'You know what weird stuff. There was a pentagram on the floor, candles, a bowl of herbs. And according to the security logs, you're the one who took it in to her.'

'I took her a few things that her psychiatrist said might help her. The guards checked everything I took in. Even had a sniffer dog go over it.'

'You helped her escape. I know you did.'

'Yeah, and what exactly did I do? I smuggled in a hacksaw so that she could saw through the bars, did I?'

'The bars were fine, all the doors were locked, there's nothing on the CCTV. She didn't walk out, she just vanished.'

'And you think I had a hand in that?'

'Where were you last night?'

'I was in Gosling Manor until about midnight.'

'You had a party there, did you?'

Nightingale shook his head. 'I was alone.'

'On New Year's Eve?'

'I just wanted some quiet contemplation,' he said. 'I was making my New Year resolutions, if you must know.'

'Can anyone confirm that you were there?'

'I told you, I was alone. Then I came back here.'

'What time?'

'About two o'clock.'

'Still alone?'

Nightingale nodded.

'So no witnesses?' said Chalmers.

'Chalmers, if I was up to something I'd have sorted out an alibi for myself, wouldn't I? I was in the Job, remember? I know how it works. But I drove, so I'm sure you'll be able to catch me on CCTV somewhere.'

'What's going on, Nightingale?'

Nightingale shrugged. 'I've no idea what you're talking about,' he said.

'Where is she?'

Nightingale put his hand on his heart. 'I have no idea. And that's the truth. Scout's honour.'

'You know who her last visitor was?'

'I'm guessing that would be me.'

'Yeah, well, you guess right. On Thursday you go in to see her. Saturday morning and she vanishes. I don't believe in coincidences, Nightingale. Let's go.'

'Go where?'

'Gosling Manor.'

'Not without a warrant,' said Nightingale.

Chalmers reached into pocket and took out a second envelope, which he thrust at Nightingale. 'Get your coat,' he said.

88

Graham Kerr lit a match as he watched. He was standing in a clump of trees overlooking the house and had seen the MGB, patrol car and police van arrive. He breathed in the fragrance of the match and shivered with anticipation. At his feet was a can of petrol. He wasn't happy about using petrol. Petrol was the blunt instrument in an arsonist's armoury, the equivalent of a sawn-off shotgun or a machete. Kerr preferred subtlety, but in Jack Nightingale's case there was no time to be clever. Mistress Proserpine wanted him dead and she always got what she wanted.

Kerr loved to watch his victims. Watching them going about the business not knowing that their days were numbered was part of the pleasure. It was almost as satisfying as the setting of the fires that took their lives. Almost, but not quite.

Kerr let the match burn down almost to his fingers before blowing it out and slipping it into his back pocket. He didn't like using petrol but at least he could use his Swan Vestas matches. First he'd have to wait for the police to leave. If Nightingale stayed in the house, that's where he would die. If he went back to his flat in Bayswater, he'd die there. But one way or another, Jack Nightingale would die.

89

Nightingale climbed out of his MGB. 'Nice of you to let me use my own car,' he said to Chalmers, who was walking towards the front door.

A Surrey Police van with half a dozen uniformed officers had been waiting for them at the gates and had followed them in.

'We've got better things to do on New Year's Day than run a taxi service for you,' said the superintendent. 'Now open the front door.'

'Anything to stop you doing the chinny-chin-chin thing.' Nightingale took out his keys and opened the front door as the uniforms piled out of the van. They were led by a bruiser of a sergeant, who glared at Nightingale as if blaming him personally for having to work on New Year's Day.

Chalmers put a hand on Nightingale's shoulder. 'You hang on outside with me while the men give it the once-over. If she's in there you'd best tell me now.'

'She isn't,' said Nightingale.

The uniforms filed through into the hallway. Two of them went upstairs and the rest spread out on the ground floor.

Nightingale tapped out a Marlboro and lit it. 'Happy New Year, by the way,' he said.

'What's going on, Nightingale?' asked Chalmers. 'What's this all about? You inherit this house from a mystery man who blows his own head off. People around you have a nasty habit of coming to a sticky end. A serial killer tries to slit your throat. And your long-lost sister escapes from the most secure mental hospital in the country a couple of days after you pay her a visit. And all this happens over – what, four weeks?'

'It's been an eventful month, that's true.' He blew smoke towards the mermaid fountain.

'Is there something you want to tell me? Something that would explain it?'

'I'm as baffled as you are,' said Nightingale.

'I'm trying to help you here,' said the superintendent.

Nightingale held the cigarette away from his mouth. 'No, you're not,' he said. 'You're playing good cop in the hope that I'll give you something you can use to send me down. You didn't like me when I was in the Job and you don't like me now, so you can just search the house and then get the hell off my property.'

Chalmers opened his mouth to reply but then the transceiver he was holding crackled. 'Superintendent, you need to see this. Third bedroom on the left.'

Nightingale gritted his teeth. That was the bedroom where he'd summoned Frimost, and he hadn't cleaned up.

Chalmers noticed his discomfort and he grinned triumphantly. 'Something there you hoped we wouldn't find, huh?' He jerked a thumb at the door. 'Inside,' he said.

Nightingale flicked away his cigarette and went into the hall. The superintendent followed him up the stairs.

The panel that hid the secret passageway down to the basement was still in place and Nightingale avoided looking at it. They turned left at the top of the stairs. A constable was standing outside the door to the bedroom, his arms folded. A sergeant was inside the room, looking down at the pentagram and the candles. He nodded at the superintendent.

'No sign of the girl?' asked Chalmers. The sergeant shook his head. 'Okay, search the rest of the rooms while I have a word with Mr Nightingale here.'

The sergeant left the room and Chalmers kicked the door shut, then turned and shoved Nightingale in the chest with both hands. Nightingale staggered backwards. He regained his balance and pulled back his right hand in a fist.

'Go on, do it!' shouted Chalmers. 'Do it and see what happens.'

Nightingale relaxed his hand. 'You assaulted me.'

'Yeah, and I'll do it again if you don't start telling me the truth.'

'So PACE goes out of the window?'

'Screw PACE and screw you.' He pointed at the pentagram. 'You did this?'

Nightingale didn't say anything.

'There was a pentagram like this in your sister's room. And candles, and the same strong smell of burned crap. What's going on? What does it mean?' Chalmers jabbed his finger at the pentagram. 'Did she do this? Was she here?'

'I did it,' said Nightingale quietly.

'Why?'

'I can't tell you.'

'Can't? Or won't?'

'Both,' said Nightingale. 'So what are you going to do? Hit me again? Because if you do, I'll break your sodding arm and take my chance in court. I could always say you tripped and fell – that worked for me when I was in the Job.'

Chalmers glared at Nightingale, then reached for the door handle. 'I'm going to get you for this if it's the last thing I do, Nightingale.'

'Good luck with that,' said Nightingale, taking out his pack of Marlboro.

Kerr watched the police car and van drive away from the house. He looked at his watch. It would soon be dark. Nightingale was alone in the house and if he stayed there then that would be where he died. He hoped that Nightingale stayed where he was because it was a lovely old house and Kerr would love to see it burn. Kerr sat down with his back to one of the trees and shook the box of Swan Vestas matches. He felt his groin tighten with every rattle of the matches. He stared at the house and licked his lips. 'Soon,' he muttered to himself. 'Soon.'

Nightingale took his phone out of his pocket and rang Jenny.

'It's on the news,' she said before he could speak. 'They had her picture and said that she could be dangerous.'

'I know. Chalmers picked me up this afternoon. I'm at the house.'

'What if they find her?'

'They won't. That was the deal she did. Escape and freedom. They searched my flat and Gosling Manor and they'll have her red-flagged at the airports and ports but she's already fled the coop.'

'Do you know where she is?'

'I don't want to know,' said Nightingale.

'Now what?'

'Now's the hard part,' he said.

'Do you want my help?'

'You can't help, kid. I have to do it myself. Tonight, at midnight.'

'Be careful, Jack.'

'Always,' he said, and ended the call.

He walked downstairs to the hall, switching on the lights as he went. He pulled open the panel that led to the basement. He flicked on those lights too, then went slowly down the wooden stairs.

He had taken careful notes of what Aleister Crowley had written in his diary about summoning Lucifuge Rofocale. The pentagram was identical to the ones he had used when calling up Proserpine and Frimost, but the mixture of herbs was different, the candles had to be black and not white, and the incantation was longer and more complex. But the crucial part was a parchment that had to be prepared and burned at one of the two north-facing candles at the stroke of midnight.

The parchment had to be prepared from a virgin goat, and luckily Mrs Steadman at the Wicca Woman shop had been able to supply him with some. On the parchment there had to be a drawing that looked like a pentagram but with various rune-like scrawls in the centre and below it. Nightingale had sketched it from the diary and Crowley had stressed that it had to be copied perfectly onto the parchment on the day that it was required, ideally within an hour of the ceremony. The drawing could be done in the blood of a sea turtle, or the blood of the person summoning the devil. Mrs Steadman had laughed when he'd asked her if she had any sea-turtle blood and told him that there wasn't much call for it.

Nightingale sat down at the book-strewn desk, opened one of the drawers and took out a new razor blade and a swan's feather. He used the razor blade to clip off the end of the feather to make a workable nib, then slowly drew the blade across the tip of his left index finger. He winced as the blood flowed.

92

Kerr looked at his watch. It was just before midnight. There were lights on in the downstairs hallway and upstairs at the front of the house and he had waited, hoping that they would go out, but eventually he had walked around to the rear of the building and seen candlelight flickering in one of the upstairs bedrooms, and he figured that was where Nightingale was. He reached for the handle of the front door, turned it and smiled when he realised that it wasn't locked. He opened the door and slipped inside, his heart racing. The house was bigger than anything he'd ever torched in the past, and he knew that to be sure of killing Nightingale he'd have to go upstairs.

He eased the door shut behind him. In his left hand was the red petrol can. He'd filled it almost to the top and he heard the liquid slosh around as he headed for the stairs.

93

Nightingale took a piece of paper from his pocket. On it were instructions that he'd copied from Aleister Crowley's diary. He looked around the pentagram to check that everything was in place, then he ignited the mixture of herbs that he'd placed in a brass crucible. They caught fire easily and crackled and hissed as they burned.

Nightingale began to read from the paper. '*Osurmy delmausan atalsloym charusihoa,*' he said, trying not to stumble over the unfamiliar words. He spoke for a full minute, taking care over every syllable. When he'd finished, he took a deep breath. 'Come, Lucifuge Rofocale,' he said. He held the parchment with its bloody drawing over one of the north-facing candles and watched as it burned. 'Come, Lucifuge Rofocale,' he repeated. 'I summon you.'

He narrowed his eyes, not sure what to expect. In the diary Crowley hadn't been able to describe what Lucifuge Rofocale looked like, saying that he chose one of many forms depending on the circumstances. The burning parchment scorched his fingers but he barely felt the pain.

The thick smoke rippled and then began to spin in a vortex at right angles to the floor, faster and faster in a motion that was almost hypnotic, and Nightingale found himself leaning towards it. He took an involuntarily step forward and then another, but he gritted his teeth and forced himself to stand still.

There was a deep booming laugh that echoed around the room and then the vortex folded inside out and a short, squat figure appeared, less than four feet tall. At first Nightingale thought it was a child, but as it moved through the smoke he saw that it was a dwarf, with a large head topped with curly black hair, a thick body and short bow legs. The dwarf thrust his chin square out as he stared up at Nightingale with blood-red eyes. He was wearing a crimson jacket with gold buttons up the front, black jodhpurs and shiny black boots that made Nightingale think of a toy soldier.

'You are Lucifuge Rofocale?' asked Nightingale. 'I command that you speak the truth.' In his diary, Crowley had said that the devil sometimes sent emissaries in his place but an emissary could not lie about his identity.

There was a blast of heat, so hot that Nightingale gasped. A wall of flame flickered along the edge of the pentagram, red at the bottom, yellow at the top, then the flames leaped higher, sucking the air from the room. Nightingale put his hands over his face and he could feel the heat singeing the hairs on his skin. The flames grew higher until they were as tall as he was, then they began to swirl until they formed an impenetrable mass of fire. Nightingale whirled around but, whichever way he faced, the heat was unbearable.

'I summoned you to talk!' he screamed, and in an instant the flames vanished.

The dwarf was glaring at him. 'You dare to summon me?' he hissed. 'Do you know who I am?'

'You are Lucifuge Rofocale and I command that you speak the truth.'

'You command?' roared the dwarf.

The ground shook and the walls fell away and then the floor vanished and Nightingale was standing on the pentagram in the middle of darkness. There was nothing above him or below him and the air was ice-cold. There was no sign of the dwarf.

'You are Lucifuge Rofocale and I command that you speak the truth!' shouted Nightingale. His voice echoed into the distance. Then suddenly the pentagram began to plummet down in free-fall, the air rushing past his face so quickly that he couldn't pull it into his aching lungs. Nightingale closed his eyes. 'This isn't happening,' he said. 'I'm in Gosling Manor, inside the pentagram. None of this is real.'

He opened his eyes again and he was back in the bedroom. The flames had gone. He looked at the back of his hands; the hairs there were singed and the skin blackened.

The dwarf's upper lip curled back. 'Happy now? Or do you want more?'

There was a flash of light so blinding that it hurt, and Nightingale shaded his eyes with his hands. The dwarf had gone and in its place was a creature so large that its head was against the ceiling and its leathery wings scraped the walls on either side of the pentagram. It had a pointed snout, jagged teeth and reptilian eyes, and when it roared the stench was so overpowering that Nightingale almost passed out.

'Do you want more?' the creature screamed and Nightingale staggered back.

'I want only what is my right: to summon you and for you to speak the truth.'

'Right?' roared the creature. 'Who are you to talk of rights?' The creature opened its mouth and a stream of flame flashed over Nightingale's head.

'My name is Jack Nightingale and provided I stay within the pentagram you cannot harm me!' shouted Nightingale.

The creature roared and there was another flash of light. Now the dwarf was back, scowling up at him. 'The pentagram is a sanctuary and a prison,' he hissed.

'I've been told that,' said Nightingale. 'I want to talk.' He fought to steady his breathing; he could feel his heart pounding in his chest as if it was about to burst.

'You are either very stupid or very devious,' said the dwarf. 'Which is it?'

Nightingale shrugged. 'I'm not sure,' he said. 'A lot depends on the way things go over the next few minutes.'

There was a loud bang and a flash and a foul smell, like a bad drain.

Lucifuge Rofocale folded his arms. 'You tricked Sugart and he is not happy.'

'I didn't do anything. My sister summoned him. My sister sold her soul in exchange for escape.'

'While you distracted Frimost, who had first claim on her soul.'

'It's hardly my fault if Frimost took his eye off the ball, is it?'

Lucifuge Rofocale glared at Nightingale. 'You planned this. You planned it all.'

Nightingale wrinkled his nose. 'It's not my problem, is it? They're both your subordinates. All you have to do is choose which one gets my sister's soul.' He put his hands in his pockets. 'Of course, whoever loses out is going to be pretty pissed off, right? And I reckon no boss wants a pissed-off subordinate, even in Hell.'

'You know nothing of Hell, Nightingale,' said Lucifuge Rofocale. 'Yet. But your day will come.'

'This isn't about me,' said Nightingale. 'This is about my sister. Her father sold her soul to Frimost thirty-one years ago. She has now sold it in good faith to Sugart. It seems to me that they both a have good claim on it. Both can make a good case and neither is going to take kindly to being told that he's lost out.' Nightingale grinned. 'So you're going to have to decide, right? And I'm guessing that souls are indivisible, which means that there's no judgement of Solomon.'

Lucifuge Rofocale said nothing. He stared up at Nightingale, his lips set in a tight line.

'So here's the thing,' Nightingale continued, taking his hands out of his pockets. 'They both have a claim on her soul, no question about that. And neither will accept the other taking it from him. The way I see it, there's only one thing you can do.'

'Neither of them gets her soul,' said the dwarf.

'It's the only way to keep the peace,' said Nightingale. 'It's the only decision that they'll both accept.'

'You're a clever man, Nightingale.'

'Not really,' said Nightingale. 'But I've been involved in a few negotiations over the years. So we're agreed? My sister gets her soul back?'

'This won't win you any friends, you know.'

'I can live with that,' said Nightingale.

'Sugart and Frimost will blame you. They will want revenge.'

'They know where to find me,' said Nightingale.

Lucifuge Rofocale nodded slowly. 'So you have what you want. Your sister has her soul back. You must be feeling very pleased with yourself.'

'Not really,' said Nightingale. 'I just want this to end. I want this threat lifted from her so that she can get on with her life.'

He took a piece of paper from his pocket and began to read.

'Wait!' said Lucifuge Rofocale.

Nightingale frowned. 'What?'

'We haven't finished,' said Lucifuge Rofocale.

'I have,' said Nightingale. 'There's nothing else I want from you.'

'Are you sure?'

'I'm sure.'

'What about Sophie?' Nightingale shivered as if an icy finger had been drawn down his spine. 'Don't you wonder what happened to her?'

94

Kerr shuffled backwards down the corridor in a low crouch, gently pouring petrol over the bare floorboards. The wood would burn quickly, he knew, but not as quickly as carpet. Someone had stripped out all the floor coverings, along with the furniture and pictures that had once lined the walls. It was a nice house, thought Kerr, as he shuffled and poured, and it would make a lovely fire.

The petrol fumes were making him a little light-headed. He loved the smell of petrol almost as much as he loved the smell of burning matches, but petrol fumes came with a price: a searing headache that sometimes hung around for days.

He reached the bedroom where he'd seen the candle-light through the window. Kerr could hear voices inside and that confused him because he'd thought that Nightingale was alone in the house. He couldn't hear what was being said but it didn't matter anyway. He continued backing down the corridor towards the stairs.

Kerr had calculated it perfectly and as he reached the top of the stairs he poured the last of the petrol onto the floorboards. He took a step back, put down the can and took out his box of Swan Vestas. He shook the box, then slid it open and selected a match. He sniffed the match and felt the muscles in his groin contract. He took a deep breath and gasped as the petrol fumes filled his lungs. He took another step back, struck the match and flicked it down the corridor. It span through the air, and as it hit the floor the petrol ignited with a whooshing sound like a train rushing down a tunnel.

Kerr wanted to stay and watch the flames but he forced himself to pick up the can and walk down the stairs.

95

Nightingale tensed and relaxed his fingers as he stared at the dwarf. Lucifuge Rofocale grinned up at him, showing yellowed, pointed teeth.

'Sophie's dead,' whispered Nightingale.

Lucifuge Rofocale laughed. 'And dead's dead, is that it?'

'Isn't it?'

'You really don't understand anything, do you?'

'Apparently not.' He fiddled with the piece of paper he was holding. 'What does she have to do with any of this?'

'Everything,' said Lucifuge Rofocale. 'Haven't you realised that yet? Everything changed on the day she died, didn't it? Your life was heading in one direction, but after she jumped from that balcony everything changed, didn't it?'

'So?'

'So it was a pivotal moment. And she was a pivotal person. If she hadn't died, you would never have left the police, never become a private detective. So many things would have been different.'

'But we would still be standing here, wouldn't we?'

'Maybe. And maybe not.'

He waved his hand lazily and time folded in on itself,

then Sophie Underwood was standing next to him, dressed exactly as she had been when she jumped off the balcony, her Barbie doll dangling from her right hand. She had her head down and her long blonde hair covered her face.

The dwarf leered up at her. 'Pretty little thing, isn't she?' He reached out to stroke her dress with a hand that was festooned with jewelled rings.

'Jack,' she moaned. 'Help me. I don't like it here.'

'That's not her,' whispered Nightingale. 'It can't be.'

'Why do you say that?' said the dwarf, running his hand along her hair.

'Because she fell thirteen stories,' said Nightingale.

'Is that how you'd rather see her?' said Lucifuge Rofocale. He waved his hand again.

Time folded and Sophie's dress was drenched in blood. 'Jack . . .' moaned Sophie. 'Jack, it hurts.' She turned to look up at Lucifuge Rofocale. Nightingale saw that the left side of her face was crushed and her eyeball was half out of its socket. Her jaw had been shattered and her teeth broken.

'Don't do this,' said Nightingale quietly.

Lucifuge Rofocale smiled. 'Do what?'

'Use her to hurt me. Anyway, that's not really her.'

Sophie turned to look at him. 'It is me, Jack,' she said.

Nightingale forced himself not to look at her. He glared at Lucifuge Rofocale. 'Make her go away.'

'Jack, please, you have to help me,' sobbed Sophie. She reached out her left hand and took a step towards him.

'We're done,' Nightingale said to the dwarf. 'You can go.'

'We're done when I say we're done, Nightingale,' said Lucifuge Rofocale, his voice a throbbing roar that hurt

Nightingale's ears. He waved his hand and Sophie went limp, her arms at her sides, her hair hanging down over her face.

It went suddenly quiet and Nightingale could hear his own breathing. He was panting like a horse that had been ridden hard and he fought to steady himself.

'There's one more thing,' said Lucifuge Rofocale. 'About your sister.'

'We agreed what you'd do,' said Nightingale. He felt as if all the strength had drained from his upper body and his legs were shaking. 'Neither can claim her soul so it remains unclaimed.'

'Yes, you are right,' said Lucifuge Rofocale. 'Her soul will not be claimed by either party. But nobody gets something for nothing. Your sister is getting back her soul, so there is a price that will have to be paid.'

'By whom?'

Lucifuge Rofocale's lips curled back into a snarl. 'By your sister, of course.'

96

Kerr jogged towards the clump of trees from where he'd first watched Gosling Manor. He put down his empty can and took out his box of matches. He lit one and smelled the smoke as he looked at the house. There was no sign of smoke yet, no flames flickering at the windows. The corridor would burn first, he knew. The wooden floorboards would catch, and then the doors, and then it would spread up through the ceiling and into the attic and sideways into the bedrooms. It would be at least ten minutes before the fire really took hold. The match went out and Kerr lit another. He felt himself grow hard between his legs and he reached down with his left hand to touch himself as he stared at the house.

97

There was a bright flash and the dwarf vanished. Sophie stayed where she was, her head down, her body wracked with silent sobs. Then Lucifuge Rofocale's laughter echoed off the walls, there was a second blinding flash and Sophie disappeared.

Nightingale's chest ached and he realised that he'd been holding his breath. He opened his mouth and tilted back his head, sucking in the foul-smelling air. His ears were buzzing and crackling and his legs felt as if they were about to give way under him. He looked around the room and then stepped gingerly out of the pentagram.

He took his pack of Marlboro out of his pocket and lit one, then opened the bedroom door. Flames billowed into the room and across the ceiling and a blast of heat hit him in the face, making him gasp. His cigarette fell from his fingers and he slammed the door shut.

Nightingale stood where he was, his mind racing. How the hell had a fire started? And so quickly? He went over to the window and tried to open it, but it was locked. He'd never bothered opening any of the windows in the house and had no idea how to unlock them. He looked for something to break the glass with. He picked up the metal crucible that he'd used for the burning herbs and smashed it against one of the panes of glass, but it didn't break. Nightingale cursed and tried again. The glass steadfastly refused to shatter. He threw the crucible to the side and it clattered onto the bare floorboards. Gosling must have installed unbreakable laminated glass as part of his security arrangements.

Nightingale took out his mobile phone. He dialled nine nine nine and asked for the fire brigade. As he gave them directions he saw that smoke was pouring through the gap under the door. Nightingale had left his raincoat in the bathroom and he rushed to get it. He could use it to block the gap. But as he picked it up he knew that he would only be delaying the inevitable. Even if he plugged the gap he was still trapped in the room, and he'd be overcome by the smoke or the heat long before the firemen arrived.

He put his phone on the washbasin, pushed the bath plug into place and turned on the cold tap. He held his raincoat under the torrent of water until it was soaked and then climbed into the bath and lay down, submerging himself in the water.

He wiggled his arms and legs, thrashing around to make sure that his clothes were totally soaked, and shook his head from side to side, then climbed out of the bath, grabbed his phone and coat and ran to the door.

He stood by the door, taking deep breaths, then draped his soaking-wet raincoat over his head. He took a final deep breath, ducked down low and pulled the door open. The fire roared and flames burst over his head. He kept low as he ran out into the corridor, his mouth closed and his eyes narrowed to slits.

The fire roared and he could feel the heat on his wet skin. He turned to the right and ran, pulling the raincoat down low. He couldn't see where he was going but he could make out the floorboards and kept to the middle of the hall, counting off the steps in his head. Three bedrooms. Each bedroom about fifteen feet wide. Each pace three feet. Five paces one room. Fifteen paces and he should be at the stairs.

His hands were burning as the flames dried out the water and the heat got to his skin. He kept them bunched into fists and curled them so that they were covered by the coat. His chest was aching but he forced himself not to breathe because the air would be blisteringly hot and would damage his lungs.

He turned to the right and reached the stairs, charging down them. He had to take a breath as he ran down but the air wasn't hot any more, though it was thick with smoke and made him gag. He hurtled to the bottom and headed for the door, coughing and spluttering.

He pulled open the front door and fell out into the cold night air, gasping for breath. He threw his raincoat down onto the steps, where it lay smouldering, and staggered over to the mermaid fountain, thrusting his hands into the water.

Nightingale looked up at the house but there was no sign of fire or smoke, no indication of the blazing inferno within. He took his hands out of the water and shook them. The flesh was red but that was all. His phone rang and he pulled it out of his pocket. It was Jenny.

'Jack, how did it go?'

Nightingale began to laugh. He sat down on the edge of the fountain. In the distance he heard a siren.

'Jack, what's wrong?'

'I'll call you back, kid. I'm in the middle of something right now.'

98

Kerr groaned as he saw Nightingale stagger out of the house. He picked up the empty petrol can and jogged across the lawn to the gates. He slipped out into the road and walked along to the field where he'd left his car, muttering to himself. He stopped when he saw the young woman dressed in black who was standing by his car, a border collie on a chain sitting at her side. She was wearing too much mascara and black lipstick and had a black choker with an upturned silver cross over her throat. Her black jeans looked as if they had been sprayed on and there were silver chains hanging from her black leather motorcycle jacket. The dog growled at him and the girl made a shushing sound.

Kerr lowered his eyes, not wanting to meet her gaze. 'I failed you, Mistress Proserpine,' he said.

She smiled. 'Yes, Graham, I know.'

He dropped the petrol can, went down on his knees and put his head on the ground. 'I beg your forgiveness, mistress.' He heard sirens, off in the distance.

'Get up, Graham. There's no need for that.'

Kerr got to his feet. Tears were running down his face.

Proserpine looked at him sadly. 'You know what you have to do now, Graham?'

The sirens were getting closer. The sirens of a fire engine and two police cars. Kerr knew the difference.

'Yes, mistress. I know.'

He walked to the back of his car, an old Renault. He opened the boot, took out a fresh can of petrol and methodically poured it over himself, from head to toe. He drew a deep breath, relishing the intoxicating aroma, and then turned to face Proserpine. He fished his box of Swan Vestas from his pocket.

Proserpine nodded her approval and her dog growled softly.

Kerr rattled the box, then pushed it open with his thumb and took out a single match. He looked at Proserpine and shivered with anticipation as he rubbed the match along the striker. He heard the whoosh of the petrol igniting and then smiled as he felt the searing pain of his flesh as it began to burn.

99

Nightingale let himself into his flat and went straight into the kitchen. He kept a bottle of Russian vodka in the freezer and he took it out and poured a big slug into a glass, adding a splash of Coke. He drank it in one go and then poured himself another. He went through to the sitting room and phoned Jenny.

'Where are you?' she asked.

'The flat. Can you come round? I need to talk.'

'Before you wouldn't tell me what was going on and now you want to talk?'

'Just come round.'

'What's wrong, Jack?'

'Just come, yeah? I don't want to tell you on the phone. Too much has happened.'

He ended the call and took another long pull on his drink. He sat down on his sofa and flicked through the TV channels but couldn't find anything that he wanted to watch.

The fire brigade had arrived in time to save the house, though there was extensive damage to the upper floor and the firemen's water had flooded the ground floor. Nightingale hadn't been able to check on the state of the basement but he figured that the damage there would be extensive.

He finished his drink and went back into the kitchen

to make himself a fresh one. This time he took the bottle of vodka into the sitting room and put it on the coffee table. As he sat down the entryphone buzzed. He frowned and looked at his wristwatch. It was too soon to be Jenny. He pushed himself up off the sofa and went over to the intercom. 'Yes?'

'Mr Nightingale? It's Janet Bethel. Greater Manchester Police.'

'Yes?'

'We met at your aunt and uncle's funeral.'

'I remember. What's up?'

'I'd like to talk to you, if you don't mind. We have some new information on the case.'

'Case? Which case?'

'Your aunt and uncle.'

'I didn't realise there was a case,' said Nightingale.

'It'd be easier if I could sit down and talk to you,' she said.

'It's late,' he said. 'I was just about to go to bed.'

'It's important, Mr Nightingale.'

Nightingale pressed the buzzer to let her in. He had the front door open for her by the time she reached his floor. She was wearing the same fawn belted raincoat that she'd been wearing in church and carrying the same black shoulder bag. Nightingale showed her into the sitting room. She put her bag on a chair and took off her coat, revealing a dark blazer with a grey skirt. She looked more like a holiday rep than a detective.

'What on earth are you doing here at this time of night?' he asked.

'I heard about the fire so I figured you would be up. Do they know what happened?'

'Arson,' said Nightingale.

'While you were in the house?'

'Yeah. It was a close thing.' He frowned. 'You said you wanted to talk about my aunt and uncle? What's so important?'

'I couldn't trouble you for a glass of water, could I? I'm parched,' she said. She draped her coat over the back of the chair. 'I got the train and it took forever.'

'Sure,' said Nightingale.

'Or coffee,' she said. 'I could really do with a coffee.'

'Milk and sugar?'

'Lots of milk and no sugar.' She smiled. 'Sweet enough already.'

Nightingale went through to the kitchen and made her a mug of coffee. When he took it through to her, she had put a sheet of paper on the table and was holding a pen. 'I couldn't be a nuisance and ask you to sign this, could I? They're being a real pain over expenses at the moment.'

'It's not a confession, is it?' he said, picking up the sheet. It was on Greater Manchester Police headed paper and confirmed that he was being interviewed by Detective Sergeant Janet Bethel.

'Why would it be a confession, Mr Nightingale?'

'I was being flippant,' said Nightingale. 'Which, under the circumstances, probably wasn't the wisest move.' He scrawled his signature at the bottom of the letter and gave it back to her.

'I'm sorry about that,' she said, putting the letter into her bag. 'But we have to get a signed receipt every time we conduct an interview outside our area. No receipt, no expenses.'

Nightingale sat down on the sofa and sipped his vodka and Coke. 'So why are you here?' he asked.

'Frankly, Mr Nightingale, I'm not convinced that your uncle took his own life. And if that's the case, it casts doubt on the assumption that he killed your aunt.'

'I thought the forensic evidence was conclusive.'

'It was, but, as I'm sure you know, evidence can be planted or removed.'

'That's certainly true,' said Nightingale. He took another drink.

'And I understand that you were in north Wales recently. Abersoch.'

Nightingale nodded but didn't say anything.

'You know what's going on there, I assume.'

'The serial killer? I heard.' He frowned. 'What are you saying? The same guy killed my aunt and uncle?'

'It doesn't fit the profile completely, I know. The killings in Wales have all been of women and they have all been made to look like suicides. Your aunt was murdered, and your uncle's death appeared to be a suicide.'

'Plus it's quite a way from Wales to Manchester. Most serial killers tend to stay in an area that they're comfortable with.' Nightingale yawned. He was feeling tired. He took a long drink and stretched out his legs.

'I'm sorry for getting here so late, Mr Nightingale. I can see that you're tired.'

Nightingale put a hand up to his head. He was finding it difficult to concentrate. 'No, it's okay,' he said. 'What were you saying? About my aunt and uncle?'

'There is a possibility that they were both killed by a third person,' said Bethel.

'And do you know who that might be?'

'I was going to ask you the same thing, Mr Nightingale. You were in Connie Miller's house just after her death. And you were there a few days later, weren't you?'

'How do you know that?' asked Nightingale. His legs were going numb and he couldn't feel his feet. He drained his glass.

'My opposite number in north Wales told me,' said Bethel. She stood up and went over to her bag.

Nightingale's head started to spin. 'They didn't know,' he mumbled.

'Didn't know what?'

'They didn't know that I went back to Connie's house. They knew I went around to her parents' home but they didn't know that I was in her house.'

The glass tumbled from his fingers and bounced on the carpet. He looked up. The detective was standing in front of him, a roll of tape in her hands.

'You were there,' said Nightingale. 'You were watching the house.' He tried to stand up but his legs had gone numb.

She bent down and used the tape to bind his wrists together. He tried to resist but there was no strength in his arms.

'What are you doing?' he asked.

'Keep quiet. It'll all be over soon,' said the detective. She went over to her handbag again and returned with a plastic bag. She pulled it down over Nightingale's head.

Nightingale tried to shout but it felt as if there was a heavy weight on his chest.

Bethel started to wind tape around his neck, sealing the bag shut. Nightingale heard a buzzing. It was his door intercom. He tried moving away but Bethel slid onto his lap, her thighs pinning his legs as she continued winding the tape. The intercom buzzed again.

The plastic bag began to mist over and it started pulsing in and out in time with his breathing. Nightingale knew that he had to breathe slowly so he fought the panic that was making his heart race.

Bethel smiled as she watched his discomfort. She placed her hands on his shoulders and put her face close to his. 'Not long now,' she said.

She was wearing gloves, Nightingale realised. Black leather gloves. 'Why?' he asked, but then had to gulp for air. His breathing was fast and shallow and his lungs were burning.

He felt himself start to pass out. Bethel was grinning at him in triumph, staring at him with a wild look in her eyes. Nightingale's eyes were just closing when he saw movement behind Bethel. There was a cracking sound and Bethel tumbled off his lap and fell to the floor. Hands pulled at the plastic bag and ripped it apart. Nightingale gulped in fresh air.

'Jack, are you okay?' It was Jenny.

'She put something in my drink.' He groaned as the room began to swim.

Jenny hurried to the kitchen and returned with a pair of scissors. She used them to cut the tape around his wrists. Bethel lay on the floor face down, not moving.

'You were lucky I had a key,' Jenny said. 'I'll call for an ambulance. You should try to throw up.'

She picked up Nightingale's mobile phone, called nine nine nine and spoke to the operator, but Nightingale couldn't hear what she was saying and his eyelids fluttered as he slipped into unconsciousness.

100

Nightingale opened his eyes and blinked under the fluorescent lights. He swallowed, which hurt, and there was a bitter taste at the back his mouth. A familiar face loomed over him. Jenny. She smiled.

'Welcome back,' she said.

'Where am I?'

'Hospital,' said Jenny.

'Water,' croaked Nightingale.

Jenny picked up a glass of water and helped him drink.

'What did she give me?' he asked as she took the glass away from his lips.

'It was Valium, that's all,' she said. 'Not enough to kill you, just to make you really relaxed. They had to pump your stomach, though, just to be sure. It was the plastic bag that was going to do the damage. She was planning to make it look like you had killed yourself. She had a typed suicide note in her bag, with you blaming yourself for your aunt and uncle's death.'

'She got me to sign a form saying that I'd spoken to her. She was probably going to forge my signature on the letter.' He groaned. 'How long was I asleep for?'

'Fifteen hours.'

'You hit her, right? I remember that much.'

'That's right. Riding to the rescue, like the cavalry.'

'What did you hit her with?'

'My fist.'

'Your fist? Since when did you know how to fight?'

'Jack, I've got a black belt in tae kwon do. You really should read my CV some time.'

'And who was she? I'm assuming she wasn't a real cop.'

Jenny shook her head 'Her warrant card was a fake. I had a look at her driving licence before the cops came. Her name's Katherine Whelan. She lives in Caernarfon.'

Nightingale frowned. 'She didn't sound Welsh.'

'She didn't sound like she was from Manchester, either. But she's definitely the killer.'

'But how did she know we were after her? We thought the killer was a man, remember?'

'I used the office computer to talk to Caernarfon Craig. That was her. If she knew what she was doing she could track the computer down. Once she had the office address she must have done some digging and found out about your aunt and uncle's funeral and then traced you here. I'm guessing she'd have got my address too.'

Nightingale winced. 'My head hurts,' he said. 'Can you raise the bed a bit?'

Jenny pressed a button to adjust the bed. It made a metallic grinding noise and slowly levered Nightingale into a sitting position.

'Anyway, the Welsh cops are over the moon,' she said. 'Her flat was full of souvenirs. Every time she killed she took something from the victim's home as a reminder. And her computer was chock-a-block with emails and website stuff. She's already got a lawyer and they're working on an insanity defence.'

Nightingale forced a smile. 'Maybe she'll end up in Rampton.'

Jenny grinned. 'She can have your sister's room.' She sat down on the edge of the bed. 'Yesterday you said you wanted to talk about what happened. With the deal.'

Nightingale nodded. 'Yeah. He agreed. Neither gets her soul. It was bargained twice, both times in good faith. So neither deal can stand and Robyn gets her soul back.'

'That's great,' said Jenny.

Nightingale looked uncomfortable.

'What's wrong?' she asked. 'What aren't you telling me?'

'He wasn't happy,' said Nightingale.

'I'm sure he wasn't, because at the end of the day you tricked them. But all's well that ends well, right?'

Nightingale looked even more uncomfortable.

'Jack, what is it?'

'It's not as simple as all's well that ends well. I had to negotiate.'

'What do you mean?'

Nightingale reached over for the glass of water and took another drink. He wiped his mouth with the back of his hand. 'I need a cigarette.'

'You're in hospital, Jack. Smoking isn't an option. Tell me what happened.'

Nightingale sighed. 'He wasn't prepared to let Robyn walk away without some payback.'

'Payback? You're not making any sense.'

'Jenny, please don't push me. You weren't there.

You didn't see what he was like. The power he had . . .'
He ran his hands over his face. 'He let Robyn have
her soul back. It's hers again. No one has any claim
on it.'

'But? There's a "but", isn't there?'

Nightingale nodded. 'Yeah.' He sighed again. 'Here's
the thing. Robyn gets to keep her soul but she dies on
her thirty-third birthday. In two years' time.'

Jenny opened her mouth in astonishment.

'There was no room for manoeuvre. That's what he
wanted. It was a deal-breaker. He said that if I didn't
agree then he'd let one of them take her soul and to hell
with the consequences.'

Jenny stood up, her eyes blazing. 'You gave away your
sister's life? How could you do that?'

'It wasn't mine to give, Jenny. Don't you see that? If
I hadn't done anything she'd have died in two years
anyway. Only they'd have taken her soul as well. This
way, at least . . .'

'At least what, Jack? She's got two years to live? Does
she know?'

Nightingale shook his head. 'And she won't ever know.
I don't even know if I'm going to see her again.'

'Where is she?'

'I don't know. And so long as everyone thinks she killed
those kids, I don't want to know.'

'So she stays underground, lives her two years and then
dies? How is that a good deal for her?'

'She gets to keep her soul.'

'We don't even know what a soul is, Jack. We don't
even know if there are souls.'

'If there aren't, then what is all this about?'

'I wish I knew,' said Jenny. 'But I know one thing: no one has given you the right to play God.'

'That's not what happened.'

'That's exactly what happened. You did a deal with a devil and as a result of that deal your sister is going to die in two years.'

'You're playing with words.'

'No, Jack, that's your prerogative. I'm telling you how I see it. You sold your sister out.'

'I did a deal to save her soul.'

'You had no right to do a deal like that. You should have talked to your sister first.'

'That wasn't possible. I had to do what I had to do.'

'As always, Jack Nightingale is at the centre of the bloody universe.'

'Jenny . . .'

Jenny shook her head and held up her hand. 'Enough.'

'You don't understand.'

'No, I do understand. That's the problem. I'm out of here.' She turned and walked away.

'Jenny!'

She didn't look back and walked out of the room.

Nightingale cursed as a plump West Indian nurse walked in. She grinned mischievously at him. 'Girlfriend trouble, honey?' she asked.

'She's not my girlfriend,' said Nightingale.

'There's a spark,' said the nurse, looking at his chart. 'A definite spark.'

'She's always like that just before she bursts into flames,' said Nightingale. 'Speaking of which, I really need a cigarette.'

'This is a hospital, honey.'

'I know. But there's a smoking room, right?'

She chuckled. 'You do know that smoking is bad for you, don't you?'

'Lots of things are bad for you. Life is bad for you. At the end of the day, everyone dies.'

The nurse frowned and put down the chart. 'Honey, what made you so cynical? Life is to be lived to the full and then you have an eternity with the Lord.'

'What's your name?'

'Mary-Louise.'

'You believe that, Mary-Louise?'

'Of course I do.'

'Even working here in a hospital? You must see people die every day.'

'I see people go to meet their maker. And I see miracles. And if you had your eyes open you'd see them too.'

'And what about angels? Have you seen angels?'

She smiled at him, her eyes twinkling. 'I've seen doctors send home people who'd come here to die, and I've seen them turn suffering into release. If that's not the work of angels then I'd like to know what is. What about you, Mr Nightingale, have you seen angels?'

'Not yet,' he said.

'Well, keep looking, because they're out there.'

Nightingale swung his legs over the side of the bed. 'I might just do that,' he said. 'In the meantime I'm checking myself out. And before you ask, I didn't take anything from the minibar.'

'We don't have minibars,' said the nurse.

'Exactly,' said Nightingale. 'Now, where are my clothes?'

101

Space folded in on itself amid the swirling clouds of smoke and then she was there, dressed in black, her black and white collie at her side. She was wearing a black T-shirt with a gold inverted cross on it, a black leather miniskirt and thigh-length black boots with stiletto heels. Around her neck was a black leather collar with chrome studs.

'Why do you always dress like a cheap hooker?' Nightingale asked.

She walked up to the edge of the pentagram. 'I could ask you why you always dress like a cheap gumshoe,' she said. The dog growled softly and Proserpine bent down to scratch it behind the ear.

Nightingale ran his left hand down the front of his raincoat. 'It was raining earlier,' he said.

'I meant the suit. And the shoes.' She pointed at his rain-flecked Hush Puppies. 'Suede? Didn't suede go out of fashion in the seventies?'

'They're comfortable,' he said. 'I do a lot of walking. Goes with the job.'

She looked at him and slowly walked around the edge of the pentagram, her heels crunching on the bare floorboards. 'So what do you think, Nightingale? All's well that ends well?' Her smile hardened and she stared at him with her black, featureless eyes. 'I told you before that I don't like being bothered for nothing. You can't summon me whenever you've a question you want answering.'

'I don't have a question for you,' said Nightingale. 'There's something I want to give you.'

Proserpine frowned. 'Give me? What could you possibly have that I'd want, Nightingale?'

Nightingale's hand appeared from behind his back, holding a long-stemmed red rose. He tossed it high in the air and she caught it easily.

'What's this?' she asked.

'A flower,' he said. 'By any other name.'

Proserpine sniffed the rose. Nightingale reached into the pocket of his raincoat and brought out a small box. He threw it towards her and she caught it with her other hand. She smiled when she saw what it was. 'Perfume?' she said.

'Mademoiselle by Chanel,' he said. 'The girl in Harrods said it was very popular.'

'It is,' she said.

'She said Chanel Number 5 was heavier.'

'Much,' she said. 'Too much jasmine for my taste.'

'I'm crap at presents,' he said. 'I told you that before.'

'Much as I appreciate the gift, you know that we eternals don't celebrate birthdays,' she said. 'We measure time differently.'

'Yeah, you explained that to me. It's not a birthday present.' He smiled and took out his pack of Marlboro and his lighter. 'It's to say thank you.'

'Thank you?'

He tapped out a cigarette and slipped it between his

lips. 'You sent three guys to kill me. Well, two guys and a girl.'

'That was the deal,' she said. 'Three questions answered; three killers.'

'Yeah, but you decided who to send, didn't you? You could have sent anyone, and I'm pretty sure that, doing what you do, you'd be spoiled for choice.'

'I do know some mean motherfuckers, that's true.'

Nightingale grinned. 'I love it when you talk dirty.'

'Don't flirt with me, Nightingale,' she said. 'I choose this form because, like your cheap suede shoes, I'm comfortable with it. It's not the real me.'

'It's not about the way you look,' said Nightingale. 'It's about what you did. You could have had a sniper blow me away or have a bomb put under my car, but you didn't. You gave me a fighting chance.'

Proserpine shrugged. 'I wouldn't read too much into that if I were you,' she said.

'You could have sent killers who wouldn't have given me a chance. They could have killed people close to me. Collateral damage. But you didn't do that, did you? You sent people you knew I could beat.'

'You're reading too much into it, Nightingale.'

Nightingale shook his head. 'I don't think so,' he said. 'But, whatever the reason, you went easy on me and I just wanted to say thank you.'

'With perfume and a rose?'

'I had absolutely no idea what else to get you,' he said. 'Okay. That's all I wanted to say. You can go now, and I promise not to bother you again.' He flicked the lighter.

'You know that cigarette smoke is an impurity,' she said. 'It'll weaken the protective circle.'

Nightingale flicked his lighter again, lit the cigarette and then blew a cloud of smoke into the air. 'You know what, honey?' he said. 'I trust you.'

'I'm not sure that's a good idea,' she said.

Nightingale shrugged. 'I'll risk it.'

'Up to you,' she said. 'But I have to say that you're being a little presumptuous.'

Nightingale frowned as he blew smoke. 'Why?'

'I answered three questions for you.'

'And you sent three killers. Chance, Katherine Whelan and the arsonist.'

Proserpine smiled. 'Whelan was nothing to do with me,' she said. 'She had her own agenda. The other two were mine, though.'

Nightingale's cigarette froze on the way to his lips. 'So there's still another killer out there?' he said.

Proserpine smiled and blew him a kiss. 'Be lucky,' she said, then turned and walked away.

Time folded in on itself and she and the dog vanished.

Nightingale took a long pull on his cigarette and let the smoke escape slowly from between his lips. 'That didn't go quite as well as I'd hoped,' he said. He flicked ash onto the floor and stepped out of the circle.